WESTERN

Rugged men looking for love...

That Maverick Of Mine

Kathy Douglass

Courting The Cowgirl

Cheryl Harper

MILLS & BOON

Kathy Douglass is acknowledged as the author of this work
THAT MAVERICK OF MINE

First Published 2024
First Australian Paperback Edition 2024
ISBN 978 1 038 92176 5

COURTING THE COWGIRL

First Published 2024
First Australian Paperback Edition 2024
ISBN 978 1 038 92176 5

Published by
Harlequin Mills & Boon
An imprint of Harlequin Enterprises (Australia) Pty Limited
(ABN 47 001 180 918), a subsidiary of HarperCollins
Publishers Australia Pty Limited
(ABN 36 009 913 517)
Level 19, 201 Elizabeth Street
SYDNEY NSW 2000 AUSTRALIA

Printed and bound in Australia by McPherson's Printing Group

That Maverick Of Mine

Kathy Douglass

MILLS & BOON

Kathy Douglass is a lawyer turned author of sweet small-town contemporary romances. She is married to her very own hero and mother to two sons, who cheer her on as she tries to get her stubborn hero and heroine to realise they are meant to be together. She loves hearing from readers that something in her books made them laugh or cry. You can learn more about Kathy or contact her at kathydouglassbooks.com.

Visit the Author Profile page
at millsandboon.com.au for more titles.

Dear Reader,

Welcome back to Bronco, Montana, home of the famous Hawkins sisters. These rodeo stars have been falling in love recently, and now it's Faith's turn. After years spent traveling the rodeo circuit, she's considering settling down in Bronco to be near her family. That new lifestyle is enough of a change for her. She's not looking to add romance to the mix. But she's not opposed to having a good time with the right man.

Enter Caleb Strom. Although he is completely attracted to Faith, he's not interested in a romantic relationship. He is on a mission to find his birth father and can't even think of falling in love until that matter is settled.

Don't you love it when two people who are perfect for each other agree that they aren't interested in romance? Come along and watch as Faith and Caleb's friendship turns into love. Of course, there are a few bumps and bruises as they travel the road to their happily-ever-after, but that just adds to the fun.

I hope you enjoy reading *That Maverick of Mine* as much as I enjoyed writing it.

I love hearing from my readers. Drop me a line at kathydouglassbooks.com to let me know what you think about Faith and Caleb, and I promise to get back to you.

Happy Reading!

Kathy

DEDICATION

This book is dedicated with love and appreciation to my husband and sons. Thank you for always supporting my dreams and encouraging me to follow them.

CHAPTER ONE

CALEB STROM STEPPED into the arena of the Bronco Convention Center and looked around. The arena, which held about four thousand seats, was packed with a raucous crowd who'd come to honor Brooks Langtree, one of rodeo's legendary cowboys. Thirty years ago, Langtree had won the Golden Buckle, a special tribute reserved for the profession's most promising new stars. From all accounts, he had gone on to have an illustrious career, winning numerous awards, being named Cowboy of the Year several times, and serving as a role model for another generation of rodeo riders. Now he was back in Bronco, Montana, and was being celebrated as part of the Golden Buckle Rodeo.

Caleb pulled the flyer announcing Brooks Langtree Day from his pocket and studied it again even though everything there was seared into his mind. He'd folded and unfolded the paper so many times that he'd worn creases in it. He remembered the first time he'd seen the announcement. He and some of his friends had been going to lunch at the diner back home in Tenacity, a town about one hundred miles away from Bronco. One of his buddies had picked up the flyer from a stack by the cash register and shared it with the others. They'd pointed out that Caleb and Brooks Langtree looked so much alike that the two of them could be related. The guys had teased him about hitting up his famous relative for a loan. Caleb had thought that his friends had been pulling his leg until he'd taken a glance at the flyer for himself. The face on the advertisement seemingly looking back at him had made him dizzy. The eyes, nose, chin and cheekbones were the same. Brooks Langtree looked like Caleb imagined he would in twenty years.

At first, Caleb tried to ignore the resemblance. What was that famous saying? Everyone has a twin somewhere in the world. The fact that his lookalike happened to be a famous rodeo rider twenty years his senior didn't mean that they were related. It could be pure coincidence. Physical resemblance wasn't proof. It didn't mean that Brooks Langtree was his long-lost biological father.

Even so, Caleb had begun investigating the other man. He'd gotten his hands on everything he could find. He'd found and devoured old interviews in rodeo magazines and newspaper articles. He'd watched a couple of short videos on YouTube. He'd studied the information so intently that he practically knew every word by heart. By all accounts, Brooks Langtree was honest and honorable. A man with a stellar character.

Not at all the kind of man who would abandon his own months-old infant. And certainly not the type to insist the child be given no information about him.

Iris and Nathan Strom had adopted Caleb as an infant. He couldn't have asked for better parents. They'd given him a wonderful childhood filled with love and joy. They had never hidden the fact that he had been adopted. It hadn't mattered to any of them. They were a real family.

The adoption had been closed and the Stroms knew next to nothing about Caleb's birth parents. In the past, he had been satisfied with the little that he'd known about them. His birth mother had died a few months after he'd been born, and his father had given him up for adoption shortly thereafter. It was only after he'd turned thirty that

Caleb had begun to want to know more about where he'd come from.

Even so, the resemblance couldn't be ignored. Not only that, it was the only clue Caleb had to go on in his search to find his biological family. He hadn't been successful before now. Brooks Langtree was as good a place to resume the search as anywhere.

Was it possible that Brooks Langtree was the man Caleb was searching for?

Caleb refolded the paper and slipped it into his pocket, then gave his head a mental shake. He needed to slow down and stop jumping to conclusions. Caleb had come here in order to get a good look at the man in person. Given the size of the crowd, many of them already occupying the seats nearest the makeshift stage that had been erected in the middle of the arena, an up-close-and-personal look wasn't going to happen.

Caleb was so busy staring at the stage that he didn't notice the person in front of him had stopped walking until he bumped into her. The woman turned around and stared at him. An apology was forming on his lips as he looked into her face. Then every thought in his mind vanished except one. She was the most beautiful woman he had ever laid eyes on. He searched his mind for words to say, but he couldn't form a coherent sentence to save his life. The woman was staring at him with wide brown eyes. Wide, *beautiful* brown eyes. He noticed the expectant expression on her face a second before she shook her head in obvious disgust and turned away.

Caleb had never had trouble sweeping a woman off her feet, so being speechless and inept was a new experience for him. He could only attribute his clumsiness to being shook up at possibly seeing his birth father for the first time in thirty years.

As much as possibly seeing his birth father after all this time had him rattled, Caleb knew that was only a small part of the reason he was so flummoxed. The other was the stunning woman who was currently laughing and talking with several other women. One glance at her was all that it had taken to make his heart lurch. If he didn't want her to think that he was a total loser, he needed to do something fast. He knew it was impossible to make a second first impression, but hopefully, there was still time to improve on their initial interaction.

He tapped the woman on her shoulder. She spun around and stared at him, her right eyebrow raised. The expression on her face was a mixture of annoyance and curiosity. And it was totally sexy.

"I want to apologize for bumping into you earlier. I was a bit distracted and didn't watch where I was walking. I hope I didn't hurt you." He gave her his most charming smile—the one that generally had women eating out of his hand.

She stared at him for a long moment, and he held his breath as he awaited her response. Then she nodded and smiled. "I'm okay. I guess in a crowd this size a person should expect to be bumped into."

She started to turn back to the women with her and Caleb feared that he was about to lose the opportunity to get to know her better. He extended his hand and blurted, "I'm Caleb Strom."

Glancing over her shoulder, she smiled and then turned back to him. She took the hand he offered. "I'm Faith Hawkins."

"It's nice to meet you, Faith." Her hand was soft and warm and he was reluctant to release it. But he didn't want to look like a creep either by holding on too long, so he released her fingers. “Are you related to the Hawkins rodeo family?”

Faith nodded and smiled. “I am indeed.”

“Your family is legendary.” Caleb wasn’t much of a rodeo fan, but he recognized the name from his rodeo research on Brooks Langtree. He’d seen a few references to the Hawkins women. Although he hadn’t done more than skim the articles that mentioned their names, he knew that they—especially Hattie Hawkins, the matriarch of the family—had been influential in the sport.

“Some of us are. My grandmother was a trailblazer. My mother and aunts followed in her footsteps, making names for themselves as the Hawkins Sisters. The women of my generation are trying to live up to their illustrious reputations.”

“From what I gather, you ladies are well on your way.” Caleb smiled, grateful that he’d spent the time studying up on rodeo so he could be conversant.

“Thank you. We do our best.”

He was searching for something to say to extend the conversation when the crowd erupted in cheers and applause. Caleb had been so focused on Faith that he hadn’t noticed that everyone else had settled into seats. Caleb’s eyes darted around the stage, searching for Brooks Langtree. The older man was leaning against the side of his armchair, chatting with the woman seated beside him. Langtree said something that amused the woman and they both laughed. For a reason that escaped him, Caleb was irritated by the sight. He wasn’t even sure if Brooks Langtree was his biological father, so the sight of him enjoying himself shouldn’t be an annoyance. Not only that, it was ridiculous to expect the man not to have a good time on a day designed to celebrate his accomplishments.

Besides, Caleb surely didn’t expect his biological father to be miserable after all this time. Thirty years had passed since Caleb had been given away. That was more than enough time for penance. By now, the man surely had come to grips with what he'd done and moved on with his life.

That is if Brooks Langtree actually was his father—something that had yet to be established. If all went according to plan, Caleb would discover the truth today. And if Brooks Langtree wasn't his biological father? Then Caleb wasn't any worse off than he'd been this morning. He'd simply spent an hour or so in the presence of a rodeo legend and his legion of fans. Not only that, he would have met a gorgeous woman.

Faith and the women sat down. Faith was in the aisle seat next to where Caleb was currently standing.

"Do you mind if I sit with you and your friends?" Caleb asked.

Faith nodded up at him and then spoke to the other women. As one, the others rose and scooted over a seat, leaving the aisle seat—next to Faith—vacant for Caleb. He couldn't have planned it better.

"Thank you," Caleb said, leaning over so he could whisper in Faith's ear. Her sweet scent filled his nostrils, wrapping around him and filling him with sudden desire so strong it shocked him.

"You're welcome," she whispered back. Her low, sultry voice suited her perfectly. With high cheekbones, full lips, dark brown eyes and clear brown skin, she was absolutely breathtaking. She was only about five foot two, but every inch of her was perfect. She looked delicate, but he knew she had to be strong in order to compete in rodeo like her family. He'd followed in his father's footsteps and was co-owner of Strom and Son Feed and Farm

Supply, so he understood how important it was to carry on the family legacy.

Would he feel drawn to rodeo if he had been raised by Brooks Langtree? Would he be a bull rider or a bronc rider, competing in rodeos every week? Those questions couldn't be answered, even if it turned out that Brooks and Caleb were related. Greater minds than him had participated in the nature versus nurture debate.

Faith put her arm on the armrest between their seats, nudging his arm aside. When he looked at her, she flashed him a disarming smile. His heart skipped a beat in response. What was that about? This wasn't the first time an attractive woman had smiled at him. Not to be vain, but from the time he'd been a tyke, the opposite sex had been drawn to him. It wasn't something that he controlled. It just was.

Caleb couldn't allow Faith's grin to sweep him off his feet. Nor could he allow her armrest aggression to go unchallenged. As she'd done earlier, he raised a questioning eyebrow. When she acted as if she didn't get the message he knew he had to be more direct. "What are you doing?"

"This is my armrest. Yours is on the outside."

He looked around her. Her other arm was on the other armrest. "But you're using that one."

"Elizabeth doesn't care. Besides, you have the aisle seat. That is a bonus in and of itself."

"I didn't realize there was a rating system for arena seats."

She laughed, a sweet sound that sparked warmth inside his chest. "You don't expect me to believe that. Even little kids know the hierarchy."

"Let's pretend I don't know and you can enlighten me."

"It's fairly simple. Aisle seats are the best. The closer you get to the center, the worse the seats become. I had the ultimate seat, which I very generously gave to you, so naturally I get to use the armrest."

He didn't care about the armrest—or the aisle seat. He'd just wanted to sit beside her. But he was enjoying talking with her. "In that case, the armrest is yours."

"Thank you."

Geoff Burris, currently rodeo's biggest star and a resident of Bronco, approached the podium and Caleb and Faith turned their attention to the stage. Geoff welcomed everyone to the opening day of the Golden Buckle Rodeo and then began to talk about Brooks Langtree. The older man had quite an impressive biography. Not only had he been a huge star on the rodeo tour for years, he'd been a pioneer. He'd been the first Black cowboy to win the Golden Buckle.

As Geoff listed his numerous accomplishments—some of which Caleb had been unaware of—images of Brooks on horseback or riding bulls flashed on enormous screens around the arena. Watching the nearest screen, Caleb couldn't help but be impressed by the man's obvious skill.

"It is my honor to announce that today is Brooks Langtree Day," Geoff said, bringing his remarks to a close. "So please, let's give Brooks a Bronco welcome."

The crowd roared as Brooks Langtree rose from his seat and approached the podium. Geoff and Brooks embraced before the latter stepped up to the microphone.

Although Brooks Langtree was fifty years old, he had the muscular build of a much younger man. There didn't appear to be an ounce of fat on him. He was about six foot tall, with an erect bearing. Only a sprinkling of gray in his short-cropped black hair indicated his true age. A close-up of Langtree's face filled the screens and a shiver raced down Caleb's spine as he once more noticed the similarities to his own face. The pictures on the flyers hadn't lied.

Langtree's eyes sparkled with humor and his smile was friendly as he glanced around the arena, soaking in the applause.

When the cheers died down, Brooks spoke. "I'm honored to be here. It has been a very long time since I've been in Montana. Thank you so much for welcoming me back home."

The crowd erupted in applause again. Brooks was clearly affected by the love the audience sent in his direction. He wiped a tear from his eye and then waved, starting at one side of the arena and turning slowly so that he included each corner in his greeting. Caleb's heart raced when Brooks turned to his section. He willed the other man to look directly at him, but Brooks didn't. Even if their eyes met, Caleb knew Brooks Langtree wouldn't know who he was. To him, Caleb would simply be another face in a sea of faces. A complete stranger.

Even if he was his biological father, Brooks Langtree hadn't raised Caleb. Nathan Strom had had that privilege. Nathan was Caleb's father in every way that mattered. Even so, the need to know where he had come from had grabbed on to Caleb and wouldn't release him no matter how desperately he struggled to get free. He wouldn't be at peace until he'd gotten answers from the man who had sired him and then walked away without a second glance.

Caleb sent those thoughts away and managed to keep them at bay as the ceremony continued. After other commendations, Hattie Hawkins, Faith's grandmother, approached the microphone. Caleb had expected her to add her praise of Langtree, so Caleb was surprised when she said, "Faith Hawkins, I need you to come to the stage."

Faith sighed, and Caleb turned to look at her. She'd buried her face in her hands and was shaking her head as she slid down in her seat. "I can't believe she did this."

"Go on," one of the women with her said.

"You know she isn't going to budge until you do," added another. "Unless she decides to come off that stage and drag you up there with her."

Hattie put a hand on her forehead and began to search the crowd. Spotlights began moving around the audience. "I know you're out there somewhere. Don't be shy."

Caleb stood and stepped into the aisle. Instantly a spotlight landed on him and Faith.

"Thanks a lot, traitor," Faith muttered, looking at him. Although she was frowning, her eyes sparkled with mischief, assuring him that she didn't consider him a traitor after all.

"You're welcome," he said, flashing her a cheeky grin.

She stood and passed in front of him. Once more he inhaled a whiff of her sweet scent. Soft and slightly floral, it was enticing enough to get his imagination going in a manner totally inappropriate for the moment.

The spotlight followed Faith as she walked down the aisle and Caleb's eyes did the same. Her perfectly round bottom filled out her faded jeans and swayed with each step she took. She jogged up the stairs to the stage and stood beside her grandmother.

"You didn't think I was going to let this day pass unnoticed, did you?" Hattie asked. Although she was speaking to Faith, the microphone picked up her words so that the entire arena was privy to the conversation.

"I was hoping," Faith said, softly.

Hattie gestured to someone offstage. "Bring it out."

Two men wheeled a table holding an enormous, six-tiered cake onto the center of the stage. Two big numbers—a three and a zero—were in the middle of the top layer. Clearly Faith was thirty years old, the same age as he was.

"Since everyone is here, I thought we should celebrate your birthday with the entire town."

Faith shook her head. "But it's Brooks Langtree's day. I don't want to steal the spotlight from him."

"Nonsense," Brooks said. "There's plenty of attention to go around." He joined Hattie at the microphone and together they led the crowd in a rousing rendition of "Happy Birthday."

Faith stood there, looking uncomfortable, then relieved when the last strains of the song faded away. As she hugged her grandmother and shook Brooks's hand, several people began cutting the enormous cake and placing the slices on paper plates. They handed a few to Faith along with several paper napkins. Faith then returned to her seat and distributed the cake to the women with her. After she'd done that, she held two plates in her hands. She grinned and then offered one to Caleb.

"Thank you," he said, taking the cake from her. "You had me worried there for a minute."

"I had to make sure I had enough. As the saying goes, sisters before misters."

He laughed. "Is that right?"

"You'd better know it. But you wouldn't have been out of luck. There's cake enough for everyone."

The lights in the arena were turned up as people wearing shirts advertising the Golden Buckle Rodeo began passing out servings of cake to the audience.

"Maybe," Caleb said with a smile. "But somehow I think this piece will taste sweeter."

FAITH SNEAKED GLANCES at Caleb from the corner of her eyes. He had to be the best-looking man she'd ever seen. Surely he was in town specifically for today's event or new to town. If he lived in Bronco she would have noticed him before today. Men this attractive didn't generally fly under the radar for long. Even though she was certain she'd never seen him before today, there was something vaguely familiar about him. Try as she might, she couldn't put her finger on what. She had an excellent memory and never forgot a face or a name. If they'd met before, she would know. Still, she couldn't shake that feeling.

"Excuse me," a man distributing cake said, coming to stand behind Caleb.

"Sorry," Faith said, stepping out of the aisle and taking her seat. Caleb sat beside her and his shoulder brushed against her. Her skin heated and tingles raced down her spine. What was that about?

Caleb took a bite of cake. "Delicious. And by the way, happy birthday."

"Thanks." This wasn't the quiet celebration she'd had in mind, but she should have known her grandmother would do something like this. Hattie was nothing if not a showman. Decades removed from her groundbreaking rodeo career, Hattie Hawkins still knew how to command the spotlight. That ability to hold a crowd in the palm of her hand had been passed on to her daughters and granddaughters. Faith's cousin Audrey, rodeo's biggest star on the woman's circuit, had her wedding to Jack Burris as part of the Bronco Family Rodeo a couple of years ago. Faith didn't mind the attention—that was part of the job—but in her mind that was a bridge too far. Some parts of her life were too personal to share with her fans.

"How else are you going to celebrate? Besides having the world's biggest birthday party, that is," Caleb asked.

"This isn't my birthday party. Today is Brooks Langtree Day, remember? It just sort of got hijacked."

A strange expression crossed his face and vanished so

quickly that Faith could have imagined it. "I got the impression that he didn't mind sharing the spotlight with you."

She shrugged.

"So," he said, when she only sat there, "what do you have planned for the rest of the day?"

"My sisters, cousins and I will be performing in the rodeo this afternoon."

"That sounds nice."

"Have you lived in Bronco long?" she asked, still trying to place him.

"I don't live here," he said, confirming her earlier thought.

"So you just came for this event?"

"Yes. I saw flyers announcing Brooks Langtree Day. I decided to come by and see if he lives up to the legend."

"Where do you live?" she asked. Faith didn't want this conversation to turn into an interrogation, but she was curious about Caleb. And more than a little attracted to him. She was still a relative newcomer to Bronco and he was the first man that she'd found remotely interesting. Not that she was looking to add a man to her life. A relationship was the furthest thing from her mind. She'd been burned enough times to last a lifetime and was more than a little gun-shy. But Caleb was interesting. And he didn't appear to be flirting with her. It was possible that they could become friends. A girl could never have too many friends.

"Tenacity."

She shook her head and grinned ruefully. "True confession. I haven't lived in Montana for long and I have no idea where that town is. Honestly, I've never heard of it."

"It's about an hour and a half away. It's not as upscale as Bronco, but it's home."

"If you're looking for a tour from a local, you've come to the right place," her sister Elizabeth said, leaning over

Faith and talking to Caleb. "Faith is just the person to show you around. You might even stop and get a cuppa."

Faith kicked her sister's foot. Since they were each wearing boots, she knew Elizabeth didn't suffer a bit of pain. In fact, she only grinned.

"Cuppa?" Caleb asked.

"Elizabeth lived in Australia for years," Faith said. "Every once in a while she slips up and uses an Aussie term. She means coffee."

"I would love a tour from a local," Caleb said. "And I wouldn't say no to a cup of coffee."

"Like I said, I'm relatively new to Bronco."

"You've spent more time here than I have," Caleb said reasonably.

"True." Faith actually liked the idea of spending more time with him, so she didn't resist too much. "I'll tell you what. If you come by after the rodeo, I'll be glad to show you around."

"That sounds like a plan."

Caleb had finished his cake and he stood. The crowd had begun to disperse and he stepped into the aisle. "I need to get going. Ladies, thanks for letting me sit with you. I'll see you later, Faith."

Faith watched as he walked up the stairs, her eyes glued to his broad shoulders, trim waist and firm backside. His muscular physique was just one more thing to like about him. Not that she was counting.

Once Caleb had walked through the doors of the arena, Faith spun around to look at her sisters. "What is wrong with you guys?"

"What do you mean?" Tori asked, innocent as a baby.

"You know exactly what I mean. Why were you trying

so hard to push us together? Foisting me on him like an unwanted Christmas fruitcake."

The others laughed. After a moment, Faith joined in.

"That man is gorgeous," Amy said.

"Consider putting the two of you together our birthday gift to you," Tori said with a wicked grin.

"I was looking forward to getting that pair of earrings I saw in Cimarron Rose," Faith said.

"If you don't want him, I'll take him off your hands," Elizabeth said.

"Like anyone would believe that. You're so in love with Jake that you can't see anyone but him," Faith said. Her sister had married Jake McCreery just a couple months ago, combining their respective children into a busy family of seven. "If Caleb had even looked in your direction, you would have run away so fast you'd set a new land speed record."

Elizabeth grinned. "True. But since there is nobody in your life right now, there is no reason why you can't hang around with Caleb."

"Exactly," Tori added. "He was nice and seems like he's a lot of fun."

"He is gorgeous," Faith admitted, agreeing with Amy's assessment. There was no sense pretending that she didn't find him attractive. That would be a blatant lie. He seemed to possess all of the qualities that she liked in a man. Funny. Kind. Considerate. At slightly over six feet, he was neither too tall nor too short. He was muscular, but not overly so. He still had a neck. She absolutely loathed those guys who looked like they swallowed steroids daily and somehow ended up with no neck.

She also liked the way he dressed. His jeans were casual and his polo wasn't too tight or too loose. Like Goldilocks said, he was just right. And given her decision not to become involved with anyone, he was completely wrong.

But then, she'd always liked to live dangerously. Besides, what was the harm in a little fun?

CHAPTER TWO

FAITH BRUSHED HER horse one last time before handing her reins over to Glenn, the stable employee who led Sugarcane into the trailer. Although she loved her horse, the house she rented in Bronco didn't have the acreage a horse needed to be happy. So, like her sisters, cousins and their numerous in-laws who competed in rodeo, she boarded her horse at one of the local stables. Faith had confidence in the owner and the employees who cared for Sugarcane, but she went to the stables each day to care for her horse and to practice her skills.

Once Glenn drove away from the convention center, Faith went to the locker room where her sisters and cousins were gathering up their belongings. Today's event had been an exhibition as opposed to a competition with ranking points, but they had done their best to put on a good show. It was never a good idea to slack off at any time. Bad habits were easy to develop but hard to shake off.

"Good show," Audrey, Faith's cousin said, giving her a hug. Audrey worked hard to maintain her status as the undisputed champion on the women's circuit.

"Thanks. But you'd better watch out. I'm coming for your crown."

Audrey laughed and winked. "It's good to have a goal."

"So I've been told."

"Happy birthday, by the way. Let's get together for lunch one day next week. My treat."

"Sounds good."

"Elizabeth wanted me to tell you that she spotted your birthday gift in the audience. She said you would know what that means."

Faith waved off the comment. "You know my sister's sense of humor."

"I do. And I also know your ability to change the subject. That could only mean one thing. This gift is a man."

Faith knew it would be futile to deny it. She and her cousins had grown up together. They'd spent so much time with each other that they were as close as sisters. There was no fooling each other. "Yes."

"This man wouldn't by chance be Truett McCoy?"

"Tru McCoy? The Hollywood actor? Are you kidding me?"

Audrey nodded. "Jack told me that he might be here today."

"Why would a big star be in Bronco of all places?"

"I figure since he stars in cowboy movies he might want an up-close-and-personal view."

Faith only shook her head. Audrey's husband, Jack Burris, and his brother Geoff were famous both inside and outside of rodeo circles and they might hobnob with celebrities, but Faith didn't. "No such luck. We met a guy this afternoon. He sat with us during Brooks Langtree's presentation. Before I knew what was happening, Elizabeth had volunteered me to show him around town."

"How do you feel about that? If you don't want to be bothered, I can have Jack and his brothers get rid of him for you." Audrey grinned. "I didn't mean that as sinister as it sounded."

"Actually I don't mind. He seemed like a good guy." Yet there was something about him that was a bit off. Not that she thought he was up to no good. She could read trouble from a mile off. Her sisters had equally good Spidey senses too, so one of them would have known if Caleb wasn't a good guy. He just seemed to be a bit distracted, which, considering he'd driven over an hour just to attend the ceremony, was a bit odd. But there was no crime in being distracted. She'd found her own attention straying to Caleb once or twice this afternoon.

"Well, then, let your hair down and go enjoy your birthday present." Audrey flashed a mischievous smile, shimmied her shoulders and then walked away.

Shaking her head at her cousin's antics, Faith changed out of her rodeo garb and into her most flattering pair of jeans and a new top that she'd gotten the other day at Cimarron Rose, her favorite Bronco boutique. She freed her hair from the scrunchie that held it away from her face, ran a comb through her hair, touched up her lipstick, then went to meet Caleb.

As she headed into the arena, her heart began to pound and her tingles skipped down her spine. *Don't be ridiculous. This isn't a date and Caleb isn't a potential love interest.* They were simply going to spend an hour or so together while she showed him around Bronco. If things went well, they might grab a drink at Bronco Java and Juice. If things went *very* well, she might suggest they grab a burger. If not, they'd go back to their cars, say good-night and go their respective ways.

Caleb was sitting in the front row when she entered, his long legs stretched in front of him. There were a few stragglers lingering at the back of the arena as if unwilling for the night to end. A number of workers were raking the dirt floor, getting it in shape for tomorrow's events. It was so quiet now that it was hard to believe that thousands of cheering people had been in here only thirty minutes ago.

When Caleb noticed her, he stood and walked over.

He smiled and Faith instantly felt comfortable. There was something about him that put her at ease. Suddenly she couldn't wait to get the night started.

"That was some spectacular riding you did," Caleb said by way of greeting. "You're a great barrel racer."

Warmth flooded her and she smiled. "Thanks. Sugarcane and I have been working together for years. She knows when and how I want to move, which saves valuable seconds."

"You're a great team."

"Thank you again." She looked at him. "What would you like to see first?"

"I wasn't kidding earlier when I said that I didn't know anything about Bronco. I don't know what to ask to see. Perhaps a better question would be what do you want to show me?"

"That depends on whether you want to see Bronco Heights or Bronco Valley."

"I didn't know there were two Broncos."

"I'm still learning the difference, so take what I say with a grain of salt."

"Where did you live before, if you don't mind my asking."

"South America. I traveled the rodeo circuit there for a while. My cousins actually settled in Bronco first. Then more of my family followed. I guess the Hawkins family is gradually taking over."

He laughed. "A stealth invasion."

She laughed with him. "In a manner of speaking."

They talked easily as they walked side by side to the parking lot. Her Escape was parked near the entrance of the arena. A late-model pickup truck was parked a few rows away. The Bronco Convention Center was on the outskirts of town, so in order to get to any of the places Faith wanted to show him, they would need to drive.

"I know you don't know me well," Caleb said, "so if you would feel more comfortable, I can always follow you to town."

Faith smiled. She may have just met him, but she knew she was in no danger from him. At least not physically. She wasn't as sure about her heart. There was something about him that appealed to her on an elemental level. But since she wasn't going to open herself up for a romance, her attraction was immaterial. "I feel perfectly safe with you. But we are a ways from town. It makes more sense for each of us to drive there, so we won't have to double back later."

He seemed disappointed, but he nodded. "I'll follow you."

"Which side of Bronco would you like to see?"

"You were going to explain the difference to me." He shifted his Stetson away from his forehead and lifted one side of his mouth in a half smile. The expression was so sexy that her heart skipped a beat. She ordered her body to knock it off.

"Bronco Heights is where the rich folk live. Big houses. Big lots. All that. Bronco Valley is where the middle-class people like myself and my family live. Older homes and smaller lots. For the most part, everyone gets along well. Friendships aren't based upon class or anything like that."

He nodded, so she continued.

"Each place has its own downtown area with its own restaurants and stores. People from Bronco Valley go to Bronco Heights and vice versa. It just depends on what you are looking for. So, Caleb, what are you looking for?"

He shrugged his massive shoulders and her mouth went dry. She reminded herself that tonight was a one-time thing. She wasn't in the market for a man. "Just take me to your favorite places."

"I can do that."

Once they were in their cars, Faith led the way to town. Traffic was light and before long she'd reached Bronco Valley. She pulled onto a side street with plenty of parking spots, got out of her car and waited while Caleb parked his pickup.

"This looks nice," Caleb said once he was beside her.

"I enjoy walking around Bronco. There are so many interesting shops and good restaurants. Even though I haven't lived here long it already feels like home."

"Where did you grow up?" Caleb asked as they walked down the street. There were a few other pedestrians taking advantage of the beautiful fall evening, but the pavement wasn't crowded.

"Everywhere. My mother and her sisters were also on the rodeo tour and my sisters, cousins and I traveled with them."

"What was that like?"

She paused as she gave his question some thought. "There were things I enjoyed. I liked seeing different places and meeting new people. The adventure of it all. It's a big world and I want to see as much of it as possible. But there were times when I wished we didn't travel as much. Times when I wanted to live in one place for years instead of just a short time. But even as a child, I knew that it wasn't possible to do both things at the same time. Choices had to be made."

"Are you planning on settling down in Bronco or will you be moving along?"

"That's a good question. I do like Bronco. Some of my family members have begun to put down roots. They've either married local men or are involved in serious relationships. My parents came to town for my sister's wedding and they decided to stay for a while. I like being around my family and having a home base. As long as I'm competing on the rodeo circuit, I'll be able to satisfy my wanderlust."

"So you have the best of both worlds. It can't get much better than that."

"No, it couldn't." Of course, having a special someone to share that world would be nice. Not that she would say that out loud. She didn't want Caleb to think that she wanted him to fill that role. To be honest, she wasn't sure she wanted anyone to fill that spot in her life. She'd tried getting serious once before and the relationship had been an unmitigated disaster. Besides, she was enjoying the single life. There was plenty of time to fall in love in the future.

"This place looks interesting," Caleb said, stopping in front of Cimarron Rose boutique.

"It's one of my favorite stores. They sell the most beautiful boho chic clothing and jewelry. Some of it is a bit pricey, but it's all exquisite."

"I don't know boho chic from regular chic, but the stuff in the window looks nice. I could find some nice gifts here."

For whom? Did he have a girlfriend? It suddenly occurred to Faith how little she knew about Caleb. "If you're looking for something special for that certain someone, this is the place to go. Of course, if you're looking for high-end jewelry, I'd suggest Beaumont and Rossi's Fine Jewels."

Caleb gave her an odd look and she knew her fishing expedition had been very obvious. "I was thinking about my mother. She loves antique jewelry."

"Oh. Okay."

He looked her straight in the eyes. "And just for the record, there is no *certain someone* in my life."

Caleb's voice rang with sincerity and his eyes were clear and honest. Faith had no doubt that he was telling her the truth, and she appreciated his truthfulness. "Even though you haven't asked, there is nobody special in my life either. To be honest, I'm not looking."

"I sense a story there."

She shrugged. "It's not an original one nor one worthy of sharing. Suffice it to say that the last guy I dated was seeing me and someone else at the same time. He didn't tell either of us. When I found out, it hurt."

"Were you in love with him?"

"Not even a little bit. My heart wasn't broken. It was the fact that he lied to me that disappointed me. I don't think anyone should stay in a relationship that they don't want to be in. Not everyone is made for commitment or monogamy. But I do think that people should be honest about what they want. If they no longer want to be in an exclusive relationship, they should let the other person know. Deception hurts."

He nodded. "I agree. For the record, I'm not looking for a special someone either. And now that we've established that we're on the same page when it comes to relationships, can we go inside and look around?"

"Sure."

Caleb held the door for Faith before following her inside. There were only a couple of other shoppers, so they were free to walk about at their leisure. Faith loved it here. All of the items might not be her style, but they were all elegant in their own ways.

"What do you think?" Caleb asked, holding up a pair of silver chandelier earrings.

"I like them. They go so well with your skin tone."

"You think?" Caleb asked, not the least bit fazed. "Maybe I should get the gold."

She laughed. His sense of humor matched hers.

"Nah. Stick with silver."

"I think my mom would love these."

"She has good taste. They're beautiful."

They looked around a bit more, checking out other pieces of jewelry. In the end, Caleb decided to stick with the pair that he'd picked out initially. He paid for the jewelry and they continued their tour of the town, stopping in random businesses on occasion. Eventually they came upon Bronco Burgers.

"Would you like to get something to eat?" Caleb asked.

"Yes. I can't tell you how hungry I am. I'm always starving after I ride."

"Why didn't you say something earlier?"

She shrugged. "We agreed that I would show you around town, not that we would go out to dinner."

"Faith." The way he said her name spoke volumes. It also sent shivers racing down her spine. "That didn't mean that we couldn't grab a bite."

"I think I knew that."

"Do you want to get a burger here or would you rather go somewhere else to eat?"

"I would love a burger," Faith said. "I've eaten here a couple of times before. They have the best shakes."

"Sounds perfect."

The minute they stepped inside, the wonderful aroma of grilled beef surrounded them. Faith's stomach rumbled. "Sorry."

"Don't worry about it."

They grabbed seats and then placed their orders.

"I've told you a bit about Bronco. Can you tell me about Tenacity?"

"Sure. The name suits the town. People there are strong with a never-say-die attitude. Tenacity is a blue-collar town made up of ranchers."

"Are you and your parents ranchers?"

"No. We actually own a store. Strom and Son Feed and Farm Supply. I know that's a mouthful. We serve the ranchers in Tenacity as well as those in the vicinity."

Faith gave him a long, searching look. "I can totally see you doing that. You have a calm demeanor and a way of putting people at ease. More than that, you're honest yet diplomatic. You probably get a lot of repeat business because of that."

He seemed flustered. "I don't know whether you're pulling my leg or not."

"Not at all. I'm being completely honest."

He exhaled. "We do get a lot of repeat business. But that has more to do with my father than it does with me. My father only gets the best supplies so customers never have to worry about quality. He anticipates what people will need and stocks it ahead of time. If someone makes a special request, he does his best to fill it in a timely manner."

"That's good business."

The waitress brought their meals and they didn't speak until she had walked away. Faith took a big bite of her burger and then sighed. Delicious.

Caleb bit into his too, and his eyes closed briefly. "This is really good."

"It's the perfect after-rodeo meal."

"I know that Bronco has a couple of other rodeos. One at Christmas and one in the summer. Did you compete in those?"

"The one in December is the Mistletoe Rodeo. The other is the Bronco Summer Family Rodeo. And no, I didn't participate in either of them. My sisters Tori, Amy and I were touring in South America last year. I only moved to Bronco recently and was still getting a lay of the land this past summer."

"This must be a big change."

"In some ways. But rodeo is rodeo. Same events. Same scoring system. Same smells. And rodeo people are the same all over the world. Close-knit and caring. Supportive. We compete against each other in the ring, but once the event ends, we're friends. Family, really. We all try to do our best, but we're happy for whoever wins."

"Why did you decide to come back to the States?"

"It was time. Don't get me wrong, I enjoyed being in South America. I saw a lot of tourist sights and had a lot of experiences I wouldn't have had otherwise. But my family seemed to be gathering in Bronco. My sister Elizabeth was actually touring in Australia before she came here. She was widowed a few years ago and has five-year-old twin daughters. Now she's married to a local rancher with three kids."

"Wow. That's a lot of kids."

"Elizabeth has a big heart and plenty of love for all of them."

"That's good. Kids deserve love."

"Speaking of kids. Do you have any brothers or sisters?"

He hesitated ever so slightly as if unsure how to answer. "No. I'm an only child."

"What was that like?"

"Good. I have great parents."

"Did you ever feel lonely?"

"Of course. Didn't you?"

She started to say that with four sisters and numerous cousins someone was always around, but that simply meant that she was seldom alone. Their presence didn't keep her from experiencing occasional bouts of loneliness. "Yes. I guess I did."

"I don't think the presence or absence of others keeps us from experiencing the whole range of emotions. We can try to use others to avoid feelings we don't want to acknowledge, but they're always there, lurking in the background until you deal with them."

"Impressive." She looked into his intelligent eyes. "What are you, a psychologist or a business owner?"

"I'm just a man."

A man she was beginning to like. Although she wasn't looking for a relationship, she now realized that by avoiding men altogether, she'd given her most recent ex-boyfriend control of her future. Since she hadn't been willing to give him a say over her life in the past, why would she give him that power now?

"How long are you going to be in Bronco?" Faith asked.

"I'll be going back to Tenacity Monday morning. I have a few things to take care of this weekend."

His words were vague, and Faith waited, expecting him to clarify them or give more details. Rather than do that, he picked up his cup and drained his strawberry shake. She shoved down her curiosity. They were little more than strangers. She wasn't entitled to know his itinerary. Nor did he owe her an explanation. Even so, they had talked so easily tonight it was disappointing for him to clam up now. Her Spidey senses went off but she told herself she was overreacting. His behavior didn't warrant her suspicion.

The waitress brought their bill and Faith reached for her purse.

"I have it," Caleb said, pulling his wallet from his pocket.

"That's not necessary."

"It *is* necessary. I enjoyed the pleasure of your company."

"I enjoyed your company, too," she said.

"Then consider this my birthday present to you."

Before Faith could argue further, Caleb handed the waitress several bills. "Keep the change."

The waitress looked at the money and then flashed Caleb a wide smile. "Thank you. Have a wonderful evening. Both of you."

Caleb nodded, then he and Faith left the restaurant. The October evening was pleasant and the air was crisp. As they walked down the street, dried leaves crunched under their boots. Faith glanced up at Caleb. "I love this time of year."

"Do you?"

"Yes. It's not too hot and it's not too cold. After a long, hot summer, it's nice to have cooler weather. And I'm a pumpkin spice kinda girl, so that's also nice."

"I have no idea what that means."

Laughing, she shook her head. "Pumpkin spice is a flavor. It's hard if not impossible to find in the spring and summer. But come autumn, it's everywhere. There are pumpkin spice lattes, cookies, biscuits, and even cereal to name a few things."

Caleb made a face.

"I take it you aren't a fan."

"It doesn't sound like something I would like, but I'm not going to say no without even trying it."

"If you like coffee, there is pumpkin spice creamer. That's my favorite."

"I prefer my coffee black."

"You aren't going to make this easy, are you?"

He chuckled. It was a happy sound that sent butterflies loose in her stomach. "Where would the fun be in that?"

"Fine. You like cookies, don't you?"

"I wouldn't say no to an oatmeal raisin or sugar cookie."

"Good. As soon as it's available, I'm getting some pumpkin spice sugar cookie dough. I'm going to bake a batch of cookies and you're going to love every bite. In fact, you're going to beg me to make you some more."

"You must be pretty confident in those cookies."

"I am actually underselling them."

"I have an excellent memory, so I'm not going to forget this brag."

"I don't want you to. I want you to remember every word that I've said."

He gave her a sexy smile that made her toes tingle. "I'm going to remember everything about tonight."

So would she.

They talked and laughed as they walked for another block before turning and going back the way they'd come. When they reached her car, he leaned against the hood. She leaned beside him. A breeze blew and his scent wafted around her. His cologne was slightly woodsy and totally enticing. Her knees wobbled. If she hadn't been propped against the car, she might have slid onto the ground.

While they'd been strolling around town, the sun had set and the moon had risen in the deep blue sky. Stars were beginning to pop out all over. Suddenly everything around them felt romantic.

Faith turned to face him. "I had a great time tonight, Caleb."

"So did I. Thank you for taking the time to show me around." His voice was deep. Husky.

"You're welcome."

They stood there for a moment, staring into each other's eyes, not talking. Words weren't necessary as they basked in the pleasure of each other's company. She could happily stay here all night, but she needed to get home. She sighed. "I suppose it's time to say good-night."

"I know." He pushed away from the car and held out his hand. When she took it, he led her around the car to the driver's door. She fumbled through her purse until she found her car keys. She pressed the key fob, disengaging the lock. Caleb opened the door and held it while she slid inside. He waited until she'd fastened the seat belt before speaking.

"Would you mind texting me to let me know you made it home safe?"

"I don't mind, Caleb." Touched by his concern, Faith couldn't make her voice rise above a whisper.

They quickly exchanged numbers. Then Caleb closed her car door. Faith watched as he ambled over to his truck and hopped inside.

When Caleb was out of sight, Faith blew out a breath, turned the key in the ignition and drove away. As she went down the street, one thought played through her mind.

She really wanted to see Caleb again.

CHAPTER THREE

CALEB DROVE THE short distance to the Bronco Bed and Breakfast where he was staying the weekend. The B and B was in a six-bedroom, yellow Victorian house. The owner, Claire, a single woman in her midthirties, explained that she'd recently inherited the house from a long-lost uncle and had converted it into this B and B. She was friendly and respected her guests' privacy, something that given his situation, he appreciated.

His second-floor room was small yet cozy and the blue-and-cream color scheme was relaxing. The queen bed was comfortable and there was an old-fashioned rolltop desk where he'd set up his laptop. Stepping out of his boots, he settled into the armchair in front of the window and propped his feet on the footstool. He needed to update his parents. When he'd told his parents of his plans to find his birth father, they hadn't been surprised. It was as if they'd always known the day would come.

The funny thing was, until he'd turned thirty, he hadn't given the idea much thought. Sure, he'd occasionally wondered about his birth parents, but the notion had always been fleeting. This time had been different. Once the idea had entered his mind, he couldn't shake it. He still didn't understand why. His parents were the best and he'd grown up surrounded by their unconditional love. They'd never once treated him as anything other than their precious son.

So why was the need to find his biological parent so strong?

When he'd decided to go in search of his past, he'd debated long and hard before he'd approached his parents. He hadn't wanted to make them feel like he was rejecting them. The words had still been making their way out of his mouth when his mother had shushed him, pulling him into her familiar embrace.

His father had patted him on his shoulder, something he'd done for years as a way of conveying his affection. "We know that, son. Nothing and nobody will ever be able to change the love between us. But we also know that you want to know more about your birth parents. We'll help you in any way that we can."

"I have all of the paperwork from your adoption," his mother had added. "Let me get the file and we can go through it together."

Just like that, all of Caleb's worries had vanished. He'd known that finding his birth father wouldn't break the bond he and his parents shared, but confirmation had gone a long way toward putting him at ease.

His mother had gone into her office, a room decorated in soothing creams with black accents, and returned holding a large manila folder. "This is everything we know about your birth parents."

"Do you want to read it alone or would you like company?" his father asked.

"I'm not sure." He'd wanted to read everything alone, just in case there was something in there that would break his heart. The last thing he wanted was for his parents to witness his pain. At the same time, he'd needed their support.

"How about we let you read everything on your own

first," his mother had said after a moment. "If you have any questions or want to talk about anything, we'll be here."

"That sounds like a good plan," Caleb had agreed.

The only problem was there had been no new information in the file. He still knew only that his mother was deceased, and his father had wanted to maintain his anonymity. Caleb had tried to get his original birth certificate, but he hadn't been successful in that either.

His mother had been the one to suggest that he write a letter to his birth father in care of the adoption agency. He'd sent the letter the following day, but weeks later he hadn't gotten a response. With each passing day, his hope of hearing from his biological father dwindled. As a last desperate measure, he'd tried one of those DNA tests, hoping to find a relative that way, but had come up empty. If he had any biological family, they weren't trying to figure out where they'd come from. But then, they probably already knew.

He'd come up against an impenetrable brick wall and had been ready to admit defeat when pictures of Brooks Langtree had sprung up all around Montana. No matter where Caleb went, he couldn't escape the image. There was a resemblance between the two that couldn't be denied. Since he was all out of options, he'd decided to try to meet with Brooks Langtree and get his question answered.

Was Brooks his biological father? The resemblance between the two had made Caleb believe it was possible. But the more he learned about Brooks Langtree, the less likely it seemed. Brooks didn't seem the type to give away a child and then make it next to impossible to be found.

But then, who knew the kind of person he'd been thirty years ago. Langtree was a good-looking man, even at fifty. He'd probably been even more so in his youth. No doubt he'd had women chasing after him at twenty. After all, he had been a rising star with a bright future. That would make him even more appealing to a whole segment of women. Perhaps a rodeo groupie had gotten pregnant. Perhaps once she'd died, Brooks Langtree hadn't wanted the responsibility of raising a child on his own.

Caleb shook his head. He'd promised himself not to let his imagination run wild. He would deal with facts, and *only* facts. If he couldn't prove a theory, then he would discard it. That was the only way to ensure that he didn't travel down the wrong path, ending up farther away from the truth than he was now.

Pulling out his phone, he punched in his parents' number. He was a grown man, but he still turned to them for support and advice.

After two rings, his mother's familiar voice came over the line. Although Caleb had lived in his own place ever since he'd graduated from college, he saw his parents all the time. They were just as close as ever.

"How are you, son?" Iris asked. That was the first question she'd asked him for as long as he could remember. The first thing she'd always wanted to know.

"I'm actually good," Caleb said. He might not have stood face-to-face with Brooks Langtree, but he had seen close-up images of the man on the video screen. There was enough of a resemblance for Caleb to believe they could be related.

But that wasn't the only reason Caleb was so elated. The other reason was Faith Hawkins. Just being around her had made him feel emotions he hadn't experienced in a long time—if ever. She was so easy to be with. So much fun. She was a light that brightened dark places in his heart. Being with her felt good. It felt right. Although he hadn't been looking for a romantic entanglement when he'd come to Bronco—and he still wasn't—meeting Faith had been an unexpected bonus.

He wished he'd made plans to see her again. He'd had a chance when she'd texted him to let him know she had arrived home safely but he hadn't taken it. Instead of setting up another date, he'd wished her good-night and sweet dreams. He was on a mission and couldn't allow himself to be distracted.

"Hold on so your father can pick up the extension," Iris said.

Her muffled voice came over the phone as she covered the receiver with her hand and called for her husband to get on the phone. Caleb couldn't help but smile to himself. Although his parents had cell phones, they insisted on keeping their landline. After a moment his father's voice came over the phone. "How are things going?"

"Everything's fine."

"Did you get a chance to meet with Brooks Langtree?"

It was just like his father to get to the heart of the matter. Nathan believed in facing a problem head-on. Get it all out there and find a solution. That was his motto.

"No. But I didn't really expect to. I just wanted to see the man in the flesh instead of just looking at pictures."

"And?"

"The resemblance is there. The pictures didn't lie. He might be my biological father."

"Don't get your hopes up," Iris cautioned. "Even if that's true. You might be excited to meet him, but he might not feel the same."

"I know." The idea stung, but it couldn't be denied.

"I don't want to have to hurt that man if he hurts my baby," Iris continued.

Caleb and Nathan laughed. Iris talked tough, but she

was the sweetest person in the world. Of course, nobody had ever hurt someone she loved.

"I'll keep that in mind," Caleb said.

"So you only saw him from a distance?" Nathan asked.

"Yes. On the big screen."

"So why are you in such a good mood?" Iris asked.

Was he going to mention Faith? After all, there wasn't that much to tell. And then there was the risk that his mother would jump to conclusions. Iris was normally a rational person and never allowed her feelings to get the best of her. Unless the topic was romance. Then her brain short-circuited, and logic was replaced by emotions.

It hadn't always been that way. Then about four or five years ago, her friends' children began getting married and having babies. Caleb had always dated, but never seriously. That was no longer good enough for his mother. Suddenly Iris was all about Caleb finding a nice girl, getting serious and settling down. She wanted grandchildren while she was young enough to enjoy them.

"I made a friend. We hung out a little bit and went out to dinner."

"Would this be a female friend?" His mother's voice was filled with hope.

"Iris," Nathan said with a chuckle. "You aren't going to start that, are you? With everything going on, Caleb doesn't have time to focus on romance."

Caleb appreciated his father's support, but knew it was futile. Reasoning wasn't going to work with his mother.

"Caleb is a bright boy. He has the ability to multitask."

Nathan and Caleb laughed again. Iris was on a mission and nothing would deter her.

"Tell me about this girl," Iris said.

"There's not much to tell. Her name is Faith. She competes in rodeo."

"That can be dangerous," Iris said.

"She knows what she's doing. I saw her in action this afternoon. She's really good."

"Does she have to travel a lot?" Nathan asked. "That can be hard on a relationship."

"I don't know how much travelling she has to do. I do know that she toured South America with her sisters not too long ago."

"I didn't know that rodeo was popular all over the world," Nathan said.

"I didn't either," Caleb admitted. There was a lot he didn't know. But if he was going to get closer to Faith, that would need to change.

"Maybe you should think about meeting a girl with a less dangerous job," Iris said softly. "And one who doesn't travel as much."

"I'm not thinking about marrying Faith, Mom. I just met her a few hours ago."

"That's time enough to know if there was a spark," Nathan said. His mother might be the one urging Caleb to settle down, but his father was the more romantic of the two.

Nathan remembered the exact date and time he and Iris met. He vividly recalled every detail of her outfit down to the earrings and bracelet she'd worn. Nathan often surprised Iris with jewelry, flowers and other *just because* gifts. He was the one who scheduled twice-monthly date nights and romantic weekend getaways for the couple.

"That's true," Caleb conceded. It was useless to argue. Especially since his father was right.

"So, was there a spark?" Nathan asked.

Caleb could evade the question, but he wouldn't. Even though he wasn't looking for a relationship, for some odd reason he wanted his parents to know about Faith. "There was. I can't explain it. I've been attracted to women before, of course, but what I felt for Faith was different. Stronger."

"She could be the one," Nathan said.

"Don't jump to conclusions," Iris said. "He barely knows her."

"And she might travel for her dangerous job," Caleb said, voicing his mother's true concern.

"Exactly."

"What else do you know about her?" Nathan asked.

"Not much." He could tell his parents that she was petite with the sexiest body that he had ever seen. Or that she had a sultry voice, a happy laugh, and smelled like Heaven, but he knew that wasn't the kind of thing they wanted to know. "Oh. I do know a bit about her family. Her grandmother was a big star in rodeo a while ago. Hattie Hawkins. And Faith's mother and aunts used to compete as the Hawkins Sisters."

"Faith is a Hawkins?" Iris asked.

"Yes. Does that make a difference?"

"Of course it does. Anyone with even a passing knowledge of rodeo knows about Hattie Hawkins. She helped to make rodeo safer and more humane. She had great influence in her day. She still does. Her daughters were very talented and skilled. They're all very professional. From what I hear, this new generation is just as talented. They generally win their events, but they never take foolish risks."

"So I take it that you're no longer opposed to me spending time with Faith," Caleb said.

"No. Not that I thought it would make a difference. You're your father's son when it comes to romance. Stubborn as a mule. Besides, if Faith is a Hawkins, I know she'll be careful. And I know that I'll like her."

Caleb smiled at the not-so-subtle hint. Now that Iris approved of Faith, it was full steam ahead. Iris was ready to march him down the aisle this year and help him build a nursery the next. "Slow down, Mom. It was only one date. Besides, I'm focused on finding out if Brooks Langtree is my biological father. If so, the search is over. If not, I need to keep looking. Until this is settled, I'm not in a position to start a relationship."

"Humph," Iris replied, clearly displeased by his answer.

"What's your plan for tomorrow?" Nathan asked.

"I'm going to try to meet with Brooks Langtree. I just have to figure out a way to make that happen."

"Is there anything I can do to help?"

"No, Dad. Thanks for offering. I'll find a way." He hoped.

"Good. I hope he can give you the answer you're looking for."

"So do I."

FAITH LEANED AGAINST the back of the tub, then sank down until the warm, sudsy water brushed against her chin. Closing her eyes, she let the sound of the saxophone playing over the speaker wash over her. Nothing soothed her like a long, scented bubble bath accompanied by smooth jazz, especially after a day of competition. Though today had simply been an exhibition, her muscles still appreciated the relaxing bath.

Brooks Langtree Day had been great. Faith had enjoyed seeing the older man get the recognition he deserved. He had grinned the entire time, joy bursting from every pore as the crowd acknowledged his accomplishments. But that hadn't been the best part of her day. Nor had being serenaded by the audience, although that had unexpectedly been fun. Meeting Caleb had been the highlight of the day.

He was by far the most interesting man she'd met in years. He had a quick sense of humor and an easygoing demeanor that made him fun to be around. His handsome face and muscular body appealed to her on a basic level. In simple terms, he was good to look at.

That thought made her laugh. How many times had she said that she wanted men to look at her as a person and not focus so much on her looks? Yet here she was, doing the same thing to Caleb. Oh, well. Life was like that sometimes.

She'd really enjoyed herself tonight. Everything had been perfect. The burger, fries and shake had hit the spot. Walking around town and sharing some of her favorite spots with Caleb had been fun. She remembered how impressed she'd been when she'd seen Bronco for the first time. How at home she'd felt. There was something about Bronco that felt familiar. Every person was so warm and welcoming. The town was like a big hug. She wondered if Caleb had felt the same way. Not that it mattered. He hadn't given any indication that he was looking for a new hometown.

Faith soaked until the water turned chilly and her bubbles had faded away. Then she dried off on a fluffy towel, smoothed on her favorite scented lotion and put on a pair of orange pajamas. She had just settled in her bed with a cup of tea and a mystery novel when her phone rang. She glanced at the screen and smiled.

"Hi, Elizabeth. What are you doing up this late?"

"I finally have a moment of quiet. The kids are asleep and I decided to give you a call to see how your date went."

"It wasn't a date," Faith was quick to point out.

"Did you prearrange a time and place to meet?"

"Yes."

"Did you have an established agenda?"

Faith sighed. She knew where Elizabeth was going. She also knew that Elizabeth was relentless and there was no way to stop her. "Also yes."

"Then it was a date."

"Okay, smarty-pants. It was a date."

"And? How did it go?"

"It was wonderful," Faith said. If she'd thought before answering, she might have been less effusive. She didn't want to give her sister the wrong idea. Not that she thought Elizabeth would jump to conclusions. Her sister was well aware that Faith wasn't looking for love. Once burned, lesson learned.

"Oh. *Wonderful*," Elizabeth echoed. "Tell me more."

Faith piled her pillows behind her back and then sighed. "There's not much to tell. We walked around town for a bit and then stopped for burgers and shakes."

"Ah. Dinner."

Faith rolled her eyes. "Why are you so determined to make a bigger deal out of this than it is?"

"I'm not. I'm simply summing up what you're saying."

"No. You're spinning what I'm saying. You're in love, so now you have romance on the brain."

"That could be true. Remember what I told you when Jake and I started dating. Your Mr. Wonderful could be right around the corner. Who knows, it could be Caleb."

"We just met."

"But do you like him?"

Faith smiled. "I do. I felt really comfortable with him."

"I knew it," Elizabeth crowed. "I had a good feeling about the two of you."

"Don't get ahead of yourself. I'm perfectly content to take things slowly."

"Even that is a big change for you. Before you met Caleb you weren't willing to even think about having a relationship."

"Right. So don't make me nervous or I might turn tail and run."

Elizabeth laughed. "I'm not worried about that. You've never run away from anything in your life. Especially not a man."

"There's always a first time."

"And," Elizabeth continued as if Faith's words weren't worthy of acknowledgement, much less a reply, "you have never run away from happiness."

"You sound so sure that Caleb is offering me happiness." Of course, there was no reason for her to suspect that Caleb would bring her unhappiness. He'd been so honest and open today. People who were up to no good generally weren't so forthcoming.

That sliver of doubt returned to nag at Faith. She still suspected that Caleb was holding something back. She believed him when he said that it wasn't another woman. Even if he was withholding something, so what? She didn't expect him to bare his soul to her on their first date. There was a time and a place for everything. An order to things. Too much information might have sent her running for the hills. They were still in the getting-to-know-each-other phase of their relationship. If indeed there was a relationship. They hadn't made plans to see each other again, so she could be worrying about nothing.

But they could get together. Caleb was staying in town this weekend. And she had his phone number. She could call him. But when she'd texted him that she was home, his answer had been perfunctory. He hadn't made an effort to get a conversation started. But then, neither had she.

"I don't know what he's offering you," Elizabeth said honestly, pulling Faith's attention back to the conversation. "But I do know that life seldom goes according to our plans. My life is proof of that. Bad things happen. I lost Arlo to an undiagnosed heart condition with no warning. I didn't think I would ever recover emotionally or that I would be able to love again. But I did. Sometimes good things are waiting to happen. All we have to do is be open to them."

"That sounds so easy."

"It is. The question you need to answer is this: Are you willing?"

"I don't know," Faith admitted.

"And on that note, I'm going to say good-night," Elizabeth said. "Morning comes early around here."

Elizabeth's words echoed in Faith's head long after they'd ended the call. Something good could be waiting for her right around the corner. All she had to do was be open to it.

Was she willing to take a chance and possibly find love?

CHAPTER FOUR

CALEB STARED AT his phone. For the past ten minutes he'd been debating with himself, trying to decide whether or not to reach out to Faith. Today was the second day of the Golden Buckle Rodeo and Caleb expected Brooks Langtree to be in attendance. If he was there, Caleb might have a chance to talk with him. Even with that idea in mind, Caleb couldn't stop thinking about Faith. But should he call her? Or should he stay focused on the task at hand and the reason he was in Bronco?

Debate over, he tapped in her number and waited while the phone rang. There really hadn't been much doubt what he was going to do. The minute the notion struck him, he'd known he would eventually break down and reach out to her. He reasoned that if she hadn't wanted him to call her, she wouldn't have given him her number.

"Hi, Caleb. What's up?" Faith's voice was slightly breathless as if she had been running. Hopefully, he hadn't interrupted something important.

"I was just wondering if you would be interested in going to dinner with me tonight." That wasn't exactly why he'd been calling, but he did want to see her. Besides, he had no idea how she would react if he told her that he'd thought about her all night and had longed to hear her voice from the moment he'd awakened this morning. He was probably better off not saying that he wanted to spend time with her to find out if the feelings she'd stirred in him yesterday were real and just how deep they went. No, asking for a date was much more appropriate.

"I would like that very much," Faith said. "Where do you want to go?"

"Let me do some checking and get back to you."

"Oh, a man who is willing to do some research about the town. I like that."

His heart warmed at the pleasure in her voice. He'd learned from watching his father that when it came to women, the little things were actually the big things. "What time is good for you?"

"I'm free around seven," she said.

"I'll call you around six if that works for you."

"It does. I'll talk to you then."

After the call ended, Caleb smiled. Although there was still a lot unsettled in his life, just talking to Faith made his concerns seem that much smaller. That thought brought him up short. Faith shouldn't be able to impact his mood like that. And yet she had.

Deciding that this was a puzzle to solve at another time, Caleb grabbed his Stetson and jacket, then headed downstairs. The B and B provided breakfast for the guests of course, but Caleb was suddenly much too edgy to sit down to eggs and bacon. That would consume too much time.

Grabbing a bagel and an apple from the buffet set up in the dining room, Caleb nodded at Claire and left. He took a big bite from the juicy fruit and then headed to the convention center. When Caleb arrived, Brooks Langtree and his people were already in place, seated in their private box away from the crowd. Disappointment that he wouldn't have a chance to "bump into" Langtree swamped Caleb and for a moment he considered leaving. He shoved the idea down. It wasn't his nature to give up without even trying. He would create an opportunity to meet the man.

That decided, he found his seat and then looked over the program. Today's exhibition was limited to the men.

Caleb flashed back to Faith's appearance yesterday. She'd been impressive. Masterful. It had been a pleasure to watch as she confidently circled the barrels placed around the ring. She'd steered her horse very close to the barrels, but never once had either she or the horse touched one. When she'd finished her ride, the crowd had risen to its collective feet and given her a well-earned standing ovation.

Caleb had never cared much about rodeo. Before yesterday, he had never attended an event nor watched one on TV. He was a football fan. Even with his lack of knowledge, he could tell when someone was merely good as opposed to being exceptional. Faith fit firmly in the latter category. But she wasn't the reason he was here today, he reminded himself. Brooks Langtree was.

The lights dimmed and the crowd cheered. An unseen announcer welcomed everyone to the second day of the Golden Buckle Rodeo. He then acknowledged Brooks Langtree, who waved to the crowd from the VIP section. Although it made no sense, Caleb waved back.

The cowboys came out and began to compete in the first event. Caleb was impressed by the skill the riders displayed as they took turns lassoing a running calf while remaining on horseback. When that event ended, the next one started. Caleb was surprised to find himself on his feet cheering when riders managed to stay on the back of a spinning and bucking bull for eight seconds. This weekend was turning him into a rodeo fan.

When the rodeo ended, the lights came up. Caleb turned and looked to the VIP section. Brooks Langtree and his party were leaving their private box. Perhaps if he hurried, Caleb could catch him backstage.

Caleb went against the tide of the exiting crowd and

worked his way backstage. As he grew closer to the stage door, his heart began to pound and sweat beaded on his forehead. Was he about to meet his biological father? What would they say to each other? Would Brooks Langtree be happy to be reunited with the son he'd given up for adoption three decades ago? Or would he be angry that Caleb had managed to track him down? Would he say that he'd made it clear that he wanted the adoption to remain closed because he had no interest in ever seeing Caleb again? That horrible thought stopped Caleb in his tracks and he considered turning around and leaving.

Caleb took a steadying breath and ordered himself to slow down. He was making a huge leap here. There was still no proof that Brooks Langtree was his father. He needed to discover that first. Caleb started walking again, not stopping until he reached the backstage door. A security guard blocked entry.

"How can I help you?" The guard didn't smile, but he didn't appear particularly menacing either.

Caleb didn't know why he had expected to just walk up and talk to Brooks Langtree. He should have anticipated encountering a barrier. This may be a town with friendly people, but security was a necessity everywhere these days. Not to mention that Brooks Langtree was a celebrity.

"I was hoping to meet Brooks Langtree."

"I see. And is he expecting you?" The guard picked up a clipboard and glanced at a paper secured there. Caleb knew his name wouldn't be on any list.

"No."

"Are you a reporter?"

"No."

The guard gave Caleb a searching look. Perhaps he saw something on his face, because he held up a hand. "Hold on a minute. Obviously I can't let you past. But Mr. Harvey, Mr. Langtree's agent, is coming this way. You can speak with him."

Caleb looked over the guard's shoulder at a well-dressed older man who was striding in their direction. He held a cell phone pressed to his ear and appeared to be listening intently to whoever was on the other end. The guard waved at the man, who nodded. When he finished his conversation, he slipped the phone into his jacket pocket and strode over to them.

"What can I do for you?" the agent asked the guard.

"Mr. Harvey, this young man wants to meet with Mr. Langtree."

"I see." The agent gave him a once-over. "Are you a reporter?"

"No." Caleb and the guard answered at the same time.

"What business do you have with Mr. Langtree?"

Caleb hesitated. "It's personal."

"Is that right?" Mr. Harvey sucked his teeth.

"Yes."

"I handle Mr. Langtree's business affairs."

"If this was a business affair, I would talk to you. But it's not. It's personal," Caleb said firmly, hoping that answer would be good enough for the man. Caleb couldn't just blurt out that he might be Brooks Langtree's son. Especially since he wasn't sure it was true.

"I don't think you understand, son," Mr. Harvey said quietly. "Nobody gets to see Mr. Langtree without going through me."

Caleb bit back his frustration and swallowed harsh words. Being rude wouldn't accomplish anything other than getting him kicked out of the building.

"I get it. I do. And I'm not trying to be difficult. The matter I was hoping to speak to him about is personal. I'm not sure he would want anyone else to hear."

The security guard and the agent exchanged glances and all friendliness vanished. Mr. Harvey's slightly impatient expression morphed into one of undisguised suspicion and hostility. Clearly they were protective of Mr. Langtree.

"Is that supposed to be some kind of a threat?" Mr. Harvey asked. His voice was hard and his eyes narrowed into slits.

"Not at all," Caleb said quickly, hastening to erase the impression he'd just made and defuse the tense situation. "It's nothing like that. Look, I just need ten minutes alone with him."

"As I said earlier, that's not going to happen," Mr. Harvey said. "Now, if you're not going to tell me what you want, there is no need to continue this conversation." The agent pulled out his phone, tapped in a number and walked away.

"That didn't go the way I'd hoped," Caleb muttered to himself.

"No, I imagine it didn't."

Caleb jumped. For a moment there, he'd forgotten that the security guard was still around. Not that it mattered. He'd already gotten the only answer he was going to get.

"I just need to meet with him."

"Good luck with that," the guard said dryly.

"Yeah." Caleb walked away. That was a bust. He needed to regroup and come up with a better plan. Actually, this hadn't been much of a plan. Did he think that he was just going to walk up to a rodeo legend and have a private conversation about a secret child? He must have been delusional.

When he reached the parking lot, Caleb leaned against his truck and looked up. One big puffy cloud floated in the clear blue sky. When Caleb had been a kid, he and his father used to go on fishing trips to a lake near Tenacity. While waiting for the fish to bite, they would point out shapes in the clouds. Those had been great times and Caleb smiled at the happy memories. More often than not, they hadn't caught more than two or three fish between them. Without exception, Nathan had taken one look and declared the fish was too small—no matter how big the fish looked to Caleb—and said that they needed to throw it back.

Caleb was thirteen before he realized that while Nathan enjoyed their father-and-son time, he wasn't a fan of fishing. Or more accurately, he didn't like the idea of killing the fish. His big, strong father had a heart as mushy as a marshmallow. Caleb loved that about Nathan. His father wasn't embarrassed to show his gentler side. He had never tried to make Caleb into a hard man. Nathan let Caleb know that it was okay to cry when he was sad and that it was perfectly fine to experience every emotion, even the softer ones. Especially the softer ones.

Although Nathan had assured him that he wasn't being unfaithful by seeking out his birth father, Caleb still felt as if he was being disloyal to the man who'd raised him with such love. The man who had patiently taught him how to knot a tie, listened as he cried over a girl who had broken his heart, and taught him how to drive a stick shift.

Given the love that Nathan had shown him, why was Caleb consumed with the need to know more about his birth father? Meeting him wasn't going to change anything. Caleb wasn't going to start turning to his biological dad for advice. He wasn't going to start confiding in him about his hopes and dreams. No man would never replace Nathan Strom in Caleb's life or affection. So why was he so determined to meet his birth father if he didn't expect anything in his life to change?

What if Brooks Langtree—or whoever Caleb's birth

father was—wanted things to change? What if he wanted to have a part in Caleb's life? Would Caleb make a place for him? And how would that make Nathan and Iris feel? Was Caleb opening a can of worms that should remain closed? Caleb loved his parents more than anyone else in the world. He would sacrifice his happiness for them. If they didn't want his biological father to be a part of his life, then no matter how much Caleb wanted to know about his past, Caleb would keep him away. So why was he doing this?

Frowning, he forced the thoughts from his mind. This line of thinking was giving him a headache.

Caleb's stomach growled and he checked his watch. Hours had passed since he'd eaten that apple and bagel, which hadn't been much of a breakfast to begin with. Time enough for him to get good and hungry. He'd spotted a diner in town earlier and been eager to give it a try. Hopping into his truck, he drove there. It was past lunchtime but the dining room was still nearly full.

"Take any table you want and I'll be right with you," the waitress said as Caleb stepped inside the Gemstone Diner. He contemplated taking a seat at the counter since he was alone, but then decided against it. The booth by the windows would be perfect for people-watching. Although he was only in town for a little while, it wouldn't hurt to get a better feel for the place. Especially since Faith had decided to call Bronco home.

What was it about Bronco that appealed to her? It had to be more than the boutiques and eateries. You could find those anywhere. It couldn't be the weather. Winters in Montana could be long and brutal even for the hardiest of souls. That left the people. What characteristics did they share? He didn't expect the answer to show up on their faces—unless you counted the smiles they wore.

Maybe that was it. The happiness. The belief the people in town had that tomorrow would be just as good as today if not better. The sense that good things were waiting right around the corner. A feeling that the people of Tenacity seemed to be lacking.

"What will you have?" the waitress asked, standing beside his table. Her name tag read Mandy.

"How is your meat loaf?"

"Just the best in the state," she said with a bright smile.

"You mean, second to my mother's," he said with a grin.

"That goes without saying."

"In that case, I'll have meat loaf."

Mandy took his menu and promised to be back with his meal soon. While he waited, Caleb tried to come up with a new plan for meeting Brooks Langtree. Obviously Brooks's agent wasn't going to allow Caleb to get near him, so he couldn't use the typical lines of communication. Writing a letter was out because he didn't know who would open it. Brooks Langtree might have a person for that. The same was true of an email. Too bad Mr. Harvey had been so protective today.

While Caleb stared out the window, his mind wandered. Naturally he ended up thinking about Faith. He was looking forward to seeing her tonight, but he didn't want to ask her for a restaurant suggestion. He needed to take the initiative so she would know that he cared enough about her to put in the effort.

Mandy set his plate in front of him with a smile. "Here you go. Let me know if I you need anything else."

"Will do."

After the first bite, Caleb leaned back and smiled. The meat loaf was good. While he ate, Caleb tried to come up with a plan for meeting Brooks Langtree. Unfortunately each idea he came up with had too many hurdles and relied upon luck.

"How was it?" Mandy asked, coming up to his table.

"As good as advertised."

Mandy smiled. "Told you."

"Earlier you said I should let you know if I needed anything else."

"Sure." She reached for her pencil and pad. "What else can I get for you?"

"Actually, I would like a bit of help."

"Sure." She put a hand on her hip. "What do you need?"

"This is going to sound odd, but I'm not from here. I live in Tenacity."

"That doesn't sound odd. Lots of people come to Bronco from time to time. Especially when there is a rodeo in town."

"Okay. I'm looking for a place to eat."

She looked around. "I'd say you found one."

He grimaced. "That didn't come out right. I have a date tonight and was looking for a restaurant. Do you have a favorite place?"

She gestured broadly. "Apart from here, you mean?"

"Yeah."

"Depends on your wallet. There's Coeur de l'Ouest, which is quite expensive but worth every penny. Great food. Wonderful ambience. Scenic views. Impeccable service. And there is no way you'll be able to get in without a reservation. It's too late to get one now. There's also the Association. I heard that their food is really good but I've never been there. It's a private club. If you're not a member—"

He held up a hand, stopping her before she could continue. "Maybe I wasn't clear. I'm looking for places that I *can* take a date, not someplace that I *can't*."

She nodded. "If you like Italian, there's Pastabilities. That's a nice family restaurant and reservations aren't required."

He pictured a lot of kids running around and noise that would probably not be conducive to conversation. "What else do you have?"

"There's always DJ's Deluxe. It's a great rib joint. There's a chance you could get a reservation." She winced. "But it's the weekend, so..."

"You're killing me here. Surely there has to be another option."

"There's another place in town. Lulu's BBQ. It's not fancy, but the food is great."

"How not fancy is it?"

"It's really down-home. Paper towels on the table. That kind of thing."

What would Faith think if he suggested a place like Lulu's BBQ for their first official date, especially since they had gotten burgers and shakes the other day? Would she think he was a cheapskate? He might like Lulu's, but he doubted Faith would be impressed. And he really wanted to impress her.

"Thanks for your suggestions," Caleb said.

"You're welcome." Mandy gave him the bill.

He opened his wallet and pulled out some cash. "Keep the change."

"Thanks. And good luck finding the perfect place for dinner."

It was hard if not impossible to find a place to take a date when you didn't know your way around. Pulling out his phone, he did what he had hoped to avoid. He called Faith for a suggestion.

"Hello," Faith said. At the sound of her voice, Caleb smiled. There was a slight fluttering in his stomach that startled him. His body had never reacted like that to a woman's voice. Her legs. Yes. Her face. Definitely. But not her voice. "How are you?"

"I could use your help," he admitted.

"Go ahead."

"I know that I told you that I wanted to plan our date but I'm having a bit of trouble finding a restaurant."

She laughed. "So you're telling me that it's hard to find a place to eat in a town that you're not at all familiar with?"

"That about sums it up."

"Good thing I have a couple of ideas."

"Go ahead."

"Lulu's BBQ. It's not fancy but they have the tenderest ribs and the best sauce I have ever tasted."

"I heard about that place. You'd be happy going there for a date?"

"Absolutely. Unless you don't like ribs."

"I love ribs."

"Then it's set."

"You really are a surprise."

"Because I'd rather go to a regular restaurant instead of some hoity-toity place with white linen tablecloths?"

"Well...yeah."

"Don't get me wrong. I like a fancy restaurant just as much as the next girl, but they aren't the only places I go. I go to restaurants for the food. And today I would like to eat ribs. Lulu's are top-tier."

"I like the way you think." He'd been willing to follow the expected playbook when it came to first dates, but it looked like he didn't have to this time.

"That's a point in your favor," she said with a laugh.

"Would you like me to pick you up or would you rather meet there?"

"Do you think you know your way around town well enough to find my house?"

"I have GPS."

"In that case, you should pick me up. It is a date after all." He smiled at the humor in her voice, a clear sign that he was going to have a great time tonight. "I'll text you my address."

"Okay." His phone buzzed. He looked at the screen. "Got it."

"Good. Then I'll see you tonight."

They ended the call and Caleb's spirits soared. He might not have gotten the opportunity to meet with Brooks Langtree, but he would be having dinner with Faith.

In his book, that was a win.

CHAPTER FIVE

FAITH HELD THE phone for a few seconds after she and Caleb ended the conversation. Anticipation flowed through her body and she smiled. She'd dated her share of men, but she'd never felt this attracted to one before. She had never experienced such a strong connection so soon after meeting someone. And she'd certainly never felt such an intense longing to be with anyone. This feeling wasn't entirely comfortable but she couldn't seem to shake it. She wasn't even sure she wanted to.

One thing was certain—she wasn't going to make a big deal of it. Nor was she going to try to figure out what any of this meant. Caleb's six-feet-plus of muscles weren't the only things he had going for him. He was a good man—one she hoped would become a good friend.

Realizing that she was wasting time, she set down the phone and headed to her bathroom. She took a hot shower, using her favorite scented soap that calmed her jumpy nerves. When she was done, she smoothed on lotion and then released her hair from the shower cap. Though she wasn't looking for a relationship, she did enjoy male company. She loved her sisters and cousins and they spent a lot of time together. But there was something different about hanging out with a man. Something special. She liked getting a man's perspective on things. With the right man, discussions could be spirited and fun. Caleb had already shown that he was intelligent and a good conversationalist, so tonight held lots of promise.

Faith also liked dressing up. When she and her female relatives and friends went out, she generally didn't spend a lot of time on her appearance. A bit of lipstick, some mascara and maybe some color on her cheeks and she was ready to go. Even though she and Caleb were going to a casual dinner spot, this was still a date and warranted her full beauty regimen.

Going into her bedroom, she slipped on her silk underwear and then a satin robe. Taking her time, she dabbed on foundation, brushed on blush and eye shadow. She put on mascara and lipstick and then smiled at her reflection, pleased by what she saw. She pulled on her new purple blouse, tight black jeans and boots and spritzed on her favorite perfume. She had just put on silver earrings and bangles when her doorbell rang.

She glanced at the clock on her bedside table. Right on time. Grabbing her purse, she descended the stairs and headed for the front door. She swung it open and barely managed to hold back a gasp when she saw Caleb.

Dressed in a white long-sleeved pullover that hugged his broad shoulders and solid chest before it tapered to his flat stomach, and faded jeans that emphasized his muscular thighs, he was temptation on two legs. Telling herself not to make a fool of herself by drooling, she held the door open so he could enter.

"Thank you." He stepped into the room and she tried to see it through his eyes. The eclectic space had been designed for comfort, not fashion. She'd furnished her house with items that she had accumulated on her travels over the years. Each knickknack, piece of furniture and rug held special meaning for her.

"I'm ready. I just need to grab a jacket," she said, heading for the closet.

"Take your time." He looked around. "I don't know what I was expecting, but this room suits you perfectly."

"How so?"

"It's a little bit of everything." He gestured first to her large, striped sofa with its carved wooden arms before pointing to the tan leather chair with the blue striped throw draped across the back. Then he pointed to the miniature carved figures serving as bookends for her signed novels. "The pieces are a bit different from each other, and not at all what you would see anywhere else. Everything is unique. Just like you. And they all belong together, working together to create one cozy room. I like it."

"You totally get my style." In a way, he had summed up her personality. She wasn't predictable. She had lots of different facets. Not that she was going to let him know that. She needed to keep him guessing, at least for a while. Especially since there was still something mysterious about him. Of course, that could be her overactive imagination at work. Perhaps she should lay off the mystery books and movies and replace them with comedies.

Caleb helped her put on her jacket and they stepped onto her front porch. Once the door was locked behind them, they walked to his pickup and climbed in.

"Nice," Faith said, touching the butter-soft leather seats.

"I spend a lot of time on the road for the store. I'm either visiting customers, in search of new ones, or meeting with suppliers, so I need a comfortable ride."

This top-of-the-line vehicle was definitely that. It had all of the bells and whistles including a few features she had never seen before and wouldn't mind having in her car.

Lulu's BBQ was only a short ride away, so they were only able to discuss surface topics before he was parking in the lot behind the red brick building. Faith looked forward to having more in-depth conversations as they ate.

"You are going to love this place so much," Faith said as they walked through the door. The aroma of smoked meat, spicy sauce and frying potatoes filled the air, and she inhaled deeply.

"It smells so good I'm already in love," Caleb said.

There were lots of people in the dining room, and they had to wait for a few minutes for a vacant table. Disco music from the seventies played on invisible speakers and Faith tapped her toes to the beat.

Once a table had been cleared, Caleb pulled out the padded stool for Faith and then took the seat across from her. Instead of placemats, there were brown paper napkins on the wooden table. Where other restaurants had autographed photos of celebrities who'd dined at their establishment on their walls, Lulu had framed pictures of the smoking process on hers. Clearly she was as proud of her food as other restaurant owners were of their famous customers.

Caleb and Faith pulled laminated menus from between the paper napkin holder and the salt and pepper shakers and perused them. Patrons could order a meal by the number or create one from the slabs, tips, sandwiches and variety of sides on offer. A waitress dressed in black jeans, a white shirt and an apron with Lulu's logo embroidered on the top approached them. She set tumblers of ice water on the table, then grabbed a pencil and pad of paper from her apron pocket. She smiled at them. "Are you ready to order?"

Caleb and Faith exchanged glances. She nodded. "Yes."

They placed their orders and then the waitress nodded. "I'll be right back with your drinks."

Once they were alone, Faith turned back to Caleb. She had a million questions, so she voiced the first ones that came to her mind. "What brings you to Bronco? Are you trying to get more business for your store? Will you be coming back?"

CALEB TOOK A swallow of water as he tried to decide how to answer those questions. He was always looking for more customers, so he could say yes. It wouldn't be a lie, but it wouldn't be the truth either. He didn't want to deceive Faith. But he didn't want to tell her that he believed Brooks Langtree was his birth father. "I was hoping to get a feel for rodeo. I've never been a fan, even living in Montana, believe it or not, and Brooks Langtree Day seemed to be a good opportunity to see it up close. He is something of a legend. Being in his presence was special."

"Judging by the turnout, a lot of people felt the same way. I'm glad that people came to show their appreciation for all that he's done in his career. He helped pave the way for lots of today's competitors."

"I know. And it turns out that I got to sit with one of those competitors. But that's not the only reason I came to Bronco."

"No?"

He inhaled deeply and then blew out a slow breath. He couldn't believe it, he certainly hadn't planned it, but he was going to tell Faith the truth. Though he hadn't known her long, he could tell that she was a good person. A trustworthy person. Even so, he needed her to know how serious the matter was. And he needed to make sure he wouldn't be overheard. The restaurant was a good size and all of the tables were occupied. Fortunately, there was lots of space between the tables. Not only that, the other diners were talking to each other. Nobody was paying the least bit of attention to Faith and Caleb.

"You seem to be struggling," Faith said. "Feel free to

tell me however much or how little you feel comfortable sharing. Or we can change the subject entirely."

Before he could reply, the waitress set their meals in front of them. After giving them extra napkins and containers of sauce, she excused herself and walked away. By unspoken agreement, Caleb and Faith each tasted their rib tips. A groan of pleasure slipped through his lips. "This is so good. I might never be the same."

Faith grinned. "I told you that you'd like it."

"Don't tell my dad, who is the grill master in our family, but these are the best ribs I have ever tasted."

Faith pretended to lock her lips and the action drew his attention to her full mouth. It looked so soft he longed to press his lips to hers in a hot kiss in order to find out if it was as soft as it looked. "Lots of people feel the same way. Even so, Caleb, your secret is safe with me."

He hoped so, because he was about to share another secret. "You asked why I was here in Bronco."

"I did. But I didn't mean to pry."

"You didn't. The truth is…" His voice trailed off. The words were harder to say than he'd expected. Once he'd said them, there would be no taking them back. Exhaling a deep breath, he forced out the words. "I'm here looking for my birth father."

"Okay." She nodded as if what he'd just said wasn't a big deal. Maybe to her it wasn't.

"I'm adopted," he repeated, just in case she needed clarification.

"So am I."

"You are?" His mouth dropped open.

"Yes. So are my sisters and many of my cousins. My mother and her sisters are adopted too."

"I didn't know that."

She gave him a wide smile. “You really aren’t into rodeo, are you?”

“No. But what does that have to do with anything?”

“Our adoptions aren’t a secret. They really couldn’t be, since we’re not all the same race or ethnicity. My mother is white, two of her sisters are Black, and one is Latina. Same with my sisters. Elizabeth and I are Black, Amy and Tori are white, and Carly is Latina.”

“Sorry. I’m more of a football fan,” he admitted with a half smile.

She laughed. “That’s no skin off my nose. But if you aren’t interested in rodeo, and clearly don’t know much about rodeo riders, why were you so intent on seeing Brooks Langtree?”

He didn’t want to lie, but he wasn’t ready to mention his belief that Brooks Langtree might be his father, just in case he was wrong. “I was given up for adoption thirty years ago. I have reasons to believe my father was on the rodeo circuit thirty years ago. I figured a lot of old-timers might show up to the event. Maybe one of them would have known him.”

She nodded slowly as if considering what he’d said. “That’s possible, I suppose. But lots of people travel the rodeo circuit. Take it from me, a rider could be here one day and in another town the next. That’s the nature of the beast.”

“I have to start somewhere. My hometown is only a hundred miles away, so here seems as good a place as any. I don’t have any facts to back up my belief. I’m still in search mode.”

“What are you looking at? If you don’t mind my asking.”

“I don’t mind at all. It’s nice to be able to talk to you about this, especially since we’re in the same boat.”

She tilted her head and her dark hair drifted over her shoulder. "What do you mean?"

"You're adopted too."

"Yes. But mine was an open adoption. I know who my birth mother is."

"Oh." He felt a twinge of envy, which was ridiculous. "Is she a part of your life?"

Faith shrugged. "Yes and no. I see her from time to time and we email occasionally, but she has her own family and I have mine. She's married and she and her husband have two sons. And I'm a Hawkins through and through. They're my family."

"I understand that. And I feel the same way about my parents."

"That said," Faith continued, "I think I would wonder about her if I didn't know her. That knowledge has kept me from having a lot of unanswered questions."

"That's it exactly. I'm not looking for a new family. Or even to be a part of my biological father's life. I just want to meet him so I can find out about him. Hopefully, he'll tell me something about my birth mother. All I know is that she died when I was a baby." He sighed. "Maybe I'm barking up the wrong tree. He might not have anything to do with rodeo. That's just a guess." He shook his head. "You probably think I'm being ridiculous. And maybe I am."

She grabbed his hand and gave it an urgent squeeze. "Don't do that, Caleb. Don't put yourself down. Whatever you feel is totally understandable. Naturally you want to know where you came from."

"That's just it. I've always known I was adopted. My parents called me their chosen child. I never thought about my biological father until I turned thirty. Then it was like a switch flipped on. It was all that I could think about and I became curious about my past. What were my birth parents like? I know my mom died, but is my father still alive? Does he wonder about me? Does he wish he had kept in touch with me?"

She nodded, sympathy in her eyes. "Do you know anything else about your birth parents?"

"I only know that my father insisted that the adoption be closed. He didn't want me to be given any information about either of them."

"That's not a lot to go on."

"I know." He swallowed some of his cola, trying to wash away the disappointing reality. Because the truth was if Brooks Langtree wasn't his dad, Caleb really had no other clues to follow.

"So, what's your plan?" she asked quietly.

He sighed, forcing down the nagging stress that was never far from him. "I don't have one. If you have an idea, feel free to share it. I'm open to suggestions."

"Nothing comes to mind right now, but if I think of something, I'll let you know."

"Thanks. I mean that sincerely. I feel better now that I've told you."

"Do your parents know that you're looking for your bio dad?"

"Yes. They say they're okay with it."

She gave him a searching look. "Do you believe them?"

"For the most part. I know they would never stand in my way of doing something that I need to do. My happiness matters to them." He grimaced. "But it can't be easy on them. They've had me all to themselves for thirty years. I don't want them to worry about losing their place in my life."

"I don't know your parents, but I doubt they're worried about that."

"How do you know that?"

She smiled gently. "Because as you've said, they've been your parents for thirty years. The love you all share won't vanish simply because you meet the man responsible for half of your genes."

"They said the same thing, although they said it slightly differently."

"Then you know I'm right. So take them at their word."

He took a swallow of his cola and then looked into her eyes. "How does your adoptive mother feel about your birth mother? Does it hurt her when your birth mother comes around?"

"I don't think so," she said slowly. "But our situations are not the same. They met before I was born. My birth mother actually chose my parents. I think they feel grateful to her."

Caleb frowned. "I don't think my parents will feel gratitude if they meet my biological dad."

"Are you planning on making him a part of your life?"

"I haven't thought that far in advance," he admitted. "To be honest, it depends on him. Just meeting him and getting a few questions answered might be enough."

"*Might* be enough?"

He shrugged. "I don't know how I'll feel. Will just having him acknowledge me and tell me why he gave me away be enough? Is it enough for you?"

"My birth parents were teenagers," she said, with a half smile. "They were still in high school when my bio mom got pregnant. Their parents convinced them that it would be best for me if they gave me up for adoption. Best for them too. My birth mom insisted on an open adoption so she could always know where I was and that I was okay."

"You mentioned your birth mother. What about your birth father? Are you in touch with him?"

Faith shook her head, sending her hair cascading over

her shoulders. "No. But neither is my birth mom. I guess it was easier for him to walk away and forget I ever existed. Or maybe knowing that I was out there and that he could never be my father was too painful for him. I don't know. Either way, the result is the same."

"Which way do you think my birth father feels?"

She lifted one slender shoulder. "I have no idea. The only way to know for sure is to ask him."

"Which I will do if I find him."

"*When* you find him."

Her confident words comforted him in a way he hadn't expected. Though he'd been uncertain about telling her about his adoption, he was glad that he'd done so. "On that positive note, let's change the subject."

"That works for me. What do you want to talk about?"

"Can you tell me about life on the rodeo circuit?"

"Sure. What do you want to know?"

"Whatever you want to tell me. What are your days like? How does it feel to live and work with the same people that you compete against day after day?"

"They're my friends. Some are my family. I often compete against my cousins and sisters."

"I don't get it. How can you try to beat someone one minute and then act as if you didn't the next? How does that work?"

"It might seem strange to you, but I'm not competing against them. I'm competing against myself. I'm trying to get the best score that I can."

"I get that, but the others are trying to get better scores than you. Someone is going to win and someone is going to lose."

"That's the football fan in you talking. One team battling against the other in a zero-sum game."

"It's competition. Isn't rodeo the same way?"

"Of course, we all want to win. But unlike football, we're all on the same team. We leave it in the ring. We can root for each other to do well because we're friends. If they do great, it doesn't affect my score. If they do poorly, same thing. My score doesn't change. So I can cheer for them. And they cheer for me. Not only that, we often compete in towns where we don't know anyone else. It would be pretty lonely if we couldn't be friends."

"Everything you're saying makes sense." He admired her even more now. "And it makes me believe that you are one special woman."

CHAPTER SIX

FAITH TRIED NOT to read too much into Caleb's statement. After all, they'd just had a very emotional conversation. After that personal revelation, his feelings were probably all over the place. The fact that she was sympathetic—indeed empathetic—to his experience had no doubt affected him. He probably didn't mean the words the way they sounded. Even so, her heart was racing.

A moment passed before she realized he was waiting for her reply. "None of what I said makes me special. All the riders on the circuit feel the same way."

"How long do you want to compete?"

"Now, that's a question." She sighed and leaned her chin into her palm. "I've seen so many places and had some wonderful experiences in my travels. I wouldn't have had these experiences without rodeo. I know some people have wanderlust. I'm not one of them. At least not anymore. In fact, I'm turning into quite the opposite. I'm starting to feel the need to put down roots. I'm not thinking about retirement per se. I'm only thirty after all. There are lots of things I still want to do. But I'm thinking about making a few changes in my life."

"You've already made a big one when you moved back to the States."

"That was big," she agreed. "But it was time."

They'd eaten while they'd talked, and now only the bones remained on the plates. Not even one French fry or baked bean had remained uneaten. The waitress returned with their bill, interrupting their conversation. After Caleb paid and left a tip, they exited the restaurant. Faith would have enjoyed lingering for a while, but there was a line of people waiting for the table.

Once they were outside, the subject of her life was dropped and they made small talk on the drive back to her house. Her nerves jangled as they got closer to her block. Although this had been a friendly date, her excitement began to build as she contemplated the way it would end. Would they kiss? Did she want to? Yes and no. Right now she was comfortable with their budding friendship. A kiss, even a perfunctory one at the end of a date, might change that dynamic. Good friends were hard to find, and she didn't want to ruin this friendship by making a mistake. And kissing would definitely be a mistake.

On the other hand, there was no denying the attraction between them. The air practically crackled with sexual tension. Would it be so wrong to act on it just this once in order to see what happened? If they decided that a romantic relationship was wrong for them, they could always take a step back into their old friendship. No harm no foul.

She nearly laughed out loud at the thought. When in the history of the world had that ever happened? Once you stepped over a line, it was impossible to cross back.

"I can practically hear the wheels in your head spinning," Caleb said, bursting into her thoughts. And not a minute too soon.

She turned in her seat so she could look at him while he drove. There was sufficient light from the moon and streetlamps to make his profile visible. With carved cheekbones, full lips and a strong jaw, he was just as attractive in profile as he was straight on. "Is that right?"

"It is."

"Then what am I thinking?"

He grinned, and a dimple appeared. Faith knew there was an equally sexy one in his other cheek. "You're wondering whether you should invite me in when we reach your house. You're also wondering whether I'm going to kiss you good-night."

"Is that right?" She arched an eyebrow.

"Yep."

She decided not to deny it. "Well, are you?"

He laughed. "I'm not going to tell you that now."

"Why not?"

"That would totally ruin the moment. Don't you find the suspense exhilarating?"

She shook her head. "That's one way to describe it."

"What's another?"

She huffed out a breath. "Nerve-wracking."

"Why? It's just a little kiss." He gave her a wicked grin. "What could possibly go wrong?"

"So many things." She pressed her lips together. "That's it. I've decided. I'm not kissing you."

"Wow. That's the first time a woman has said that to me."

"Well, write it down in your diary tonight so you don't forget."

"You think your rejection is something I want to remember?" Caleb asked, an incredulous expression on his face.

"Maybe you should think of this as a learning opportunity."

"What's the lesson? You know, for future reference."

"I'm not sure what you're supposed to learn," she admitted with a wry smile. "When I figure it out, I'll let you know."

"What if I'm not the one who is supposed to learn anything? Perhaps the lesson is yours to learn."

"Maybe. So tell me what bit of wisdom I'm supposed to take from tonight."

He didn't hesitate for a second. "To just go with the flow and not look too far ahead. Don't worry about things that haven't happened yet."

She wondered if he followed that advice. "I'll take that under advisement."

"You do that." Caleb parked in front of her house and turned off the engine.

They got out of the truck and walked side by side up the stairs and to her front door. The sun had long since set and the moon was shining in the starry sky. A gentle breeze blew, knocking a few leaves from the trees lining the street. The wind chime hanging from her porch roof tinkled softly. The night couldn't be more romantic if they were on the set of some romantic movie.

When they reached her front door, they paused and stared into each other's eyes. He was standing so near that Faith actually felt the warmth from his body. Suddenly, she yearned to lean against his muscular chest. Longed to feel his strong arms wrapped around her. Her desire must have shown on her face because he chuckled.

Ever so slowly, he lowered his head until his lips were mere centimeters from hers. Then he froze. "Too bad you decided not to kiss me tonight, because I have a feeling it would have been electric."

Before she could reply, he straightened and took a step back. Eyes dancing mischievously, he held out a hand to her. "Good night, Faith. I had a wonderful time. I would love to see you again when you're available."

"What?" She blinked and sputtered. "What is even happening here?"

"I'm saying good-night to you."

"Oh." She hid her disappointment. He really wasn't going to kiss her.

His cocky grin faded and his expression turned serious. "Thanks for listening to me talk about the search for my biological dad."

"I'm always here if you want to talk."

"I appreciate it." He leaned over and whispered into her ear, "Good night, Faith."

His breath brushed against her neck and her skin tingled. Her knees grew weak and she had no doubt that a kiss would be earth-shattering.

She considered reaching out and pulling his head down to hers while she rose on her tiptoes and kissed him, but before she could act, he turned on his heel and walked down the stairs. Shaking her head in disbelief, she went in the house and leaned against the front door.

Wow. That good-night hadn't gone the way she'd expected. But then, she tried not to have expectations when it came to men. She'd been let down one too many times. It was better to expect nothing and be surprised when something good happened. But Caleb was better than good. He was one of a kind. She'd had so much fun with him and couldn't wait to hang out with him again.

She wasn't one to delude herself about a man's feelings—been there, done that—but she believed that Caleb was as attracted to her as she was to him. And not just physically. She sensed an emotional connection between them. Surprisingly, she wasn't tempted to head to the hills in order to protect herself. She was willing to see where the attraction led. At least for the time being. There was little danger she would fall in love and get hurt while Caleb was trying to find his biological father. That could be a full-time job.

Not only that, it had to be emotionally draining, leaving little energy for a romantic relationship.

She recalled his concern for his parents' feelings. Although she'd kept it to herself, she knew they couldn't help but be a little bit hurt even as they supported him. It was only human. Even though her own mother knew Faith loved her to the moon and back, Suzie had admitted to feeling a twinge of jealousy whenever Faith and her birth mother got together. Suzie acknowledged that the problem was hers and that the sensation never lasted long. Gratitude for being chosen as Faith's adoptive mother outweighed the rare negative emotions.

Faith grabbed a glass of water and then checked the time. Suzie was a night owl, so Faith knew she would be awake. Her mother had been on the rodeo tour thirty years ago. Though there were many rodeos going on simultaneously across the country and lots of riders on the circuit, it was still a tight-knit community. Secrets would have been hard to keep. If Caleb's biological dad had actually been on the rodeo circuit back then, her mother might have met him. She might even have known Caleb's birth mother. If she hadn't known either of them, she might have heard some scuttlebutt that could help Caleb fill in some of the blanks. It wouldn't hurt to ask.

She picked up her phone and then punched in her mother's number. Suzie answered on the first ring.

"Hello, my darling daughter," Suzie said. That was her standard greeting for Faith and her sisters and it had been for as long as Faith could remember. There had been a time when Faith had thought her mother called them all "darling daughter" to keep from getting their names mixed up. She wouldn't be the first parent to do that.

When she was fifteen, Faith had asked her mother why she referred to them that way. Even now, recalling Suzie's answer made her smile. "Aren't you my darling daughter? Aren't your sisters? Then why shouldn't I call you that?"

"Hello, my darling mother," Faith replied. She could hear the television in the background. After a moment, the canned laughter vanished, a sign that she had her mother's full attention.

"What are you doing up this late?" Suzie asked. "You always were my early-to-bed, get-up-way-too-early child."

"I just got in from a date."

"Do tell," Suzie said, a smile in her voice.

"Are you sure you want the details?"

"I'm your mother. There's nothing you can't tell me. Besides, I know you all too well, Faith Clementine Hawkins. I doubt you even kissed the man good-night."

Even now, she still regretted her hastily spoken words. She'd only been teasing. "True."

"Oh ho. And from the disgust and disappointment in your voice, you were hoping for a kiss. That's a surprise."

"Maybe. But that's not why I called."

"Are you sure you didn't call so I could go over and lecture that young man on the proper way to say good-night to a Hawkins woman?"

Faith laughed. "You would, too. I forget how much like Grandma you are."

"I don't see how. My mother raised me to take the bull by the horns."

Faith couldn't stop the groan. "Horrible rodeo pun. When did you start telling dad jokes?"

"I've got talents I have yet to share with the world."

"You might want to keep stand-up comedy to yourself for a wee bit longer."

"I'll admit that wasn't my best material." Suzie chuckled. "Now, if you don't want me to educate your date, how can I help you?"

"Actually, it's my date who needs your help."

"How do you think I can help him?"

Faith hesitated for a moment. "This is confidential."

"Are you asking me to keep this a secret?"

"Yes."

"And did he ask you to keep this a secret?"

"No. I wouldn't say anything to you if he had. But I don't think he wants me blabbing his personal business all over Bronco either. I wouldn't mention it if I didn't think you could help. I know you won't tell anyone."

There was a long pause and Faith knew her mother was giving this matter some thought. Finally, she replied. "All right. Spill."

"Caleb is adopted. He's trying to find his birth father."

"Where is his birth mother? Can't he ask her?"

"No. She'd dead. She died when he was a baby."

"Oh. I'm sorry to hear that." Suzie's voice was filled with sympathy.

"The adoption was closed and the adoption agency won't give him any information. But he wants to find out about his birth father. He wants to meet him if he's still alive."

"How do you think I can help?"

"He thinks his father might have been in the rodeo. Since you were traveling the circuit back then, you might know him."

"Why does he believe that his father was in the rodeo?"

"I don't know. He didn't say. Maybe he pieced that information together over time. Or maybe the adoption agency told him. I didn't want to press him to tell me more than he felt comfortable sharing. But since you were competing all across America thirty years ago, I thought you might have heard some gossip."

"The circuit is quite big," Suzie said slowly. "Hundreds of people participate in almost as many rodeos. You know that."

"I do. But for the most part it's one big family."

"More like a small town made up of several families," Suzie said.

"But still. Word had a way of getting around."

"Giving up a child for adoption is a personal matter, so the people involved are going to be discreet. They might not talk about it to many people outside their immediate family."

"That's true," Faith admitted. "So you didn't hear anything about it?"

"Think, Faith. I was pretty busy thirty years ago. Your father and I had just adopted you. And Elizabeth was already two years old and getting into everything. Tori was ten and was involved in her own activities. I was much too busy raising my family to keep up with the goings-on of the rest of the rodeo circuit."

That made sense, but something in her mother's tone sounded…off. Her voice was strained, as if talking about the subject was uncomfortable. It was more than not liking to talk about adoption or birth parents. Not only that, Suzie loved gossip. Not the mean kind that hurt people. She didn't have time or patience for that kind of nonsense. But even with kids to raise, Suzie had always had her finger on the pulse of the rodeo community. Not much went on that she didn't know about. If someone was looking for a truck or was having trouble making ends meet, word eventually found its way to Suzie's ear. Inevitably she *had a guy* who could help. Given what Faith knew about her mother, it was hard to believe that Suzie hadn't heard a whisper of something about the adoption.

"Wait until you have children of your own," Suzie continued. "Then you'll realize that with only so many hours in the day, something has to give. I guarantee it won't be your family."

Faith didn't fail to notice how adeptly her mother had shifted the subject. Nor did she fail to notice that Suzie hadn't really answered her question. Faith decided not to press. "I know we aren't having the get-married-and-have-kids discussion right now."

"Why not? You just went on a date with an interesting man, didn't you?"

"Yes. But it was only a first date. I'm certainly not going to start planning a future around him now."

"The way I hear it, you've been out with him already. Unless this is a different man you're talking about."

Faith sighed. "It's the same man. Which one of my sisters or cousins told you that?"

Suzie's laughter floated over the phone. "I never divulge my sources. You should know that by now."

Although Suzie couldn't see her, Faith nodded. One thing she'd always admired about her mother was her ability to keep a confidence. You could bare your soul to Suzie and never have to worry about hearing your words coming from someone else's lips. There were things that Faith had told her mother as a child that Suzie still kept to herself. Those things that no longer mattered to Faith were still sacred to Suzie.

"Fair enough. He's from Tenacity and wanted to see some of Bronco. So I obliged."

"You don't have to explain anything to me. You know I'm all for you meeting a man worthy of your love. Tenacity isn't as close to Bronco as I would like, but it's in this country. If you settle down with him, I'll see you more than I did last year."

"You're the one who raised me to be a free thinker and to follow my dreams."

Suzie chuckled. "I'm pretty sure that was your father."

"I'm sure it was both of you, for which I will be forever grateful. The two of you raised strong women who know our own minds." Faith's father had been forced into an early retirement from the rodeo because of a leg injury, but he hadn't become bitter. Instead, Arthur had devoted himself to making his daughters the best athletes—the best people—they could be.

"Being your own woman doesn't mean you can't have a family of your own," Suzie said gently.

"I know. And believe me, when the right man comes along, I'll welcome him with open arms."

"How do you know you haven't met him already?"

"Good question. One I'll need to think about. Is it okay if I get back to you in say a year?"

Although she couldn't see her mother, Faith knew Suzie was shaking her head. "I don't think it will take that long, but okay."

"On that note, I'm going to say good-night. As you pointed out, it's way past my bedtime. Have a good night."

"You too, my darling daughter."

After ending the call, Faith closed her eyes and blew out a long breath, sad on Caleb's behalf. She'd been so sure her mother would be able to help, so Suzie's lack of knowledge was disappointing. Faith could ask her aunts. They'd been competing on the circuit thirty years ago too. But they'd been raising families back then as well. If Suzie didn't know anything, Faith doubted her aunts would either.

But there was still her grandmother. Thirty years ago, Hattie hadn't been performing as much as she had in her heyday, but she'd still been active in rodeo circles. Perhaps she would be able to help Caleb find the truth.

Faith didn't know why she was so determined to help

him. They were barely friends. But his happiness mattered to her. One way or the other, she was going to help him find the answers he was looking for.

CHAPTER SEVEN

Caleb woke early the next morning, feeling quite happy. He was no closer to meeting with Brooks Langtree today than he had been yesterday. Nor had he come up with a new plan to make such a meeting a possibility. Given all of that, he should be discouraged. Despite the situation, he was grinning from ear to ear. It didn't take a genius to know why he was in such a good mood. It was all due to Faith Hawkins.

Just thinking about her made his already broad smile stretch even wider. Faith possessed a certain something that set her apart from everyone else. Something that made her special. Caleb was a simple man from a struggling Montana town yet somehow, he had managed to meet and capture the attention of this extraordinary woman. Any man in the world would be thrilled to spend time with Faith, yet she had chosen him. He wasn't going to question why. Instead he was going to thank his lucky stars and enjoy the ride for as long as it lasted.

He showered and dressed quickly. He was buttoning his shirt when his phone rang. He checked the screen and his smile returned, accompanied by a strong desire. *Faith.*

"I hope I didn't wake you," she said in that voice he was coming to love.

"Nope. I generally get up early. Most of our customers are ranchers, so we've got the store open before they start work."

"That's probably convenient for them. And good for business."

"Yes to both."

"Are you busy today?"

"No. I don't have any plans." That would have been disappointing before he'd met Faith. Now he was glad to be free.

"Good. I invited us to my grandmother's house for lunch."

"Don't tell me you're already trying to get me to meet the family?" he teased. "This when you wouldn't even kiss me last night. I don't think you understand how this dating thing works."

"Are we dating?"

"If you have to ask, then I guess not," he said dryly.

She laughed, a happy sound that touched his heart. "Maybe I was just seeking clarity."

"I'll accept that answer."

"So, are you interested in meeting my grandmother? You know, to talk to her about the hunt for your bio dad."

"You didn't mention this to her, did you?" Caleb managed to keep the panic from his voice, but just barely. He should have told Faith that he didn't want word getting out. He couldn't risk people guessing that he thought Brooks Langtree was his father when there was no proof. Brooks had to be the first person to learn about Caleb's suspicion.

"No. I figured you could tell her what you wanted her to know. But she knows everyone who was anyone in rodeo. She was also familiar with people who were just passing through. You know, the ones who liked the idea of being in rodeo more than the reality of constant travel and injuries."

"Then I would enjoy meeting her." Who knew what

could come of that. Maybe Hattie Hawkins would be of some assistance. Even if she wasn't, he would be spending more time with Faith today.

"Hold on," Faith said. "That's her calling now."

As he waited, Caleb pictured Hattie Hawkins as she'd appeared on the stage during the Brooks Langtree Day ceremony. He guessed that she was in her early to middle seventies, although he couldn't be sure. She had that smooth skin that certain women had that defied age. From the easy way she moved, it was clear that she'd been an athlete in her younger days. Though he'd only seen them from a distance, Hattie and Brooks seemed to be enjoying each other's company. Maybe they were friends. If so, maybe she would know if Brooks had given up a child for adoption. Of course, he couldn't come out and ask her. That would raise too many questions he wasn't sure he could answer.

He was trying to come up with a way to broach the subject when Faith's voice came over the line. "That was Hattie. Something came up and she needs to reschedule. Do you mind?"

Disappointment threatened, but he shoved it down. Before Faith had called, he hadn't had an expectation of meeting with Hattie Hawkins. Nor had he even considered it was something he should do. Now he knew it was a possibility. If he had to wait a bit longer to talk to her, so be it. "That's fine by me."

"Good. Since I know you're free, do you still want to get together?"

"Are you asking me on a date, Ms. Hawkins?" he asked in a formal voice.

"I am indeed, Mr. Strom," Faith's replied, her tone mimicking his. "So, are you going to grace me with the pleasure of your company?"

"Absolutely. What did you have in mind?"

"I thought we could go apple picking. Unless that sounds too much like work."

He smiled. "We own a feed and farm supply store, so there is not much apple picking involved. Besides, a little physical activity is good for our health."

"I agree. I don't want to do too much sitting around. Being active keeps me in shape."

And what a good shape it was. "Then let's do it. It sounds like fun."

And not at all something he'd expected to interest Faith. Perhaps it was time for him to rid himself of his preconceived notions about her and relax and get to know her. She might be gorgeous, but she was also fun. Two qualities he found quite appealing. After setting a time for him to pick up Faith, Caleb called his parents and updated them on his progress or lack thereof. As usual, they were supportive and encouraged him to keep going. According to his mother, success was right around the corner. He might have agreed if he'd been able to meet with Hattie Hawkins.

He ordered some farm equipment that one of their customers had expressed an interest in, then reviewed online feed catalogues until it was time to head over to Faith's house. Although he had just seen her yesterday, and talked to her a few hours ago, he couldn't wait to see her again. There was no denying what was happening. He was falling for Faith. Hard. Given all that was going on in his life, that probably wasn't wise. He didn't need the distraction. But his heart rebelled at the idea of not seeing her again.

The drive to Faith's house was quick, and before long, he was ringing her doorbell. As he waited for her to answer the door, he looked up and down her block. The houses were of average size and each was well maintained, surrounded by trees ablaze with red, gold and orange leaves, proof that Fall had arrived in full force. Leaves were strewn on the sidewalk and scattered across the small, neat lawns. Two boys stood on opposite sides of the street, tossing a football back and forth. A young couple pedaled down the road on bicycles. They waved to him as they passed by. The entire scene felt optimistic.

He heard the locks disengage and turned around as the door swung open to reveal a smiling Faith. She was dressed in a tan and black print sweater, tight black jeans and tan cowboy boots. Her black hair was free around her shoulders, framing her face. Her bold red lipstick emphasized her irresistible, full lips. Her eyes sparkled with joy. Caleb felt his mouth gape open, but he was powerless to do anything other than stare. Faith was the sexiest woman he'd ever laid eyes on. She was petite, not even five foot three, but she was a dynamo with personality to spare.

Caleb had dated lots of women and not one made him laugh as much as Faith did. She managed to find the humor in every situation without making light of serious matters. And she was easy to talk to, open and candid. Just telling her about his search for his biological father had relieved some of his stress. He wasn't exactly relaxed about the situation, but he was no longer overwhelmed either.

Realizing that his mouth was still wide-open, he snapped it shut. "You look beautiful."

Faith smiled with pleasure. "Thank you. You don't look too shabby yourself."

"This old thing?" he asked, striking a pose.

"I like a man in faded jeans."

He liked her in everything. Caleb was positive he would *really* like her in his arms, and that he would *love* her in his bed. He shooed the thought away. There was no sense in getting ahead of himself. Especially when he wasn't in the position to maintain a relationship. "That's good to know. Especially since that describes a good portion of my wardrobe."

"Not mine. I have lots of clothes. You name the occasion and I have an outfit to wear."

"I like a woman who's prepared. No need for any last-minute shopping."

She put on her jacket and pulled her purse strap over her shoulder. "I didn't say that. Last-minute shopping is how I got such an extensive wardrobe."

As they drove to their destination, they talked about anything and everything under the sun.

"Turn at the corner and then head for the highway," Faith directed. "The pick-it-yourself orchard is about forty-five minutes from here."

He nodded. "Have you been apple picking before?"

"No. It just seemed like something fun. I like to keep myself open to new experiences. I don't want to fall into a rut, even doing things that I enjoy."

"You're adventurous. I like that about you."

"I don't know another way to be. If it sounds good, I'm willing to give it a try. What's the worst thing that could happen?"

He nodded. A sedan in front of them was traveling rather slowly, so Caleb passed it before looking back at Faith. "Does that adventurous nature ever get you into trouble?"

She hesitated a moment and then laughed. "More often than I care to admit. Although not as much lately. I remember when I was about fifteen and we were living in some small town. I don't remember which one exactly. It was a fall day and this girl who was my nemesis dared me to jump off of this ledge into a pond. This older boy we both liked was there with some of his friends. He was pretending not to be paying attention to us, but I could tell that he was."

Faith glanced over at Caleb and he nodded.

"Anyway, I couldn't let that dare stand. I've never enjoyed swimming all that much, especially in the cold water, but I rolled my eyes at her, adjusted my T-shirt and shorts, and then jumped in."

"It was a challenge so what else could you do?"

"I was in the middle of the air when my father's words telling me not to let my ego get me into trouble came back to me. He'd told me more than once that every adventure wasn't a good adventure. I hit the water and immediately began to sink. It was freezing and I gasped in a mouthful of water. I was struggling to get back to the surface when out of nowhere these strong arms grabbed me."

"The boy you liked?" Caleb guessed.

"Yep. Now, I could swim mind you. My parents started me in lessons at the Y when I was three. But I figured I should let him play the hero."

He laughed. "I'm sure he appreciated it."

"Of course, it wasn't all pretense. Flying through the air was the scariest hour of my life and I felt weak."

"Hour? I don't know how high that ledge was, but I doubt it was longer than a second or two."

Faith flashed a cheeky grin. "Time stretches when you're terrified."

"I'll have to take your word for it."

She shook her head. "You are such a guy. Of course you've never been terrified."

"Not that I'll admit to. So what happened next?"

"The guy, whose name I can't remember, invited me to sit around the bonfire with him and his friends so my clothes could dry and I could get warm. My nemesis watched on with envy. I would have laughed in her face if I hadn't been shaking so badly."

"I guess no big romance resulted since you can't even remember the guy's name."

"No. After spending an hour or so with him and his friends, I discovered that he was kind of a jerk, so I invited my nemesis to join us." She chuckled at the memory.

"One jerk deserves another?"

"Yep." Faith sobered. "But I decided that moment that being adventurous was not the same as being reckless. I made up my mind not to be so willing to try everything. At least not for the wrong reasons. I've had more fun since then."

"I bet you were a handful growing up."

Faith's beautiful smile returned. "I refuse to answer that on the grounds that it might incriminate me."

"Yeah. I got my answer."

"Enough about me. What about you?" She gave him an assessing look and he wondered just how he came across to her. Would he appeal to her or would she find him to be boring? After all, his life experiences didn't compare to hers.

"What about me?"

"What kind of kid were you?"

He smiled. "I was a good kid. A rule follower. I didn't get into much trouble."

She nodded slowly. "I can see that about you. Don't worry. Stick with me. I'm sure I can find some mischief for us to get into. That is if you're game."

"I'm not a kid any longer. I'm sure I'll be more than up for whatever you come up with. The question is, will you be daring enough to do whatever I come up with?"

She gave him a look hot enough to melt steel. "I guess you'll have to wait and see."

That was all right with him. He just hoped there wasn't a lot of waiting before they got around to the seeing part.

They talked about other things until they spotted a sign for the apple orchard. There were numerous arrows directing them, so he found the parking lot rather easily. They climbed from his vehicle and walked through the lot and to the entrance. Bushel baskets were stacked inside and they each grabbed one. A teenager wearing earbuds and clearly not interested in conversation handed them each a map before looking back down at his phone.

Caleb and Faith exchanged glances before walking away.

"I so recognize that age," Faith said.

"Me too. I bet that he's the owner's son and has no choice but to work here."

"Did you act that way when working for your dad?"

"As a teenager? Yep. I wanted to be somewhere where I could meet girls. Believe it or not, they didn't frequent the feedstore."

"I know that. I am a girl, remember?"

He looked her up and down, taking note of her sexy body. Even dressed casually, she was the most gorgeous woman he had ever seen. "I don't think I could ever forget that."

She smiled and then, clearly flustered, she looked down at her map. "They have a couple of different types of apples growing here. Which type do you want?"

"It doesn't matter to me. I'll eat whatever kind you want."

"Honey crisp it is."

There were lots of people walking about, taking advantage of the nice fall weather. Faith and Caleb found several trees in a secluded area near the edge of the orchard.

A step ladder was leaning against the trunk of each tree and they each grabbed one.

Caleb glanced over at Faith who grinned at him. Her smile was so bright, so open, that he couldn't look away from her to save his life. There was a vibrancy to her that struck him to his core. He could get used to having her in his life. Of course, until he settled the issue of his father, he would have to put that interest on the backburner.

He stood by her as she climbed onto the lowest rung. They were eye level and her luscious lips were tantalizingly close. It would be so easy to lean in and kiss her. Before he could decide whether that was a good idea or one he should ignore, she poked him in the shoulder with a perfectly manicured nail.

Her eyes danced with mischief. "I'm not going to fall so I don't need you to stand guard over me."

"How do I know you're not scare of heights?"

"I'm not. Are you?"

"What do you think?" He stepped onto the bottom rung of his ladder and then looked down at her.

"I think I liked it better when we were the same height."

So did he.

They picked apples in silence for a while, but he didn't feel the need to fill the space. There was a connection developing between them that didn't need conversation in order to remain intact. Besides, he liked the quiet. It was comfortable and relaxing in a way that he hadn't experienced before with another woman.

The day was perfect with a clear, blue sky. Every once in a while a cool breeze blew, filling the air with the scent of dry grass and leaves.

After a while, Faith stepped off her ladder and used the rung as a seat.

"Finished?" he asked, coming to stand beside her.

"Yes." She looked into her nearly filled basket and then over at his. He'd climbed up and down the ladder more quickly than she had and his basket was full. "What are you going to do with all of those apples?"

"Good question." He hadn't thought that far ahead. In fact, he hadn't thought about it at all. He'd simply been enjoying himself and the beautiful day. Now he rubbed the back of his neck and looked up at the sky as if searching for inspiration. "What are you going to do with yours?"

"My horse likes apples. So do my sisters' and cousins'. I suppose I could give the ones I don't eat to them."

"I don't suppose you would be interested in baking a pie or two?"

"Do you mean *with* you or *for* you?"

"Whatever answer will get me a pie."

She laughed. "With you."

They leaned their ladders back against the tree trunk, grabbed their baskets and headed for the exit. After paying for the apples, they loaded the fruit into his vehicle and he drove back to her house.

Once they were in her kitchen she leaned against the counter and smiled sheepishly. "I suppose we've reached the part of the program where I confess that I have never baked an apple pie from scratch in my life. Or any pie for that matter."

He threw his head back and laughed. "What about all that big talk you spouted about making cookies so good I would lose my mind after just one taste?"

"I stand by what I said. But cookies and pies are two different things. Surely you know that."

"I do. Lucky for you, I can make apple pie."

The look of surprise on her face was one he would never forget. It was quickly replaced by sheer joy. "Really?"

He nodded. "I love apple pie, so my mother insisted that

I learn how to bake them for myself. That way I can have a pie whenever I want."

"For the record, I love your mother."

"So do I. Now let's get to work. I'm getting hungry."

The first time Caleb had baked an apple pie, he'd been with his mother. She'd been a patient teacher and he'd enjoyed himself. Once he'd mastered the task, he'd made pies on his own.

Neither of those experiences compared to working in the kitchen with Faith. She took things to a whole different level. She'd turned on some music and bobbed her head as she peeled apples. When a popular song came on, she set the apple into the bowl and used her knife as a microphone, singing gustily and shaking her hips to the beat.

Caleb put down his knife, leaned against the counter, and watched with amusement mixed with a hint of lust.

"Don't tell me you don't know this song," Faith said.

"Of course I do. It only comes on the radio every hour if not more."

"Then grab a mic," she said. "I could use a backup singer."

Grabbing his knife, he went and stood behind Faith and began to blast out the background vocals. His eyes strayed to her round bottom as she danced and he admitted it was a pleasurable sight to see.

She turned and caught him staring. The uptempo song ended and a ballad began to play. Setting down her knife, she held out her hands to him. Without hesitating, he dropped his knife on the counter and took her into his arms. As they slow danced, her sweet scent floated around him. She fit perfectly in his arms and he closed his eyes, enjoying the feel of her soft body pressed up against him.

The urge to kiss her was strong, but he wouldn't act on it. He wasn't in the position to offer her a relationship.

When the song ended, he forced himself to release her and get back to the work.

Once the pie was baking, they put together a quick dinner and then sat at the table to eat. The kitchen was small and Caleb appreciated the intimacy. Though he'd enjoyed their time at the apple orchard earlier, nothing felt as good as being alone with her.

They ate in silence for a couple of minutes. Then Faith looked at him. "You've seen my town. Now tell me about yours. What is it like?"

"Different from Bronco."

Faith scoffed. "That's like saying it's different from Chicago or Paris. It tells me absolutely nothing."

"Okay. Before I answer, tell me this. Are you still in touch with your friends from high school?"

"Yes. A couple of them. Why?"

"I've done a lot of walking around Bronco over these past couple of days. I've seen lots of young people here. Couples in their twenties are settling down and starting families. People are starting careers and opening businesses."

"Yes."

"That's not happening in Tenacity. I don't think a single member of my high school graduating class still lives there."

"Really? Are you serious?"

"That might be a bit of an exaggeration, but not by much. There aren't many opportunities there, so once kids graduate they move and don't come back. My parents insisted that I get my college degree, so I went away to Howard University. When I came back I didn't see many familiar faces. I didn't see any new ones either. The kids I used to hang out with on Friday and Saturday nights had packed up and moved in search of greener pastures. I joined the family business. We hire as many local people as we can, but there's only so much a small business like ours can do."

"Wow."

"I know we're only a hundred or so miles apart, but the differences between Tenacity and Bronco are stark. We've had some bad financial luck in town for well over a decade or so, and nobody in town seems to know how to reverse the trend. But the mayor and the city council are trying to attract younger people and more businesses."

"Surely there must be something good happening there."

He thought for a moment. "Well, we have the Tenacity Winter Holiday Pageant."

"What's that?"

"It's a holiday program. Last year the choir's multi-cultural presentation went viral."

"Cool."

"We all thought so."

"Do you plan to stay there or are you going to join the exodus?"

"I'm staying," Caleb replied instantly. "I love Tenacity. Despite all of its flaws and its current state, it's home. Besides, I'm not the type to abandon ship simply because the waters are a bit rough. I know there's a way to turn things around, and I plan to be a part of it."

Faith smiled and held up her glass in toast. "Here's to the future being even better than the past. I hope you get everything you want."

So did he. And suddenly Faith Hawkins was at the top of that list.

CHAPTER EIGHT

"I'M SORRY THAT I had to cancel our meeting yesterday," Hattie said as she held out a hand to Faith, welcoming her into her home. Hattie had moved to Bronco a year or so ago, but her house was filled with items that gave the comfortable home a familiar feeling. Faith had learned over the years that it wasn't the building that made a home. Or even the furnishings. It was the family that lived there. The love that they shared. Whether she'd been on the road with her parents, sleeping in a hotel room in some small town off the highway, or in her bed at home, it was the love that made her feel secure in the knowledge that she belonged. Bronco was home now, but she knew any place in the world would feel the same as long as people she loved were there.

"I understand," Faith said. "I just hope you can help me out."

"I will if I can. Would you like a drink?"

"Yes."

"So, will your friend be joining us, or will it be just the two of us?"

"Just us."

Caleb had returned home to Tenacity early that morning, as planned. Even though his father had claimed to have everything under control at the store, Caleb had insisted on going back to work. He was an active partner and wanted to pull his weight. Faith appreciated how responsible he was even though she'd hated watching him drive off.

"Well, maybe next time."

Faith nodded and followed Hattie into the kitchen. Her grandmother always made everything special. While others might nuke a cup of water, dunk in a tea bag and call it a day, Hattie used a teapot and loose leaves. And she also always had cookies to go with it. It was a production that always made Faith feel valued. As a little girl, tea with Hattie had always made her feel grown-up and sophisticated.

Hattie filled the kettle and then set the water to boil. She withdrew several homemade cookies from an old-fashioned, bear-shaped ceramic cookie jar and put them on a plate. Faith grabbed napkins from a drawer that held the kitchen linen and set them on the coffee table in the living room. Hattie soon followed behind, pushing a cart with the porcelain tea set on it through the narrow room. She poured tea into two delicate, gold-rimmed cups, handed one to Faith and kept the other for herself.

"Help yourself to some cookies."

Faith grinned as she placed two maple cookies on a delicate saucer. These had always been her favorites. Knowing that Hattie had baked them especially for her made them taste twice as good. "Thank you."

As they sipped their tea, they chatted about recent events.

"So, what is this favor?" Hattie asked, setting her empty cup on the table.

Faith swallowed her bite of cookie and dabbed her mouth with her napkin before answering. "It's for a friend. He was given up for adoption thirty years ago and knows very little about his birth family. He believes that his father was in the rodeo back then. I asked Mom, but she doesn't have a clue."

"Really?" Hattie's eyebrows disappeared beneath her salt-and-pepper bangs. "That doesn't sound like Suzie."

"I didn't think so either. But she said she'd just adopted me and she was busy with her family."

"I suppose..." Hattie said, but she didn't sound totally convinced. "Well, anyway, what do you need from me?"

"Do you remember hearing anything about that?"

"No." Hattie pursed her lips and slowly shook her head. "It's possible that his father didn't have a connection to the rodeo at all. He might have been a local laborer who helped out while the rodeo was in town. Many people did that."

Faith shook her head. "He's certain that his father was part of the rodeo. He didn't tell me why and I didn't want to pry."

"I understand. The man is entitled to his secrets." Hattie folded her hands in her lap and closed her eyes, thinking. Then she opened them again and looked at Faith. "My memory isn't what it used to be, so nothing comes to mind."

Faith sighed. Though she'd been disappointed when her grandmother canceled the initial meeting with Caleb, now she was glad that he wasn't here to hear what her grandmother had to say. Her stomach churned with regret for getting his hopes up when she didn't have any answers for him. Next time she would keep any information she received to herself, until she had something solid.

"Thanks anyway."

"Don't be so glum, Faith. I might not remember details right now, but I've collected lots of souvenir programs, pictures and newspaper clippings from over the years. I can go through my trunk and see what I have from thirty years ago. That might refresh my memory."

"I hope it's not too much trouble."

"It's no trouble at all. I'll take any excuse I can get to

take a trip down memory lane." She tapped a manicured fingernail against her forehead. "This is filled with wonderful memories."

"In that case, I'm glad to be of service."

They laughed together. Hattie refilled their cups and then they reminisced about happy times they'd shared together, laughing and talking long after the last of the tea and cookies were gone.

After a while, Faith stood. "I suppose I need to get going. Let me help you with the dishes."

Hattie swatted aside Faith's hands. She had a certain way of washing and putting away her tea service. "You know I have it covered."

"I do. But Mom would have a fit if I didn't at least offer."

"I'll be sure to let her know that the lessons in manners took."

Faith laughed because she knew her grandmother would do just that. Whenever the grandchildren spent time with Hattie, she'd always given a report to their parents. Of course, she'd always edited out misbehavior, claiming it was not worth mentioning.

"It's always good to see you," Hattie said later as they walked to the door. Faith carried a plastic container with a half dozen cookies inside.

"Same." They embraced before Faith left, her spirits high with expectation. Perhaps her grandmother could turn up valuable information after all. Hopefully, she would have something good to tell Caleb soon. She was looking forward to the day when he came back.

Faith put her desire to see Caleb on the back burner as she drove to the stables. She wasn't scheduled to appear in a rodeo for another couple of weeks, but she liked to keep her skills sharp. Several of her family members also boarded their horses at the same stables, and if she was lucky, one or more of them would be there too. It would be good to have someone else to talk to about Caleb. It was one thing to talk to her mother and grandmother about him, but as open-minded as they were, she doubted that either of them would be comfortable listening to Faith lust after him. Not to mention that she wouldn't feel comfortable talking about it either.

Imagining that conversation, Faith laughed out loud as she got out of the car.

"What's so funny?"

Faith turned as her cousins Corinne and Remi and her sister Amy approached her. Corinne and Remi competed as the Hawkins Sisters here in the United States with their sisters Audrey and Brynn. The two often competed together in team events. Faith grinned. "I was just imagining telling grandma and my mother about a guy I like. Can you picture their faces as I talked about his cute butt?"

"The guy from Brooks Langtree Day?" Corinne asked.

"How do you even know about that? You weren't there."

"Surely you weren't in South America long enough to forget how things work around here. If one Hawkins woman knows something in the morning, we all know by noon."

Faith laughed. "Oh, no."

"Caleb isn't supposed to be a secret, is he?" Amy asked, and Faith wondered if she'd located the source of the information.

"No. In fact I was hoping that I would run into someone to talk to about him."

"Lucky for you, you've run into three of us," Corinne said. "I'm sure everyone is tired of hearing me talk about Mike."

"I'm not," Faith said. "I would love to hear more about your fiancé, the future doctor."

Corinne smiled. "We can talk about him later."

"For the record, I'm not tired of listening to you talk about Mike either," Remi said, proving why she was a favorite of all the cousins. She was loyal to a fault and sweet as pie.

"That's good to know," Corinne said. The two linked arms as they walked toward the stables. "And I'm going to take you up on that very soon. Right now I want to hear all about Faith's new man."

"Fair enough," Remi said, looking at Faith. "It's decided. We're going to talk about your guy first. Then we can talk about Amy and Tru McCoy."

Faith stopped walking and turned to look at her sister. "Tru McCoy? The actor? Why am I just now hearing about this? What happened to the Hawkins Sisters telling each other everything?"

Amy held up her hands, stopping Faith before she could ask her any more questions. "I'll tell you the same thing I told Corinne and Remi. There is nothing to tell."

"But you were talking to him at the Golden Buckle Rodeo. Remi and I saw the two of you together."

"Only for a minute. It was nothing," Amy insisted, her eyes darting around, never meeting any of them in the eyes. "So let's change the subject."

Faith exchanged glances with Remi and Corinne. Neither of them believed Amy's denial. It was clear that she was holding something back. But they all loved and respected her too much to push, especially when she was clearly uncomfortable.

"Okay," Remi said. "Let's get back to talking about Faith's boyfriend."

"Whoa. You're a few steps ahead of me," Faith said. "I wouldn't exactly call Caleb my boyfriend."

"Call him whatever you want as long as you tell us

all about him," Corinne said, a mischievous grin on her face. "I want to know everything. Don't leave out a single detail."

"Don't worry. I won't," Faith said and then laughed. "I love having a willing audience even though there isn't that much to share."

Their horses were housed in stalls in the same aisle. The grooms took excellent care of them, but the Hawkins women had been raised to be responsible for their own horses. The horses were their partners and were treated as such. The four women checked the animals' hooves and brushed them before saddling them and leading them into the corral. Once the women were all in the saddle they let their horses trot. As they rode, Faith told them about Caleb.

"He sounds like a good guy," Corinne said when Faith concluded. "A kind guy."

"A hot guy," Remi said. "He wouldn't by chance have a brother, would he? I haven't been able to find a good man on my own."

Faith shook her head. She intentionally hadn't brought up Caleb's search for his birth father. For all she knew, he might have another sibling out there somewhere. But she wasn't going to speculate. She was going to stick with the information that he had provided her. "He's an only child."

"Darn. How about a cousin? Or maybe even a young uncle?" Remi said, chuckling.

"Not that she's desperate or anything," Amy said with a grin.

"Not at all," Remi said. "I'm just expanding my search parameters."

They laughed together before Faith sobered. "I don't know anything about that."

"If the opportunity arises, feel free to ask on my behalf." Remi winked.

"I'll be sure of it."

They teased Remi for a few minutes more before they got down to work, putting their horses through the paces. When they were finished, they led their horses back to their respective stalls. After removing their saddles and blankets, they brushed their horses and inspected their hooves. After checking their water and food, the cousins left the stable.

"It was good to see you guys," Faith said as they walked back to their cars. "We need to have a cousins night out soon."

"Agreed. Now that you and most of your sisters are back in the States we should get together at least once a month," Remi said.

"I'll tell Tori and Elizabeth if you guys tell Audrey and Brynn," Amy volunteered. "Maybe we can all get together in the next couple of weeks."

"That sounds like a plan," Corinne said.

Faith climbed into her car while Amy and her cousins walked to theirs. Today had been nice, but now that she was alone, she was thinking of Caleb. She missed him and her heart ached to see him again.

And that was a problem.

CALEB SAT DOWN at the dinner table in the same chair he'd used every night from the time he was a child until he'd moved out a few years ago. The familiarity felt good, especially considering everything else that was going on in his life. He and his parents usually ate dinner together on Sunday nights, but since he'd been in Bronco last week, he'd been unable to come. He and Faith had made plans to spend this weekend together, so he wouldn't be around this upcoming Sunday either, so he made sure to be here for dinner tonight. Now, of all time, he didn't want to do anything to make his parents feel neglected. He was very careful to make sure they knew just how important they were to him.

"It's been good to have you home," Iris said, setting the green beans on the table beside the pot roast, mashed potatoes and rolls.

"It's good to be back." Instead of a typical Thursday night meal, his mother had gone all out. There was a chocolate cake sitting on the kitchen counter, waiting to be served with the homemade vanilla ice cream.

Nathan held Iris's chair for her before taking his own. Once they were all served, they talked about the goings-on in town. Eventually the conversation turned to his search for Caleb's biological father. Not that there was anything new to tell. He still hadn't met the man. Despite his best efforts to remain positive, doubt was beginning to creep in. Maybe he'd gotten as close to Brooks Langtree as he was ever going to get.

"So, what do you plan to do?" his mother asked when he'd finished with his recap.

"Faith thinks that she has a way to help. She's asked her mother but the woman didn't know anything. She's going to ask her grandmother next. Hopefully, she'll be able to help. I guess I'll find out when I get back."

He and Faith had talked on the phone several times this past week, but he hadn't wanted to talk about his search. He wanted their relationship to be about more than that.

"And if things are still at a standstill?" Nathan's question hung in the air for a moment.

"What do you mean?"

"Will you stay in Bronco so you can spend more time with Faith?"

"Don't matchmake," Iris said. "Caleb is quite capable of finding a good woman without your encouragement.

He knows how much we want grandchildren to spend the weekends with us before we get too old."

Caleb smiled at how slickly Iris chastised Nathan while simultaneously mentioning her desire for grandchildren.

"I wasn't thinking about grandchildren spending the weekend with us," Nathan denied. "I like having my best girl all to myself."

"Oh, you," Iris said, smiling like a teenager.

Caleb watched the interaction between his parents. They hadn't changed a bit in thirty years. His father was romantic and flirtatious while his mother was more reserved. They were the perfect couple. Caleb wondered if he would ever find his perfect mate. *Perhaps you've found her in Faith.* The thought, although appealing, wasn't appropriate right now and he refocused on the conversation.

"I'll stay the weekend either way. As you pointed out more than once, finding my birth father might take a while. I'm in it for the long haul."

"You might have a bit more success if you actually told the man what you believe. If he's not your biological father, you'll know and be able to continue your search elsewhere."

"That's my plan. But I want to tell him and *only* him. If I'm wrong, I don't want to be the source of gossip that might reach his family and friends. And I definitely don't want it to reach the media who might run with it. Especially after all of the accolades that he just received."

Iris patted his hand. "You always were a good and considerate child. You're an even better man."

Caleb's heart warmed at his mother's praise. "Thank you."

"When are you leaving?"

"I figured I'd leave tomorrow afternoon. Faith and I have plans to spend the evening together."

Iris smiled and patted Nathan's hand. "It looks like we might be getting those grandkids after all."

"Don't get ahead of yourself, Mom," Caleb said, rolling his eyes. "One thing at a time. We're still getting to know each other. Besides, with everything that's going on, I don't have time for a serious relationship."

Iris only nodded and Caleb knew that she was going to think whatever she pleased. Surprisingly he wasn't annoyed. In fact, he liked the idea of Faith having a more permanent role in his life. But first, he needed to know whether Brooks Langtree was his biological father. Until he knew that, romance was off the table.

CHAPTER NINE

"How do you feel about Halloween?" Faith asked Friday night as she and Caleb walked around the Bronco Fairgrounds, taking in the sights. They'd spent the past few hours enjoying the Bronco Harvest Festival. They'd played a few games, winning a few strings of beads, and gone on a hayride. It was slightly chilly, but nothing their cups of warm cider couldn't chase away. There was a stray piece of hay clinging to the front of her sweater and she brushed it off.

Caleb shrugged and Faith's eyes were immediately drawn to his massive shoulders. "I don't feel any kind of way. We always give out candy at the store and at home. Other than that, it's just a normal day."

"Do you wear a costume?"

"I haven't since I was a kid."

"But you aren't opposed to dressing up, are you?" she asked, mentally crossing her fingers.

Caleb stepped in front of Faith, stopping her progress. A kid holding a pink cotton candy nearly ran into him, veering away at the last minute. "I get the feeling there's something behind these questions. Why don't you just get to the point?"

"I want to invite you to a Halloween party."

"With costumes?"

She nodded.

"Sure. It might be fun."

"Great. I was hoping you would say that. It's tomorrow."

"*Tomorrow?* Tomorrow isn't Halloween. In fact, Halloween isn't for weeks. That is if we're talking about the same Halloween that we observe in Tenacity and the rest of the country."

"Ha ha. You're cute."

He puffed out his chest and struck a model pose. "Think so? My mother always says I'm her most handsome son. But then, I'm an only child, so…" He gave a half smile.

"You don't fool me for a minute. I bet the women in Tenacity are falling all over themselves to get to you."

He actually looked embarrassed. *Was he blushing?* "I do all right."

She laughed. It was good to know he wasn't vain.

"If we're comparing looks, you're going to win by a mile, Faith. You're more than cute."

Her heart skipped a beat and she struggled to calm down. She didn't want to let herself be led astray by one comment, so she forced herself to get back on track and started walking again. "Back to the party. It's more of a pre-Halloween party if you want to get technical. But there will be costumes and decorations."

"Is there a reason for the early date?"

"Yes." She held back a grin.

"Are you going to share that with me or is it a state secret? You know, you'd tell me but then you'd have to kill me."

She laughed. "It's the last day of the Bronco Harvest Festival. The organizers decided to have a costume party to cap off the event. Why? Are you a purist? Are you philosophically opposed to attending a Halloween party on any day but October thirty-first?"

He snorted. "A purist? No, I'm not."

"Then you'll go to the party with me tomorrow?" She

held her breath as she waited for his response. When she realized what she was doing, she exhaled forcefully. There was no need to make this a bigger deal than it was.

"Sure. But I don't have a costume. Or are costumes optional in this newfangled Halloween party?"

"I don't think that costumes are required but wearing them will make the party a lot more fun."

"What are you going as?"

"I don't know. I don't have a costume yet." She hadn't even planned on going until Caleb had come into her life.

"I have an idea. You can go as a rodeo star and I can go as the owner of a feed and farm supply store." His dimples flashed in his cheeks and she held back a smile.

"I'm going to pretend that you didn't say that. I don't wear work clothes to a party."

"Then what are we going to do for costumes? There's not much time."

"We're going to make them."

"You mean like sewing? Because if that's what you have in mind, I need to warn you that I'm useless with a needle and thread."

"For shame. I can sew. But that's not what I had in mind. There are some great shops in town where we can buy some vintage clothing and create our own costumes. I heard there'll be prizes for best costume and most original. Things like that. If we make our own as opposed to getting one at a store, we'll have a better chance of winning."

"And winning matters?" Caleb looked at her, a question in his eyes.

She shrugged. "It doesn't hurt. Besides it'll be fun to get our pictures taken with one of the trophies. You'll see."

She stopped and looked into his eyes. They were still a bit wary but he appeared to be warming up to the idea. So she continued. "Here's the plan. Tomorrow morning we'll hit some vintage clothing shops. If we don't find what we need there, we'll branch out. We can get any other supplies we need at the hardware store." She was winging it, but the more she thought about it, the more exciting the prospect became.

"So I guess we won't be cutting eyeholes in sheets and going as ghosts," Caleb quipped.

"Ghosts are invisible. Everybody knows that."

"Really? I must have been absent from school the day they taught that."

"Good thing you met me."

He grinned slowly. "Yes, Faith, it is."

Her stomach fluttered and she made herself ignore the feeling. "Anyway, we need to come up with something original."

"Hmm. I do like a challenge. I like the rodeo theme. But maybe with a twist. Instead of going as a horse, we could go as a camel. Our heads will be the humps."

Despite herself, Faith laughed. "What do camels have to do with rodeo?"

"Good point. But remember I'm a rodeo novice."

"Clearly."

"How about two peas in a pod?" Caleb said. He looked serious for a good three seconds before he burst into laughter. *Thank goodness.*

"I'm glad that you're getting into the spirit of things," she said with a wry smile.

"Totally. Maybe we could go as two pieces of bread. Heck, we could ask one of your sisters to join us and go as a sandwich."

Faith laughed. "Now you're just being silly."

He came up with one outrageous suggestion after the other, making her laugh uproariously, which drew the attention of several passersby.

Faith's sides were aching from laughter by the time Caleb finally ran out of suggestions.

"Do you want to eat breakfast together tomorrow before we hit the stores?" she asked.

"Absolutely. We can't start Operation Costumes on an empty stomach." Caleb stepped closer and whispered. "Should we synchronize our watches? Maybe have a secret code word in case anyone is looking?"

"I don't wear a watch. Not to mention the clocks on our phones are synchronized. But a code word is a good idea. What do you have in mind?"

His eyes widened in surprise. "You're kidding, right?"

"That's kind of long, but I suppose it'll work in a pinch."

Caleb shook his head. "You know, I like you, Faith Hawkins. I like you a lot."

And just like that, the playfulness fled and was replaced by a warm sensation. His sincerely spoken words were exactly what she'd longed to hear. At the same time, it was exactly what she was afraid of hearing. The emotions he awakened in her were strong. She hadn't felt anything like them before, yet they felt oddly familiar. They were simultaneously comforting and terrifying. But she knew she had nothing to fear from Caleb. She might not have known him for long but she knew he was a good man. A man she could trust.

"I like you too, Caleb." They'd stopped walking and were now facing each other, standing so close that she could feel the warmth from his body reaching out and surrounding hers. With each breath she took, she inhaled his enticing, masculine scent. She tried to fight back a sigh but it escaped her lips.

Caleb reached out and caressed her face. His touch was gentle and she leaned into his palm. "So, Faith, is the no-kissing rule still in effect?"

"No. It actually expired that night."

"That's good to know." His voice was a hoarse whisper that sent chills racing down her spine.

Her heart pounded in anticipation. "So, what are you going to do about it?"

Rather than answer, he leaned over and brushed his lips against hers. Her lips began to tingle and heat blossomed in her stomach before flowing throughout her body. Her eyes drifted shut. After a few seconds, he moved away, ending the kiss.

Opening her eyes, she looked at him, not bothering to disguise her frustration. A self-satisfied expression was written on his face. Clearly he knew that she was expecting more than that simple kiss. She poked him in his chest, absently noting just how hard and muscular it was. He laughed.

"What did you expect?" he asked. "We're in the middle of the Festival. Kids are running around and I don't want somebody's parents giving me the evil eye. And don't forget that every phone is a camera. I didn't think you would appreciate being the topic of conversation for the next couple of days and possibly even going viral."

"I don't care about that. I'm a Hawkins Sister. People are always talking about one of us."

"And that doesn't bother you?"

She gave a one-shoulder shrug. "If you can't stand the attention, don't compete in rodeo."

"So you wouldn't mind people talking about you making out in public with some strange—although incredibly handsome—man? You wouldn't care if that gossip reached your parents and grandmother?"

"I didn't say that. Besides, we weren't exactly making out."

"Not yet." Grinning mischievously, he reached for her. "But there's nothing stopping us."

She dodged his grasp. Turnabout was fair play. "It's too late now. The mood has passed."

He dropped his hand and his grin fell away. "That was fast."

"As my grandmother likes to say, you snooze, you lose."

"I wasn't exactly napping. But now I know I have to move fast with you."

"Sometimes and in some ways. Other times, slow is better. I'll leave it to you to determine which is which." She realized just how suggestive that comment was, but she didn't take it back. There was no sense denying the sexual attraction between them. The only question was how long it would simmer before it boiled over.

He nodded slowly. Then without saying a word, he grabbed her hand and they began walking across the fairgrounds again. His firm palm pressed against hers felt heavenly. She could get used to this.

CALEB'S HEART BEGAN to race as he walked beside Faith to her front door. It had taken all of his self-control to limit himself to a brief kiss earlier. The feel of her soft lips had sent his imagination into overdrive and he'd yearned to pull her into his arms and deepen the kiss. But his common sense had overruled his urges. Faith might not mind being the subject of gossip, but he did. He preferred to keep some things private. Especially since he might be the long-lost son of a big rodeo star. Caleb didn't want anything he did to sully Brooks Langtree's pristine reputation. If they were related, Brooks would come under scrutiny for everything that Caleb did, so he had to be sure not to step out of line.

But that was a worry for another time. Caleb and Faith were no longer standing in the middle of a busy festival.

They were alone on her secluded porch and not another soul was around. The mature trees blocked out a great deal of the moonlight, casting romantic shadows that shifted as the wind blew. The smell of smoke from a neighbor's fireplace filled the crisp autumn air.

Faith leaned against her front door and looked up at him. There was a gleam in her eyes that made his pulse race. She placed a hand on his chest and his heart began to pound. A small fire ignited inside him. His desire for her grew by each passing second and his control began to weaken.

She leaned closer, her sweet scent teasing his senses. "Just in case you need a hint, this is where I would like you to make a move."

"Is that right?" He placed his hands on her waist and pulled her closer to him. Her soft body molded against his, and his desire nearly consumed him. And yet he prolonged the moment, tormenting both of them. "I think I can handle that."

Ever so slowly, he lowered his head, drawing out the moment until the sexual tension between them fairly sizzled. Then their lips met. Instantly the fire inside him blazed hotter and intense desire spread from his head to his toes. He wrapped his arms around her, pulling her small, soft body even closer to his.

Caleb licked the seam of Faith's lips and she opened her mouth to him. Immediately he swept inside and their tongues tangled and danced. She tasted sweet and hot and his desire threatened to overwhelm his good sense. Caleb knew he should slow things down, but his body wouldn't let him. Instead, he deepened the kiss, indulging the pleasure he'd waited all day to feel.

Way too soon, he felt Faith easing back from him. Though his mind was hazy with lust, he understood her message and immediately loosened his hold on her, ending the kiss. Instead of backing away as he'd expected, Faith leaned her head against his chest. He was breathing hard, inhaling big gulps of air as he sought to catch his breath. He was vaguely aware of Faith doing the same. After a moment, she took a step back. Instantly Caleb missed the physical connection. He longed to reach out and pull her back to him but he resisted.

"Wow." Her quivering voice was filled with wonder.

"You took the word right out of my mouth." His voice sounded hoarse to his ears and he cleared his throat. A part of him wanted to continue this inside and see where things might go, but he shoved that thought aside. Faith had made herself clear and he respected her right to end things here. Besides, he was in the middle of searching for his birth father. He didn't know where that would take him. For all he knew, he might not be in Montana next week. He didn't want to start something with Faith he might not be able to finish. She deserved someone who could give her all of his attention. Someone who could promise to always be here for her. If things were different, he would pursue her in a heartbeat. But until he found his birth father, there would be no woman in his life.

"I suppose I should go in now." Faith's voice was reluctant and she didn't move.

He brushed a strand of her hair away from her face, letting his fingers skim over the soft, warm skin of her cheek. It wouldn't take much for him to get her aroused again, but he wouldn't. He took a step back and shoved his fist into his pocket to keep from reaching out to her again.

Faith pulled her keys from her purse, fumbling with the ring. She sorted through the keys until she found the right one. She held one and aimed it for the lock. And missed. Caleb covered her hand with his, steered the key into the lock, then turned the knob. Faith pushed open the door and looked back at him. Her eyes were dark and dreamy and his earlier resolve threatened to crumble.

"Thank you for a good day, Caleb. I had a wonderful time."

"So did I."

"I'll see you in the morning."

"Yes." Nothing would keep him away.

She raised on tiptoes and brushed a kiss on his lips. She lingered for a moment and then broke the contact. His lips were still tingling when she stepped inside and closed the door behind her. He leaned his head against the frame for a moment before turning and jogging down the stairs, hoping the brisk night air would cool him off.

Tonight had been great. Tomorrow promised to be even better. He couldn't wait.

CHAPTER TEN

"BACON AND EGGS? Really?" Faith pressed her lips together as she struggled to hold in her laughter. It slipped out anyway. She placed a hand on her hip. They were in the middle of a secondhand shop trying to find something to make their costumes with. They'd already hit a couple of stores in town but hadn't met with success. "What is it with you and food costumes?"

Caleb held up the pants in front of him and looked at her. He dragged his hand over the various shades of brown wavy stripes. "You cannot tell me that these pants don't look like slices of bacon."

He had a point, but she wasn't going to tell him that. That would only encourage him to make more outrageous costume suggestions. Not that she minded much. Caleb was a one-man comedy show. She couldn't remember the last time she'd laughed this hard or as much. But time was slipping by and they needed to find a costume. "I'm not going to answer. We have work to do."

Caleb hung the pants back on the rack. Then he smiled. "Be right back. I see something."

"That sounds ominous," Faith said, following him across the store.

"You aren't the only one who will know it when you see it," Caleb said, echoing the words she'd said earlier.

She still believed them to be true. But she needed to see "*it*" soon. "So you say."

Caleb grabbed a hanger from a rack and then whipped it around with a flourish. He smiled confidently at her. "Great, huh?"

She looked at the yards of dark blue velvet fabric in his hands. "What is it supposed to be?"

"It's curtains," he said, the "duh" unspoken yet understood.

"You want to go as window treatments?"

"No. That makes no sense. We can go as opening night. We can each wear one panel. We can pull them apart and reveal the moon and stars on T-shirts. Get it? *Opening night?*" He looked so proud of himself she almost hated to burst his bubble.

"I do. But it's way too complicated. If you have to explain the costume then it's no good."

"That's what you said before. I still disagree about the Milk Duds."

"Me dressing as a carton of milk and you as an unexploded grenade? Do people even eat Milk Duds anymore?"

"I can't believe you just asked that. They're one of my favorite candies ever."

"Sorry for offending the junk food addict in you."

"You're forgiven." Caleb looked at the curtains again. "I still think opening night can work."

She shook her head. "It would be too hard to dance. And how would we go to the bathroom if we were stuck together? And before you ask, I still don't want to go as radio waves. I'm not wearing a box with painted-on knobs while you get to wear big hands. Nor do I want to switch."

"I have the perfect solution. I can smoke a cigar and wear glasses. You can wear a slip. You can dance in that and going to the bathroom won't be an issue." He brushed his hands together as if it was a done deal.

She frowned. "I don't get it."

"I'll be Freud. We'll be—"

"—a Freudian slip."

"Yes." He smiled.

"No."

"Well, then, I'm fresh out of ideas."

"Thank goodness."

"I'm ignoring you," he said with a laugh and began searching through the shelves. Clearly he was not offended by her comment. But then, they had been kidding each other all morning. He'd arrived at her house bright and early this morning. She'd cooked waffles, eggs and sausage. After taking his first bite, Caleb had begun proposing one wacky idea after the other, taking up from where he'd left off yesterday. Many of the ideas had been clever, but she didn't see how they could actually make the costumes. Given that the party was tonight, they were running out of time.

"How about we go to the party *as* a party?" Caleb asked.

She'd been digging through a box. She stopped and looked at him. "What does that even mean?"

"You can use that fabric to make a dartboard shirt. You can wear pants and still be able to dance. People play darts at parties."

"What kind of parties do you go to?"

"Okay. Not a party. A sports bar."

"That's good. That has possibility. What will you go as?"

He held up a T-shirt with a vintage beer logo on front. "I can go as a bottle of beer."

"A T-shirt is not really much of a costume."

"Or..." He held up the curtains in his other hand as if weighing their options. "Opening night?"

"When you put it like that..."

Caleb laughed.

"I actually like the idea of a beer bottle T-shirt, but I think we can do a bit better than that. I can make a hat that looks like a bottle cap." She rubbed her hands together. "This is going to be so good."

They paid for everything and then headed back to her house. She pulled her sewing machine out of the closet, then searched through her fabric box until she found what she needed. Fortunately the costumes were pretty simple and it only took an hour or so to complete. Caleb insisted on making them something to eat while she sewed. It felt nice to have a man prepare a meal for her. Having him bustling about her kitchen should have felt strange, but it didn't. It felt cozy.

She was pressing the last seam when he set a plate on the edge of the ironing board. "Dinner is served."

"Just in time. I'm finished. And starved." She washed her hands and then picked up her plate. They sat on the couch and started on their grilled cheese sandwiches, salad and tomato soup.

"This meal is my specialty," he said.

"And one of my favorites. I generally don't mind cooking, but there are times when I'm too hungry to make a big dinner."

"I get it. My mother loves to cook and she's taught me how to make a number of different dishes. But unlike her, I don't like spending hours in the kitchen unless I'm baking a pie. Fifteen minutes is all I'm willing to do."

"Same."

"My mom makes a big Sunday dinner every week. I wouldn't want to hurt her feelings by not taking home leftovers. Those generally last a day or so."

Faith smirked. "You're such a good son."

"I try to be."

He sounded so serious that Faith looked up, spoon in

hand. "You are," she repeated. "I suspect you're feeling guilty again about looking for your bio dad. Let me remind you to stop it now."

He was silent for a moment, staring into space. Then he smiled. "Thanks. I needed that."

"Of course."

He smiled and polished off the last of his sandwich. "That should hold me until the party. Hopefully, they'll have more than candy."

Faith laughed. "They will. Remember, we can't leave until after they announce the winners."

"If we don't win, don't blame me. I still think we should have gone as movie tickets."

"Or bowling pins. I know." She waved him off with a stifled smile. "Don't worry. I won't get upset if we don't win. It's all in good fun. Plus, this will be a way for you to meet some of the people in town."

"True."

They grabbed their dishes and put them in the kitchen sink. "Let's get changed. We don't want to be late."

Faith showed Caleb to her guest room where he could change then she put on her costume in her bedroom. She stood in front of her full-length mirror and checked her appearance. Not too shabby for a last-minute job.

She grabbed her purse, then headed for the living room. Caleb was already there, sitting on her sofa. He stood and applauded when Faith entered. "You look so good. I have no doubt you'll win first place."

Faith took a bow. She'd made the dartboard out of two foldable paper fans, covering them with black and red cloth. Now she closed the fans and unfastened them from her shirt and then dropped them into her large purse where they wouldn't get bent.

"You look pretty good yourself." She adjusted the silver cap on his head. "I'm not much of a beer drinker, but if I was, yours is definitely the brand I would pick up."

"You say the sweetest things." Caleb grinned and held out his arm. "Shall we get this show on the road?"

Faith looped her arm with his. "Absolutely."

Once they were settled in his truck, Faith leaned back against the seat and smiled at him. "We're going to have the best time."

"I'm already having the best time," Caleb said. "Being with you is always fun."

Those quietly spoken words made Faith's heart skip a beat. Caleb wasn't flirting or spouting a line. She heard the sincerity in his tone and felt it. His openness gave her the courage to be as honest as he'd been. "I feel the same way about you."

Caleb looked pleased as he turned his attention back to the road. Neither of them spoke for a while as if basking in the glow of their shared feelings and trying to figure out what came next. At least that was what she was doing.

When they arrived at the Bronco Community Center, Caleb parked and Faith reassembled her dartboard costume before they entered the building. Strips of black and orange crepe paper dangled from the ceiling. The walls were decorated with black cats, orange jack-o'-lanterns and colorful scarecrows. Bales of hay were stacked at random intervals down the hall. The lighting was dim, casting spooky shadows on the walls.

"They went all out," Caleb said.

"Of course. We don't do things halfway here in Bronco."

"It's nice that the town has the funds to decorate this way. It's a little thing, but it goes a long way when you set the mood. The right ambience makes a difference." He frowned. "I wish we could afford special events like this in Tenacity. I think it would help strengthen the sense of community and build morale. Maybe more young people would be inclined to stay. But when you only have so much money, choices have to be made. Do you spend the cash on a three-hour party or do you fill potholes?"

"I get your point. Hopefully, Tenacity will find the magic it needs to increase the funds in its coffers. That way they won't have to choose. They can do both things."

He nodded. "Enough talk about that. We're at a party, so let's enjoy ourselves."

They followed the sound of up-tempo music down the hall and then stepped into the party room. The decorations were just as elaborate as the ones in the hallways. Round tables interspersed with orange and black tablecloths were arranged around the perimeter of the room with a dance floor in the middle.

The dance floor was filled with costumed merrymakers moving to the song blaring over the speakers. There were only adults present. There was a separate party for the kids in another room.

"Do you want to find a seat or would you rather dance?" Caleb asked.

"Dance. Definitely dance." Faith shimmied her shoulders and wiggled her hips. It had been a long time since she'd been to a party much less danced and she didn't want to wait another minute.

"Well, then, let's go. I don't want to keep you from shaking your groove thing."

Faith laughed. "My *groove* thing?"

"You know what I mean." He wiggled his eyebrows suggestively as his gaze swept over her hips. Butterflies immediately began soaring around her stomach and the blood began to pulse in her veins. Caleb held out his hand and led her to the dance floor where they managed to find a spot that wasn't too crowded. They immediately began to move to the beat and Faith was pleased to note that Caleb could more than hold his own. One song blended into another and they danced to several up-tempo tunes until the notes of a slow song filled the air.

Caleb extended his arms and Faith held up a hand. She unpinned her dartboard costume before going into his arms, sinking into him. She leaned her head against his chest and sighed as his arms wrapped around her. She felt his heart beat beneath her ear. It was steady and strong. His torso was hard and muscular and she felt his abs move in and out as he breathed. His cologne hinted of the outdoors. It smelled so good she would be happy to stand here breathing it in all night. Everything about this moment was perfect and she wished it could last forever.

After the last notes of the song faded away, the DJ announced that finger food was now being served. Faith and Caleb joined the buffet lines at the front of the room. Faith introduced Caleb to the people around them and they chatted until they reached the trays of food. Faith and Caleb grabbed glasses of fruit punch and filled their clear plastic plates with mini subs, pizza rolls, chips and carrots.

They were headed for a dining table when Faith spotted Elizabeth sitting with her rancher husband, Jake McCreery. Faith turned to Caleb. "Hey, there's my sister. Do you mind sitting with her and her husband?"

"That's fine with me."

They crossed the room and stood beside two empty chairs. "Can we join you?"

Elizabeth smiled, stood, and then embraced her sister. "You know you can. I didn't expect to see you here. You said you weren't coming."

"It was a last-minute decision." Faith introduced Jake to Caleb and then they sat down.

Faith popped a sausage pizza roll into her mouth. *Delicious.* "Are the kids here?"

"Of course. The five of them are in the kids' party. Although Halloween is becoming more popular in Australia, the girls and I never made a big deal of it. They were over the moon when Jake's kids told them how they celebrate here."

"I imagine they're thrilled to be filling up on pizza and candy," Faith said.

"You know it. Dressing up as mermaids with Molly was the icing on the cake."

"I bet they look so cute."

"They do."

Faith glanced from Elizabeth to Jake. "And where are your costumes?"

"I love a good party as much as the next person," Elizabeth said, "but wearing a costume is where I draw the line."

"That explains why you came as a rodeo star."

"It was either that or a tired mother."

Faith shook her head and then turned to her brother-in-law. "And what are you supposed to be, Jake?"

Jake shrugged. "I'm a rancher. Can't you tell?"

"I tried to convince Faith to come as a rodeo star," Caleb said, "but she shot me down."

"My sister always has to do things the hard way," Elizabeth said.

"Trust me, I know," Caleb said and then began telling them about the costumes that Faith had vetoed.

Jake laughed. "My boys would have definitely preferred to go costume shopping with you instead of me. They had to settle for coming as superheroes. Next year I'll get with you for ideas."

"As long as you and Caleb are the ones making the

costumes," Faith said as Elizabeth nodded in agreement. "Those brilliant suggestions of his will be hard to make."

Caleb held up his hands in front of him. "Sorry. I'm just the idea guy. Manufacturing is a separate department."

The others laughed. As they talked, they enjoyed the tasty finger food and drinks. Several of their friends came up and spoke to them and Faith was pleased to note how well Caleb fit in with everyone.

"He's definitely a keeper," Rylee Parker, one of Faith's friends, said as they sat together. Faith hadn't seen her friend since the Golden Buckle Rodeo and they took a moment to catch up.

Faith laughed and glanced over at Caleb. He was talking with Jake so Faith didn't have to worry about him overhearing. "We're having fun now. I'm not making plans for the future."

"You might want to rethink that. Good men don't come along every day." Rylee glanced at her engagement ring, a smile lighting her face. She looked over at her fiancé, Shep Dalton, who was talking with one of his brothers before looking back at Faith.

"Speaking of good men, how are the wedding plans coming along?" Faith asked.

"Good. But busy. With searching for a dress, choosing the menu for the reception, and so much more, I barely have a free minute. Not to mention work. I'm busy working on the Mistletoe Rodeo." Rylee was the marketing director for the Bronco Convention Center where the rodeo was held.

"I'd volunteer to help but I don't know the first thing about weddings."

Rylee glanced at Caleb and then back at Faith. "I have a feeling that might change soon."

"You're as bad as the Hawkins women."

"I'll take that as a compliment," Rylee said, before she gave Faith a hug and walked away to join her fiancé.

Faith was still contemplating Rylee's comment about Caleb when the DJ announced the judges were about to award the prizes. Faith looked toward the makeshift stage where the judges, holding clipboards, were huddled. The room began to buzz as everyone speculated who would win. The head judge approached the microphone and a hush came over the room. Faith and Caleb exchanged grins and he lifted his hands to show his crossed fingers.

Before the judge could make an announcement, a person dressed in a purple floor-length costume and face mask entered the room. Gray hair flowed around her shoulders and big earrings dangled from her ears. There was something vaguely familiar about the way the woman moved, but Faith couldn't put her finger on what it was. The masked woman slowly strode around the room as if searching for someone. Then, without saying a word, she turned and walked out the door.

All of a sudden the room was abuzz and people spoke over each other.

"Did you see her?" a man called.

"Was it her?" a woman asked in an excited voice. "Was it Winona?"

"I couldn't tell with the mask. But it could have been."

"Somebody needs to catch up with her and find out."

"Where is Stanley? Somebody should call him and let him know that Winona was here."

"What's going on?" Caleb asked.

"People think that woman was Winona Cobbs," Jake said. When it was clear the name didn't mean anything to Caleb he continued. "Winona went missing several months ago, hours before her wedding to Stanley Sanchez."

"So she's a runaway bride?" Caleb asked.

"Nothing like that," Elizabeth corrected him. "I was at her bridal shower. Winona was as excited as any bride I've ever seen. In fact, she expressed regret for making her fiancé wait so long to finally set a date. She loves Stanley. There's no way she would simply disappear without a word to him."

"So, what do people think happened?"

"Speculation is running rampant but nobody really has a clue. You know how people love to be the first to know something and then spread their information around even if there are no facts to support it. Winona's been gone since July and with each passing day, the stories grow a little bit more desperate and more outrageous."

"Winona is a little bit eccentric, but she's well liked in town," Jake added.

"Well, if she's back in Bronco, maybe she'll explain where she's been," Faith said.

"I hope so," Elizabeth said.

The commotion gradually died down and a man Faith didn't recognize returned to the room. His breathing was heavy and it took a minute for him to catch his breath. The room grew quiet again as everyone waited to hear what he had to say. "I don't know if that was Winona or not. By the time I got into the hall, she was out of sight. I searched the whole building. Then I checked the parking lot. I even walked around the block but she was gone."

"So you didn't get a look up close?" The woman's voice was unfamiliar, but Faith recognized the sorrow and disappointment in it.

"No," the man admitted.

"But if that was her, I'm sure she'll let us know in her own time," someone else said.

"And if it wasn't?"

"Then we're in the same place we were an hour ago, wondering what happened to Winona."

That comment was not especially satisfying, but it was the truth.

After the potential sighting, the judge announced the winners of the contest, which Faith had to admit now seemed anticlimactic. She and Caleb didn't win anything, but they were having too much fun to care. The music resumed and after a bit of a lull, the gloomy mood lifted and once more people returned to the dance floor.

"I hate to be a party pooper, but I think it's time for us to grab the kids and head home," Elizabeth said as she got their attention.

"Already?" Faith asked. She'd been having a good time with her sister and her brother-in-law.

"I'm afraid so. Remember, our kids are little. It's already past the twins' and Ben's bedtime." Elizabeth's daughters were five and Jake's son Ben was six. His other two kids were eight and ten. Not exactly the age to party the night away.

"I hope you aren't expecting them to go right to sleep."

Elizabeth grimaced. "With all the sugar they've eaten tonight? No. I dream big, but not that big."

"We can always let them run around the backyard. That ought to help them burn off some energy," Jake suggested with a mischievous grin.

"Or we can drive around with the heat on high," Elizabeth countered. "That might make them drowsy."

Faith and Caleb exchanged glances as they laughed at the other couple. "Tell them all good-night for me," Faith said.

"I will. Of course, you can always come into the kids' party room and do it yourself."

Faith shook her head. "I'll pass. I can only imagine how hectic and loud it is in there."

Elizabeth laughed. "Chicken."

Faith flapped her arms like wings and squawked.

Elizabeth hugged Faith and whispered, "I'll catch up with you later. I need an update on this romance of yours."

"It's not a romance," Faith whispered back, sounding more definite than she felt.

Elizabeth only nodded as she stepped away.

"It was good meeting you," Jake said to Caleb.

"Same."

Caleb and Faith watched as the couple left, arms around each other. Then Faith and Caleb headed for the dance floor, and joined a line dance. When the song ended, several people began streaming out the door. Most of them were parents who no doubt were picking up their children from the kids' party. Since neither she nor Caleb had children, they were free to party for the rest of the night. Even so, all too soon, the last song ended. Faith and Caleb put on their coats and joined the exodus to the parking lot.

"I had such a good time tonight," Faith said once they were ensconced in Caleb's truck.

"So did I," Caleb said.

As they rode back to Faith's house, they recounted the highlights, laughing as they talked about the other costumes they'd seen. A good number had been clever, and quite a few had been elaborate. Faith had to admit that the winners of the contests had deserved their victories.

"We'll win next year," Caleb said, "but we'll have to get an earlier start."

Faith tried not to read too much into that comment, but she couldn't stop her heart from skipping a beat. Nor could she stop the hope that bloomed inside her. Was Caleb planning on being in her life a year from now? Did she want him to be?

Caleb parked in front of Faith's house and her body began to tingle. It was getting harder and harder to keep her feelings for Caleb friendly. The attraction was simply too strong. While she wasn't interested in a romance, perhaps they could have a casual relationship. After all, they were both adults. There was no reason they couldn't have a physical relationship while keeping their hearts out of it. That is, if Caleb was amenable.

Caleb had already made it clear that he didn't have the bandwidth for anything serious. With everything going on in his life, she believed him. Weren't men supposed to be expert at keeping the physical and emotional separate? Maybe Caleb would be able to do that.

Caleb parked in front of her house, then glanced over at her. His eyes were dark and mysterious. "I suppose I need to say good-night," he said. Faith heard the reluctance in his voice.

"You don't have to. You can always come inside for a while."

Caleb grinned. "I was hoping you would say that."

They climbed out of the truck and walked side by side up the stairs and into the house. After hanging their jackets in the closet, Faith gestured for Caleb to have a seat. She rubbed her hands over the front of her thighs. "Would you like a drink?"

"I wouldn't mind."

"Good. I'm in the mood for some warm cider."

He frowned. "That's not my idea of a good drink, but don't let that stop you."

"The thought never crossed my mind." She smiled. "What can I get for you?"

"I wouldn't say no to coffee."

"Of course."

She quickly made their beverages and returned to the living room. They sat side by side on the sofa, his denim-clad leg brushing against hers. Her skin heated at the contact and the blood began to race through her veins. She'd been attracted to men before, but it hadn't felt anything like this. In the past, she'd never had a problem controlling her body and thoughts. Caleb's simplest touch made her burn with desire and sent her imagination running wild. Faith had to face facts. Caleb Strom was irresistible. And she was tired of trying to keep him at a distance.

Faith glanced out the corner of her eye and caught Caleb staring at her. She turned her head in his direction, expecting him to look away. He didn't. Instead he met her stare head-on. The heat in his dark eyes melted her bones to liquid and her hand shook, sending cider sloshing over the side of her mug.

Caleb took her mug, set it on the coffee table, then placed his next to hers. With each passing second, the longing she'd fought to contain grew stronger, threatening to overwhelm her, and her breathing became shallow. He sat back and she looked into Caleb's face, noting the intense desire on his face. Then, as one, they reached out for each other. Their lips met in a hot, passionate kiss that turned the fire inside her into a raging inferno. She pulled him closer, needing to feel more of him, but no matter how close she pressed against his body, she couldn't get enough of him.

Her heart was pounding and blood was racing through her veins. Unexpectedly Caleb broke the kiss. A cry of protest burst from her lips. Confused and vibrating with desire, she reached out to pull his face back to hers. He took her hands and held them in his. He looked into her eyes, his own hazy with yearning. "We need to slow down before I can't stop."

"And if I don't want to stop?"

His chest rose as he inhaled deeply. Her eyes were drawn to the muscles his shirt barely contained. She'd run her hands over his chest and knew just how strong and firm it was. "You need to be sure, Faith. Because as much as I want you, as much as I like you, I can't offer you a relationship. You deserve commitment. Actually, you deserve the world."

"I'm well aware of your limitations, Caleb. I have similar ones of my own. I'm not willing to put my heart on the line right now. But I am willing to have a casual relationship. No strings. No expectations. No risk of heartache. But a whole lot of fun. That is, if you are willing."

He pressed a searing kiss against her lips, sending a flow of heat throughout her body. "I'm not just willing. I'm completely able."

She stood and held out her hand. He took it without hesitation and they raced up the stairs to her bedroom.

CALEB BLINKED AT the sunlight streaming though the curtains. For a moment he didn't know where he was. The warm woman lying beside him instantly cleared that up. He was in Faith's bed. He closed his eyes as pleasant memories of the night they'd just shared flashed through his mind. He'd slept with women in the past, although not nearly as many as people tended to believe—but he'd never found making love as fulfilling as he had with Faith.

Faith was a generous and spontaneous lover. What could have been an awkward first time had been fun. Their friendly and comfortable relationship had not stopped at her bedroom door. They'd been completely in tune with each other. After satisfying their physical needs, they'd talked and laughed late into the night until Faith had fallen asleep with her head on his chest. Now, despite how at ease they'd been with each other last night, he experienced a bit of trepidation. It was easy for Faith to say she could keep things casual *before* making love. Would she actually be able to do that now that she'd given herself to him so fully?

"Stop thinking so hard," Faith said, startling him.

"I didn't know you were awake."

She stretched languidly and opened her eyes. "I wasn't. But you tensed up and I could practically hear the wheels whirling in your head."

He glanced at her face. Even without a hint of makeup, she was positively gorgeous. "Is that right?"

She propped herself on one elbow and looked down at him. She walked two fingers across his chest, leaving a trail of fire behind. "Yes."

He captured her fingers and brushed a kiss against her palm. "So, what am I thinking about?"

"You're worried that I won't be able to keep from falling in love with irresistible you. You're afraid that I can't separate the emotional from the physical. But I can. I want things to be casual between us. More than that, I *need* for things to be casual. That's the only way that this works for me."

Relief washed over him at her words even as his ego chafed a bit. A small part of him wished that she would fall madly in love with him. That same part knew he could fall head over heels in love with her in a heartbeat. But then what? He wasn't in a position to give her the love and attention that she deserved. And he certainly couldn't put her on hold.

"Then we're in agreement," he said finally.

"Yes." She sat up, pulling the striped sheet up over her

perfect breasts, hiding them from view. "I suppose we should get up."

He sat up and dropped a kiss on her bare shoulder, then nuzzled her neck. "How about I take you out to breakfast?"

"I wish I could take you up on that. I'm meeting my sisters to practice for an upcoming rodeo in an hour." She gave him a glance that set his blood on fire. "But there's time to shower before I need to hit the road. You're invited. Unless you'd rather grab your clothes and go."

Caleb looked around. His clothes were scattered around the bedroom, evidence of the rush they'd been in last night. His T-shirt was draped over the arm of a chair, coming close to dragging the floor. His pants were inside out near the closet and tangled with Faith's.

Not waiting for an answer, Faith tossed off the sheet, then got out of the bed wearing nothing but a smile. She glanced over her shoulder at him, an invitation in her eyes, one brow raised in a dare. Caleb was never one to walk away from a challenge, especially one that came wrapped in such a delectable package.

Standing, and as naked as she was, he walked across the room, his eyes never breaking contact with hers. He held out his arm and they walked side by side to her cozy bathroom. The tiled shower was small, but big enough for two and Caleb stepped aside as Faith turned on the water and tested it with her hand. When she found the temperature satisfactory, she stepped inside and winked at Caleb, who followed her.

She grabbed a bar of soap and a washcloth and he did the same. Once their cloths were lathered up, they began to wash each other. He'd touched her in every place possible last night, his hands often pausing in the most sensitive spots. Watching her dissolve with desire had been extremely pleasurable. Even so, rubbing the terry-cloth square against her smooth brown skin was just as exciting and stimulating today.

Faith rubbed her cloth across his torso, her sensual touch leaving a trail of suds behind. She followed the cloth with a fingernail, dragging it through the bubbles. The water from the showerhead pounded on his back and shoulders, running in rivulets down his legs and to the drain. The heat rose between them as they washed each other. Her hand wandered down his chest and over his stomach, and his muscles clenched in response. Flames of longing licked inside him and the pounding water was powerless to douse it.

What started out as harmful play quickly turned passionate and their laughter faded away. Caleb captured Faith's lips in a searing kiss. When she sighed and opened her mouth to him, his desire raged even hotter. He lifted her into his arms and she wrapped her legs around his waist. Stopping to turn off the water, he carried her from the bathroom and into the bedroom. He tossed her onto the bed, then jumped in beside her. Familiar with her body, he knew exactly what to do to drive her wild and focused on giving her the utmost pleasure.

"I could get used to starting the day like this," Faith said some time later.

"You and me both."

Her stomach growled loudly and she frowned. "Of course, that might mean I'd miss more meals than I can afford to."

"Nah. It just means we need to wake up earlier." He brushed a kiss on her damp shoulder and then sat up. "But that's a sacrifice I'm willing to make."

She ran a hand across his abs, a devilish expression on her face. He forced himself to resist. Covering her hand with his, he stopped her progress. "Not now. We need to get dressed so we get out of here. You have to meet your sisters, remember."

"I do." She scrambled from the bed and headed for her bathroom. After watching her walk away with a bit of extra swing to her hips, Caleb gathered his clothes and headed for the guest bathroom. The shower stall was smaller but it served its purpose. He quickly washed and dressed, then went downstairs to wait for Faith.

There were lots of knickknacks and pictures on the tables and bookshelves. He picked up a framed photo of Faith. Dressed in rodeo gear, she looked to be about twelve or thirteen. She held the reins of her horse in one hand and a giant trophy in the other. Her smile was wide and her eyes shone with pride at her victory.

He set down the picture and picked up another. She was older in this picture—but only slightly taller. The outfit was different, but the expression on her face was the same. Instead of a trophy, she was holding a belt buckle. Time had changed a few things, but she was still a champion.

Faith stepped into the room. He turned to look at her and smiled. She was dressed in a floral flannel shirt that she'd tucked into faded jeans that showcased her small waist. Even dressed casually, she was temptation personified. But more than lust, he felt a strong—and growing—affection for her.

He had agreed to keep things casual between them. Now he wondered just how long he would be able to keep it up.

CHAPTER ELEVEN

FAITH WAITED ON the porch for her mother to answer the door. As she did, her mind replayed the message Suzie had left for her earlier that day. "I need you to stop by after practice. We need to talk in person."

Although she'd told herself not to worry, she couldn't stop the thoughts that assaulted her. Was Suzie sick? That idea, though terrifying, didn't make sense. Why would she only want to talk to Faith and not all of her daughters? Or at least the four of them that lived in Bronco? It had to be something else. While she was trying to come up with an alternative answer, the door swung open.

"Sorry. I didn't realize that the door was locked. Come on in." Suzie stepped aside and Faith quickly entered.

"Thanks." Faith looked at her mother. As usual, Suzie looked radiant. Her ash-blond hair brushed against her shoulders. Her fair skin was just as clear and glowed as always. Suzie was the picture of health. Even so, Faith's nerves were still on edge. She couldn't bear not knowing for another moment. "What's going on? Is everything okay? You aren't sick, are you?"

Suzie gave a little laugh. "No. Whatever gave you an idea like that?"

Relief surged through Faith's body and she sighed before answering. "Your message was a bit cryptic to say the least. 'We need to talk. In person.'"

Suzie shook her head as she and Faith sat on the sofa.

"I forgot how dramatic you can be. You always did have a wild imagination."

"And that imagination got the best of me," Faith admitted. "So if there's nothing wrong, what did you need to talk to me about so urgently? What couldn't we discuss over the phone?"

A sober expression replaced the smile on her mother's face and Faith's stomach began to churn again.

"I was thinking about your friend, Caleb."

Faith's heart skipped a beat at the mere mention of Caleb's name. Images of the two of them wrapped in each other's arms flashed through her mind. His touch had been erotic and his kisses had been stimulating. Making love with Caleb had been more pleasurable than anything she'd ever experienced before. She was longing to feel that way again. Before she could get flustered, she forced her mind back to the conversation at hand. "What about Caleb?"

"I heard that the two of you were together at the Halloween party."

"Word travels fast."

"I take it that you like him a lot."

"I do. You don't have a problem with that, do you?" Faith frowned. Was this why her mother needed to talk in person?

Suzie shook her head. "Not at all."

"Then what is it?"

"I was thinking about his search for his biological father."

Of course Suzie would wonder how things were going. She had a big heart. "It's not going that well. He's hit a wall. But he's not going to give up. He's determined to find his biological dad."

"That's not a good idea."

"What do you mean? Why do you say that?"

"He should stop searching."

"Stop? Why?" That was the last thing Faith expected her mother to say.

Suzie was quiet for a long moment. She picked at the cuticle of her perfectly manicured nail, then brushed imaginary lint from her pants. Finally she looked up at Faith. She appeared to have a hard time meeting Faith's eyes. "I wasn't entirely honest with you before. I know who Caleb's biological father is."

"You do? How did you find out? Who is he? Is he alive?" Faith asked excitedly. She couldn't wait to tell Caleb. He was going to be so happy.

"Yes, he's alive. And I'm not going to tell you who he is."

"Why not?"

"Because I have no doubt that you'll go straight from here to Caleb. You'll tell him. I don't want you to. It will only cause him pain."

"How do you know that?"

"Because I knew the man." Suzie's voice was flat.

"You knew him?" Faith asked, at once outraged and disappointed in her mother. "You said you hadn't heard a word about an adoption. You told me that you were so busy raising your family that you didn't have time to keep up with gossip."

Suzie's cheeks pinkened. "I remember what I said, so you don't need to replay it for me. And I'm not telling you his name. That's not why I wanted to talk."

"Then why?" Faith folded her arms over her chest.

"To get you to convince Caleb to stop looking."

Faith shook her head. "I won't do that."

"And I won't tell you his name."

"Forget about his name for the moment. What *are* you willing to tell me about him?"

"He wasn't a good man."

"I'm willing to accept that you believe that. But I need more than that."

Suzie shook her head and pressed her lips together.

"Please, Mom. What aren't you telling me?"

Suzie sighed. "I knew Caleb's biological mother."

Faith's heart stuttered. "Really?"

"Yes. She was such a sweet woman. A girl really. She was in her teens when I met her. And she was only twenty when Caleb was born. She loved Caleb's father with her whole heart. There was nothing she wouldn't do for that man." Suzie's voice turned bitter. Hard. "But he didn't want to make their relationship public. Even after she had the baby, he insisted on keeping their marriage a secret. Now, she adored him, so naturally she did as he asked. All she wanted was to be with him. If he was happy, then so was she."

"So their marriage remained a secret," Faith surmised.

"Yes."

"Then how did you know about it?"

"I told you. I was friends with Caleb's birth mother, so I saw everything firsthand." She paused only a moment before she continued. "After she died, Caleb's father left the child behind. He continued to travel on the rodeo circuit and never looked back. I doubt he ever thought about that baby again."

Faith thought of Caleb's need to find his father and decided to try again. "You should tell me his father's name."

Suzie shook her head. "No good will come from Caleb getting in touch with the man."

"I could understand keeping the information a secret if Caleb was still a child and needed protection. But he's a grown man. It should be his decision."

"He's my friend's son. She's not here, so she can't protect him. But I can. I'm not going to do something that I know will hurt him. I owe her that much."

"You said she loved Caleb's father. She wouldn't want you to keep them apart."

Suzie folded her arms against her chest, a move that Faith recognized. She was not going to budge from her stubborn position. "Did you hear a word I said? Surely you don't think this is the kind of person Caleb needs in his life."

"Mom," Faith said, gently, reaching out to touch her mother's arm. "Try to put yourself in Caleb's position. He only wants to know more about his birth family. He needs to know where he came from. Surely as someone who was adopted, you know how important that is."

"Are you saying that you don't know where you came from? Or where you belong? That you don't feel like you're a part of the Hawkins family?" Suzie sounded at once angry and hurt. That wasn't at all what Faith wanted. She'd simply been trying to get Suzie to put herself in Caleb's shoes.

"No, Mom. And I believe you know that. But you were adopted as a teenager, so you know about your birth parents."

"Yes. And they were no picnic. Getting adopted by Hattie Hawkins was the best thing that ever happened to me. I can't tell you how glad I am that the state of Oklahoma didn't see fit to get in the way of that."

Faith nodded. Hattie was Black and allowing her to adopt a white teenager had been unusual for the times. Perhaps her fame on the rodeo circuit was part of the reason. That, and the fact that Suzie had been dirt-poor and without other family.

"They might not have been the best people in the world, but you knew them. You don't have to wonder who you look like. You don't have to wonder what behaviors you inherited from them."

"None. Thank God. If I act like anyone, it's my mother, Hattie Hawkins."

Faith blew out a breath. Suzie didn't like to talk about her birth parents at all. As far as she was concerned, they weren't worth remembering. Her anger toward them and her bad childhood were no doubt coloring her perspective now. She truly believed that she was protecting Caleb from unnecessary pain. Suzie didn't understand that having unanswered questions was painful too.

"In his position, I would wonder about my birth parents," Faith said.

"Meaning what?"

"Just what I said. I would wonder what they looked like. I'd wonder about their likes and dislikes. I'd question if they would want to know me, or if they never gave me a second thought once I had been adopted. So many things would eat at me. Maybe not all the time, but often enough. It wouldn't keep me from loving you and Dad, or being happy with my life, but it would be there. Like a ghost haunting me."

"You know your birth parents. Or at least your birth mother."

"Yes. And because I know her, I understand why she gave me up for adoption. In her position, I might have done the same thing. Her life could have turned out so differently if she would have had to care for a child at her age. Instead, she gave me to a loving family."

Suzie huffed out a breath. "And your point is?"

Faith covered her mother's hands with her own, giving them a gentle squeeze before replying. When she did, her voice was soft. "My point is that Caleb needs to find out about his past. You should help him."

Suzie pulled her hands away. "No. I can't do that."

"Is that your final word?"

"Yes."

"In that case, I'll see you later."

Feeling helpless, Faith kissed her mother's cheek and left. She didn't know what else she could do or what else she could say. And who knew—perhaps Suzie was right. After all, she'd been there and seen it all. Caleb did say his father had wanted to keep his identity a secret from him. Perhaps it was best if Caleb didn't meet the man.

That thought stayed with Faith the rest of the day and long into the night. She wished she knew what to do. One thing was certain. She didn't want to cause Caleb unnecessary pain. She considered telling him what her mother had said about his father, but decided against it. Besides, what did Faith actually know? She didn't know the identity of Caleb's father; she didn't know his mother's name. Most importantly, she didn't know how to convince her mother to share the information she was holding close to her heart.

When you added it all up, Faith didn't know anything. At least nothing helpful.

CALEB SMILED AS he exited the highway and turned onto the ramp leading to Bronco. Although his father had told him he could take a leave of absence while he tried to make contact with Brooks Langtree, Caleb had decided against it. Who knew how long that would take. From what Caleb could tell, Langtree had left Bronco sometime after the Golden Buckle Rodeo ended. Not that it made a difference. Caleb hadn't been able to reach Brooks when he had been in town.

Even though he was disappointed about his failure to connect with Brooks, Caleb was very happy with how things were going with Faith. Dating her was the most fun he'd had in his life. No other woman had made him laugh the way Faith did. Not that every conversation was a party. They'd also discussed serious matters. He'd been impressed by her insight and compassion. He appreciated the way she made him consider different perspectives.

The past week without her had dragged, but going to work had been the right thing to do. Running the store took a lot of effort and was more than Nathan could handle alone. Not only that, Caleb enjoyed the work. Strom and Son Farm and Feed Supply was a successful business and Caleb intended to keep it that way. His family, employees and the citizens of Tenacity were depending on him and he wasn't going to let them down.

But it was Friday night and the store was closed and the weekend belonged to him. Faith had invited him to stay at her house, but he'd turned her down, choosing to stay at the B and B again. Staying with Faith would have flown in the face of their decision to keep things casual. Caleb didn't want to send mixed signals. Crossing lines could lead to confusion and pain, something they were each trying to avoid.

Caleb checked into his room and then phoned Faith. His pulse sped up as he waited for her to answer. *That was ridiculous.* This wasn't some great love story. They were just two friends getting together tonight. Their plans were nothing special. They were going to go to Doug's, a local dive bar that Faith liked and wanted to show him, for burgers. It wasn't romantic, but then, he wasn't aiming for romance.

Faith answered on the second ring. The moment Caleb heard her voice, a sense of contentment enveloped him and he relaxed. He couldn't quite put his finger on why but just talking to her made his worries fade away.

"Are we still good for tonight?" he asked.

"Of course. I've been looking forward to seeing you all week. I'll be ready in a few minutes."

Just knowing that she was as eager to be together again made the loneliness of being apart worth it.

Faith was standing on her front porch when he arrived. She was dressed in tight jeans, over-the-knee black boots, a cable-knit purple sweater and a purple jacket. A purple-and-black headband held her hair away from her face. She was even more gorgeous than he remembered and his blood heated. He might not want to become emotionally involved with Faith, but his body had made a deep connection with hers.

He was getting out of his truck when she started jogging down the stairs. When he realized that she wasn't going to stand on formality, he restarted the engine and waited for her to climb in beside him.

"Hi," she said, turning a bright smile on him.

"Hi yourself." Unable to resist, he pressed a gentle kiss against her soft lips. His mouth tingled at the brief contact. The urge to pull her into his arms was strong, but he resisted. The sexual attraction between them was intense. It wouldn't take much to set them both ablaze. They wouldn't make it to their destination if he gave in to temptation now. Besides, there was plenty of time to satisfy that hunger later tonight, so he pulled away from the curb and headed for the bar.

"You're going to love Doug's. It's not fancy, but the food is good. Plus there's a pool table and a small dance floor. Most of the people are regulars, but they're very welcoming of new people."

Though they had either talked or texted every night this past week, they still had a lot of catching up to do. Faith had just finished telling him about an upcoming rodeo she and her sisters were going to compete in when she directed him to park.

"This is Doug's?" he asked, unable to keep the shock from

his voice. There wasn't even a sign on the old building. If Faith hadn't pointed it out to him, he would have passed right by.

"Yep. You aren't one to judge a book by its cover, are you?"

"I try not to judge at all."

Faith sighed. "Just when I thought I couldn't like you more than I already do."

Caleb held the door for her and they stepped inside. There were a good number of patrons inside.

Faith and Caleb grabbed a table near the small dance floor where he anticipated they would spend a lot of time tonight. He couldn't decide if he wanted to slow dance and hold her delectable body pressed against his, or if he wanted faster dances where he could watch her wiggle her sexy bottom. Why not both?

"Why not both what?" Faith asked, a confused smile on her face.

"Did I say that out loud?"

Faith nodded. "Yep."

"I was actually thinking of whether I would prefer to dance fast or slow with you."

"Ah. And you decided on both."

"Yes."

She leaned back in her chair and stretched out her curvy legs in front of her, crossing them at the ankles. "You're assuming that I want to dance. I might just want to sit and talk."

"I know you too well to fall for that. You want to dance."

"You're right. I've been looking forward to dancing all week."

The waitress approached their table, took their orders and was back with them before long.

"That's absolutely delicious," Caleb said after swallowing the first bite of his burger.

"Nothing tastes better than that first bite," Faith agreed.

"I didn't say that," Caleb said, staring at Faith's luscious mouth. "I can think of one thing."

Faith's cheeks grew darker as she blushed. Then she gave him a look so hot he felt his temperature rise. "Is that right?"

"You know it. And later I hope to taste it again."

"For dessert?"

"Absolutely."

"I look forward to it."

Anticipation was great and simultaneously terrible. But making love with Faith later would be worth the wait.

After they'd eaten every bit of their burgers and fries, Caleb dumped a handful of quarters in the jukebox and selected a mix of fast and slow songs, and they headed for the tiny dance floor. Watching Faith dance was almost as pleasurable as holding her in his arms and swaying to a ballad. Once the jukebox was quiet, they grabbed pool cues and headed for the pool table.

"I'm a really good player," Faith said, racking the balls.

"Is that right?" Caleb had been putting chalk on his cue. Now he paused, leaned on his stick, and looked at her. "Care to make a friendly wager?"

She looked at him from toes to head. Incredibly, his skin began to warm. It was as if she'd dragged a red hot coal across his body. "What do you have in mind?"

"How about the loser has to do whatever the winner wants?" he suggested.

"For how long? A day? A week?"

He chuckled. "One game. One thing. One time."

"That's all? Why? Are you scared you aren't going to win?"

"Oh, I'm going to win. I just don't want to take advantage of you. That wouldn't be gentlemanly."

She flashed him a grin. "It's also not gentlemanly to brag, but that doesn't seem to bother you."

Unable to resist, he reached out and cupped her chin and caressed her soft cheek. "That wasn't a brag, sweetheart. That was me giving you a warning. This is your last chance to back out."

She leaned her face into his hand for a moment. Then she straightened. "Don't try to distract me."

"I wouldn't dream of it." If anyone was in danger of being distracted, it was him. The way her round bottom filled out her tight jeans was ruining his concentration.

He moved aside as she stepped up to the table. She took her shot, sending two solid balls into the pockets. After she'd taken two more shots, he knew that he was in for a challenge. Good. He liked knowing that winning would require all of his skill.

She took another shot and missed. He lined up his shot and knocked two striped balls into the pockets. And then another. He was clearing the table when she came to stand by him. Her sweet scent wafted over to him, and he glanced over at her, then turned back to the pool table. As he was taking his shot, she dragged her hands over her breasts, smoothing out her sweater, and wiggled her hips. Those moves were so enticing that he momentarily lost track of what he was doing. The stick tapped the cue ball, but the contact wasn't hard enough to knock his ball into the pocket.

"Oh. Too bad, so sad," Faith said, nudging him aside. "My turn."

He was still sputtering when she took—and made—her next shot. And then sank the eight ball. "I win. It's going to be so good to make you do whatever I want."

"You distracted me on purpose."

She grinned. "All's fair in love and pool."

"I'll remember that."

"Do that."

"What did you have in mind for me to do?"

"I don't know. You'll have to wait and see."

"I can wait. I'm a very patient man."

"Good things come to those who wait." She winked. "Or at least that's what people keep telling me."

They played two more games and he won both of them. "So I guess I get to tell you what to do twice."

She shook her head. "Nope. The bet was for one game. There's one winner. Me."

"In that case, let's leave. Ready to go?"

She nodded and gave him a look hot enough to boil his blood. "I'm more than ready. I'm willing and able."

He took her hand and led her to his truck. His heart thumped hard as he drove to her house where they could be alone. Although he'd had a good time hanging out with her at Doug's, he was looking forward to getting reacquainted with her body.

When he reached her house, he parked and they jumped from the vehicle and dashed across the lawn and up the stairs to her front door. When Faith jammed the key into the lock, he pushed open the door, scooped Faith into his arms and, kicking the door shut, he carried her through the front room and up the stairs to her bedroom. They fell on the bed together, laughing and pulling off each other's clothes.

It took less than a minute for them to shed their clothes and go into each other's arms. As they touched and caressed, the heat inside Caleb grew and intensified until he was near to exploding. Faith cried out in pleasure mere seconds before his cry joined hers. He wrapped her in his arms and pulled her close to him. For now, all was right in his world.

CHAPTER TWELVE

FAITH WAS IN TROUBLE. She was falling hard for Caleb. She'd spent the past week trying to convince herself that her feelings hadn't grown, but she knew she was lying to herself. Despite her best intentions, she was unable to keep their relationship purely physical. Somehow her feelings had become involved. She cared about Caleb more than she wanted to. Much more than was safe for her heart. But that was her problem. One that she didn't intend to burden Caleb with. They'd both agreed that there was no room for emotions in this relationship. She couldn't even consider changing the parameters of their relationship when she was keeping a huge secret from him.

She parked and walked to the front door of the B and B. Caleb was waiting for her in the main room. Her heart skipped a beat as she looked at him. No matter how much time she spent with him, she was always struck by how handsome he was.

They met in the middle of the room and he brushed a gentle kiss against her lips. As usual, desire surged through her and a tingling sensation danced up and down her spine.

He led her to the room he was renting and she looked around. The room was quite charming.

"How are you today?" he asked, closing the door behind him.

"Good now that we're together." Faith draped her arms

over his shoulders. Looping them around his neck, she pulled his head down for a proper kiss. He didn't disappoint.

Slowly, they ended the kiss and she looked in his eyes. "What's the plan for the day?"

It was Sunday afternoon and he would be returning to Tenacity in the morning. She wished he could stay longer, but she knew he needed to go to work. So did she. She wanted to be at her best in her upcoming rodeo.

"I thought we could go to the corn maze and then visit the Happy Hearts Animal Rescue."

Faith smiled. She hadn't visited a corn maze in years. It was always fun getting lost in one and trying to find her way out. Though she wasn't interested in getting a pet, she did enjoy spending time around the animals. "That sounds like fun."

Caleb's room phone rang. Giving her a confused look, he crossed the room and answered it. He listened and then smiled broadly. "Sure. Come on up."

When he ended the call, Caleb stared into space for a few seconds, a smile on his face. Faith tapped him on the shoulder. "Have our plans changed?"

"What?" Caleb blinked. "Sorry. Maybe not changed but definitely delayed. That was actually your grandmother. She's here with something she wants to show me."

Faith wondered how her grandmother knew that Caleb was staying here. Then she dismissed the question as ridiculous. News traveled fast in Bronco. Plus, there were only so many places in town that Caleb could be staying.

There was a knock on his door. Caleb hurried across the room and then ushered Hattie inside. She was carrying a cloth shopping bag in each hand.

Hattie's eyes darted from Caleb to Faith. She smiled slowly. "I hope I'm not interrupting anything."

"Not at all," Caleb said.

"It's good to see you." Faith kissed her grandmother's cheek. "What do you have there?"

"Patience," Hattie said. "Didn't your parents tell you that good things come to those who wait?"

Faith smiled as she recalled saying those very words to Caleb right before their torrid night of lovemaking. "All the time. But I was the daughter who didn't believe that."

Hattie laughed. "No. Now that I think of it, you weren't very patient. But it's never too late to change that."

"Would you like to sit down?" Caleb asked as he pulled the chair from the desk and turned it to face Hattie.

"I would." Hattie sat down. "Such a gentleman."

Faith sat on the foot of the bed and Caleb sat beside her. He smiled at Hattie. "I have to admit that I'm sharing Faith's curiosity."

"Well, then let me put you both out of your suspense." Hattie leaned one bag against the chair and put the other on her lap. She reached in and pulled out a handful of programs. "After Faith and I talked, I searched through programs of rodeos that I'd participated in."

"You have quite a collection," Caleb said.

"I had quite the career," Hattie said. "I brought programs from rodeos from thirty years ago too. I wasn't competing then but I like keeping a historical record on the evolution of rodeo. I also like keeping souvenirs of rodeos where my daughters and granddaughters competed."

She handed over those to Caleb and then reached inside her tote and pulled out even more. Those she gave to Faith.

"Thank you," Caleb said.

"I figured that looking through these would be a good place to start."

Faith opened the first program and began to flip through the pages. She read through the list of competitors, pausing when she saw her mother's name and picture. Suzie was years younger and had a confident expression on her face. Faith had seen plenty of pictures of her mother in photo albums, but those photos, taken at birthday parties, graduations and Christmas mornings were snapshots of Suzie as a mother. These were of Suzie as a rodeo competitor.

"Are we looking for someone in particular?" Faith asked as she turned the page and continued to peruse the pictures.

"Yes," Hattie said. "But I don't want to influence either of you. I might be seeing something that isn't there. I'll wait to see what you both have to say."

Caleb didn't appear to be listening to the conversation. He was scanning the pages as if looking for a certain individual. He turned a page and stopped. He sucked in a ragged breath and froze.

Hattie walked over and Caleb handed the program to her. She glanced at the picture and then smiled. "You see what I do."

As if unable to speak, Caleb only nodded.

"What do you see?" Faith asked. Hattie handed her the program. Faith looked at the picture of Brooks Langtree. "Wow. You look exactly like him. In fact, you could be twins."

The expression on Caleb's face said it all. He'd found his birth father. "I've been trying to get in touch with him. His people won't let me near him unless I tell them what I want to talk to him about. Naturally I don't want to do that. This is personal."

"I know Brooks," Hattie said. "I'll have no trouble getting past his gatekeepers. I'll reach out to him for you."

"You'd do that for me?"

"Of course I will," Hattie said. She patted Caleb's hand. "You just leave everything to me."

Caleb's expression was so hopeful that Faith could

barely stand to look at him. She hated the idea of that hope being shattered if what her mother had said was true.

"I don't think that's a good idea," Faith blurted out.

Caleb and Hattie looked at her as if she'd suddenly sprouted a second head.

"Why do you say that?" Caleb asked, his voice ringing with the same confusion that was written all over his face.

"What if he doesn't want to meet you? Did you ever think of that? Perhaps he doesn't want to know you at all." Faith tried to control her voice, but as she grew more desperate, her voice reflected that. She glanced at Caleb. His eyes were wide with surprise. She inhaled and then blew out the breath. She needed to be calm and logical if she intended to convince him.

She grabbed his arm. "He walked away from you when you needed him the most and then forbade the adoption agency to give out any information about him. He hid his relationship with your mother from everyone even after you were born. Your mother adored him and he didn't do right by her then. What makes you think that he will do right by you now?"

Caleb looked at her, no longer surprised by her speech. Now he looked angry. His lips were turned down and his eyes were narrowed. He stepped back, breaking the contact and her hand dropped to her side. "How do you know any of this?"

"Does it matter how I know?"

"Of course it matters." Disappointment and anger mingled in his voice. Then it lowered in warning. "I'll ask you again, Faith. How do you know anything about my past?"

Faith exhaled and then confessed in a weak voice, barely above a whisper. "My mother told me."

His chest rose and fell with his angry inhalations. "When?"

Before she could answer, Hattie interrupted. "I can see

that I'm no longer needed in this conversation. I'll leave so the two of you can talk in private."

Caleb nodded. "Thank you so much. I appreciate all of your help. It's nice to know that I can depend on you."

Although he'd been speaking to Hattie, Caleb's last comment was directed at Faith. She felt the sting of his words.

Hattie gave Faith a look that spoke to the depth of her disappointment in her before leaving. Neither Caleb nor Faith spoke until the door was firmly closed.

"Let me explain," Faith implored, reaching out to Caleb. He dodged her hands and took several steps back. The room wasn't very big, but suddenly the gulf between them was a mile wide. She let her hands drop futilely to her side.

"What can you possibly say to defend yourself?"

"I didn't know his identity until just now."

"Right," he said sarcastically. "You know all about my past—more details than even I know—but you didn't know who my father was. Surely you don't expect me to believe that."

"I asked my mother, but she wouldn't identify him."

He looked at her, his eyes so cold she shivered. The warm relationship they had built up might never have happened. "You knew about my father, and my mother, but couldn't be bothered to tell me."

"I didn't know," she continued, needing him to understand the spot she'd been in. "What was I supposed to do?"

"You could have told me."

"Told you what? My mother wouldn't tell me his name. Or anything else about him no matter how many times I asked. And I did ask. The only thing she would say was that he's bad news and it will be best if you keep away from him."

"So you decided that you were the person to make the

decision for me. That you somehow know better than I do what's right for my life." Although Caleb spoke quietly, the anger in his voice was unmistakable.

She shook her head. "I know it looks bad but that's not what happened. I was just trying to keep you from getting hurt."

"No. You put yourself in charge of deciding what was good for me and what wasn't."

"That's not true."

Caleb leaned over so that their faces were mere inches apart. She easily read the anger in his eyes. "The truth is you didn't respect me enough to tell me what your mother said. You didn't think I was strong enough to handle it."

"I didn't know who he was."

"*You* might not have known, but *I* had an idea that it was Brooks Langtree."

"You never said anything." Despite knowing she didn't have a right to know, Faith was still hurt by how little she mattered to him. They might be sleeping together, but that didn't make her special to him. Her feelings might be growing, but not his. It was safe to say he no longer felt the same affection he had before.

"I know you didn't just say that to me. Not after the secret you've been keeping. This is *my* search. My life. I don't owe you any information. I don't have to bare my soul to you. Given the fact that you've just proven yourself to be untrustworthy, I'm glad that I didn't tell you more. In fact, I regret sharing what I did."

"Really? Because if not for me, Hattie wouldn't know a thing about you. Nor would she be using her relationship with Brooks Langtree to set up a meeting between the two of you."

"Great. Thanks." His voice was anything but grateful and Faith knew that she and Caleb were veering close to a place where they would say things they would each regret. Words that they wouldn't be able to take back when their tempers cooled. That might not matter to Caleb now since he was positively furious with her, but it mattered to her. She was falling in love with him.

"I should go," she said softly.

"Yes, you should."

That harsh answer was painful, but she knew she'd earned his wrath. If she could go back and do it over, she would do it differently. She wouldn't keep anything from him. Better yet, she'd mind her own business.

She grabbed her purse and draped the strap over her shoulder. The hope that Caleb would say something to her dimmed as she crossed the small room. When she reached the door, she turned the knob and looked back at him. "I really am sorry, Caleb."

He only stared at her, his eyes icy. Realizing that she wasn't going to get an answer, she opened the door and left.

She trudged down the stairs and found Hattie sitting on the sofa in the main room. She stood when Faith entered.

"I didn't expect you to be here," Faith said.

"I figured you could use a friend." Hattie looped her arm with Faith's and they walked outside together.

"How did you guess?"

"Things were going pretty poorly between you and Caleb. I had a feeling they were only going to get worse."

"You were right. They did. He's furious with me."

"Do you blame him?"

Faith forced herself to admit the truth. "No. At the time I thought I was doing the right thing. Now that things have blown up in my face I realize that I should have handled it differently."

"So should your mother. I'm really disappointed in her."

"I tried to convince Mom to tell me the name, but she

wouldn't. She was so sure that she was protecting Caleb from getting hurt."

"Like mother, like daughter I suppose." Hattie nudged Faith's shoulder affectionately. "Do you want to go to the diner and have an early lunch? It might make you feel better."

Faith nodded. "I really don't want to be alone. Caleb and I had plans for the day. Now I'm wondering if he'll ever forgive me."

"Of course he will. Now get in your car and follow me. I'm in the mood for a good salad."

As Faith drove to the Gemstone Diner, she tried to keep her mind from straying to Caleb and the disaster that their relationship had become. Hattie was getting out of her sedan when Faith arrived and they walked inside without speaking. After they'd placed their orders, Hattie looked directly at Faith. "Tell me what you plan to do next."

That was a surprise. She'd expected a lecture or some other form of recrimination. "Nothing. It was my 'doing something' that created this mess. Maybe I should just bow out and let Caleb take the lead."

"I wasn't suggesting that you try to run things. You're a Hawkins. It's not easy for us to sit back and let things happen, even if that is what the situation calls for."

"Is this one of those situations?"

"Yes. Give Caleb space for now. He needs it. I'm sure his emotions are all over the place. That might account for the intensity of his anger. Be there to support him if he needs it."

"I can do that." Faith toyed with her French fry. "Do you really think he'll forgive me? Or do you think this is the end? Tell me the truth. I can handle it."

"I saw the way that man looked at you. Your relationship is far from over."

Faith blew out a relieved breath. "I hope you're right."

Hattie smiled. "When am I wrong?"

"Well, I can safely say not once in my lifetime."

"Right. Now let's eat and talk about something else. Unpleasant conversation is bad for digestion."

"Done."

The impromptu meal with Hattie was just what Faith needed.

They'd just finished eating their desserts when Hattie's phone rang. She answered and then smiled. "Thanks for calling me back, Brooks. I was hoping that we could meet."

Faith's heart sped up at the mention of Brooks's name. She tried to make sense of the conversation when she could only hear one side. She didn't want to get too excited but it sounded as if Hattie and Brooks were scheduling an appointment.

"I'll see you then," Hattie said and then ended the call.

"I take it that you're going to meet with Brooks Langtree."

Hattie nodded. "In half an hour. Without Caleb."

Faith grabbed the bill, perused it and then tossed money on the table to cover it as well as a generous tip.

"I'm going with you."

"Are you asking me or telling me?"

"Whichever works best."

Hattie raised her eyebrows. "What if neither does?"

"I'll follow you." When Hattie only stared, Faith knew that tactic wouldn't work. She folded her hands and tried again. "Please let me go. Please."

"Are you the same woman who just said you were going to step back?"

"Yes. And I meant it. I'll tell Caleb about this meeting. That is if he ever talks to me again."

"Why do you want to go?"

"I have to see for myself that Brooks Langtree is a good man. My mother says that he didn't treat Caleb's birth mother very well. She really doesn't like him but you seem to. Or at least you don't dislike him."

"I didn't know his wife, but from what I gather, she and your mother were friends. Naturally Suzie holds a grudge against him."

"I guess I understand that. But I still want to look into his eyes. Hear his voice. That way I'll feel more comfortable about the situation."

"And if you don't like him? Then what? Are you going to try to keep him and Caleb apart?"

"No way. I've learned my lesson."

Hattie nodded.

"So I can come?"

"Yes." Hattie stood and held out her arm, ushering Faith out of the diner. "We got lucky. He's in town to shoot a commercial for Taylor Beef. We're meeting at his hotel room."

Faith's heart thudded as she drove to the Heights Hotel. By the time she parked behind Hattie's car and got out, it was racing. She could possibly be meeting Caleb's birth father. She really hoped that he was a good man.

Hattie took one look at Faith and patted her hand. "Calm down. You look like you're about to keel over."

Faith inhaled deeply and then blew out the breath. "I just really want him to be everything that Caleb hopes he is."

"Let's go inside so you can find out."

Faith and Hattie walked into the hotel. Hattie gave Brooks Langtree's name to the front desk clerk. The smiling woman called Brooks's hotel room before she gave them the room number. Faith crossed her fingers as they rode the elevator to the second floor.

Hattie knocked on the appropriately numbered door

and it immediately swung open to reveal a smiling Brooks Langtree. He looked so much like Caleb it made Faith's heart ache.

"Hattie. I was so pleased to get your call. Come on in."

"Thank you." Hattie stepped inside and Faith followed. "I brought Faith with me. I hope that's okay."

"Of course it is." Brooks gave Faith a warm smile. "Welcome. I hope you had a nice birthday."

Faith returned his smile. "I did. Thank you."

Brooks had a suite and he led them to the comfortable seating area. "Can I get you something to drink? A soda? Water?"

"I wouldn't mind some water," Hattie said, sitting on the silver-and-black striped love seat.

"And you, Faith?" Brooks asked.

She really wanted to get to the reason they were here, but it would be rude to say that. She sat beside Hattie and folded her hands in her lap. "I'll take a water too, please."

"Three waters coming up," Brooks said, heading for the mini fridge. He handed Hattie and Faith bottles of water, keeping one for himself. He sat in the chair across from them, a smile on his face. "To what do I owe this pleasure?"

"I'm not usually at a loss for words," Hattie said, "but suddenly I'm not sure how to start."

"That sounds ominous," Brooks said, stiffening.

She shook her head and replied quickly. "It's nothing bad. At least not to me."

Brooks leaned back in his chair, and blew out a breath. "In that case, take your time. I don't have any plans for the next few hours."

Faith was impressed by the older man's calm demeanor and the patient way he treated her grandmother. That raised her estimation of him. In the quiet, Faith took the opportunity to study Brooks. She couldn't get over how much he looked like Caleb. Or rather, it was more accurate to say that Caleb resembled Brooks. They both had rich deep brown skin, carved cheekbones, deep brown eyes and an identical smile. They also had similar builds. Both were each about six feet tall with broad shoulders. They even had similar mannerisms. No wonder Faith had felt like she'd seen Caleb before.

"Well, I suppose I should just get to it," Hattie said at last.

Brooks nodded. "Whenever you're ready."

"I recently met a young man who believes he might be your son. If I'm wrong and I've offended you, I apologize."

Brooks's face lost color and his hands began to tremble. The bottle began to slip from his fingers and Faith jumped up and grabbed it before it hit the floor. Tears began running down Brooks's face, but he didn't seem to notice. "You know my boy? You know Caleb?"

Faith was shocked that Brooks knew Caleb's name. That emotion was quickly followed by relief that Brooks admitted to being Caleb's birth father.

"Yes," Hattie said. "I do. He's been trying to meet with you for a while now."

"So that's who it was." Brooks nodded, then explained, "My agent mentioned talking to a young man one day, but it never occurred to me that it could be Caleb."

"It was," Hattie said gently.

Brooks shook his head and spoke in a soft voice as if to himself. "I feel like I'm dreaming. I've been waiting for this day for the longest time. Practically from the moment I placed him in the social worker's arms and forced myself to walk away."

"I don't understand," Faith said. "You chose to give him up for adoption."

Brooks didn't take offense at her words or her accusatory tone. "I did."

"Why?"

"Faith. That's none of your business," Hattie admonished, sending her a look.

"It's okay. I don't mind answering," Brooks said. He turned his gaze to Faith. His eyes were turbulent with emotion. "I was so young when he was born. Only twenty. But I loved him from the first time I laid eyes on him. And I loved his mother. The three of us were a happy little family. But the rodeo promoter convinced us—or rather convinced *me*—to keep our marriage a secret. I was a rising star. They thought it would hurt my career if the public knew I had a wife and a child at my age. They liked the idea of a playboy bachelor image." His mouth twisted in obvious disgust. When he spoke again, his voice was filled with remorse. "It sounds so ridiculous now. I never should have agreed to it."

"You're looking at it with the wisdom of a fifty-year-old instead of the inexperience of a twenty-year-old," Hattie said gently.

"Even back then I had my doubts. But I also had a family to support, so I went along with it. So did Genie. And then Genie went back to work. I should have protested. It was only a few months after Caleb was born. But she said she was ready and that she missed competing. So I agreed." His sigh was filled with remembered pain. "One freak accident and Genie was gone. Suddenly I was a single father. Caleb was only a few months old. Barely able to hold up his head. He needed so much and I wasn't sure I could give it to him. I was broken, grieving the loss of the woman I loved."

Faith heard the agony in his voice and she experienced a rush of sympathy. He'd really been in an impossible situation.

"The only way I could support him was in the rodeo. But I couldn't care for him alone on the road.

"Then the social workers started coming around, telling me that it would be best for Caleb if I put him up for adoption. Genie and I didn't have any other family. All we'd had was each other. I might have made a different decision if I'd had someone else to turn to. But I didn't. Sure, there were my rodeo friends, but they were traveling just as much as I was. And what Caleb needed was stability. A home. A mother and a father. The social worker promised that he would be placed with a good family who would love him. From what I can see, they kept their word."

"How do you know that?" Faith asked.

"I've kept tabs on him from a distance. Although I couldn't be a part of his life, I needed to be sure that he was happy. That he was cherished."

"Why didn't you ever contact him? It's been thirty years." Faith knew that she didn't have a right to ask that question, but she couldn't help from advocating on Caleb's behalf. She was going to tell him about this meeting and she wanted to provide him with as much useful information as she could.

"It wasn't my place. I had no right to interfere in his life. When he was a kid, I didn't want to confuse him. I didn't know whether or not the Stroms had told him that he was adopted. If they hadn't I didn't want to be the one to break the news to him. Who knows what kind of harm that would have caused? It could have hurt Caleb and his relationship with his parents. I didn't want to do that." Brooks paused and blew out a long breath. "He had a father and it wasn't me. I didn't want Caleb to have to split his loyalties between the man who'd helped to create him and the man who'd raised him. That would have been a horrible thing to do to a child."

Brooks's voice grew low. If possible, he sounded even sadder. "Besides, I always thought he was better off without me. I was a rodeo rider, spending months at a time on the road, scratching out a living. A couple of days in this town, a couple days more in another. His adoptive father owned a successful business. He was at home every night for dinner with his family."

He looked at Faith, as if waiting for her next question. But she could only nod and wait for him to continue at his own pace.

"Then there was the question that I couldn't answer. Would Caleb even want to know me? Would he want me to be a part of his life? I didn't know, so I decided to let things be. If Caleb and I were ever meant to meet, it would happen on his terms and without interference from me."

"He has been searching for you for a few months," Faith said, quietly. "He wants to meet you."

"I want to meet him too." Brooks's voice quivered with emotion and more tears filled his eyes. Faith was elated as she realized that Brooks and Caleb wanted the same thing.

They wanted to meet.

"I'll call Caleb today. If it's okay with you, I'll give him your number," Faith said. She'd overstepped before and had learned her lesson. She was going to check with both parties before she made a move.

"That would be great," Brooks said, his smile bright despite the tears that stained his cheeks.

It was clear that the older man was overcome with emotion, so Hattie and Faith stood. Hattie said, "We're going to leave now, so you can have time to yourself. I know this has been a lot to absorb."

Brooks nodded absently. It was as if he were already

imagining the reunion with his son. Then he shook off his stupor and jumped to his feet. He shook Hattie's hand effusively. "I'll never be able to thank you enough for what you've done for me and Caleb."

"You're quite welcome," Hattie said before she and Faith left.

Once they were alone in the hall, Faith turned to Hattie. "I have to tell Caleb about this. Or do you want to?"

Hattie laughed. "You know as well as I do that you want an excuse to call Caleb. This good news is the best reason of all. You should deliver it alone."

"You know me so well." Faith gave her grandmother a big hug. "I'll call him as soon as I get home."

"Good luck." Hattie said.

"Thanks. I'm going to need it."

On the drive home, Faith rehearsed what she planned to say. The second she stepped inside her house, she whipped out her phone and called Caleb. Her heart began to pound with tension as the phone rang. When she heard Caleb's voice, her practiced speech flew out of her head.

"This is Faith," she said.

"What can I do for you?" Caleb's voice was devoid of any emotion and her heart sank lower than she thought possible.

"Hattie and I met with Brooks Langtree just now. She told him about you and he wants to meet you. I told him that I would give you his telephone number. I hope that's all right."

Caleb didn't reply and Faith wondered if she'd overstepped again. As the silence stretched, her fear that he was never going to forgive her grew. Perhaps it really was over between them.

CHAPTER THIRTEEN

Caleb heard Faith's words, but he wasn't sure he actually heard them correctly. *Brooks Langtree wanted to meet with him?* The words echoed in his mind for a few moments before he was able to speak. "Say that again."

"Brooks Langtree is your father." Faith's voice was filled with glee.

"Did he say that?" Caleb asked cautiously and his back stiffened. The entire turn of events was shocking. Thirty years ago, the man had insisted that Caleb be given no information about him. And today he'd just told Hattie and Faith that he was Caleb's father. That was unbelievable.

Caleb's knees weakened. Suddenly woozy, he stumbled across the room and fell into a chair.

"Yes. I have his number if you want to talk to him."

Of course he wanted to talk to him. That was the entire reason he'd come to Bronco initially. Though he was elated beyond belief, his heart still ached from Faith's deception. Just thinking about how she'd withheld vital information from him still hurt. Secrets had kept him from his biological father for thirty years. The social workers and adoption agency had known the identity of Caleb's father, but hadn't shared it with him no matter how many times he'd asked. Faith had done the same thing.

She'd claimed that she'd been trying to protect him. He hadn't needed her protection. He'd needed her honesty. "What is the number?"

Faith gasped audibly and Caleb knew she'd been hurt by his abrupt response. He searched inside himself for some compassion for her, but he couldn't find any. His feelings were too raw at this time. Maybe later, he might be able to extend her some grace, but not now.

"Of course. I'll text it to you when we finish talking."

"Is there something more you need to say? Is this a power move on your part? Withholding the number until I've listened to you?"

"Of course not. I only wanted to apologize again. But clearly you don't want to hear it."

"You're right. There's nothing you can say to me right now. The only thing I want from you is Brooks Langtree's telephone number."

Faith didn't reply and he realized that she'd ended the call. He frowned but he had to admit that she'd only done what he'd requested. The phone beeped as a message came through.

His hand shook as he read the number. *His father's telephone number.*

Beads of sweat broke out on Caleb's forehead and he wiped his brow. His nerves jangled and he inhaled deeply and blew out the breath, trying to calm himself. His hand was trembling so much it took three attempts before he successfully tapped in the number. As the phone began to ring, Caleb's heart was pounding. And then a firm voice said hello.

"Brooks?" Caleb said, suddenly at a loss for words. He closed his eyes and started again. "This is Caleb Strom. I, uh… Hattie and Faith Hawkins spoke with you about me today. I…uh… I'm…"

"I know who you are, Caleb. You're my son." There was a long pause. Then Brooks continued in a shaky voice. "I've been waiting to talk to you for thirty years."

Brooks's emotional words dissolved Caleb's fear. Brooks—his father—had missed him. He hadn't turned his back on Caleb as he had often feared. There had been another reason. Now Caleb would finally learn the truth from the man himself. Caleb's vision blurred and he wiped away unshed tears. He hadn't expected to cry, but suddenly he couldn't stop the tears from falling. Before he knew it, big sobs were wracking his body.

"It's okay, son. I'm here." Brooks's voice broke and Caleb knew the older man was crying too.

Caleb took several deep breaths. Finally he regained sufficient control of himself to talk. He supposed he should give Brooks a quick summary of his life up to this point. Instead, he blurted out, "Why did you give me away? Didn't you love me? Didn't you want me?"

"Oh, Caleb," Brooks said and then sighed.

"Forget I said anything," Caleb said quickly. He didn't want to offend Brooks and get the conversation off on the wrong foot. Brooks might decide getting to know Caleb wasn't worth the recrimination. What was the point in bringing up a past they couldn't change? What mattered was the present. And possibly the future.

"No, son. I don't want to forget it. You have every right to ask that question. Ask me anything you want to know. Anything. Nothing is off-limits."

"Okay."

"And to answer your questions, I loved you with every fiber of my being. You and your mother were my world. After Genie died I wasn't in any position to take care of a baby. So I gave you to a loving couple who could give you what you needed."

"Did you ever regret giving me up?"

Brooks sighed. "Regret doesn't begin to describe my

feelings. I wished there could have been another way. But there wasn't one. So I had to let you go."

"What was she like?"

"Your mother? I'm sorry. Is it okay to refer to Genie that way?"

"It's okay. So…her name was Genie?"

"Yes. Regina actually, but everyone called her Genie."

"Regina." Caleb tried the name on for size. He liked the way it sounded. "What was she like?"

"Genie was a tiny little thing, but she had the heart of a giant. She was gutsy and bold. Perhaps too bold for her own good. And ours."

"What do you mean?"

"Genie and I were still in our teens when we got together. We would have told the whole world about our marriage, but the rodeo managers advised us to keep it a secret. Very few people even knew about the baby—I mean you—and us."

More secrets.

"But it didn't make a difference to us. We were happy living in our private little world."

Caleb smiled at the picture that Brooks painted. It sounded so perfect. If Genie hadn't died, he might have spent his formative years on the rodeo circuit. He might have become a rider himself. It's possible that he could have met Faith years ago. Just thinking of her was painful and he shoved the thought aside.

"Genie was one of the best woman competitors on the tour. She didn't compete much when she was pregnant, so she was itching to get back into the ring. She started competing again when you were only a few months old. I shouldn't have let her."

"Why?"

"Because she was killed in a freak barrel racing accident. Her horse tripped. When they fell, the horse landed on her."

"I'm sorry to hear that." It sounded so cold and impersonal, especially since he was talking about his own mother.

"I know I have no right to ask this," Brooks said hesitantly, "but is it possible to meet in person?"

Caleb's heart leaped with hope. "When?"

"Anytime. Now if you can. I'm actually in Bronco. I can come to where you are. Or you can come here. I'm staying at the Heights Hotel in Bronco Heights. Whatever works best for you."

Caleb would lose it if he had to sit in this room, counting the minutes until Brooks arrived. He needed to do something. Driving to Brooks's hotel was preferable to waiting. "I'll come to you. I can be there in a few minutes."

"I look forward to seeing you soon."

After saying goodbye, Caleb grabbed his keys, raced from the room, jogged down the stairs and hopped into his truck. Before he turned on the ignition, he took several calming breaths, trying to slow his racing heart and quiet his mind. He didn't want to get into an accident.

When Caleb was sure he could drive carefully, he turned on the truck and started down the road. His mind was a jumble of thoughts and his emotions were scrambled. He forced himself to concentrate on his driving and tune out everything else.

Caleb reached the hotel and parked in the first spot he saw and then hurried into the lobby. He'd forgotten to ask Brooks for his room number, so he had to wait for the desk clerk to call Brooks for permission to give Caleb the room number. With the information in hand, Caleb climbed the stairs, two at a time. When he reached Brooks's floor, he stepped into the corridor and looked around, trying to get his bearings before heading down the hall.

Before he had taken two steps a door opened and Brooks Langtree stepped into the hall. Caleb stopped. Time froze as the men stared at each other. Then before he knew what was happening, Caleb found himself moving down the hall. At first he was walking. Then he was jogging. Running. Brooks must have been running too because they met in the middle. Brooks held out his arms. Without thinking, Caleb fell into the outstretched arms and felt Brooks's arms wrap around him. The embrace was strong and Caleb struggled to contain his emotions. He couldn't. Once more his body was shaking with sobs.

Eventually he became aware that Brooks was rubbing his back and murmuring soothing words to him. "I'm here, Caleb. I'm here."

Caleb sniffed and then pulled away, dragging his sleeve over his wet face. He waited for embarrassment to swamp him, but the feeling never came. Brooks was wiping his own eyes and Caleb knew he had been just as affected by the meeting.

"Come on into my room," Brooks said, extending his arm.

"Thanks."

Once they were inside the hotel room with the door closed behind them, Brooks stared into Caleb's face. Slowly he smiled. "You look just like your mother."

"I was thinking that I look like you." Caleb took a breath. "Do you have a picture of her?"

"Just one with me." Brooks took a wallet out of his pocket, reached inside, pulled out a faded photograph and handed it to Caleb. He gave Caleb a crooked grin. "You're actually in this picture too."

Caleb eagerly looked at the tattered photo. There was

an indentation from the wallet and he wondered how often Brooks had pulled it out over the years to look at. Though Brooks was also in the picture, Caleb's eyes instantly zeroed in on the woman's sweet face. Brooks had said they'd only been twenty when he'd been born, but that fact hadn't really sunk in. Now looking at his mother's image, he realized that she'd been barely out of her teens when he was born. As had Brooks. A decade younger than Caleb was now.

Although he'd tried to understand what Brooks had been telling him when he'd talked about that time in his life, Caleb had held onto a sliver of resentment at his father for giving him away. A part of him believed he should have tried harder to hold onto him. Now, seeing them smiling at the camera while Genie held a baby—him—in her arms, he finally got it. They had been young. Too young.

Genie was radiant with joy that could only come from loving and being loved. The contentment on her face couldn't be faked. Caleb studied her face, looking for features they shared. He spotted some right way, although hers were more feminine. Delicate. Ever so slowly, he dragged his finger over the lines of her face, trying to connect with her. The picture was cool beneath his hand as expected, filling him with a deep sorrow. He wanted to know more about her.

"She was so happy to be your mother," Brooks said. "This may seem hard to understand, but she loved you a lifetime in the few months that she was blessed to be with you. I just wish you could remember that time."

So did Caleb. He would give anything to have a memory of sleeping in his mother's arms. He wished he could recall the sound of her voice or the smell of her skin. *Anything.* "Are there any videos of us together?"

"No. We didn't have a lot of money back then for things

like that. People may have cameras on phones now, but they weren't as prevalent thirty years ago."

"I should have known that."

"I have a few more pictures. I can make copies for you if you want."

Caleb nodded. "That would be great."

They sat down and Brooks poured them drinks that neither of them touched. Brooks sighed and then glanced at Caleb with sorrow-filled eyes. "I felt guilty about her death for a long time. If she hadn't been in the ring that day she would still be alive today."

"I don't know much about rodeo, but I know that accidents happen and that they aren't anybody's fault," Caleb said.

"Taking care of a newborn is a lot of work. I knew she wasn't getting enough sleep and that she was worn out. But she insisted on competing. And I let her. Then she was gone. The pain in my heart was unbearable. Every time I looked into your beautiful face, I saw hers. I truly believed that giving you up was my punishment. After what I let happen to Genie, I didn't think I deserved to be your father. Not when she wasn't around to be your mother."

"That's not true. You didn't deserve to be punished. And neither did I."

Brooks gasped. "Please don't tell me that your parents weren't as kind to you as I have been led to believe."

Caleb shook his head. "No. My parents were great. Are great. They love me as much as any two people ever loved a child. But I deserved to know where I came from. I deserved to know about my biological parents. And since my birth mother was dead, you were the only person alive who could tell me. And you made it all but impossible for me to find you."

"You're right. I know a lot of time has passed, but I can tell you all about her now."

"And about you. The only things I know are what's available in the public record and that's limited to your career."

"That's pretty much out of habit. It was drilled into me as a young man to keep my private life private. I suppose I got used to keeping secrets."

"Are you married? Do you have other kids?" Caleb felt a strange ache in his chest as he awaited Brooks's answer.

Brooks smiled. "Yes. And I want you to meet them. That is if you want."

"I would like to." The idea that there were more people in the world who were genetically related to him was mind-blowing. He knew that shared love could create a family of people who didn't share genes. Iris and Nathan Strom were his parents. They were a family. Nothing would ever change that. But still he liked knowing that there were more people in the world who were related to him. More family.

"Then I'll tell them about you and set up a meeting."

"How do you think they'll react? If learning about me will upset them, you don't have to do it. I don't want to cause any problems for you."

Brooks shook his head. "There won't be a problem. My wife knows that I was married when I was a teenager."

"Does she know about me?" Caleb held his breath, trying to ignore the dread creeping down his spine.

"Of course. You weren't a dirty little secret. You were my son."

Caleb breathed out a sigh of relief. "And your kids?"

"I have a son and two daughters. I can guarantee that they will be pleased to discover that they have an older brother. Especially my son, who has been outnumbered by his sisters."

The thought made Caleb smile. Over the years, many of his friends had told him about battles of the sexes in their own homes. As an only child, he'd listened to their complaints with a bit of envy. Now he knew that he actually did have siblings.

"How old are they?"

"Isabel is nineteen, Angelique is seventeen, and Craig is sixteen."

Caleb nodded. They were younger than he'd expected. But then, Brooks probably hadn't wanted to have kids as a young man again.

"It took me a while to get my head on straight after losing your mother and then you," Brooks said as if he'd read Caleb's mind. "I was numb for years. I didn't think that I deserved to be loved. I closed off my heart, unwilling to risk the pain. Rodeo became my life and I gave it my all. When I wasn't competing, I was traveling or practicing. That's it. That was my entire life for years."

"Did you win a lot?"

"I won just about everything. But having a great career didn't bring me even a bit of joy. I didn't come back to Bronco. Bronco was where I'd lost everything that mattered to me and being here hurt way too much."

Caleb nodded in understanding. He wouldn't want to visit the place where he'd lost his entire family either.

Brooks smiled. "Then I met Judith."

"Is she in rodeo, too?"

Brooks shook his head. "No. She's a tax accountant. We met at the movies and were friends for a long time. She helped me to forgive myself. It took a while, but she finally convinced me that there was nothing I could have done to prevent your mother's accident. After a while, I started to believe that I had the right to have a life again. A life that included love. The next thing I knew, we were dating. Then we fell in love. There's not much more to say about that."

Caleb could use his imagination to fill in the rest. Although he was only getting to know Faith, he could picture how it would feel to fall in love with her. That thought shocked him. He wasn't going to fall in love with Faith. They'd agreed that their relationship was going to be casual. Strictly physical. She'd been clear that she wasn't looking for romance. Neither was he.

He'd been trying to find his birth father and didn't have time for anything else. But now he had met Brooks and the search was over. His situation was different. Of course that didn't mean Faith had changed her mind.

Not that it mattered. He wasn't sure she was actually the type of woman she'd led him to believe she was. She'd kept secrets from him. He might forgive her for that one day. But today wasn't that day.

Brooks and Caleb talked a while longer, unwilling to part company. Then Brooks received a business call.

"I should go," Caleb said, pushing to his feet.

"Call me when you get back to the B and B so we can set up a time for you to meet everyone."

"I will," Caleb promised. He was walking on air as he strode down the stairs and back to his car.

He'd finally met his father. He would give anything to share the moment with Faith. Too bad he couldn't.

FAITH EMPTIED THE bucket of dirty water into the toilet, flushed it and then yanked off her rubber gloves. She squatted on her haunches and sighed. Although she'd never kept score, this had to be the worst week of her life. She had hoped to hear from Caleb by now, but with every passing day, hope had seeped out of her. His silence was an unmistakable sign of how badly she'd hurt him. Proof of just how angry he was at her. At least, she prayed that was all it was. Otherwise his silence might mean he'd actually cut her out of his life.

She shoved that heartbreaking thought aside. She'd spent several days and nights checking to make sure that her phone was working. As if a broken phone was the reason she hadn't heard from him. She'd tried to focus, but she couldn't keep Caleb off her mind. Whenever she found herself thinking about him, she made herself do something else. Anything else. After eating more ice cream and potato chips than she should have, Faith decided to turn to constructive activities. She now had the cleanest home in the city of Bronco, if not the entire state of Montana.

This morning Faith had decided that she wasn't going to keep thinking about Caleb. If their relationship was over, there was nothing she could do to change it. She certainly wasn't going to force herself into his life.

She was returning the mop and bucket to the broom closet when her doorbell rang. Her heart leaped as she thought that Caleb had finally come to see her. Faith glanced in the mirror hanging over her sofa, hoping that she didn't look like she'd just mopped the kitchen and bathroom floors. She was sorely disappointed. Her ratty T-shirt gaped away from her torso and her jeans were threadbare in spots. Her clothes were damp in places and she looked like Cinderella before her fairy godmother worked her magic. Pausing for a moment, she removed the scrunchie, ran her fingers through her hair and then redid her ponytail, looking slightly less bedraggled.

She turned away from the mirror. This was as good as it was going to get.

"Coming," she called as she rushed through the spotless front room. Inhaling deeply, she pulled open the door. And sagged. It wasn't Caleb. "Oh."

"Is that any way to greet your mother?" Suzie asked.

"Sorry." Faith forced a smile. "Come on in."

"Don't mind if I do." Suzie swept inside and paused. She inhaled. "Furniture polish. Window cleaner. Bleach. What's wrong?"

There was no sense in pretending. "Caleb and I had a falling-out."

"Oh no. I'm sorry to hear that. What happened?" Suzie sat on the sofa and then patted the seat beside her.

Sighing, Faith sat down. As she spoke, she struggled to keep her voice steady. "He was angry when he discovered that I had kept information about his birth father from him. I tried to explain that I didn't have any facts to share, but he wasn't hearing that. Hattie arranged a meeting with his father, but that didn't change things between us. We haven't talked in a week."

"Oh, Faith. I'm so sorry."

Faith shrugged. It would be easy to blame her mother for what happened—she'd withheld vital information from Faith—but Suzie really wasn't at fault. It had been Faith's choice to keep what little she'd known from Caleb. Besides, assigning blame wouldn't change things. "It's over now."

"I was trying to keep from hurting Caleb. Instead I ended up hurting you."

"You aren't the one who hurt me."

"Maybe not directly, but I put you in a position to be hurt. If I'd either told you everything I knew or told you nothing, Caleb wouldn't have a reason to be upset with you."

"Maybe. But hindsight is twenty-twenty and all that. The main thing is that he has found his father. He and

Brooks Langtree have been in contact." Faith turned to her mother. "Brooks is nothing like you said. He's a good man."

Suzie sniffed. "Time changes people. Sounds like it was for the better in his case."

Faith imagined that was as good as it was going to get. Suzie's loyalty to her late friend wouldn't allow for much else. "I guess. Anyway, it worked out for them. Everything else is secondary."

"You're saying what you think I expect you to say, which is nice but not necessary. You can be honest about your feelings with me. I won't judge you."

Faith blew out a breath. "I'm feeling hurt and left out. Caleb would never have gotten to meet with Brooks Langtree if not for Grandma. Grandma wouldn't have been involved if I hadn't asked for her help on his behalf."

"And you want his gratitude?"

"No." She wanted his love. "But I think he should at least give me the benefit of the doubt. He should have given me a chance to explain why I did what I did."

"Maybe given time he will."

"I've given him time. It's been a week. How much time does he need?"

"I don't have the answer to that question. But maybe you're spending too much time focusing on him and not enough time focusing on your own life."

"What do you mean? I'm taking care of my life. I've been working hard on my career. I've also been taking care of my home. You can't possibly think that I'm neglecting anything."

"This place is spotless. Evidence that you're trying to keep yourself busy so you don't have to face your feelings. That in and of itself is a sign that you need to get yourself together."

"Meaning?"

"You've been spending a lot of your time and energy helping Caleb."

"He's my friend."

"And more?"

There had never been a good time to lie to her mother. Suzie was much too astute to be fooled. Besides, apart from a few rough years when Faith had been an angsty teen who hadn't been on good terms with most people, she and her mother had always shared a close relationship. Suzie would understand how she felt.

Faith sighed. "I was beginning to consider the possibility."

"I had a feeling," Suzie said slowly. She smiled and then it faded. "But he has so much going on in his life at the moment. I can only imagine the number of emotions he's feeling right now. He probably can't even tell you how he feels because he might not know."

"This has been a very emotional time for him. But he'd managed to compartmentalize before and we had a great time together."

"I don't doubt that. But now that he and Brooks have met, Caleb will be dealing with a lot more emotions. They'll probably be spending time getting to know each other. That is, if Brooks is interested in getting to know Caleb," Suzie scoffed.

"I met Brooks. He was so happy to learn that Caleb had been looking for him. He was eager to meet Caleb in person. I have no doubt that they'll be spending more time together in the future."

"With all that going on, he probably doesn't have a lot of time for a relationship," Suzie said.

"What are you saying?"

"Maybe it's best if you step back too. Stop spending so much time trying to avoid your feelings or waiting to hear from Caleb. Get back to living your life."

"I'm trying."

"I know. Of course, if you run out of things to do around here, you can always come over to my house. I've been trying to get your dad to paint the kitchen for weeks, but he hasn't picked up a roller yet. You can always take over that task. There certainly isn't any more cleaning to do around here."

Faith laughed. "I'll consider the offer."

"You do that." Suzie rose. "I need to get going. I just wanted to make sure that you're okay. I'll see you later."

Faith hugged her mother and then watched as Suzie got into her car and drove away. Though she didn't want to admit it, her mother was right.

It was time to let Caleb go and move on with her life.

CHAPTER FOURTEEN

"So, tell us everything. We want to hear everything from the beginning," Iris said, settling on the sofa beside Nathan. Caleb sat in a chair across from his parents. He'd called his parents right after he'd met with Brooks, but he'd been so emotional that he couldn't express himself correctly. He and Brooks had spent time together every day this past week, eating dinner or just sitting and talking so they could get to know each other better. Though his parents had been overjoyed for him, and would have understood if he'd stayed in Bronco even longer, he'd made it a point to be here for Sunday dinner.

"It's been good. And strange." Caleb leaned forward and clasped his hands together. After he and Brooks had gone their separate ways that first day, Caleb had been too amped up to sit still. He couldn't call Faith and discuss his feelings. He was still upset with her and was unsure how the conversation would go. Their last one had been pretty bad. So he'd called his parents. They'd deserved to know that he had met his birth father.

"Strange? You're going to have to explain that answer a bit," Nathan said.

Caleb nodded, took a deep breath and then started over, recounting the entire story from beginning to end. The first time he'd told them the story, he'd glossed over a lot of what Brooks had told him. Now he didn't leave out a single detail. Every once in a while, one of his parents would ask a question for clarification, but for the most part he was able to just tell the story without interruption. When he finally reached the end, he felt a little bit wrung out as if he'd relived that emotional moment. And relieved.

Iris took a sip of her coffee and then set the mug onto the coaster. "That explains a lot."

"It does?" Caleb asked. He wasn't exactly sure what his mother was referring to, but he had no doubt she would explain.

"Yes. After blaming himself for the tragic loss of his wife, and feeling unable and undeserving of raising you, I understand why he didn't want to make it easy for you to contact him."

"Now you've totally lost me," Caleb said, shaking his head. Did his very own mother agree that Brooks had been right to make it hard for Caleb to find him? "That is one thing that I still don't understand. If he loved me, but couldn't take care of me, it seems like he would have wanted to stay in touch. Or at least make it possible for me to find him."

"Imagine how horrible he would feel if you knew how to get in touch with him but you didn't reach out. By making it hard, he could always tell himself that you might want to meet him but were unable to. I know it doesn't make a lot of sense to you, but it was his way of protecting himself from further pain."

"I see your point even if I don't agree with his decision," Caleb said after a while.

"So, what's next?" Nathan asked.

"He wants me to meet his wife and kids. His wife knows about me, but his kids don't, so he's going to tell them about me this week."

"How do you feel about that?"

"I'm okay with meeting them if they want to meet me.

When I went in search of my biological father, I didn't think about anything else. It never occurred to me that he might have a family that would want to meet me. I didn't want to get my hopes up too high."

Nathan nodded. "That's reasonable."

"So, you intend to keep in touch?" Iris asked.

"That depends," Caleb said slowly.

"On what?" Nathan asked.

"On how the two of you feel about it. You're my parents. You're the ones who have been here all my life. You're the ones I've always depended on. You supported me when I wanted to find my birth father, but that doesn't mean you want him or his family to become a part of my life. A part of *our* lives. Whatever happens between me and Brooks will affect all of us. If you don't want to deal with Brooks and his family, I can meet them once and then that can be the end of it."

"Don't even think that way," Iris said. "We love you too much to ever be that selfish."

"We always knew there would be a possibility that you would want to have a relationship with him," Nathan said, looking Caleb in the eyes. "And we're fine with it."

"Are you sure?"

"Positive," Iris added. "In fact, we're grateful to Brooks. If not for him, we wouldn't have had the chance to have such an amazing son. And you are our son. Brooks Langtree's presence in your life won't change that. Nor will it change our love for you. And we do love you."

Caleb's throat tightened and his vision blurred for a moment. He knew his parents loved him. They'd told him and shown him that his entire life. Their reaction now was only further proof of that. "Right back at you."

"So meet his family. Hopefully, you and your siblings

will become close friends," Iris said. "And if they're amenable, we would like to meet all of them."

"Really?" Caleb asked. He didn't know why he was surprised. His parents were the most loving people he'd ever met. Naturally they would be welcoming to Brooks and his family.

"Of course. Invite them over for dinner," Iris said and Nathan nodded. "Of if they would prefer to meet in a restaurant, we can do that too."

"You two are the best," Caleb said. He stood and gave each of his parents a big hug.

"You aren't just noticing that, are you?" Nathan asked, grinning.

"No. But I don't tell you often enough how much I appreciate you."

"We know how you feel," Iris said. "We've always known."

"And speaking of girlfriends," Nathan said, ignoring the fact that they hadn't been talking about girlfriends at all, "how is Faith? I imagine she must be pretty happy about the turn of events."

Although Caleb had mentioned the role Faith had played in his search, he hadn't told his parents that she'd withheld information from him. For an unknown reason, he still felt the need to protect her.

Now he frowned. "We aren't together any longer."

"What happened?" Iris asked.

Caleb gave them the abridged version of Faith's actions, trying to keep her from sounding bad. Though she'd hurt and disappointed him, she wasn't a bad person. And she hadn't meant to hurt him. He saw that now.

"Wow," Nathan said, tapping his fingertips together. "So when do you intend to call her?"

"I don't," Caleb said flatly. "There have been so many

secrets in my life. She knew how I felt about them, but she kept information from me anyway."

"Her heart was in the right place," Iris said. Naturally she would frame Faith's actions in the best possible light. Iris could find the good in anyone.

"That doesn't change anything. Mom, aren't you the one who always says that impact matters more than intent?"

"I am. But that doesn't mean intent doesn't matter. Especially when the action was done out of love. I haven't met Faith, but from everything you've told me, I have no doubt that she was only trying to protect you."

Those had been Faith's very words.

"You know that, don't you?" Nathan asked when Caleb didn't respond.

"Don't you, son?" Iris repeated.

Caleb looked at his parents. They had made their mistakes in the past. With him and with each other. That was the nature of relationships. Yet their love had always been enough to get them through the rough patches. Would love be enough to get him through this rough patch with Faith?

That thought came out of nowhere and it stunned him. But only for a moment. Suddenly it was abundantly clear how he felt about Faith. It made sense that he would always want to protect her. *He loved her.* Now he believed that she'd tried to protect him because she loved him, too. Was he going to let one well-meaning mistake cost him the love of a lifetime? No way. "I know."

"So, what are you going to do?" Iris asked.

"I'm going to go to Faith and straighten out this mess." There might be some groveling involved. In fact, he would bet on it. But he would gladly beg. He'd do whatever it took to get Faith back into his life where she belonged.

"That's my boy," Nathan said.

FAITH STARED BLANKLY at the television. None of the characters looked familiar. The mystery she'd been pretending to watch had gone off and been replaced by a reality show, her least favorite form of entertainment. She grabbed the remote and then turned off the TV. Silence would be preferable.

She checked the time. It was eight o'clock. She supposed it was late enough for her to go to bed. Not that it mattered. She expected to toss and turn for hours as she'd done every night since she and Caleb had broken up. Hopefully, exhaustion wouldn't take long to claim her tonight.

Tossing aside the fleece throw that covered her lap, Faith stood and headed for the stairs. Before she had taken two steps, her doorbell rang. Her heart skipped a beat, but she immediately told herself to calm down. She wasn't going to play that game again. Over the past week, each time her doorbell had rung, she'd run to the door, hoping to find Caleb standing on the other side. Each time she'd been disappointed to see her mother, sisters or cousins. Once it had been a delivery guy with the wrong address. She didn't know who was ringing her bell now, but she knew it wasn't Caleb. They were done.

Not bothering to brush the potato chip crumbs from her old comfy sweatshirt or check her appearance in the mirror, she opened the front door. And gasped.

"Caleb. What are you doing here?"

He looked so good in his black leather jacket, red-and-black plaid shirt and faded jeans. One arm was behind his back. Though it was tempting to run a hand over her messy hair, she resisted the urge. Caleb already knew that she was flawed, so he wouldn't be surprised by her less than glamorous appearance. If he even cared what she looked like, which was doubtful.

"Can I come in?" he asked.

"Sure." She stepped aside. She'd given up hoping to ever see him again. Now hope tried to sprout in her heart, but she nipped it in the bud. This wasn't some romance novel where things always worked out. This was the real world where hearts got broken.

Before he entered, Caleb pulled his arm from behind his back. He was holding a dozen red roses. "These are for you."

"Why?" she asked, automatically taking the bouquet. She held them up to her nose and inhaled. They smelled so good. So sweet. That stubborn hope tried once more to spring up. This time she let it.

He stepped inside, closed the door, then led her into her front room. She took a peek at his eyes. The anger that had filled them the last time she'd seen them was gone. Now she saw doubt. "For a lot of reasons. First, I realize that I have never given you flowers. I'm ashamed of that fact now."

"Why? We weren't dating. Our relationship has always been strictly casual. I didn't have any expectations."

The corners of his mouth turned down as if her answer displeased him. "Faith..."

She didn't have the emotional fortitude to discuss their relationship. She was still trying to accept the fact that it was over. These guilt flowers weren't helping. "And the other reasons?"

He sighed as if disappointed. "To apologize to you."

"For what?" Faith asked.

"For being such a jerk." Caleb shook his head slowly. His voice was filled with remorse. "I was wrong to treat you the way that I did. I was upset, but that doesn't excuse my behavior. There was no reason to act like I did."

"I understand. Looking back, I could have done things differently too. I should have pressed my mother for more information. And even if she didn't tell me more, I should have let you know what she'd said. Perhaps she would have been willing to tell you more than she'd told me."

"You were trying to protect my feelings. You both were. I see that now."

"Yes. But you're an adult. A man. You didn't need protecting."

He reached out and took the bouquet from her hands and set it on the table. Then he took her hands into his. Their eyes met. His were filled with warmth and affection. "Everyone could use protection at one time or another. I know you were only trying to help me. It was a lot easier to lash out at you than to face my fear of being rejected by Brooks."

"I understand."

"So, can you forgive me for being a jerk?"

Her heart, which had been lifting at his words, now began to soar. "If you can forgive me for keeping a secret."

He smiled. "Let's start fresh now."

"That's a plan I can get behind." The sorrow that had been Faith's constant companion for the past week vanished and she sighed. Caleb bent down and Faith rose on her tiptoes. Their lips brushed in a gentle kiss that soothed all of her hurts and put their conflict behind them. She pulled back, then leaned her head against his chest. It felt so good to be in his arms again.

He gave her a lopsided grin. "You know, you have a way of seeing me. The real me. You know what I'm feeling even before I do."

"I wouldn't go that far."

"I would." He slid his arms from around her back and placed his hands on her waist. "Look into my eyes. Can you see what I feel?"

She met his gaze and her heart stuttered. His eyes were

filled with an emotion she'd longed to see but hadn't dared to hope for. Instead of answering his question, she nibbled on her bottom lip. "I'm afraid to say it. I don't want to get things wrong again."

"Then I'll say it. I love you, Faith. I've been falling for you since the day we met. But there was so much going on in my life, I didn't notice. Plus I didn't think I had the emotional bandwidth to add anything else. Boy, was I wrong." He grinned briefly before letting it fade away. "That's not completely honest. The truth was I was afraid of putting my heart on the line. More afraid than I was of being rejected by my biological father."

"I was a bit wary myself," Faith confessed. "That's part of the reason I wanted to keep things casual between us. You can't get hurt if you don't put yourself out there." Or so she'd thought.

"Playing it safe doesn't work for me anymore."

"We don't have to rush things," Faith said. "I know you have a lot to deal with now. I love you, Caleb and I'm not going anywhere. We can take things slowly."

Caleb shook his head. "I don't want to go slow. This past week without you has been hell. I missed you more than I ever would have believed was possible. I don't want to spend more time away from you than I have to. I need you in my life. I realize now that I don't have to solve all of my problems on my own. That it's okay and even better to have a partner to walk beside you. A partner to help you through the troubled times."

She smiled. "I feel the same way."

"There's so much we don't know about each other and I don't want to get ahead of myself, Faith. But I think we should be each other's partners. What do you say?"

"I say, sign me up."

"I was hoping you'd say that." He lowered his head

and kissed her again. This time the kiss was hot. Passionate. Everything she'd been missing and feared she'd never feel again.

She was unbuttoning his shirt when he covered her hand with his, stopping her progress. He pulled back abruptly. She opened her eyes and glanced at him.

"I would love to introduce you to my hometown. And to my parents. How do you feel about that?"

"I would love to see your hometown and to meet your parents."

He grinned. "I was hoping you would say that."

The following Sunday

FAITH STOOD BESIDE Caleb on the sidewalk in front of the rambling house where he'd grown up. Set on a slight hill, with concrete stairs leading up to the wide porch, this was exactly the kind of place she could imagine Caleb living in as a child. From the pots of mums on either side of the front door, to the neatly trimmed bushes that lined the front porch, everything about the house was welcoming. There was an enormous tree in the center of the lawn, the perfect place for a tire swing. This was more than a house where people lived. This was a home filled with love.

Faith suddenly felt nervous, fearful that Iris and Nathan Strom would find fault with her. She was wearing a red sweater, red plaid skirt and black tights. In place of her cowboy boots, she was wearing black pumps. Suddenly she wished she had worn something—anything—else.

It didn't make sense to be filled with such trepidation. She had spoken with Iris and Nathan a couple of times this past week. They'd been more than gracious to her. There was no reason to expect them to be less than warm today.

Caleb gave her a smile that let her know he understood how she felt. “My parents are going to love you.”

Faith exhaled. “I hope so.”

“I know so.”

Before Faith could say another word, the front door swung open and a middle-aged couple stepped onto the porch and hurried down the stairs. Caleb introduced them and his mother pulled Faith into a warm embrace that soothed all of Faith’s worries. After a moment, Iris pulled back, keeping an arm around Faith’s waist. “It’s chilly outside. Let’s go inside where we can talk and get to know each other better.”

Faith immediately felt at ease. She glanced at Caleb, who smiled and nodded at her. She hadn’t been looking for love, but love had found her and she couldn’t be happier.

Her future was looking better than ever.

* * * * *

Don't miss the stories in this mini series!

MONTANA MAVERICKS: THE TRAIL TO TENACITY

Welcome to Big Sky Country!
Where spirited men and women
discover love on the range.

That Maverick Of Mine
KATHY DOUGLASS
September 2024

The Maverick's Christmas Kiss
JOANNA SIMS
October 2024

The Maverick's Christmas Countdown
HEATHERLY BELL
November 2024

MILLS & BOON

Courting The Cowgirl

Cheryl Harper

MILLS & BOON

Cheryl Harper discovered her love for books and words as a little girl, thanks to a mother who made countless library trips and an introduction to Laura Ingalls Wilder's Little House books. Whether the stories she reads are set in the prairie, the American West, Regency England or earth a hundred years in the future, Cheryl enjoys strong characters who make her laugh. Now Cheryl spends her days searching for the right words while she stares out the window and her dog, Jack, snoozes beside her. And she considers herself very lucky to do so.

For more information about Cheryl's books, visit her online at cherylharperbooks.com or follow her on Twitter, @cherylharperbks.

Dear Reader,

I've always enjoyed fish-out-of-water stories. That's probably because I identify with them at a deep, deep level. Put me in a room with strangers and my pulse races like I'm running for my life (away from the faux pas lying in wait for me as soon as I attempt charming conversation). Some people thrive on the excitement of new and different; others persevere to reach familiar and comfortable. I'm the second one!

In *Courting the Cowgirl*, LA chef Brian Caruso has been asked to help choose someone to run the Majestic's reopened restaurant. Faye Parker once experienced her own uncertainty as a newcomer to Prospect; now she's the local consultant showing the city boy how restaurant life works in a small town. They'll both learn that a change of scenery may be the only way to find the place where they truly belong.

I love this town and the characters who live there (and visit along the way). Thank you for joining me on this adventure! To find out more about my books and what's coming next, visit me at cherylharperbooks.com.

Cheryl

CHAPTER ONE

BRIAN CARUSO ARRANGED the lamp, stapler and Montblanc fountain pen—that had cost more than his first car—in precise lines on his cleared mahogany desk and ignored the amused smirk of his executive chef, Belvie. She was waiting for him to hand over control of his restaurant, and he was finding it harder than he expected to take the final step. This would be the first "vacation" he'd taken since he'd opened Rinnovato—one of the top ten restaurants in Los Angeles.

While this trip to Smalltown, Colorado, population who-knew, wasn't strictly for relaxation, the two-week break would give Belvie plenty of time to stretch her wings. His right hand was ready to fly the nest and open her own place soon.

Though Rinnovato was built exactly as he'd dreamed, it was impossible to calculate how much of his success he owed to Belvie, so he kept giving gentle nudges to encourage her, but she refused to leap. This could be the final proof she needed to step out on her own.

Brian carefully polished away all the imaginary smudges on the gleaming surface of his desk.

"Are you trying to intimidate any dust that might wish to gather here in your absence?" Belvie asked before pointing at the pen. Her lilting voice bubbled with a smile. "You shouldn't leave that out. It's expensive. How do I know? I collected the funds from your entire staff to get it. Imagine, forty-three people all agreed we wanted to give you something special to mark our restaurant's anniversary. Five years. That is an eternity in restaurant life."

Brian leaned back in his oversize desk chair. "I know and appreciate all that." He and his team had beaten stiff odds to make it past the first year. And five years was a magic number—the benchmark that suggested Rinnovato was going to enjoy a nice, long life. He'd chosen the Italian word for *renovated* or *renewed* as a name because the restaurant's success would change his life. He and Belvie and a long list of others had then done whatever it had taken to make that promise come true.

"I couldn't have done it without you," Brian said. He'd lost count of the number of times he'd said as much to Belvie. They had learned this business together.

She brushed her braids over her shoulder. "And the cost is why you will never use that pen."

"But I will always keep it on display, like fine art." He shrugged. "You know how it is. We come from nothing. We enjoy the good stuff by never, ever using it."

Belvie sighed. "Of course, but some of us can learn to live a little, too." She flashed the expensive gold bangle on her wrist. "Here I am, wearing fine jewelry to work the dinner shift."

Brian smiled. "Looks good on you."

"I know. My mother would cluck her tongue in dismay at such a waste, but I am lucky to work for a boss who generously shares the profits with his staff. Nice things are always a pleasant reward. He has also trained his loyal staff well. Successfully operating without him will be difficult but not impossible." Belvie stood. "If you don't leave now, you and your daughter will arrive late to the airport. Being late worries Gemma."

"Leaving you here alone worries me." Brian held up his

hands in surrender as she propped her hands on her hips. "Not because you can't handle it, but because it's a lot of responsibility. I don't like leaving the extra work for you."

"It's less than two weeks. Many people all over the world take similar time off. It's called a vay-cay-shun. Vacation. You aren't familiar with the word, but this will be an excellent experience." Belvie scoffed. "Besides that, the bonus you are paying me to take over? My gold bracelet is lonely. Another bangle will comfort us both while I am toiling so hard."

"We don't take vacations, Belvie, not from the restaurant. You know that. It's just not us." Brian couldn't remember ever leaving a kitchen, his or anyone else's, for so long. Not voluntarily, anyway.

"We did our trial run while you were off taping your television show. Entire days where Rinnovato operated seamlessly without Chef Caruso steering the ship." Belvie wagged her finger. "If you didn't realize that a nationally broadcast TV program would make you famous and gain such opportunities to travel and demonstrate your many skills, I do not know what to tell you."

"I'm not famous," Brian said. "It was a cooking competition on a cable network, and I didn't even win the thing." Sadie Hearst had convinced him to participate in the Best Chef in America tournament against fifteen other chefs. He and the cooking icon met when she'd popped up at his food truck, and she'd mentored him through all the bumps of opening Rinnovato. Time with Sadie had boosted his own confidence. She'd started out in tiny Prospect, Colorado, and built a respectable empire without losing a bit of spark or common sense as far as Brian could ever tell.

She'd sold him on the tournament by appealing to his practical side. Participating had provided publicity for the restaurant, as expected. It had also given him a chance to prove his skills against chefs with formal culinary training and more extensive experience.

Both of them had understood what that meant: measuring up against the best.

Unfortunately, there had also been a lot of intrusive newspaper and magazine articles focused on his humble background. That he hadn't counted on. Seeing his face on the front page of the newspaper's food section had been painful. That level of fame was bad enough. He wasn't sure what would have happened if he'd managed to win the thing; finishing third had made him temporarily recognizable on the street in some parts of LA.

Drawing people to his food was good. Landing on gossip blogs was bad.

On her last visit, Sadie had been filled with glee by the scrum of photographers staking out his restaurant to get candid shots of famous people and him, when he couldn't escape them. She had tried to coach him on using the fifteen minutes of stardom correctly, but he'd been more interested in running out the clock.

Brian missed Sadie Hearst. The death of his favorite customer and trusted advisor had hit him hard. He was certain she would have words of wisdom about raising teenage girls. Gemma remained his biggest challenge in life.

Only an opportunity to repay the numerous favors Sadie had done for him would lure him away from his kitchen for two weeks. Taking his daughter with him was a high-risk gamble.

Time was ticking. Brian could picture the worried frown on his daughter's face as she waited for him. "Are you sure you don't want this opportunity in Prospect?" he asked Belvie. "You could run your own kitchen. Create your own menu. I don't know the Hearsts well, but they would love you. Everyone loves you."

Belvie nodded as if she was accepting her due. "Of course they would love me, but I will continue to make a generous salary here while I steal all your best ideas for Italian fare and apply them to my family's recipes, until I am ready to do my own thing. I have become a mildly important influencer on the social media channels doing exactly as I please with my own twists on Ghanaian cuisine. I thank you for your vote of confidence."

Since everything Belvie made him was delicious, he had no doubt that her *mild importance* would only grow with time. She definitely had the personality to draw fans.

"We still haven't decided what to do about San Francisco," he said as he shoved the file of real estate listings, his accountant's proposed expansion budget and the rough business plan he'd been drafting for a second restaurant in northern California into his laptop case.

"Are you quite certain that we haven't?" Belvie asked as she twisted the bangle on her wrist. "It may still be California, Brian, but it's a rainy place. I don't like rainy places."

He rubbed his forehead, weary. They'd immediately fallen back into the rut of the conversation they'd been having for months. "This location is perfect. Steady. If we're going to take the next step, it's now, but we have to do it together."

"I will take excellent care of your Rinnovato while you are gone. This will reinforce your belief that I can run this while you open a new place where it is foggy and wet if that is what you wish. We can both be happy, but today is not the day to shake hands on that negotiation." Belvie pointed at the clock on the wall. Gold hands were moving steadily onward. "Gemma is waiting."

"Since the kitchen will be short-staffed, call in Robbie." Brian stood to pick up his bag.

"You are taking two of my best line chefs with you for

your new TV show and want me to replace them with one flaky boy who forgets to show up for shifts? I do not see how this is an equitable exchange." Belvie opened his office door and waited for him to leave.

"It's a web series, not a television show, and Robbie will do better. Everyone deserves another chance. And those two chefs were the only ones I could get to agree to participate in a cooking competition for a cash prize and the chance to run their own restaurant for a year in Small… Um…er, Prospect, Colorado. Losing Franky or Rafa is going to be difficult in the long run. Robbie can help." Brian knew either one of the young chefs could do the job, and he was happy to give them a shot they might not get otherwise, but they would be missed.

Robbie had messed up, no doubt. It was his first real job, and he'd never had to fight for every dollar, so losing this restaurant gig had been a real wake-up call. Belvie had been absolutely right to fire him.

Meanwhile, Brian had needed third and fourth chances and the kindness of strangers like Sadie Hearst in his life to help get him to where he was today. Giving people some grace when they had talent and good hearts was a lesson he'd learned from that. Efficient overachiever Belvie hadn't needed those do-overs yet, so they agreed to disagree whenever Brian rehired someone she fired.

Brian waited for her to agree to Robbie's second chance in the Rinnovato kitchen.

Finally, she rolled her eyes. "You're the boss. I will call him. His ability to make perfect pasta from scratch is not easy to replace."

Relieved to have that standoff resolved, Brian moved quickly through the restaurant. Out of habit, he scanned the tables and floor as he went, but everything was spotless. "You have my number. Call me if anything comes up."

He had one foot out on the sidewalk when she responded, “Everything will be fine here, thank you!” Belvie gave a curt nod and turned away. The woman could be trusted to lead battalions into war, and the rest of his staff was experienced. Leaving Rinnovato would be fine.

The concept of spending two weeks with his teenage daughter in the middle of nowhere while he ran a small cooking competition streamed online had his stomach tied into knots.

Sadie’s great-nephew, Michael Hearst, had approached him about assisting with this web series after Sadie’s death. As the new CEO of her company, the Cookie Queen Corporation, Michael was searching for online content to keep Sadie’s fans returning to the company website. Sadie and her live events had been a huge traffic driver.

Brian had heard a great deal about all of the Hearsts over dinners with Sadie, so he knew Sarah, Jordan and Brooke were her great-nieces.

He hadn’t known about their inheritance of an old fishing lodge in Sadie’s hometown of Prospect until Michael showed up one evening at Rinnovato. While Brooke was in New York, Sarah and Jordan had reopened the place and were struggling to find a chef to run the restaurant there. The debt Brian owed Sadie made it impossible to refuse to help the man. Michael had asked for three competitors; Brian had only been able to get two, but either one would be an asset to the lodge’s restaurant. He was certain this competition would turn out well.

However, nothing about this whole situation made Brian comfortable. And he’d worked hard to get to this stage in his life where everything was predictably comfortable.

Ordered.

The kind of life that had been a daydream at one point.

Leaving it in exchange for the unknown was difficult.

Bringing his daughter along? That raised the stakes.

After he loaded his laptop bag next to his suitcase in the SUV, Brian slipped into the congestion of LA afternoon traffic. When he parked, Gemma was sitting on the front steps, one hand gripping the handle of her suitcase. She immediately stood and hurried down to the sidewalk. Her mother, Monica, followed and managed to grab her for a hug before she slid into the passenger seat. "I'm going to miss you, baby. Have fun. I hope you get to ride a horse."

Brian got out of the car and picked up Gemma's suitcase.

"You said I could call you if I want to come home," Gemma said anxiously when Monica stepped back. "Remember?"

Monica met his eyes before nodding. "I did, but you are going to enjoy this. I know it."

Gemma didn't answer that, but she did glance at him over her shoulder. The worry on her face didn't boost his confidence.

Monica followed him to the back of the SUV. "Being late isn't the best start, you know. She's anxious about this trip and..."

Brian nodded. "Yeah, I know. Sorry. Tying up all the loose ends at the restaurant took time." He shut the trunk. "This trip you're taking... Exactly what are you going to do from Mexico if she decides she wants to come home? Your new husband is prepared to come back early from this honeymoon?"

Monica wrinkled her nose. "Let's not find out, okay? You two need to spend some time together and this is a great opportunity for that. If Gemma calls, I'll do my best to convince her of the positives of staying, but I need you to be committed to keeping her there and content. You can do that, right?"

Brian had done a lot of hard things in his life, but this might be a challenge beyond his capabilities. Still, he wasn't going to admit that here. "Gemma and I are going to have a great break."

"Keep telling yourself that. Eventually, you'll believe it." Monica patted his hand and moved toward the passenger side. She was waving when he buckled his seat belt.

"Are you ready, Gem?" Brian asked in his friendliest Dad voice.

Her quick glance in his direction was filled with worry, but she nodded. "Yes, we should go. We need to be at the airport at least two hours before boarding." She pointed at the clock to show him they were in danger of missing that window.

"It's more of a suggestion than an actual rule," Brian said as he hit the freeway headed to LAX. "Our first trip together, just the two of us. Are you excited?"

Her polite expression didn't inspire confidence but she nodded. "Flying can be stressful, but I love to see new places."

The urge to tell her he hadn't flown or left California until he was an adult had to be squashed. He might not know much about fathering, but no teenager ever appreciated "back in my day" stories. His "growing up in LA" lessons were so unlike Gemma's that he and his daughter might have been born on different planets, but there was no good reason to point that out right now. They were both acutely aware of how dissimilar they were.

Since he'd finally reached the point where he had the money to do it, he preferred that Gemma's experience be the best: travel, clothes, cell phone and private school. Paying the tuition and funding her extracurriculars filled him with pleasure. He and Monica had learned to talk without yelling, too. It was mind-blowing what a difference having money could make in a person's life. Hard work, long hours and a healthy dose of luck had made that change in his life. It was a privilege to pass it on to his daughter.

After they made it through security, visited their gate to allay Gemma's concern that something had mysteriously altered their departure time, and found a map of all the food and shopping options in their concourse, Brian knew immediately what would be a winning suggestion. "There's a coffee place. Want to see if they have your iced macchiatos?" Should a sixteen-year-old have an expensive coffee drink habit? Brian was no expert, but the way his daughter's face brightened immediately convinced him not to spend much time worrying about it.

She'd been stuck to his heels like a shadow all the way through the airport.

But the promise of a treat convinced her to take the lead.

They got their drinks, a couple of chocolate croissants for sustenance and settled in at their gate. Some of the tension between them was gone, so Brian relaxed in his seat and stopped racking his brain for conversation starters. Instead, he nudged her shoulder. "Look at that cool T-shirt."

When Gemma turned to see the guy walking toward them wearing a Guns N' Roses band T-shirt, he waited for her reaction. Her lips were twitching when she turned back to him. "Is that, like, classic rock?" She raised an eyebrow and he sighed dramatically to make her giggle. They used to fight over the radio controls when she was small, so it was nice to see she remembered.

"I bet they play that in the grocery store now, Dad." Gemma pulled out her tablet and slipped on headphones. Brian watched over her shoulder as some kind of reality show featuring expensive boats and a lot of alcohol played. He couldn't hear any of the conversation, but he knew he was following the plot without much difficulty.

Thankfully, the flight was on time and they landed in Denver after sunset. Picking up the rental car was the usual hassle, but he was satisfied when they pulled out onto the highway in the full-size SUV.

"You're going to have to help me navigate." Brian handed Gemma his phone. "I've got the map loaded, but I haven't done this kind of driving before." He tightened his hands on the steering wheel. "Country driving. No tourists shooting across four lanes to make a turn or bumper-to-bumper traffic for no good reason. It's weird, you know?"

The small wrinkle on Gemma's forehead reminded him that this was new to her, too. He waved a hand. "You and I together don't have anything to worry about. When it tells me to turn after the second boulder shaped like a tree, give me your best guess."

Gemma tilted her head to the side. "You don't get out of LA much, do you?"

Brian laughed as he realized no matter what happened next, he and Gemma were having a real adventure.

And they were doing it together.

He'd lost a lot of time he could have spent adventuring with his daughter, thanks to his own stupid mistakes when she was a baby, and then the drive to succeed when he'd made it out. They both deserved to enjoy every minute of this. "Navigator controls the radio station, too. Find us some classic rock to listen to."

She shook her head. "Nope. Taylor Swift, coming right up."

When she landed on a station, he surprised her by singing along with the first song. It was not by Taylor Swift and he couldn't name the singer, but he'd listened to Gemma's station often enough that he knew some of the words. She joined in and Brian felt the flutter of hope in his chest.

He'd tried to avoid that flutter for a long time. He'd

learned that hope was dangerous, but Belvie had made a good point. A smart man would teach himself to enjoy these special gifts.

When the first station faded, Gemma picked another. She helped him find the turns, and they rolled into Prospect's main street without any trouble.

"Is this town even open?" Gemma asked uncertainly.

"Who is a city slicker now?" Brian joked as he surveyed the dark street. It was early evening by LA's standards, but all the shop windows were dark. The wooden sidewalks were deserted. "I heard about places where they 'roll up the sidewalk at night.' Never seen one, but this must be pretty close."

Gemma leaned forward. "Where's the hotel? All of these buildings are short."

It was a good question. "We're supposed to drive through town and out to a fishing lodge on the lake."

The front seat was dark, but the quick snap of Gemma's head was easy to see. "Fishing lodge?" There was a wobble in her voice that would have made him smile if he didn't understand a bit of her concern.

"That's a hotel on a lake," he said confidently.

That better be what it meant.

"Jordan Hearst suggested we stop and grab dinner tonight to bring with us before we leave town because they haven't stocked the kitchen at the lodge. They're waiting on my list." Brian bent forward. "The Ace High is the name of the restaurant."

As soon as he saw it and the lights burning inside, he pulled into a parking spot.

"Ace High. What does that mean?" Gemma asked as she studied the exterior. "What kind of food do they serve?"

Brian cleared his throat, aware that this might be another symptom of Gemma's protected upbringing. She was a picky eater, so this answer was critical. "Prospect was a silver boomtown about a hundred and fifty years ago. Like in the Old West days. In the daylight, we'll see these buildings as they were back then. Ace High is a poker hand, so I'm guessing this was a saloon. In those days, it was like a…bar." He was pushing the limits of his memory of watching Western reruns. Gemma was nervously chewing her bottom lip, so he added, "Home cooking. That's my guess. You'll like it."

Instead of arguing, she reached for the handle. "I'm hungry. Let's give it a try."

Her tone was resigned, so Brian had his doubts this was going to go well. What time did the grocery store close?

When they stepped inside, they were both relieved to find the decor rustic but spotless. The host stand and dining room were empty. The bells over the door rang before he could call out. After a minute, the swinging doors leading to the kitchen burst open and a petite woman bustled out, a long ponytail swinging with each determined step she took. She was wearing jeans and a T-shirt with the restaurant name across the front.

"Hey there, we'd like to order some food to go." Brian motioned around the empty dining room. "Is it always crowded like this?"

When she frowned, he realized his usual restaurant humor might not translate outside the city.

"It is when we've been closed for almost an hour, but because of a promise to a friend, someone had to wait around for a late arrival." Her expression was polite, but he could read the irritation in her eyes. "I was getting your food ready after a very long, very busy day running the only full-service restaurant in town." She held a stack of containers in one hand and offered him the other. "You're Brian Caruso. I recognize you from the publicity shots."

Her handshake was firm and brisk. Brian nodded, caught in her blue eyes until she turned away. The woman set the other containers down and turned to Gemma. "I'm Faye, and you are?"

"Gemma. Gemma Caruso. His daughter," she answered softly.

"It is nice to meet you, Gemma. Tonight we served our world-famous fried chicken with mashed potatoes, mac and cheese, and this new salad the chef is working on with brussels sprouts in it." Faye leaned closer to Gemma. "Brussels sprouts are one of those divisive side dishes, you know? But whether you fall on the Yes side or the No side about them, this dish is pretty good."

He'd never seen Gemma try a brussels sprout, but everything else Faye had said made the cut, so dinner was a win.

Brian pulled out a credit card and offered it to Faye, but she waved it off. The smile she offered him wasn't any warmer.

"No need. I figured this is covered by the exorbitant fee the Cookie Queen Corporation is paying me to be your 'local consultant' while you're filming here in Prospect. Plus, Sarah and Jordan Hearst are pals and neighbors. Otherwise, you would have had to cook your own dinner tonight." She pulled off her apron. "If you're ready to drive to the Majestic, I'll show you the way. That's how good a consultant I plan to be."

Brian wanted to tell her he could follow the GPS, but she was gone before the first word made it past his lips. The kitchen doors were swinging and Faye returned before they settled again. "Ready?"

Instead of waiting for his answer, she marched to the door and motioned them through it. Brian glanced at

Gemma as they hurried back to the SUV and pulled out to follow Faye through the dark streets of town.

"She's intense, isn't she?" Brian asked.

Gemma grinned. "I don't know. She reminds me of you when you're in the middle of the dinner rush."

They shared a glance and they both said, "So, yes. Intense."

"Lay off the jokes, Dad. The first one didn't go over well," Gemma added with a disapproving sniff. It was good advice, so there wasn't any reason to dispute it.

He was certain they would have driven to the Majestic Prospect Lodge without much difficulty, but the deserted two-lane highway out of town gave the city boy in him the heebie-jeebies.

Not that he was going to admit that aloud. Gemma was clutching their to-go food like a lifeline already.

Following Faye's taillights was reassuring when they drove down the lane sandwiched between tall trees that blocked out the stars. The opening on the other side was the one and only Majestic Prospect Lodge.

He hadn't been completely correct about it being a hotel on the lake, but warm light glowed through the windows and there was smoke rising from the chimney. Instead of rising up, the building was spread out against a backdrop of dark mountains.

There were no big highways or skyscrapers lit up to dim the night sky, so the stars were clear and sharp. Had he ever seen a sky like this?

Faye was already beside him at the back of the SUV before he realized she was out of her car.

She moved quickly.

And silently.

"Let me help with Gemma's bag." She didn't wait for him to hand it over but hauled both suitcases out of the trunk. “Jordan and Sarah will be inside. Let’s get you checked in so you can have dinner before it gets cold. You’re probably starving and this apple pie is going to change your life.”

Brian shook his head, wondering if the laws of polite society that said men carried their own bags were suspended in Colorado, as he watched Gemma hurry after Faye. They crossed a short bridge that overlooked a stream trickling down to the shadowy lake. He followed and braced himself for whatever the interior of a half-renovated fishing lodge might present. He would convince Gemma regardless that it made perfect sense and was all part of their exciting adventure.

He was in new territory, but so far, it had been a nice journey.

As long as the Majestic Prospect Lodge didn’t scare his daughter away, he was going to take advantage of this time with Gemma. Getting to know her better was his first priority. Helping the Hearsts out with this web series and the lodge restaurant was going to be simple enough.

His efficient consultant might have the whole job wrapped up before he even made it to the lobby.

CHAPTER TWO

FAYE PARKER MARCHED into Majestic Prospect Lodge and tried to ignore the jittery nerves that had flared when she met famous chef Brian Caruso for the first time. Ever since the plan for the Cookie Queen Corporation's web streaming competition had solidified, Faye had been dreading his arrival. This was what happened when she skipped meetings run by Prue Armstrong: she was "volunteered" to consult with the town's important visitor when she already had a job that kept her busier than a termite in a log cabin.

She'd expected a celebrity chef to be arrogant. His quip about the "crowd" at her restaurant supported her judgment.

The fact that he was handsome was no surprise. Every story she'd pulled up on the internet had included a photo, and Brian Caruso was the kind of handsome that could sneak up on a woman. His dark eyes had almost stopped her in her tracks.

Though there was a world of difference between his polished headshot for the TV cooking competition or the flat lifestyle photos of him working in his LA restaurant, and the three-dimensional man with both feet planted on her freshly mopped floor.

Those feet were in polished loafers that shone like glass. Everything about him shouted expensive.

Fancy.

Superior.

Faye didn't know anything about labels or menswear beyond the jeans and button-downs sold over at the Homestead Market, right beside the Produce section, but the haircut was perfect. His beard was carefully manicured. So were his nails. The only puzzle piece that didn't fit was the tattoo covering the back of his hand. Why was she instantly curious about that part of his story?

Finding his shy daughter hiding in his shadow had made it easier to regain her composure, but she'd had to set him straight about how busy her restaurant was. She worked hard there. He would put some respect on his face the next time he surveyed her dining room.

Gemma Caruso was beautiful. Faye couldn't help but be drawn to the lanky teenager who'd appeared ready to fly away at any second.

"Whoa," Gemma whispered at her side. Faye turned to find her frozen in place, apparently transfixed by the large landscape painting of the Rocky Mountains hanging behind the check-in desk in the lobby.

Faye set both suitcases down as the chef strolled in and wrapped his arm around his daughter's shoulders. "Imagine missing a chance to see those mountains firsthand, Gem. This is going to be a big adventure, right?"

The way some of the tightness around his mouth eased when his daughter nodded enthusiastically thawed a fraction of the hard shell Faye had assembled.

For two weeks, she would assist Brian Caruso as they taped a competition in the kitchen where Sadie Hearst had once cooked, here at the lodge. In return, Sarah and Jordan would receive a generous location fee that would cover some of the repairs the lodge needed in advance of the big Western Days weekend. The whole town of Prospect pitched in for the most important tourist weekend of the year. Having the lodge reopened would increase the crowds, something everyone wanted for the festival's one hundredth anniversary.

And impressing those visitors with a restored Majestic would ensure they kept returning to Prospect and hopefully to her restaurant.

No one wanted a successful festival more than family matriarch Prue Armstrong, and what Prue wanted, she got. Faye hadn't even attempted to argue her way out of this assignment, even though her grandmother needed her running the Ace.

The restaurant and its demands ruled their lives under normal circumstances, but Prue had worked some magic and Faye had a get-out-of-the-restaurant pass until this competition was over.

Or until the extra staff she'd hired failed her grandmother's expectations.

Deciding whether she wanted them to succeed or crash and burn had occupied a lot of her spare minutes until Chef Caruso had walked in the door.

The tension in her shoulders brought on by his nearness annoyed her.

Impatient to get some service for their out-of-town guests, Faye tapped the bell Jordan had placed on the check-in desk in case visitors arrived while she was in her new office. After a second of waiting, Faye pulled out her phone. "I'll text Jordan. She can't be far away."

"We're here." Jordan led a contingent of Armstrongs down the hallway toward the lobby. "I was showing off the firepit I finally managed to build."

Before Faye could prod Jordan into moving faster to get the Carusos checked in, Clay Armstrong slipped his arm over Jordan's shoulder. "*You* built the firepit?" His eyebrow rose as if he was waiting for her to tell the truth.

Their silent stare was filled with all kinds of unspoken

back-and-forth, but Jordan finally sniffed. "We built it. Together. There? Is that better?"

"Much." Clay squeezed her shoulder. "I was the brains while you did the heavy lifting."

Jordan pursed her lips as she considered that. Clay Armstrong was the architect and builder who'd been behind the most substantial pieces of the lodge's renovation, so there might be something to his claims. "As long as you admit you could never have finished it without me, I'll agree." Jordan poked him in the stomach and ignored the way her sister Sarah and Clay's brother Wes grinned. Grant Armstrong had been whispering to the lodge's part-time employee, Mia Romero, at the back of the crowd, but he dragged his eyes away from Mia to say, "Welcome to the Majestic."

When everyone beamed at his contribution, Faye inhaled for patience. The number of satisfied couples in love in this room would have overwhelmed a smaller space. Faye might have to pull the Carusos to safety so they could breathe freely.

"While you're checking them in," Faye said to Jordan, her eyebrows raised to do some of her own silent communication to get the woman in gear, "I'll be happy to make the introductions. This is Jordan Hearst. Her sister Sarah. Mia works here at the lodge." After she pointed out each person, Brian and Gemma shook their hands, so it was a lengthy process. "And these cowboys are Armstrongs. Wes and Clay and Grant, in that order. They have the ranch next door."

When the men had completed all their hellos, Sarah turned to her. "Are you in a rush, Faye?"

Jordan snorted and muttered, "Always," as she slid behind the front desk.

"I wanted to make two weary travelers welcome." Faye

stepped closer to Gemma Caruso and squeezed her arm. "They have dinner to eat and bags to unpack."

"Right. Faye, you take Gemma and find a good table in the restaurant. We'll show the chef the kitchen and bring back some drinks. Fellas, please take their bags to their rooms, okay?" Sarah said. Sarah was the oldest sister and generally took charge of everything.

Faye tightened her arm around Gemma's shoulders and guided her into the restaurant. "Fine. We'll pick the table and seats with the best view." Gemma immediately moved closer to the windows. That made sense because Key Lake was magnetic, even after sunset. On clear nights like tonight, the moon shone down brightly enough to be reflected back with each ripple of the water. "During the day, I could sit here forever. Now that the weather's warming up, you can explore the shoreline."

Gemma smiled over her shoulder before taking a seat. "I wasn't sure what to expect when I heard 'fishing lodge,' but I'm excited to see the water."

"Every window here has a view of Key Lake, so you'll have plenty of opportunity," Faye said as she pulled out containers and arranged them on the table. "The big one is dinner. The small one is dessert." Then she crossed her arms over her chest and stood back. The urge to fuss was harder to manage since she had only one table to serve, but overwhelming this girl who had settled only lightly into her chair was a bad idea.

They were both relieved when Brian Caruso arrived at the table with four plastic glasses filled with tea. Something about the image was wrong, as if he should be holding crystal, but the tattoo on the back of his left hand reminded Faye there were parts to his story that she couldn't tell from the cover.

"Here. Please sit with us while we eat." Brian motioned

his head toward a chair before offering her a glass. Then he stood, carefully watching her. Was he waiting for her to sit down first? Surely not. No one observed such niceties anymore. She should know. As the only full-service restaurant in town these days, the Ace was the choice for date night, family dinners, celebrations… They all happened in her dining room.

When the Majestic's restaurant reopened, some of that pressure would be relieved. She was looking forward to that.

Sarah and Jordan pulled up chairs, so Faye took the seat closest to Gemma and stared out the windows as she listened to small talk about their travel day interspersed with plenty of positive feedback on the Ace High's food. It was gratifying, but not unexpected.

It did force Faye to relax her defensive posture. Even if the atmosphere didn't measure up to his usual fancy surroundings, her food was good.

"Are you the chef, too?" Brian asked as he leaned back in his chair. Faye was interested to note that even the new salad that Gran had insisted on trying had vanished from the to-go container. That empty plate was absolutely worthy of at least four stars out of five.

"No, my grandmother is the chef. She sets the menu and the recipes. I do everything else." Faye sipped her tea and watched as he considered that.

"You manage the front of the house, then. Waitstaff."

"And she runs the cash register and seats everyone and answers all phone calls and argues with suppliers and does payroll and otherwise keeps the joint running," Jordan said as she moved forward to join the conversation. "The Ace High depends on Faye. That means Prospect depends on Faye. We're all hoping Faye's side job consulting will convince her grandmother to keep on the temporary staff."

Faye sighed. Trust Jordan to drag out the dirty laundry a mere thirty minutes after their guests had parked in front of the lodge. “Holly has been promoted to assistant manager and we hired two new waiters.” She wasn’t convinced that any of them would be able to handle her grandmother for long, but she would be close by to referee as necessary, so it would be a good trial period. “I wish I’d had more time to train them, but…”

Brian Caruso’s crooked smile caught her attention. “People like us have a hard time leaving the restaurant, don’t we, Faye? Unless they’ve been on the inside, no one else can understand how the place gets in your blood.”

People like us.

She hadn’t expected him to believe they were anything alike.

Surprise robbed her of words, so Faye returned his smile and realized he might be the most handsome man she’d ever met.

His open expression and warm gaze convinced her he meant every single word. In this room, the two of them understood each other in a way no one else could. The weird flutter in her chest was another shock. It would take some time to adjust to that.

Faye was used to feeling like the different one in town. She hadn’t been born in Prospect and she hadn’t moved here to follow true love. Other people made choices to call the town home, but Faye had been dropped here…and she’d never thought seriously of living anywhere else.

Sharing something with Brian Caruso, even something as small as the restaurant ownership experience, was nice.

Gemma rescued them from awkward silence when she took her first bite of the apple pie. “Whoa.” Her breathless exhalation wasn’t out of the ordinary, but Faye felt the prickle of pride that her desserts could accomplish that.

After all this time, that reaction gave her a boost. The kind she often relied on to get through the busy lunch and dinner hours.

"I don't eat dessert, but with a reaction like that I will make an exception." Everyone at the table turned to watch Brian take his first bite. How his expression changed from curiosity to...

Faye wasn't sure what to label it. Revelation?

As if he'd finally understood the purpose of desserts after a lifetime of doubt?

"Delicious. Is this your grandmother's work, too?" he asked as he took another bite.

When everyone turned back to Faye, she could almost read their minds. There were plenty of people who wanted that recipe. Almost everyone believed Gran was behind all the magic coming from the Ace's kitchen, and Faye liked to keep it that way. Gran's kitchen was her castle, and every bit of praise for the Ace fed her creativity and her love for the place.

Faye was more comfortable with the mistaken assumption than being hounded for recipes or baking advice, so she skirted the question. "All of the desserts at the Ace High are based on Sadie's recipes. She shared them with Gran and with me." And then Faye had supercharged them here and there, much to Sadie's delight. Her additions were top secret, shared only with Sadie Hearst. Now that she was gone, Faye had the only recipe for this particular apple pie in her brain.

"I have heard tale of a doctor here in town who has made it her life's avocation to find and make this pie." Jordan draped an arm over Faye's shoulders. "She has scoured Sadie's cookbooks, testing all the likely suspects, but it eludes her to this day."

Faye shrugged innocently, but the way Brian watched

her convinced Faye that he understood that she knew the secret ingredient. The urge to impress him surprised her.

So did the decision to take some of the credit she deserved for the Ace's success. "I usually bake for the restaurant. Gran is like you. She doesn't do dessert."

Sarah and Jordan exchanged shocked glances, but they both pasted smiles on before the visitors noticed.

Brian sighed as he closed the second empty container. "I may have been converted. Add me to the list of cooks scheming to discover your secret." Their eyes locked over the table, and Faye lost track of how long they sat there frozen.

Eventually Jordan cleared her throat. "We'll pick up this conversation tomorrow when it's light outside, okay? For tonight, let's make sure you both have everything you need." The loud commotion of scooting chairs and clearing the table made it simpler to breathe again.

"Gemma, how old are you?" Jordan asked as she pulled the teenager's arm through the crook of her elbow.

"Sixteen." Gemma brushed loose strands of hair behind her ear, but Faye was happy to see she followed Jordan's lead instead of hanging back for her father.

"You're kidding! Sixteen! Me, too!" Jordan exclaimed.

They were all silent as the confusion on Gemma's face was chased away by amusement. Her happy giggle set everyone back in motion.

"I love hearing that laugh," Brian murmured.

Faye nodded. "Your daughter is adorable."

He inhaled slowly. "She is. I don't get to hear that happiness often enough."

Faye and Brian followed the crowd back into the lobby, but he stopped her with a hand on her arm.

"Thank you for helping make Gemma comfortable. We're both out of our element here and could use a friend."

Faye stared at his hand until he stepped away. "Luckily, Jordan has never met a stranger. You and Gemma will be welcome in Prospect."

He pointed around the lobby. "I expected a 'fishing lodge' to have mounted fish on display. I was afraid my daughter would see something like that and decide to sleep in the car."

Faye frowned as she did a slow circle to survey the lobby. Jordan and Sarah had been working hard on the place, and it was spotless. The dust and cobwebs from years of disuse had been replaced with fresh paint and stain. It was a beautiful space.

Comfortable but timeless and classic, too.

"There are zero taxidermied animals at the Majestic." Faye pursed her lips. "Or at the Ace. In fact, I can't think of a single mounted anything in town."

Brian grimaced. "I sound like a snob, don't I?"

He did, but his concern over that appeared to be genuine, so Faye let it go.

"I'm a city boy. That's all. Neither me nor my daughter have ventured far beyond LA's urban sprawl. She was ready to cancel the whole trip before we pulled out of the driveway, but that was mainly because of the company." Brian covered his chest with his hands. "Getting her here was the first battle. Finding a place like this to stay fills me with hope for the next one." He squeezed her arm. "Thank you for the welcome. I'm open to any other help you'd like to give."

Jolted by that simple touch again, Faye swallowed hard. "Driving in LA's rush hour once gave me nervous hives—I sympathize. Prospect is a friendly place, kinda quiet, and when you get a good view of the scenery, you'll wonder why it took you so long to visit."

Determined to regain some of herself, Faye gestured

at his glossy shoes and crisp pants. "But if you're serious about fitting in, I'd suggest a quick shopping trip through Homestead Market." She held her hands out to show her own jeans and boots. "The finest in small-town couture can be had for a bargain price."

She had a job to do. Someone needed to tell the chef to relax his dress code a bit.

He tilted his head to the side, concern easy to read there. "I'll consider it."

That consideration would clearly take some effort. His standards were high. If he was anything like her grandmother, he wouldn't relax them on a whim.

"At breakfast, we can go over the rounds of competition and discuss the supplies we'll need to bring in." Faye waited for him to agree before she headed for the door.

"I'm going to figure out your secret, Faye. I need that recipe," Brian called out to her.

Faye laughed. The genuine amusement surprised her, but it was the last thing she expected him to say. "You are welcome to try, Chef." She ducked her head to make sure he understood she'd accepted the challenge and then made good on her exit, pleased to have the last word.

As she made the short drive to her grandparents' small farm on the other side of the Rocking A—home of the many Armstrongs—Faye realized she was looking forward to seeing Brian and Gemma Caruso again.

CHAPTER THREE

THE NEXT MORNING, Brian stretched slowly as he stared out the window of his room at the Majestic. If anyone had promised him the best sleep of his life would come in a no-frills fishing lodge, he would have assumed they were up to something. This place was so far outside of his experience that he couldn't have imagined any of it.

Warm sunshine poured through the window that morning. He slipped out of bed and went over to the window. A view of crystal clear lake water sparkling brilliantly caught his attention, and he wasn't able to step away. The furnishings around the place could use some updating, and the bathroom fittings were antiques, but this view would never go out of style.

Neither would crisp sheets or the strange sense that this visit to the Majestic was resetting his life somehow.

As if the place cleared away clutter to make his priorities easy to see.

He moved to the door that adjoined his room to Gemma's and tapped lightly.

"Come in," she answered, so he opened it to find her curled into the chair in front of the window, her chin on one knee as she enjoyed the view of the lake from her window. "I never expected anything like this."

"Yeah. We don't have this at home, do we?" Brian studied her face. Some of the tension around her eyes had disappeared. "Did you sleep well?"

Gemma nodded. "I was afraid I'd be up all night, listening for weird sounds, imagining bears hunting for easy snacks." She rolled her eyes to show him she knew it was silly. "But it was like every piece here was perfect, you know?"

"Yeah." He wanted to add something eloquent, but that wasn't who he was and it didn't matter much, anyway. Both of them were struggling to understand the Majestic's impact. "Sarah and Jordan want to introduce us to the neighbors. They're popular here in Prospect, and the breakfast should be epic."

Gemma wrinkled her nose. "Was that *your* word choice? *Epic?*"

Brian crossed his arms as he tried to remember who had supplied the adjective, himself or Jordan. "Could be. The menu was long and varied. Since I'm only responsible for eating, not cooking, it becomes epic in my head."

Gemma laughed. "Okay, I'll allow it, then. Jeans? This isn't a fancy business meeting, is it?"

Brian replayed his interactions with all the people he'd met in town so far, Faye Parker beginning the slideshow and ending it somehow. "We can trust that Prospect doesn't run on much beyond business casual. Your jeans will be fine." If he'd brought any, he would wear jeans.

Brian had only three settings: gym, work and everything else. For "everything else," he preferred a classic style. Silk. Leather. Wool. He never had to worry about being judged by his clothing now because it was the best of the best.

Unless he was the only one dressed for the boardroom in a room filled with people ready for the barn.

He'd told himself before falling asleep the night before that he'd filter any snobbish comments from now on before they escaped his mouth. He was almost certain that his feelings about jeans counted, and it was a good thing that he'd kept silent.

Besides, he was in Prospect to try new things. Spending time in jeans would be an easy experiment.

"Later, when we go into town, can you help me pick out a couple of pairs?" he asked Gemma. Her shocked expression made him reconsider the request.

"Jeans? You? Here?" Her mouth dropped open.

He blinked in the face of her genuine disbelief overlaid with teenage attitude. "Yes." Even if the kid's confusion was valid, Brian wasn't sure he deserved the hard time.

Then he realized she was wearing one of his old T-shirts she'd commandeered at some point and sweatpants, so she might have an edge on him in terms of wearing what was comfortable, too.

She slowly stood and pinched at his silk pajamas. "Not sure they'll carry your brands, Dad."

"Even better." He grasped her hand. "When in Prospect, we're going to try Prospect things. Right? I'll start us off by buying jeans. When someone offers you a chance to try something new, you'll take them up on it. How's that?" Making her mother promise to come to her rescue if she called was near the top of Brian's list of things to worry about. He hoped if he made this agreement with Gemma, she'd be more open to this journey.

Gemma bit her bottom lip as she evaluated his offer. "Fine. But I need to see you wearing the jeans out in public or I will consider you in violation of the terms of our agreement."

Surprised and amused, Brian said, "Okay, counsel, I intend to make good on this negotiation. And I'm going to start researching the finest law schools because you've got natural talent."

She shrugged, a light blush tingeing her cheeks. "I don't know about that."

Seeing this uncertainty in her twisted the knife of regret in his gut. If she'd had a better father in the early days, Gemma might not be so uncertain of her place in the world. "Gem, you're smart. You can do anything you set your mind to. If it's not law, fine, but don't accept any limits on your dreams."

She met his stare and gave him a quick, awkward nod.

"Get dressed and come help me find something to wear." Brian turned to go to his room but stopped. "I don't talk a lot about how I grew up, but we didn't have money for much. Certainly not nice clothing, so maybe I've gone too far in the other direction." He glanced down at the silk pajamas he was wearing and crossed out the "maybe" in his statement. The Majestic was a hundred percent cotton kind of atmosphere.

Gemma said, "I get it, Dad. I like to fit in, too. Here, that means something different than at Rinnovato. This is easy to fix."

She was absolutely correct. His daughter kept him off-balance, the blooming maturity mixed in with the shy girl, but the common thread all the way through was her intelligence. Gemma was always smart.

Then she pointed at the framed painting hanging next to the window. It was a fall scene, with brilliant red and gold trees surrounding the lake outside the window. "It's signed 'Hearst.' Do you think Jordan painted it?"

Brian stepped closer to study the signature as he considered how easily Jordan Hearst had made a new friend the evening before. "Could be Sadie or Sarah." Or any of a whole slew of Hearst relatives, honestly. "We'll have to find out."

"I like it." Her distracted tone as she studied the artwork

was familiar. When his daughter was deep in thought, everything else faded.

Brian retreated to stand in front of his closet, but he didn't make much progress until Gemma joined him there. They agreed he should pick the "most comfortable of everything" that he'd packed. When they met the Hearst sisters in the lobby, he was relieved at how Gemma immediately followed Jordan outside.

"Jordan is intense," Sarah said as she stepped out onto the pathway to the parking lot. "People generally love her or hate with nothing in between, but she's great with kids." She sighed. "That might be because she's an adult teenager herself."

"It's working for Gemma, so I'm in the 'love' camp already. Bringing my daughter was a gamble, necessitated by her mother's delayed honeymoon to Mexico. Whatever you and Jordan and Faye can do to help my daughter blend into these new surroundings, I will be grateful."

Whatever Sarah would have said was lost as Jordan called out to them, "Gemma wants to ride over to the Rocking A on the side-by-side. You guys meet us there?"

Brian glanced at Sarah. "What's a side-by-side?"

She pointed at the little…cart that Gemma was sliding into? He watched her put a helmet on and wondered how Jordan had worked this magic. Talk about trying new things.

"It's a kind of all-terrain vehicle. Useful on the ranch and if you're afraid of horses, as Jordan is, it's nice to have here. Are you okay with this? If not, I can still stop them." Sarah moved forward as if she intended to do that, but Gemma's grin convinced him she was already making good on their negotiated agreement.

"I'll let Gemma decide and since she's strapped in…"

Brian let the words trail off because he wasn't convinced it was the right decision.

Sarah nodded firmly and cupped her hands around her mouth to yell over the rumble of the engine, "Jordan, you remember you have precious cargo. Gemma better arrive in one piece. If we have to call Keena to put her back together, I will revoke your driving privileges."

Jordan returned a sunny smile and wave. Brian muttered a quick, short prayer that Jordan followed her sister's directions. They watched Jordan give the side-by-side some gas and circle the parking lot with a loud whoop, Gemma's giggles trailing behind.

"They'll be fine." Sarah patted his arm. "And Keena is the best at her job. She's our new doctor in town, and she's probably already over at the Rocking A, waiting for breakfast to be served. She's another Armstrong by association."

Brian inhaled slowly as he settled into the SUV's passenger seat next to Sarah but he didn't relax until they were stopped in front of a sprawling ranch house and Jordan and Gemma were headed toward them at what appeared to be a steady, safe pace.

Sarah paused on the first step up to the porch that lined the front of the sprawling house. "Not sure how many Armstrongs will be inside, but it'll be a crowd. Prue and Walt have five sons. They were adopted after they fostered here at the Rocking A. You've met Clay, Wes and Grant. Travis is fostering a new generation, so this breakfast crowd might include Damon and Micah. And then there's Matt Armstrong, Prospect's veterinarian. You never know when he'll pop in."

Brian wondered how his shy daughter was going to handle that large group of strangers, but he watched as Gemma tugged her helmet off and laughed at whatever Jordan was saying. He hoped Gemma having a friend would ease her way.

Sarah squeezed his arm to get his attention. "The thing you need to know about the Armstrongs is that you're already family to them. Prue disliked me at first, thanks to my Hearst connection and how Sadie left Prospect, but now she's the mother I've been missing for so long. I would be shocked if you somehow make it out of Prospect without a new Christmas card contact at the very least."

He nodded. "That description reminds me of your great-aunt. Sadie took a special interest in my life, and I'll never be the same because of it. Those people are one in a million."

Sarah's slow smile pleased him. "I love to hear stories about Sadie."

Brian glanced down at the grass on his shoes, and then at the barn and horses moving around the nearby fenced area. "She might be the only person in the world who could have brought me here."

Sarah nodded. "I know exactly what you mean." Then she motioned him to follow her, and Gemma and Jordan joined them on the porch. They all walked in together and were met with the first crowd in a large, open living room. Comfortable sofas and chairs were filled with the cowboys he'd met the night before, plus a couple of others who must be Travis and Matt, and two boys. They made introductions. Wes said, "We've been banished to the overflow section. Mom and Dad have reserved places for the guests of honor and important Hearsts at the kitchen table."

Grant held up a biscuit. "But we did get first dibs on all the good stuff."

Gemma had returned to her close shadowing, standing inches away from him, so he was relieved when Jordan led them on to the kitchen and the gathering was much smaller.

And it included Faye. The thrill of seeing her there caught him off guard.

"Come in, come in, I've held off the starving crowd as long as I could. Let's make your plates before we settle at the table. You must be Gemma. Call me Prue. Everyone does." The older woman stirring something on the stove waved her hand to draw Gemma closer. "Young ladies always go first at the Rocking A. Tell me, how do you feel about the whole 'bacon versus sausage' dilemma?"

Gemma glanced over her shoulder at him before turning back. "There's room for both at the table."

Prue pursed her lips as the older man at her side clapped his hands. "I declare, we got a sharp shooter in our presence. No sense in choosin' only one, is there, Gemma? I like you. Call me Walt."

Brian forced his shoulders to relax as the couple made sure Gemma's breakfast plate was full.

"Faye. Brian. You're next. Get what you want because I can't make any guarantees there'll be seconds. The size of the crowds around here still catches me by surprise sometimes." Prue waved them forward, so he joined Faye.

"No breakfast at the Ace High?" he asked as they took turns at the stove.

"No, the chef doesn't enjoy cooking eggs and bacon, so..." Faye shrugged before smiling up at him. "I generally do the baking in the mornings. It works out. Today is the first day where I...am not reporting to the restaurant. At all. I am working as a consultant and my new staff will carry on without me."

Brian winced in sympathy. He could hear the deep worry in her voice. Faye repeated the words as if she'd been reminded that everything would be fine in her absence. Meaning she wasn't necessary. "Oh, I know that emotion, Faye. The first days are tough. Maybe I can keep you busy enough that you'll forget about people messing up without you there to watch."

She grimaced. "I hate it. I've worked so hard to get that place running smoothly. No one knows it like I do."

"Yeah." He nodded. "That feeling…"

"It gets better?" she asked uncertainly.

"I hope so," Brian said, "but it never goes away in my experience."

She exhaled loudly. "Stay busy. Any other words of wisdom?"

Brian grinned at her as he realized he'd spent zero time concerned about Rinnovato's dinner service the evening before, the bank deposit, or whether Belvie was getting along with Robbie since he'd been given another chance.

Even more important than that, he was enjoying the break.

Having someone to commiserate with helped him relax, and watching Gemma take her first ride requiring a helmet had been important.

"Try something new." Brian watched Faye's serious expression as she absorbed his advice. "And definitely try the bacon. It's crispy."

He offered her a piece and watched her take a bite. She chewed and shook a finger at him. "This is good advice. When we first met, I was concerned about how well you would fit in around here, but I have many things to learn from you, Chef."

He followed Faye to the crowded table and realized he was excited to find out what he and Faye could teach each other.

"All right, Chef, it's not fancy but it is good," Prue said, as she slid into the chair next to him. "Tell me how you got roped into this cooking competition over at the Majestic." She passed the jam to Gemma without taking her eyes off him, and he realized that Sarah's promise about the Armstrongs making everyone feel like family also included his daughter.

Brian sipped the fresh, pulpy orange juice and smacked his lips before he realized what he was doing.

Prue's delighted laugh sent a flush of embarrassment over his cheeks.

"Around here, that's Walt's tried-and-true version of 'my compliments to the chef,'" Prue said with a sparkle in her eyes. "Are you a man of few words, too?"

Brian cleared his throat and met Gemma's stare across the table. His daughter was giggling.

"My mother taught me better manners, but I have been known to lose them." Brian slipped his napkin into his lap and decided he needed to move on, demonstrate he knew how to act politely in public. "Sadie Hearst was the most important mentor in my life. I met her when she marched up to my food truck and demanded to know why there were so many people lined up in front of it. And for whatever reason, she sort of...adopted me." Brian glanced at Sarah and Jordan. It was important that they understood how much Sadie had done for him. "She kept coming back. She urged me to dream about an actual restaurant, what I would serve, what kind of atmosphere it would have, and when I knew the answers to that, she helped me find the loans and the people I needed to make it all come true. Serving her my mother's cacio e pepe whenever she dropped in was not enough to express what she meant to me, so when Michael Hearst pitched this idea of running a contest to find a chef to lead the lodge's restaurant for a year..." Brian shrugged. There was no sense in revealing how long he'd waited to answer Michael because he had been trying to find a gracious excuse to help...from LA, not Prospect. "How could I say no?"

Prue and Faye narrowed their eyes and convinced him that they were somehow able to read between the lines, but neither pressed for more details. Prue nodded. "Having the Majestic reopening is one of those dreams I never let myself have. Sadie closed the place when she moved to LA, and without the family around, it was hard to see how we could ever get it back to what it once was. But here we are, a couple of months away from the biggest weekend the town has, and the Majestic is poised to help bring it back to life. Pretty sure everyone at this table owes a debt, large or small, to Sadie."

Brian considered that while conversation flowed around him. Jordan, Sarah and Prue managed to draw Gemma into a discussion about her school and what kind of subjects she enjoyed.

"I like literature and algebra, but my favorite class is Art," Gemma said while she fiddled with her fork. "The paintings in the lodge… Who is the artist?"

"Do you like them?" Sarah asked. "Our father painted those. He's going to be teaching classes in Prospect."

"I do like them." Gemma brushed hair out of her face. "Maybe, if there's time, I could take a class before we leave."

"Done!" Jordan waved a biscuit in the air as she added, "But please ignore whatever horror stories he tells you about teaching his daughters to paint."

Sarah grimaced. "Every single scary tale is true, Gemma. We're awful, but he's going to love meeting you."

"Gemma's the best artist in her school," Brian said. He loved the way his daughter was opening up around these new acquaintances.

Jordan whistled. "Oh, boy, Dad won't know what to do if he gets to work with someone with actual talent."

Gemma shifted in her seat.

He couldn't tell if she was proud or embarrassed that he'd called out her accomplishments. He'd missed so many things, but he was proud of all her wins, big and small.

"I won Best in Show at my school's art exhibition." Gemma shook her head as if it wasn't all that impressive, but Prue immediately squeezed her arm.

"Congratulations! I bet you have a real eye for color. While you're here in town, I'd love to have some help in my shop. With Western Days looming, I'm scrambling to get all the quilts ready for display and my precut inventory stocked up."

Gemma nodded her acceptance, and he was happy to see the enthusiasm in her eyes.

Brian enjoyed every bit of the epic breakfast. The easy banter made him realize this group was giving him the same feeling Sadie always had. He was included, accepted and welcome.

Having Sadie in common with the people gathered around the table was all he needed to fit in. They'd taken to him and his daughter and vice versa.

Even if his clothes were too fancy and he'd been known to say the wrong thing.

He'd spent a long time fighting forward, working hard for each step.

Sadie Hearst had opened this door for him, too, and he was going to gratefully step through it. It was nice to find something not such a challenge for once.

When Jordan cleared her throat, Faye bumped his arm with her elbow. "Uh-oh, someone's decided it's time to get to work."

Brian smiled at her. "I'm ready. Are you?"

"We would have started the minute we sat down if I was in charge." She wrinkled her nose. "I'm trying to go with the flow here. I don't know how to do that or what to expect."

"I'm so glad you asked," Jordan said loudly as she handed out files. "Michael has sent outlines of the three competition rounds he'd like us to tape. The small production crew is coming tonight. We'll work on setting up the first competition in the kitchen in two days. Sarah, as the Hearst with the most polished speaking ability, will be hosting. Brian, Faye and I are judges."

When Faye stiffened at his side, he bent to whisper, "Didn't know that was part of your consulting?"

Faye cut him a glance. "No, there was no mention of screen time."

"Is this part of the flow?" He grinned as she rolled her eyes.

"Walt and Prue will be helping with transportation because the crew is going to move around Prospect to get random footage as well. Walt will lead a trail ride," Jordan explained before nodding at Prue, "or delegate it to a trusted representative."

Brian watched Prue and Walt exchange stares.

Then Faye leaned over. "They're divorced, but they're more on than off lately."

"You ain't giving me permission to show off my ranch to our visitors, Prue?" Walt raised an eyebrow.

Prue rested her elbows on the table and kept her eyes glued to her ex. "You giving me permission to give you permission these days, cowboy?"

Sarah and Jordan immediately ducked their heads, focusing intently on the scene outline, which was funny, but Brian knew it was a mistake to laugh. Eventually, a slow smile appeared on Walt's lips. "Well, now, I suppose I am. What would you say to that?"

The blush in her cheeks made the sparkle in Prue's eyes

brighter. "Lend me a hand with cleaning up these dishes so we can talk over all these transportation plans."

When the older couple moved to the kitchen sink, Jordan shook her head. "Worse than teenagers with the flirting lately. They should get marriage number two started already."

"We can hear you," Prue said sweetly.

"And we can't possibly meet at the altar until we get our sons all hitched." Walt tossed a dry dish towel over his shoulder. "Might be happening quicker than I imagined, what with all the pairing up that's happened lately."

Sarah and Jordan were having a whispered argument when Faye moved closer to say, "Four out of the five Armstrongs are so deep in love that there's an unofficial betting pool in town on who will get married first, who will get married last and who's running off to Vegas to elope. That's the one with the biggest payout."

"Are Walt and Prue included in the betting?" Brian asked. "Either for putting money down or being in the running?" From his spot at the table, it sounded like the sisters were arguing about which one of them was going to be the first to head down the aisle.

Faye's grin blossomed. "Yes. Both. Doesn't quite seem fair, does it?"

He laughed as Sarah loudly whispered, "You always make me go first." Then she cleared her throat. "Enough talk about something that may or may not ever happen."

"Oh, please, it will happen. You all need to find a preacher that offers a bulk discount on wedding ceremonies." Faye chuckled when she spotted how Gemma giggled at that.

"Today," Sarah said loudly, evidently trying to get the meeting back on track, "Faye and Brian are to start stocking the lodge's pantry with the basics. It'll mean a trip into town. Your two chef contestants have provided a list of ingredients they'd like to have on hand. Faye's got that."

Faye nodded. "I've ordered from my suppliers, so some things will be here Monday. Then, we may need to reassess the plans for the other two rounds of competition."

Everyone turned toward him. "I agree." He realized that sounded hesitant when Jordan and Sarah exchanged a worried glance. "I like the outline. We may need to discuss wardrobe. Chef coat work for me?"

Sarah studied him closely. "For the judging, yes, but when we get you out on the horses, you're going to want something more..."

"Or maybe it's less..." Jordan tilted her head to the side.

Brian waited for Gemma to chime in with her opinion but she smiled angelically.

"Authentic. We can pick that up at Homestead Market, too." Faye squeezed his hand. "I am the consultant, after all."

"Good. Good. I've had conversations with the producer-slash-director, Andre, and he is going to have firm opinions on what we're wearing, saying and doing, so let's all be flexible." Sarah nodded as she returned to scanning her list. "We have our orders for today. We will regroup tomorrow morning. Prue is on deck to provide breakfast for the crew from our apartment kitchen in the lodge. It's going to be a tight fit, but this will be fun."

"Gemma, I was wondering...would you like to be my assistant this week?" Jordan asked. "When you aren't toiling away at the quilt shop, obviously. I've never had an assistant, but I bet I'll be good at bossing one around. I don't know what we'll do, but we'll be riding around in the side-by-side quite a bit."

Gemma nodded immediately. "On one condition..."

Jordan bent forward. "A condition. I'm intrigued. If it's

a fair wage, I'm afraid you've misunderstood the depth of the budget, but go on..."

Gemma held up two fingers. "First, I want to drive the side-by-side before I go home." She looked at him, so Brian shrugged. He wasn't sure he would be able to stop her, so he might as well go with it.

"Done. A woman of my power and position definitely needs a driver," Jordan said. "Second?"

"Faye has to teach me how to make the apple pie."

When Faye's mouth dropped open in surprise, he said, "It's either law school or a bail fund. I don't know whether you will use your powers for good or bad yet, but I'm going to be ready either way."

Faye sighed. "If I say yes, I will be entrusting you with my most closely guarded secret. If I say no, Jordan will never let me hear the end of it. Not ever. I'll be eighty-nine years old and Jordan will bring up this day at every opportunity."

Brian watched Jordan consider that and nod as if it was a fair comment.

"Better be yes, then." Faye's beautiful smile as Gemma did a victory dance and smacked the hands of everyone in the kitchen in a loud high five filled Brian with...something—a warm bubbly glow that forced his lips to curl in a goofy grin.

In the space of one day, the women at this table had changed his mind about this trip.

Instead of a mistake, it might be the best decision he'd ever made.

CHAPTER FOUR

BEFORE HIS ARRIVAL, Faye had imagined how difficult it would be to work with a hotshot chef who was leaving the lofty heights of LA's restaurant scene to bless Prospect with his presence and good taste. If there was anything of this imaginary hotshot who would snap orders while he stared down his nose at her, Faye couldn't find it. If Brian Caruso believed the rave reviews of his food, he'd managed to maintain a level head. At breakfast, he'd been friendly, encouraging even, with his tips on surviving time away from the Ace.

The way he'd checked in on his daughter and made sure to brag about her accomplishments was sweet.

Right now, his body language in the passenger seat of her SUV shouted uncomfortable.

Both arms were tightly crossed over his chest, pulling his fine-knit sweater tight to outline biceps that were much better developed than Faye had anticipated.

His feet were braced against the floor, and he'd stared out the passenger-side window for the whole trip into town.

"Is it my driving or is this your first time shopping in a small-town grocery store, Chef?" Faye asked as she pulled her key from the ignition.

Brian slowly turned his head and seemed to relax a fraction. Then he smiled at her, reigniting the slow-melting sensation inside that she'd convinced herself was a fluke. "Neither. Too much in my head. Sorry."

At his answer, Faye was knocked off-track again. Since she spent a lot of time and energy on things that only happened in her head, she understood him perfectly. "Can I help with whatever you are working out?"

His eyebrows shot up. "Just like that? You want to help a stranger?"

Covering her heart with her hand, she answered, "I'm a professional, experienced consultant."

His head tilted back. "Ah, part of the job description." Then he squeezed her hand where it rested on the console between them. "But I don't believe it. You just help. Whoever, whenever, you see the need to pitch in."

Off-kilter that he'd pegged her so neatly and with so little experience, Faye frowned. "Maybe, but I would always much rather be doing something, keeping busy, than waiting or worrying or any of the things that happen when I need a solution and can't find it. Running a restaurant is good for people like us, because there's always a crisis and we can be busy instead of..." Faye wasn't sure what to call those times when there was nothing left to do but think. "We aren't stuck if we're moving."

Brian unbuckled his seat belt as he considered that. "Yeah. I get that. I've spent my whole life making decisions, choosing when to move and how to move. Messing up and cleaning up." He smiled slowly. "Coming here, though, I'm out of my depth. All those decisions I make are happening back in LA without me, and here, I'm following instructions. And Gemma... I'm starting to get my hopes up that this trip could change things between us. I go back and forth between imagining how great that could be and warning myself not to get too invested in that. That will hurt if I'm wrong."

Faye wanted to ask questions but Brian opened the door and slid out of the SUV before she could formulate the first one. The parking lot of Prospect's Homestead Market might not be the best place for deep conversation. She quickly moved to catch up.

"Livery," Brian read as they walked toward the sliding glass doors into Prospect's version of a big-box grocery-and-everything-else store. "Horses, right?"

"Yep. The town has maintained the facades of the original buildings in this section of Prospect, but new businesses have taken over the spaces. Like my restaurant, the Ace High. It was once the most expensive saloon in Prospect, serving only the finest liquor to silver miners, gamblers and everyone in between. Prue and Walt have converted the Mercantile into a hardware store on one side, and a quilt and craft shop on the other. Tourists love the atmosphere." Faye pulled a shopping cart from the corral. "And if you want to know any more about the history of the buildings, talk to Clay Armstrong."

Brian shook his head. "Architectural history isn't my thing. Or history in general. Pretty much any subject they taught in school is not my area of interest." He brushed her hands off the cart. "I like produce. Dairy. Things of that nature."

Faye snorted a laugh as she followed him and tried to figure out what to do with her hands. She always pushed the shopping cart around the grocery store. Without it, she was unmoored. "Not a great student, huh?"

"My mother says I never applied myself." Brian shrugged. "Might be some truth to that. When I see Gemma's report cards from her private academy, I wonder if smarts can skip a generation. They make her Nonna proud." He studied the layout of the store. "I like grocery stores. They always follow a pattern." Then he headed directly for the vegetables.

Faye pulled out her phone for the list of ingredients

they'd need as they navigated the bins and shelves. She realized he'd practically memorized the items at Prue's kitchen table.

"What do you think, russets and yellow potatoes?" he asked. Since he put them in the cart before she answered, Faye wondered if he was thinking out loud, but before he moved on, he turned to check, one finger pointed at the bags for confirmation, so she nodded.

When she realized she was seeing a man in his element, Faye hung back and watched him. Nothing was automatic. He touched, smelled, studied everything this way and that to make sure it met his standards. He focused on the details.

"Are you judging me? Why do I feel like you are judging me?" Brian grinned at her as he took one of the large melons out of the cart and replaced it with another. "By now, Gemma would have asked for the keys so she could go sit in the car and wait."

Faye shook her head. "Gemma hasn't had the training I've had. You and Gran will either be the best of friends, two peas in the pod together or bitter enemies."

"Introduce me sometime. I don't have enough friends or enemies." He waggled his eyebrows at her. "We've got everything on the list, right?"

Faye sighed as she scanned it one more time. "Yep. How did you do it? Memorize the whole thing?"

He shrugged. "Not sure. It's just a thing I can do." Then he frowned. "Grab some jeans and shirts and go?"

There had been a definite pep in his step as they'd cruised the grocery aisles, but it seemed to be fading at the thought of crossing over into clothes. That didn't fit with his image. Shouldn't a man who invested that much in his wardrobe enjoy shopping?

"Dreading having to touch flannel and denim?" Faye asked as she took the lead into the men's section.

"Nah, getting that fish-out-of-water feeling again. You take control, and it will all be fine." He motioned her forward.

Faye realized he hated the unknown, the uncertainty. She understood that, and this was her time to consult. "Okay, we don't need to spend a lot of time, since we've got the groceries waiting. I'll grab some jeans and shirts and bring them to you in the dressing room. How's that?" If she had his sizes, she could come back and take her time later.

The personal nature of shopping for a man's clothing struck her, but she was a good consultant. She could do this.

"I think… I'm gonna roll with it." He stopped at the jeans and grabbed four pairs, all the same size. "Toss some shirts in the cart. Large. I like dark colors. Then we can check out."

Faye didn't realize her confusion showed on her face until he stopped. "What? That's not a good plan?"

"What if nothing fits when you get home?" Faye asked.

Then he was confused. "Why wouldn't anything fit?" He went to a rack of plaid button-downs and flipped through until he found one that was navy with red and yellow threads. "Like this?" He held it up against his chest, stretched his arms out to test the sleeve length, and raised an eyebrow.

Faye nodded. The colors were good for him. He tossed it in the cart.

After he repeated the process three more times, adding two flannels and a chambray button-down, he raised his head to stare over the tops of the aisles framing the clothing section. "Shoes? I'm assuming they sell those here, too. Loafers aren't going to work with my new wardrobe."

Faye knew she was bemused as she pushed the cart behind him down the wide main aisle to the shoe section. He pulled a pair of hiking boots off the shelf, slipped his foot in, paced up and down, took it off and put the box on top of his shirts.

"That should do it." Brian brushed her hands off the cart again and led the way to the checkout. After they had loaded everything in the SUV and returned the cart to the store, Faye started the car. They were on the road, heading out of town, when he said, "You've had this adorable frown on your face, the faintest line of consternation on your forehead for a while now. What's going on in there?"

Adorable? Her? Had anyone ever thought that before? No one had ever said it, she was certain.

"You're sure all those clothes will fit? How?" she asked.

"Waist measurement and inseam for the pants. Mine haven't changed in a long time. Easy to remember. Shirts?" He shrugged. "A little loose or a lot loose—either way, it works."

Faye nodded. When he put it like that, it did seem simple.

"What did you expect?" he asked.

"Based on what you're wearing," Faye said slowly, "and how thoroughly you made your other choices, I thought you'd be..." How could she say "demanding" or "picky" without actually going there?

"Fussy?" he filled in for her. "With ingredients, yes. Clothes, no." He sighed. "I'm comfortable in the chef coat. Everything else is chosen to present an image. Growing up, I lived in hand-me-downs and thrift store finds. Being successful always seemed to rest partly on looking the part. Now that I can afford to, I try to do that."

Faye realized that as much as she understood him and how he felt about his restaurant, they were coming from completely different places. Growing up in Prospect had never given her much chance to decide how people viewed her. They'd known her for most of her life. Wardrobe choices wouldn't change their perception. There were pros and cons to that.

The better she understood Brian, the clearer her own misguided assumptions about him became.

Expensively dressed outsider rolled into town past closing time and her first reaction was to assume that he had a superior attitude.

What she was learning was that Brian asked for very little because that was what he expected. He was prepared to fit himself into a space however he could.

Did he not understand his new status?

TV chefs could make their own spots any way they chose, couldn't they?

As she pulled up to the Majestic, she realized the opportunity she might have missed if Prue hadn't commandeered her assistance for Sarah and Jordan while Brian and his daughter were in town. Instead of juggling the thousands of details for lunch and dinner service at the Ace, something she could do in her sleep, she was learning a valuable lesson from this chef.

What else would she discover in their time together?

She'd parked at the restaurant entrance and now met him at the back of the SUV, where he had both arms laden with bags. "You can make more than one trip, Chef." Her lips twitched as he barely managed to walk, carrying half a grocery store in his hands.

He paused and met her amused stare before glancing down at the load in his arms. "I tend to do too much. I like a challenge. You'll get used to it." His grin sent that sizzle through her midsection again before he maneuvered the door open and stepped inside.

Faye exhaled slowly, then she gathered up a perfectly reasonable number of bags to carry. When she met him at the doorway, her mouth dried up. He stood there, one arm extended to hold the door open for her. As she slipped past him, making sure she didn't brush up against him, their eyes locked. This close, she could see green flecks in his dark irises.

Which was knowledge she could have done without.

"I won that round." His voice was husky, close to her ear.

"I didn't know we were competing." Faye cleared her throat. The croak she'd made was embarrassing. She couldn't move away from him.

"Hey, did we get here in time to miss all the hard work?" Jordan called from the kitchen, snapping the thread that had wrapped around Brian and Faye.

Faye huffed out a breath. "There are a few bags left."

Jordan moved to follow Brian out to the car but she paused as she passed Faye. "Was that what I thought it was?"

Faye closed her eyes before scowling at Jordan. "Yes, it was work. You know what that looks like."

"I do. That was something else." Jordan's smirk would have been funny if it had been aimed at anyone else.

"Romance on the brain around here," Faye mumbled to herself as she marched toward the restaurant kitchen, shaking her head as she went. The last thing she needed was anyone matchmaking. If Prue Armstrong got a whiff of a possible attraction going on, she and Brian Caruso wouldn't stand a chance.

Unfortunately, Jordan had good vision and a tendency to tell everything she knew.

Unless Faye did a better job of keeping a professional demeanor, the chef would be fighting to remain a bachelor.

And while the idea of falling head over boots was interesting in a theoretical way, Faye was certain she was meant for a different man and a different life than Brian Caruso. Remembering that while they worked together was her only hope of keeping her heart in one piece when he returned to LA.

CHAPTER FIVE

BRIAN WATCHED AS Faye finished scrubbing the stainless steel counters in the modest commercial kitchen that would be their studio for taping this competition. Two chefs could cook here comfortably, but he wasn't sure how much space the crew would take up. It was a good kitchen. With some updating, whoever took over would have a comfortable place to serve good food.

If he'd been presented the opportunity to build this kitchen and this restaurant from scratch, there were a few things he'd change. Upgrading the walk-in freezer would have been the first thing on that list, and the table linens would be replaced with something that had a more modern style.

Every now and then, the vanilla that seemed to waft through the air reminded him that this had been Sadie's home. He understood that Sarah and Jordan were doing everything they could to keep her there.

So the linens could stay.

Even Sadie would have agreed about the freezer, though.

It didn't make any sense to consider what changes he'd make to the Majestic's restaurant. When the contest was decided, he'd sit down with that chef and plan a tight menu with three or four solid entrées to make the restaurant a standout.

Then he and Gemma would explore the town, and they'd return to LA where they could discuss their adventure and share the experience, like an inside joke only the two of them would understand.

The melancholy that hit when he imagined how the Majestic would go on without them caught him off guard. He emptied the last bag of potatoes into the bins.

"Someone on the crew could have wiped those counters, you know," Brian said as he finished arranging the last of the pantry staples. "Or even the chefs when they arrive. Both Rafa and Franky will want to inspect the kitchen to make sure it's up to their standards." They better do that before they opened up their knife bags. He'd taught them the pitfalls of trusting anyone else to set up their kitchen. Food safety came first, before creativity, before experimentation, before any service started.

That was his mother's influence.

"It's a habit. After I bring groceries into the Ace High, I scrub everything down, just in case. My grandmother would have a fit if I did anything differently here." Faye smiled over her shoulder at him. "Even when she's not around, I hear her voice in my head, you know?"

Brian nodded even though Faye couldn't see it. He definitely understood. "My mother would count to thirty while I washed my hands before I could pick up a knife. I can still hear it today." He ran through his mental to-do list. "We're in good shape for the meeting with the production crew."

"Yeah," Faye said as she rested against the counter. "I should go check to make sure Prue has everything she needs to cater breakfast and lunch for the next couple of days." But she didn't move.

He hadn't been ready to say goodbye yet, either, so he moved over to study the long line of cookbooks on the counter. "Are these all of Sadie's cookbooks? I didn't realize there were so many."

Faye moved to stand next to him and pulled one out.

"This was the first. Sadie wrote this while she was still filming the public access show here in Prospect. She told me that she tested every recipe at least ten times." She smiled at him. "And that everyone in Prospect was sick of seeing her coming with plastic baggies of her latest creations."

"Did you get to spend a lot of time with her?" He was curious.

"When I was young. You haven't met my grandmother yet, but she's…exacting. She has high standards for her kitchen. She also doesn't do desserts, like you." Faye rolled her eyes. "It's weird. You're both missing out on one of the big joys in life, I'll have you know. Sadie? She was meant to teach beginners like me. My grandmother would get so hung up on the way I chopped potatoes incorrectly that there was a good chance the dish never got made."

"In her defense," Brian said, "that's a safety issue, especially for a young girl, so I can understand why…" He held up his hands in surrender when Faye's expression turned mean. "Go ahead with your story."

She sniffed to show her disapproval. "Sadie knew enough to do the dangerous stuff herself. She could teach by making things accessible for me the way I was. See? We made cookies and cakes and pies. There was music playing. If I spilled flour on the floor, Sadie would clean it quickly without making a learning experience out of it. She wanted to teach me to love the art of baking first."

Brian watched her run a finger down the table of contents as he considered that.

"She did the same thing when she was getting me ready to open my restaurant. We built this dreamlike vision of what it could be, then broke it down into nuts and bolts."

"'Because you can't get anywhere until you know where you're going.'" Faye's smile broadened. "Sadie always had the best sayings, at least one for every occasion. She would say that when she told me to pick out a recipe that we could make together. I wanted to learn, but I didn't know what I didn't know. Didn't matter. She'd hand me a book and tell me to choose. She gave me several of her cookbooks and marked them up with special notes, doodles in the margins, funny horses, things like that."

He watched her smile slowly fade. "Talking about Sadie always reminds me of how much I miss her, too."

She nodded. "It's amazing what she accomplished. Books, TV shows, appliances, Western wear… I don't even know all the things she managed to sell as the Cookie Queen, but then you hear all these stories about individual lives she touched." She shrugged. "I was ready to adopt all three of her nieces as the sisters I never had because Sadie loved them so."

Then she tilted her head to the side. "I guess that makes you my brother?"

He studied her beautiful face before he met her stare. "Nope. Not a brother."

How long did they stand there before his phone chirped to let him know Gemma had sent a text?

He wasn't sure, but Faye's eyes were blue and darkened toward the iris. Her scent was floral but crisp, not overpowering.

And she held her breath, no doubt realizing how close he was to pressing his lips to hers.

When the text came in, the sound cut through that tension and he stepped back.

When you're all done, pick me up at the Mercantile in town.

Brian read the message from his daughter twice while he tried to understand how he'd been a second away from kissing Faye. And was he relieved or disappointed the moment was over?

None of the answers were coming, but the phone chirped again.

Please. And thank you.

He chuckled at his daughter remembering her manners in real time.

"Everything okay?" Faye asked. She was back to wiping down the spotless counters.

Almost as if she needed to stay busy.

Was she as confused by their near kiss as he was?

"Yeah, Gemma was giving me my next task—pick her up in town." He sighed. "Sometimes, she's one hundred percent teenager all the way through. A little sarcastic, older than her years, and all that. Other times, she's the painfully polite stranger who would rather not ask a soul for a favor."

He offered Faye his phone so she could read Gemma's texts. Her amusement settled some of the worry in his gut. They'd worked together well all day long.

And there'd been no kiss to possibly change that. The tension between them could be forgotten.

Except this was the second time in only a few hours that they'd stood at the crossroads of...something.

"She has good manners, Dad. You should be proud of that." Faye put her phone number in his phone. "In case you think of anything else we need to stock before taping starts." Then she texted herself so she had his number.

"Smart." And efficient. That was no surprise. "I'm always proud of Gemma. Always. Monica, her mom, has given her everything she needs to be safe and curious. She cares about people, too. I've been working for a long time to build a relationship with her. A meaningful one. I don't even mind running into a snarky teen now and then."

"Pretty sure I was lucky to survive my smart-aleck teenage phase." Faye crossed her arms over her chest. "Be careful what you wish for."

"Absolutely. Her mother always tells me to look at how far we've come instead of how much further I have to go to make up for lost time." There was no way to get that back, anyway.

Faye opened her mouth to ask the question he could see brewing in her eyes, but she stopped instead.

A faint whiff of vanilla had replaced the soapy smell of Faye's cleaner and her own floral scent. "Do you smell vanilla?" He opened the pantry to make sure the expensive bottle of vanilla extract hadn't broken or spilled.

"I do." Faye grinned brightly, wrapped her arm around his and urged him toward the exit. "Why don't you ask Sarah and Jordan about that vanilla, okay?"

Confused, Brian glanced back at the kitchen doors before Faye shut off the lights and tugged him into the dining room. Brian dug his heels in to stop her determined progress. "Is there something I need to know about the kitchen?"

Faye's lips were a tight line as she shook her head. "Nope."

Brian felt certain he could get her to spill the secret. How bad could it be?

"Okay, if you won't tell me the secret you're hiding, what were you about to say before you changed your mind?" He motioned with his head. "When I was worrying aloud about Gemma?"

Faye wrinkled her nose. "I don't think..." She huffed out a breath. "I was about to ask a personal question regarding that lost time. With Gemma. And then I realized it was none of my business. I mean, it's not like we actually kissed back there." Then she shoved her hands in her back pockets and huffed out another breath, stirring her bangs.

He hadn't expected her to bring up the kiss. His plan had been to pretend it was never a thing. What kiss?

Something about Faye made him think she preferred to face every challenge head-on.

So he might as well answer her question.

"I was in jail when Gemma was born." He watched her face closely. The reactions he'd gotten to his story ran the gamut of emotion, but there was usually a hint of judgment mixed in with each one. Faye was waiting for the next part of the story. "I was young and stupid and petty theft seemed to be the only answer to my problems. No money, no education and a baby on the way. Getting caught and going to jail made all those problems a hundred times worse. I lost the job I had worked so hard to get, learning from a guy who'd actually shown a kid who had no qualifications how to work the line in his busy kitchen. It was so stupid. When I got out, I scrambled for work in kitchens and every odd job, two or three jobs at a time, to send Monica everything I could while I was trying to catch up. It took years, but I finally managed." With a lot of help from Sadie Hearst. "Then there was the food truck and crazy hours there. Once I got the restaurant up and running, I could carve out time for my daughter, finally. Unfortunately, I still had to convince her to do the same and she's had good reason to hesitate."

Faye reached over to take his hand. "Monica is right. Lost time is one of those things that's easy to regret. I'd be surprised if most people don't have days they'd like to get back, but you kept showing up for Gemma. Believe me, that can change everything. Honestly, coming to Prospect..." She shrugged. "It's hard to put it into words, but I bet this place and the people here will help more than you thought possible when you rolled into town."

He glanced down at her thumb as it traced over the back of his hand. "Just don't insult the best restaurant in town?"

She laughed. "You're a quick learner." Suddenly, she let go of his hand. "I was on my way out. And you need to go pick up your daughter."

He trailed behind her to the restaurant door. "Since I shared, does that mean we need to go ahead with that kiss? I don't want to ruin our deepening relationship, Faye."

Her lips were twitching as she backed toward the door. "Good night, Chef."

Brian watched her leave.

"That wasn't a no." He found his car keys and moved toward the lobby, vanilla floating along in the air around him. Tomorrow would be soon enough to get the answer to the mystery of where it was coming from.

It would also be his next chance to return to that kiss.

He was already looking forward to it.

CHAPTER SIX

FAYE PARKED IN front of the barn at home, glad that her grandmother was deep in the throes of dinner service at the Ace High. The smile kept turning up the corners of her lips even after she'd sternly lectured herself on the inadvisability of kissing a chef who was only in town for a couple of weeks.

The fact that the Majestic's haunting, unexplained vanilla scent had popped up between them was a reminder of the dangers of matchmakers surrounding them on all sides. No one believed in ghosts.

Until they were faced with the scent that only appeared now and then, and to some people but not others.

Even the nonbelievers would be happy to welcome Sadie back as a ghost.

Though there was no shortage of matchmakers already available for Faye and Brian to be miserable during his stay if they decided to act.

Reminding herself of all those things still didn't wipe the smile away.

Apparently, the short drive from the Majestic hadn't taken long enough for her own cautionary words to sink in.

Faye noticed the barn door was open. It had been too long since she'd spent any of her precious free time in her grandfather's company, so she changed course for the barn. On the way in, she bent to pick up the bits of baling twine that he dropped like breadcrumbs. "Grandpa? You here?"

An indistinct answer from the shadows near the empty stall in the back sent her heart racing. She scrambled through the cluttered aisle to see her grandfather crumpled on the floor, a shovel on top of his chest. He held up an arm. "Yep. Here like an old fool caught in a bear trap."

Hearing him sound a bit more like himself made it easier to breathe, but watching him struggle to move did nothing to slow her heart rate. "Stay still. Let me get over there." She used the flashlight in her phone to pick her way through the various tools and had to shift the wheelbarrow out of the way to kneel down next to him. Closer, she could see a bright red spot on his temple. "What hurts?"

"My pride." He sighed. "And something is digging into my back. Probably the pitchfork I was huntin' for when everything went south." He tried to shift to sit up and immediately flopped back down. "Need another minute."

Faye wasn't waiting a minute longer. She found Keena's number and pressed it.

"Hey, I didn't expect to hear from you today. I figured you'd be too busy with the hot chef," Keena teased.

"Where are you? In town?" Faye asked. The tremor in her voice surprised her.

"At my house. What's wrong?" Keena asked immediately, clearly switching into emergency mode. Life as a small-town doctor required more trauma response than she'd expected when she got to Prospect, Keena had told her, but the whole town was grateful to have her.

Faye pressed her hand to her grandfather's chest to stop him from attempting to get up.

"Grandpa fell in the barn and he's having some trouble standing. Do you think—"

"I don't need a doctor, Faye," her grandfather grumbled, "and there better not be an ambulance waiting when I manage to get up."

"I'll be right there," Keena said at the same time. She didn't hang up, keeping the line open just in case.

"We have the best neighbors, don't we, Grandpa? Remember that when you greet them, please," Faye said. Soon, she heard a truck stop right next to the barn. "We're back here in the stall!"

Keena was the first one through the shadows. She held up the large black bag in her hand. "Let's see what I can do with what I've got. We may need to rethink once I assess." Travis appeared then, and helped create more space so that Keena could kneel on the other side of Faye's grandfather. "Mr. Parker, you are in a pickle here. Tell me what happened."

Faye watched her study the spot at his temple and then examine his arms and legs. "No pain here?"

Grandpa shook his head. "No. I was looking for the pitchfork. It was buried under other junk, so I was fussing and tossing stuff, got my feet tangled, and couldn't recover before I hit the floor. Something landed on top of me, but I'm winded, not hurt."

"Something is poking him in the back and he's tried to sit up and had to stop," Faye added.

Keena nodded. "Did you black out? Is any part of this fuzzy?"

"No, no, I'm clear on every part of this foolishness," Grandpa said with a rusty chuckle.

Travis said, "I once stepped on an old piece of black vinyl tubing that we used to run water out to the garden, just a spare piece. Thought it was a snake and jumped six feet in the air before landing on my backside. Took three days to catch my breath."

Grandpa grunted as Keena helped him roll to his side. "How long until your pride recovered, son?"

Keena's boyfriend shook his head. "That's a permanent injury, Mr. Parker. I hate to tell you but the memory of this will wake you up in the middle of the night for the rest of your life. But all you have to do is shake your head and roll back over to go to sleep."

Faye shook her head at Travis. "That's all it takes, huh?"

He shrugged. "I only know what works for me."

"Is anything bothering you now that you're on your side, Mr. Parker? Back? Neck?" Keena asked.

"No, ma'am." He sounded like an embarrassed kid. "Can we try standing me up now?"

Keena laughed. "That makes sense as the next step. I want to check for a concussion and need to see the puncture on your back in better light."

Travis and Faye moved out of the way, and together they got her grandfather on his feet. They carefully led him through the barn to sit on the tailgate of Travis's truck. In the late afternoon sunlight, Faye was happy to see a bit more color in her grandfather's cheeks.

Keena checked his eyes. "No loss of consciousness. No knots. Your brain might be okay."

"Least as good as it was when I went in the barn, anyways," Grandpa muttered as he eased out of his long-sleeved shirt so Keena could examine his back.

The blood there sent Faye's heart racing, but Keena immediately relaxed. "These are scratches. Are you up to date on your tetanus shots, Mr. Parker?"

"O' course, stuck enough rusted barbed wire in me that I kept Dr. Singh in regular business before you came to town." Her grandfather tilted his head back. "Believe I had a shot last year, but it for sure ain't been more than two."

Keena turned to Faye for confirmation, and she nodded.

"Good. Then let's clean these cuts and see if you need a stitch or a Barbie Band-Aid." Keena dug around in her bag for the things she needed.

"Them the only two choices, Doc?" her grandfather asked and Faye exhaled slowly. He was going to be fine.

Keena worked quickly and ended up putting a small, plain bandage over the two deepest punctures. "You'll need to watch those for signs of infection. If anything comes up, some new hurt that worries you, give me a call and we'll figure it out, okay?" Keena touched his arm. "Sure am glad you're tough."

Her grandfather rolled his eyes. "Used to be able to get myself off the floor, but I guess it could be worse."

"I'm glad I wasn't working at the Ace tonight." That was the next thing that worried Faye. How long would her grandfather have been stuck there on the barn floor before she or her grandmother got home after dinner service? Would he have been able to move eventually or would he have had to wait hours for help?

And how easily would Keena have been able to put him back together after that?

"Mr. Parker—" Travis stepped forward "—I know good and well you've got one of these handy modern contraptions." He waved his cell phone. "I keep mine in my pocket in case Keena wants to call me and tell me how much she loves me. Where is yours?"

Faye tipped her head back to stare up at the clouds after her grandfather shot her a sheepish look. "In the truck." He motioned with his head in case anyone wondered exactly which truck he was referring to.

"Hmm," Travis said, "I hope you see how unhelpful that can be and why pockets are better."

She and her grandfather had discussed this issue repeatedly, but nothing got through to him.

He sighed. "I forgot it."

Travis tipped his hat back to scratch his forehead. "Never too late to correct a mistake."

Keena hugged Faye and murmured, “He’s okay. I’m glad you called me.”

Faye nodded. “I’m glad to have a doctor in the family.” The Armstrongs, their neighbors and most of Prospect were one big family.

Travis had started a conversation with Grandpa about the fence between their properties and how the steer they’d all started calling Chuck had busted through again. The animal’s strong affection for the flower bed outside Keena’s front window was irresistible, evidently.

“You Armstrongs…we owe you a debt for all this work.” Grandpa clapped Travis on the back. “Sure do appreciate it.”

Travis waved a hand. “You’ve done the same for us and you know it. Has Grant cornered you to talk about his new rodeo club?”

Grandpa shook his head.

“Well, get ready for the arm-twisting to start after Western Days winds up. He’s rounding up volunteers to restart the high school club. It sure meant a lot to us growing up that you and Sam and Dad made time to talk rodeo with us, even if only Grant ever went for the big time. Really helped me get over my…” He cleared his throat. “Let’s call it ‘uncertainty’ regarding horses. You were particularly good at working with the city boys as I recall.”

“He had practice.” Faye pointed to herself. “He put me up on Misty’s back but forgot to tell me to hold on tight until I slid right over the other side and landed in the dirt.”

Grandpa cleared his throat. “We got off to a bumpy start. I forgot city slickers need to begin further back in the process than ranch kids, but I learned my lesson. I try never to make the same mistake twice.”

Travis waved his cell phone again to remind Grandpa to keep it in his pocket from now on.

Grandpa held his hands up in surrender.

"If you have any chores or odd jobs you're looking for help with, my foster son Damon has been making noises about hunting up a job. The kid's not old enough to be working, but I get his wanting funds of his own." Travis propped his hands on his hips. "I've made him swear up, down and sideways he's not squirreling away money to make a run for it. When I was a young foster, I did that a time or two." He smiled. "He wants to buy a game for Grant's gaming system. I imagine that it will be a Christmas gift that Funcle Grant barely gets to touch thanks to Damon and Micah."

He pointed to the large garden that was her grandfather's pride and joy. "Weeding would be right up both of those boys' alleys."

"Or reorganizing the barn," Faye added quietly. Her grandfather narrowed his eyes as if to say he'd heard that.

Keena closed up her bag. "When the ranch talk starts, the doctor exits. Good to see you, Faye, Mr. Parker."

Travis waved and the couple were on their way.

Grandpa sighed. "Never thought I'd see the day I needed neighbors to get me off the floor, Faye."

"Any one of us could end up in the same spot, Grandpa." She watched him climb the steps to the house. He was moving slowly but there was no hesitation. As soon as her grandmother got home, Faye would tell her what happened, but there was no way to explain how scared she'd been.

But the Ace, as it was now, needed her and Gran both.

Today had worked out as well as it could have, but she'd make sure her grandfather always kept his phone on him. Otherwise, how would she ever sleep?

AS BRIAN DROVE into Prospect to collect Gemma, he realized he'd missed the scenery on his previous trip when he'd been worrying over how he and Gemma would fit in and remembering not to get too far ahead of himself by picturing how much better they would be when they got back home. More like family, less like polite strangers sharing an elevator.

He had also been unusually aware of the woman in the driver's seat. How long had it been since a woman had so interested him and so instantly? It was hard to name another person who had occupied his thoughts immediately like she did.

Without those distractions, it was easy to see spring thaw happening all around him in new, bright green. Would it darken as summer came on?

LA had plenty of green, too, but it was the carefully manicured lawns and golf courses. The seasons didn't change much unless one happened to be wetter than the one before it.

"I bet it's pretty when it snows," he murmured as he headed down the straight stretch that led to the middle of Prospect. "Four seasons. What a concept."

Brian had never been far from southern California. Experiencing snow might blow his mind, but it was fun to imagine building a snowman with his daughter.

"Do nearly grown women have snowball fights?" He was pretty sure Gemma would respond to any act of snowball war by returning a volley of her own.

If they were ever near Prospect in the winter, he could test his theory.

He shook his head as he realized he was doing what he'd warned himself not to do: building a rosy future that featured a return trip to the Colorado Rockies and the two of them traveling together often. "Silly. You barely take weekends off. Trips for pleasure?" Once he made it back to his restaurant, he might remember this place fondly, especially if he and Gemma got closer, but there was no reason to pretend there'd be another vacation in his future.

Faye's pretty blue eyes flashed through his mind before he pushed the image away.

There were three open parking spots in front of the Mercantile, so he pulled in. Prue Armstrong had commandeered Gemma's help for the day and he was curious about the store.

Since it was directly across from the Ace High, he could see that Faye had been telling him the truth when she corrected his remark about the lack of business the night before. It was still early for the dinner rush, but the restaurant was filling up.

Another restaurant owner might have been nervous that reopening the Majestic's kitchen would hurt their business. Instead of helping the Hearsts, Faye could have put up stumbling blocks. Was she that good a friend to Sarah and Jordan, or was there something else going on there?

He pushed open the door to the Mercantile and stepped into a quirky hallway. It had two doors, one on the left and one on the right. A stand with a few brochures for area attractions was the centerpiece.

The door on the left opened and Walt Armstrong stepped out. Brian could see a hodgepodge collection of gardening implements and wooden birdhouses hanging from the ceiling.

To someone in the shop, Walt said, "I'll be over at the Ace for dinner. Call me if you have trouble closing down the register." Walt waved his phone and then spotted Brian. "Well, now, if it ain't the chef. Got me a new assistant manager learning the ropes in the hardware store." Brian noted the man who was rearranging items on a long wooden counter.

"Learnin' the ropes. In a hardware store. That's pretty

good right there," Walt murmured before clapping him on the back. "Roger'll have the whole place topsy-turvy by the time I return, but that's part of the charm of the place. Guessing you're here to pick up Prue's handy new helper over at Handmade." Then he tapped his phone. "I said I'd have it. I didn't say this phone would be on. If Prue's dinner is interrupted by business calls, she will not appreciate it."

Brian chuckled. "Yeah, I've experienced that myself on a date or two."

Walt nodded. "Good thing you learned your lesson before you found the woman you gotta hang on to." He swept open the door opposite for Brian. "Maybe you won't have to demonstrate that your manners have improved to win her back someday."

Prue and Gemma were talking, heads bent, thick as thieves. Bright fabrics were arranged on stands of various sizes and quilts of different styles and colors covered the walls and hung from the ceiling. More quilts were stacked in clear containers near a staircase that led to the second floor. There were craft supplies galore.

"Dad, can we come back just for the weekend? They're going to have a big festival. Look at these photos." Gemma hurried over to drag him closer to a photo album Prue was holding. His daughter was wearing some kind of glove on her left hand; he could feel a rubbery texture covering her palm.

"Kind of a long trip for a weekend, but let me see these photos," Brian said as he smiled at Prue and turned the pages. Since Gemma had never asked him to take her anywhere for a weekend visit before, he knew he'd have a hard time saying no to the request. He hoped this was a sign that Prospect was working its magic between them.

Every photo featured the preserved facades of Prospect, but they were covered with bright quilts on display.

In some of the photos, he saw people dressed in period costumes mixed in with all the tourists. There was a cowboy running some kind of contest with people on stage, and a woman in a long skirt painting a girl's face with a pink flower.

He'd underestimated the size of Prospect's festival. In addition, there were food and craft vendors, a band and singer in a huge black cowboy hat, and a parade with throngs of people lining the street.

Scanning the parade photos, he suddenly stopped. "There's Faye."

Gemma immediately stuck her head between his and the photo, so he tapped where he had last seen Faye.

"She's so young." Gemma's amazement amused Prue.

"We all start out the same way, young lady, even if it's hard to believe it." Prue squeezed Gemma's shoulder as she gave Brian a wink. "Not sure what that tells me... You picking her out of the crowd like that, even with the changes that time brings." She closed the album slowly. "But I aim to think on it and let you know."

Brian frowned as he tried to decipher her meaning. Was she suspicious he was going to hurt Faye's feelings somehow?

Walt's amused grin as he pressed his lips to Prue's convinced Brian that he might be the only adult in the room not adding one and one and coming up with the correct answer.

Some kind of intuition made him wonder if he wanted to know what he was missing.

"What have you been doing? I didn't know you could quilt." He sat at the table where Gemma was now stacking neat rectangles of fabric.

"Miss Prue needed me to help stock the quilt store and the Cookie Queen Museum." Her expression as she talked was serious. "With the festival happening next month, it's the biggest sales weekend Prospect has. Everything has to be ready."

"I wonder who she heard that from," Walt muttered and ducked Prue's playful swat. "I know it seems like you're the hot news in town, Chef, but this little competition can't hold a candle to Prue's Western Days festival. One hundred years it's been going on, after all." He beamed at his...ex-wife? Brian was almost certain that was how they'd been introduced, but neither one of them were acting very "ex" in his opinion. Then he remembered all the betting going on regarding Armstrong weddings. If he had a chance to place a wager, Walt and Prue were his frontrunners.

Gemma picked up a tool that looked like a pizza cutter but was much sharper. He asked, "What exactly are you doing to help out?"

Gemma held up her gloved hand. "Cutting fabric to bundle as fat quarters." She pointed at the neat stack she'd made. "Prue's going to run a special." Then Gemma meticulously placed a clear ruler and lined it up. When she began using the cutting tool, Brian fought the urge to remind her to be careful. She was doing that, and she had the most intense frown of concentration on her face. He did not want to mess that up.

Pleased with herself, she held up the gloved hand. "Miss Prue said I came in with ten fingers so I had to leave with ten fingers. The glove protects me from the blade." She wiggled the five fingers that were safe in the glove.

That reminded him of what Faye had said about her grandmother's teaching methods versus Sadie's. There was no denying that Gemma was proud of herself for helping and Prue had been clever to find a way to keep her safe without ruining the fun.

That was a talent he needed to improve on.

"Let's call it a day. It's dinnertime. Are you headed over to the Ace or are you making fine cuisine tonight, Chef?" Prue asked as she helped Gemma out of the glove.

Before he could ask his daughter, she answered, "Definitely Ace High. And we're getting pieces of pie to go."

Relieved that she'd made the decision that easily, Brian nodded. "Works for me."

He and Gemma trailed behind Walt and Prue. Brian tried to decide whether he and Gemma were crashing a date night or whatever was going on between Prue and Walt, but they were stopped on the sidewalk by a crowd at the door.

Prue's concern alerted him that this was not normal at the restaurant.

"What's going on?" she asked the couple at the end of the line.

"Apparently, there's no one waiting tables right now." The woman shrugged. "I guess we're all stuck until Faye gets everything back under control." Her relaxed expression was confident that it would happen sooner rather than later.

"Except Faye is off tonight," Prue muttered as she cut a path through the crowd. Walt and Gemma followed behind her, so Brian brought up the rear.

As soon as they stepped inside, Brian knew something was out of the ordinary. The dining room was silent, but the racket coming from the kitchen was intense.

A young girl was hurrying to clean up a tray of food that had crashed to the floor.

"Holly, girl, what's happening?" Prue and Walt immediately bent down to help her pick up the mess.

Holly sighed before holding up a finger at the first person in the doorway. "One more minute, everyone, and we'll get dinner service back under way."

Brian would have placed Holly's age at college freshman but her tone was assured.

"The short version is that Britt got in too big a hurry, something Mrs. Parker warned her about, so she dropped the tray. Splat."

Prue turned to him. "Emma Parker is Faye's grandmother, the chef around here. Insists the kids call her 'Mrs. Parker' out of respect, I guess." She shook her head to show her opinion of that.

Holly brushed hair out of her face. "Then Britt started crying and Mrs. Parker called her back to the kitchen." She sighed. "If I heard correctly, Britt quit and Mrs. Parker has been ordering her to stop crying and stop quitting for some time now. Oh, and Mrs. Parker told Toby not to come back to work until he cut his hair after Faye and I both told him he'd be fine as long as it was tied back because that's kind of his thing, so now we are down to only one waiter, Britt, and she's trying to make a run for the door."

Her voice rose with each word, and Brian could easily understand her stress. He'd been there himself and knew the way out.

Brian patted Holly's shoulder. "All right. Here's what we're going to do. You finish cleaning up here and then seat everyone who's waiting. Walt and Gemma can serve drinks."

Holly inhaled slowly. "Pitchers of water and tea are by the host stand, glasses are stacked next to the ice machine."

Brian waited for Walt and Gemma to nod. "When everyone is seated, Prue and Holly will take orders and pass them on to the kitchen, so that dinner service can get back on track." Then he stood. "And I'll take control of the kitchen."

Before everyone could scatter, Prue motioned them all into a huddle. "And what we won't do is tell Faye about this. At all. Downplay this mess with the people you talk to. I don't know if we can contain this story long enough for the staff to get their feet under them, but Faye will be impossible to remove from this building if she hears about it tonight."

Brian watched as his daughter nodded firmly, and decided that if Gemma could jump into these unfamiliar waters with both feet, he could brave the unknown kitchen.

Restaurant kitchens were no place to show fear, no matter how bad the situation got, so he straightened his shoulders and pushed open the doors. A tiny woman had her arm wrapped around the waist of a crying teenage girl while two young line cooks watched. They appeared to be frozen in place, one of them holding a spatula like a sword.

"Kitchen is closed." Emma Parker gave him a mean stare. It would have convinced most people to turn and exit immediately.

But Brian had spent most of his life around chefs, so he'd seen worse.

He'd probably delivered worse, too.

"Chef, I'm Brian Caruso." She tipped her chin up as if she recognized the name and understood who he was. He motioned at the two cooks. "We'll work on the orders coming in while you handle the important business. The dining room is filling up for the evening's rush."

She gave him a curt nod. "Britt and I will take a fifteen, have a cold drink and then I'll be back."

And by then I will have everything under control so I can leave your domain, Brian thought to himself as he tied a clean apron around his waist. "All right, Chefs, let's fire these tickets."

One of the things that Brian loved the most about his career was that all well-run kitchens fell into the same rhythms, no matter the food they served. Emma Parker's kitchen was no different. He called out the tickets as they came in, and his line cooks responded. They repeated his orders and delivered them promptly every single time. He plated the orders and called for service. At some point, a young woman slipped past him and out into the dining room. Prue and Holly kept the orders coming, and when Emma Parker rejoined the line, dinner service had fully resumed.

Instead of dropping his apron and heading for safety, Brian asked, "Everything okay?"

Emma Parker snapped, "You interviewing for my job, Mr. Caruso?" She snatched the ticket Prue brought up as if the two of them were running a race.

"No, ma'am, helping out where I can. That's all." He raised his eyebrows at Prue through the order window.

"All the orders are now in, Emma," Prue said, "and everyone out here is content."

Faye's grandmother smiled, and Brian could immediately see the family resemblance. She and her granddaughter shared beautiful smiles. "Thank you, Prue."

Prue nodded. "And we're all going to tell Faye that service went off without a hitch, aren't we?" She crossed her arms over her chest as she waited for Emma's answer.

Emma gave a weird, jerky shrug. "Of course, we are. It did." Then she waved her towel. "Go, sit, and enjoy your dinners on the house. Britt and Holly can handle running the orders out."

Brian slipped the apron off and put it with the other dirty linens before he headed for the kitchen door.

"Chef." Emma Parker met his eyes for a split second. "Thank you, but don't think you've got a standing invitation to my kitchen. Faye and I have this place set up exactly as we like it."

"Yes, Chef," Brian answered before he joined Prue, Walt and Gemma at a table.

"Everything okay?" Gemma asked before she stuffed her mouth with a bite of one of the Ace High's cornbread muffins.

Brian wanted to fan himself with the menu, but there was no menu. None on the table. He glanced around and didn't see evidence of menus anywhere.

"No burn marks anywhere. You must have done well. Emma's pretty protective of her space." Prue patted his shoulder. "I'm glad you survived."

"Did you doubt I'd make it out of there?" Brian asked.

Prue raised her eyebrows. "Emma loves this place like one of her kids and is just as proud of it, too. She's very particular about her kitchen and dinner service."

"Did you order already?" Brian asked.

"The nightly menu at the Ace High is the chef's choice." Gemma waved a hand as if she was totally familiar with the concept. "Tonight she prepared Salisbury steak with mushroom gravy and roasted chicken with a balsamic glaze. Steamed vegetable medley, baked potato and corn casserole for the sides."

Brian blinked as he absorbed the fact that his daughter recited the menu with the casual nature of an experienced server in one of his restaurants. Prue's eyes twinkled as she waited for him to catch up. "Chef's choice is a pretty different concept, isn't it?"

"I like it." Brian admired the freedom it gave the chef to change things up. "What am I having?"

"Chicken." Gemma shrugged. "You don't like mushrooms." Her delivery was so matter-of-fact that Brian understood it had been a simple choice for her. She knew him well enough to pick his dinner without a worry.

"Good choice, Gem," he said as he squeezed her shoulder. He loved the way her confidence was growing here, working with Prue and jumping in to help out at the Ace. How could he have accomplished the same back in LA?

In his own restaurant, he had a better chance of unintentionally making his daughter cry than prep orders for a room full of diners. He wondered if people said he was "very particular about his kitchen and dinner service" the way Prue had about Faye's grandmother. If he was half as intimidating as Emma Parker, he might need to rethink his approach to new chefs and Gemma. They were both learning important things here.

Brian relaxed as they discussed all the mishaps out on the dining room floor. Prue and Gemma both chatted with Britt when she stopped by their table, and by the time he and Gemma loaded up to return to the Majestic, they were both full and… "You had a good day, right?" Brian asked as he drove away from the Mercantile.

Gemma immediately nodded. "A great day. And now we have pie." She tapped the to-go container in her lap. "That pretty much makes it a perfect day."

Good food, a happy daughter, an easy night in the kitchen and time spent with Faye Parker. Gemma was right. He couldn't have asked for anything more.

CHAPTER SEVEN

FAYE WASN'T SURE what she'd expected being behind-the-scenes of a video production, but the amount of standing around surprised her. Jordan and Sarah had periodic, intense conversations with Andre, the director, who would pace out a few steps and issue orders. Then the people who were running sound and the camera would scurry to respond.

In her role as consultant, she expected to have someone bark orders at her, but so far, she was part of the audience.

Having Brian at her side unless he was called forward to give his opinion on the order of the shots or placement of cameras while the cooking happened made it difficult to remember the strict lecture she'd given herself before she'd walked into the Majestic that morning.

His little asides, muttered for her ears only, tickled through her nervous system.

She didn't move away because she didn't want them to stop.

"Which one is Angel and which is River?" he asked close to her ear.

Faye squashed the girlish grin that blossomed before she knew it was happening. "I think sound is Angel, camera is River, but I'm not certain enough of that to use their names yet."

He nodded. "They need jackets. In the kitchen, line cooks turn over pretty quickly." He tapped his chest, which was not covered by a white coat yet but by a nice green shirt that they'd grabbed at the Homestead Market the day before. Faye imagined that was where the name would be embroidered on a chef coat. "Helps me learn their names if I can check every time I yell at them."

Faye shook her head sadly. "Have you ever considered that it's the yelling that causes all the turnover?"

His lips were twitching as he stared at her. "It crossed my mind recently, but who am I to break with tradition? It's part of the seasoning process for the finest chefs." Then he bumped her shoulder with his. "Seasoning…did you see what I did there?"

Faye tried to control the grin that bloomed at his bad pun.

"Okay, I'm satisfied we have the kitchen shots blocked." Andre waved a clipboard. "We're going to have a stationary camera in the kitchen and in the dining room for judging so that we're always rolling on a wide shot. River will move in for close-ups and reaction shots as needed." He stared down at his notes. "Each round, Sarah will outline the rules of the challenge, make chitchat and then do a follow-up before judging. Each competitor should give a handy tip for the home cook. After the cooking is wrapped, we'll tape the introduction from Chef Caruso, meet Jordan and Sarah, and hear about the Hearst legacy at the Cookie Queen Corporation carrying out Sadie's work for a new generation. The location for those segments is still TBD." Andre paused to make sure they were following. "The competitors were delayed, so they're arriving late tonight, but we'll get them in front of the camera after breakfast for screen testing. Tomorrow we'll discuss hair, makeup and wardrobe. Since this is a shoestring budget, we have no stylists, but River and I will pitch in to make sure everyone looks good. Any concerns?"

Sarah and Jordan exchanged a glance. "No, if we have extra time, we can head into the Cookie Queen Museum to get shots of Sadie's memorabilia."

Andre made himself a note.

"Might want to watch the weather, too," Prue suggested from her spot on the edge of the crowd. "Spring showers can catch us off guard around here."

Andre marched over and gave Prue a big air-kiss on each cheek. "Prue, you darling, that is a good note. I shoot in studios, not in the wild. I like this outline, but we'll keep some flex in it in case Mother Nature wants to surprise us. River and Angel, hang back, but the rest of you are free for the afternoon."

"Free time. That's unexpected." Sarah rested against the check-in desk. "Brian, Gemma, any ideas on how you'd like to spend it?"

Jordan held her arms out. "How about…riding lessons?"

The way Prue, Walt and Sarah all swung around to stare at her made Faye chuckle.

Jordan read their collective, stunned expression and covered her heart. "I'm not going, obviously. I'm volunteering Sarah since horses are involved. Or Walt. If we're going to ask the chef to ride a horse for any of these color shots Andre wants, he should get comfortable in the saddle beforehand."

Brian leaned down. "Why is everyone so shocked? I'm fairly athletic, play pickup basketball during the afternoon lull at the restaurant at least once or twice a week. I probably won't die." Then he raised his eyebrows. "Will I?"

Faye shook her head. "They're shocked because Jordan suggested anything at all to do with a horse."

He pursed his lips. "Shouldn't teaching me fall under your consulting duties?"

Faye smiled slowly. Was he searching for a way to spend

more time with her? Why couldn't she decide whether she wanted that to be true? "Grant Armstrong is a professional rider, won big on the rodeo circuit. He's the better choice."

Brian considered that. "What father wouldn't want the best for his only daughter, Faye? Grant should focus all his attention on Gemma."

"Does Gemma know she's being included in this plan?" Gemma was helping with a project at Prue's store. If Prue returned to town, Gemma would want to get back to work on it there.

He wrinkled his nose. "Not yet. Can I convince her?"

Sarah waved her phone. "Grant is available. Jordan got lucky. He can take Brian out this afternoon."

Faye inched closer as Brian moved to murmur in Gemma's ear. Her immediate frown made Faye wonder if Gemma might be in the no-horses camp with Jordan, but Brian motioned over his shoulder at Faye. Gemma followed his gesture and chewed her bottom lip as she weighed her options. Eventually, she nodded but it was not enthusiastic. At all.

"We're both in." Brian met her stare from across the room. "Give us fifteen and we'll follow you to the ranch?"

Faye nodded and started the mental countdown in her head. She was going to be mobbed for details in three, two...

"Is this a new development?" Jordan asked immediately. She could be counted on to go straight to the heart of the matter, no hemming or hawing. "This is outside of consulting, Faye, so are you and the chef..."

"She's helping Gemma settle comfortably. You know he's worried about whether she's enjoying herself here in town." Sarah was usually the voice of reason, but something about her expression said that she hoped Jordan was on the right track.

"You didn't see The Moment they had yesterday, framed in the restaurant's doorway." Jordan's eyebrows were raised nearly to her hairline to communicate how important it was. "Locked eyes. Barely a breath of space between them. You see that in the movies right before The Kiss."

Faye was usually amused at how often she heard Jordan's words in capital letters. Being in the starring role here dampened some of her amusement.

Prue tilted her head to the side, biding her time, obviously satisfied that the interrogation was moving in the right direction.

Faye shrugged.

And waited.

The slow blink she got in response from Jordan made her laugh. "I don't know which one of you is right, honestly. Gemma is great, and I did promise to help any way I could."

"But..." Prue gave her the "continue" motion with one hand.

"We spent a lot of time together yesterday." There had also been another weird, near collision with a kiss that she regretted missing, no matter how logically she warned herself about it. He had a big career in Los Angeles, and as often as she'd daydreamed about doing other things in other places, she had her family and the farm and the restaurant to consider.

"And given the opportunity to do it again, you both jumped at the chance." Prue hmm'ed to tack on her unspoken conclusion.

"I wouldn't say jumped," Faye responded, "because why would we? Less than two weeks, and the Carusos will be a full day's drive away again."

Prue waved her hand in the air, immediately dismissing that concern.

Sarah frowned and seemed to understand Faye's point.

Jordan immediately started plotting. "We have a restaurant that needs a chef. He's a chef. Other people have relocated to Prospect because of true love." She slung her arm over Sarah's shoulders. "And any day, we'll see a proposal because of it."

"Be careful, Jordan." Prue wagged her finger. "Once the first one goes, the rest will topple like dominoes. I expect Clay, Travis and Grant are already sizing rings in their spare time."

Everyone turned to see Jordan's response to that. If Faye had to guess, Jordan would need persuading to take the marriage leap. Seconds passed and Jordan sighed. "After Western Days, we may need to start planning wedding packages around here. How long would it take to build a gazebo down by the lake?"

Sarah's mouth dropped open.

Prue hooted.

And Faye grinned.

"You forgot a domino, Prue," Sarah said sweetly.

"Oh, Matt? He's still finding his way, but it won't be long." Prue held her arms out. "By the time my other boys march down the aisle, I expect Matt's true love will have entered the picture, too."

"Not Matt." Jordan shook her head ruefully, always prepared to deliver some drama. "She's talking about Walt, Prue. The man who is glued to your side lately."

"There's been a ceasefire in hostilities," Sarah added.

"From snapping to smooching at every single opportunity," Faye tacked on. She'd had to break them up over meat loaf at the Ace last week.

Prue sniffed. "When Walt's ready to ask, I'll have an answer."

Brian and Gemma walked back into the lobby, both

decked out in the finest from Homestead Market's clothing section. Gemma had already appropriated one of Brian's button-downs. They both fit in perfectly.

Sarah touched Faye's arm. "Enjoy your afternoon. Forget about LA and Prospect, and jobs and family and all of that. Have some fun."

Faye met Sarah's stare and realized she was saying so much more. As if Sarah understood how the demands of the restaurant had eliminated the time and freedom to do anything else.

"Is Grant going to meet us in the barn?" Faye asked as Brian and Gemma joined their circle. The last thing she wanted was Prue dropping broad hints about what a wonderful match they would make.

"Yes, I told him to go ahead and saddle up Lady for you." Prue patted Gemma's shoulder. "We'll catch up tomorrow, okay? With your excellent new system in place, we'll be churning out fat quarters in no time."

Faye watched Gemma nod glumly and wondered what plans her father had rearranged in order to rope her into this riding lesson. When he grimaced for her eyes only, Faye's lips twitched but she didn't smile as Gemma trudged forward, each step heavy.

"Gemma, horses are so much fun. Want to ride over to the barn with me? Your dad can follow us to the Rocking A." Faye jingled her keys. "I'll race you to the parking lot." Then she took off running. She wasn't sure Gemma had snapped up the bait until she heard the loud thump of sneakers behind her.

They were both out of breath when they hopped in the car. Faye rolled down the windows and hung her arm out to tempt Gemma to do the same as they drove down the lane, heading for the highway.

"Did your dad rearrange your plans?" Faye asked.

"Yes, Prue and I were going to take photos of the quilts she wanted to display this year and decide where to hang them in town for the festival." Gemma shrugged. "After being cooped up in the kitchen, it would have been fun."

Faye agreed. "Prue makes everything fun. She's great."

"Yeah, even pouring drinks turns into a game with Prue." Gemma's eyes grew big as she cleared her throat. "What do you think about this filming process so far?"

Pouring drinks.

What did that mean?

Pursuing the weird comment was tempting, but Faye decided keeping the peace was more important. "It's interesting, but I hope things move along quickly when they're cooking. It could be a long day if we have as much standing around as we did today."

Gemma nodded.

They pulled up at the Rocking A. Grant was leaning against the top rail of the paddock fence. The scene could have been a postcard for ranch life, with the sprawling farmhouse that had grown so much larger to accommodate the Armstrong family. It was a pretty backdrop for the barn and flowing pastureland in the distance that led up to the mountains surrounding their little valley.

"We don't have Prue, but we will have Lady, Prue's horse." Faye winked at Gemma. "I have this feeling about you, Gemma. I think you're going to love riding." Then she leaned closer. "And we are definitely going to give your father a hard time. As soon as I tell Grant the plan, he'll be an excellent accomplice. That man loves drama the way you and I love apple pie. Doesn't that sound like fun?"

Gemma nodded eagerly, so they hurried to join Grant at the fence.

She wrapped her arm around Gemma's shoulders and

pulled her close to speak to Grant as Brian parked next to her truck. "You love a scheme, right, Grant?"

The way he immediately rubbed his hands together in anticipation made her smile.

"The chef is going to be a good rider," she told him.

"He's good at everything," Gemma added with a quick glance over her shoulder.

"One of those guys, huh?" Grant asked as if he wasn't as guilty. "What's the plan?"

Since she knew Grant Armstrong the way a younger sister did a teasing older brother, Faye immediately said, "No pain, no tears, Grant. Everything else is an option."

He sighed dramatically. "Fine. I'll give him an advanced course in mucking out stalls before we ride."

Gemma's delighted giggles convinced Faye that Sarah had been absolutely right. Why would she spend a second worrying about anything when there was so much fun to be had right here and now?

CHAPTER EIGHT

BRIAN HAD TRIED to project confidence when Jordan had suggested a riding lesson, even though he'd viewed horses in much the same way as he had lions and giraffes. They were beautiful, but they had little to no impact on his life. He'd never had to make up his mind what he thought about them as far as riding went because they belonged in other people's lives, not his.

So when he found himself shoveling manure out of a barn stall, it took him a moment to evaluate whether cleaning muck was the most important step in getting comfortable with ranch horse Charlie, or he was the victim of cowboy hazing.

The way his daughter had pointed out places he'd missed in a gleeful tone finally convinced him to offer her the shovel to finish Lady's stall. She was having a riding lesson, too. Gemma had been learning how to pull pranks on her father, so she'd waited for one of her accomplices to save her from the consequences.

Until he'd smiled at her. Then she'd ducked behind Faye, giggles trailing her, and their plot was exposed.

After that, he'd actually enjoyed his riding lesson.

As the sun was sinking in the sky, he waved at Grant and Gemma, who were trotting across the pasture toward the gate that separated the Rocking A from the Majestic.

"Are you sure you don't want to follow her?" Faye asked. "It's a short ride. Good practice."

Brian sighed. "A thing I never understood before..." He carefully urged Charlie to turn away from the fence, so that he could circle slowly around to see Faye better. "Teenagers have a limited amount of patience for their parents. It will be good to have some space. Pulling a prank on her old, innocent father lightened her spirits. We can definitely take advantage of some breathing room."

"You don't seem to be holding a grudge about the prank," Faye said as she watched him move slowly around the paddock. He followed every bit of advice Grant had given him.

"Nah, life is way too short for grudges, and how Gemma laughed was worth every second of my lesson. It's my favorite sound." Brian reached down to run his hand over Charlie's neck. This might be his first time in the saddle, but there was something comfortable about it. He and Charlie made a good team already.

"Honestly, I'm afraid that Grant and Gemma together will be hatching more plots against you, so we may regret putting them together, but if I don't get Prue's horse a little exercise, she'll be appalled. Are you up for a short ride?" Faye motioned with her chin to the break in the mountains. "Armstrong land extends past that line, and it's pretty country." Then she pointed to the left. "Or we could ride the fence line, check for any weak spots. That might save Travis extra work, since he's doing his best to help my grandfather keep it up."

Brian knew that Faye was a neighbor to the Armstrongs, but he hadn't realized how close she was with the family. "Let's save the pretty country for another day when Gemma can stand to be with me without rolling her eyes."

"Think that will happen before she turns eighteen?" Faye asked as her lips twitched.

"Well, since she was part of an elaborate plot to have

me up to my knees in dirty straw and 'road apples' today," Brian drawled, "I *think* she might be getting more comfortable in our relationship."

Faye's chuckles triggered his own grin. He'd done his best to accept Grant's intense lesson on proper stall maintenance, but as soon as he'd seen the devil in his daughter's eyes and the way she had shared it with Faye, he'd jumped in with both feet.

Then he'd chased Gemma around Faye, with some of the evidence of their teamwork stuck to his hand.

"What was the other phrase? I'm afraid there will be a test when Grant gets back," Brian asked.

"Meadow muffins." Faye's shoulders shook with another round of giggles that made him happy.

Heading beyond the pasture for the fence line, Faye dropped back until they were riding side by side. "Are you making plans to get even, Chef?"

Brian sighed. "Nope. I did ask for help making Gemma comfortable here. Pretty sure this counted."

Faye's bright blue eyes gleamed with humor as she smiled at him. "You're a good sport. She's lucky to have this time with you."

"Lucky" also applied to any man who got to ride next to this beautiful woman, one who wore a cowboy hat as naturally as he wore an apron. Sure, their differences were stark, but none of them had kept them from arriving at this same spot at the right time.

Was that a coincidence?

Brian remembered Sadie Hearst telling him that she only believed in coincidences when she couldn't see who was pulling the strings.

"The longer I stay here, the more I realize how lucky I was to get this invitation to visit. The positive change in Gemma is at the top of the list of reasons why," Brian said.

"I haven't seen the worried frown since our first morning at the Majestic."

"Did you get along with your parents growing up?" she asked softly. He couldn't see her face well, so he wasn't sure what kind of emotion was in her voice.

"It was just my mother growing up, raising me and my younger brother by herself. She worked as a housekeeper. When she decided I was old enough to take over dinner, she started teaching me her recipes." Brian shook his head. "She used to chase me from her kitchen to air out the attitude."

Her soft laugh did something to him, teased the dark places nearest his heart. He was silent as he absorbed the impact of that unfamiliar sensation.

"Maybe I shouldn't have helped Gemma tease you as much as I did." Faye shrugged. "But you're as good at riding horses as you are at everything else. It's important to keep your ego in check."

Surprised, Brian turned to face her, relieved that Charlie was a professional and kept a steady pace. "You think I'm good at everything?"

She raised her eyebrows. "Aren't you?"

He grunted. "Not at all. The three most important women in my life would be able to write a long list of failures if it was ever necessary."

"Your daughter, her mother and…" Faye prompted him to keep talking. Was he going to follow her lead or change to something less…honest? He wasn't sure what was behind her mood, but he wanted to know more.

"My mother. I love her. She loves me. But the things she wanted me to be good at and what I managed to attain do not match at all. After I went to jail, I wasn't sure we'd ever be on speaking terms again."

Faye's expression was serious as she watched him. Not

judgmental, but concerned and interested in how his story was unfolding. That was nice.

"She cried when I showed her this." Brian held out his left hand so Faye could see his tattoo better. He had a lot of regrets, but this wasn't one of them, even though his mother's disappointment had burned.

"Your tattoo? Why?" Faye urged her horse closer.

"She thought it would limit me, keep me from succeeding. Everyone in my neighborhood growing up had ink, and she didn't want me to be anything like those guys."

"What is it?" Faye asked as she took his hand. "I see letters."

Brian turned it so she could read it the way he would.

"Oh, it's Gemma's name. In script." Faye traced the letters lightly, but he felt the tickle all the way to his soul.

"Yeah. As soon as I got out of jail, I had it done. When I'm prepping in the kitchen, washing my hands for the full thirty seconds my mother taught me or paying bills on my computer, even staring into space, I can see her name. To remind me what's important." He'd gotten that part right immediately. Unfortunately, he was still figuring out what it meant to make sure Gemma came first for every decision he made.

"Granddaughters are a magic key to any locked door. All I had to do was convince Gemma, who didn't know me, to spend time with me and her grandmother to start repairing things there. And once her Nonna made Gemma her *uncinetti*..." He shook his head. He'd never forget how Gemma's eyes had widened in pleasure at his mother's cooking. "They're these knot-shaped cookies that my mom always makes for Easter. My daughter grew up with a mother who prefers to make reservations and a father who can't bake to save himself, so finding out Nonna had these treats changed everything. We went from visiting my mother on holidays, to dropping Gemma off for a week in the summer so she could learn all the family secrets, to family dinner on Friday nights at the restaurant. Me, Gemma, Gemma's mom—Monica—and her husband, my mother, my younger brother and his family…all together there. It's nice."

They were quiet for a bit. He'd never heard silence like this. In the city, there was always noise. It might rise or fall, but the underlying buzz of traffic and people was constant. Here, he heard the occasional gust of wind and the horses.

He wasn't sure he wanted to hear his own thoughts this clearly.

"There's the fence line." Faye pointed in the distance to a post with barbed wire stretching for as long as he could see. "My grandparents have the land on the other side. From here, you can see the garden."

Closer to the fence, Faye slid out of the saddle and squeezed through the barbed wire to the other side, so Brian followed.

"Welcome to Grandpa's pride and joy in the summertime. It's still early but never too soon to get ready." Faye paused outside the low gate of the fenced-in area. He guessed it'd been built in a futile effort to keep animals out of the garden. "Sweet corn, potatoes, beans, summer squash, spinach, lettuce… Grandpa tries his hand at everything." Pride lit up Faye's eyes.

"Wow, this is a chef's dream. I bet your grandmother gets all kinds of inspiration for dishes based on whatever is in season." Brian pointed at the copse along the connecting fence line. "Are those trees budding? Apple blossoms?"

Faye tugged his hand to pull him closer. "These are peach trees. See? The blooms are pink, but we also have apple trees. Almost all the apples I use for the Ace's world-famous apple pies come from these trees."

"Amazing. Is that the top secret ingredient?" Brian asked. He hadn't forgotten his promise to get the recipe.

"That's for me and Gemma to know. I hope your daughter respects the rules of Apple Pie Club after I share all." Faye grinned at him.

"First rule is that you don't talk about apple pie ingredients if you make it into this elite club," Brian drawled.

"Exactly." Faye followed him as they walked slowly along the edge of the garden.

"I guess you know the Armstrongs pretty well." Brian was curious about Faye.

She smiled at him. "For better or worse, I know every single one of them. I moved in with my grandparents before Prue and Walt started fostering, but when Wes got here, my whole life changed. I dated a couple of them for brief periods during high school, but we all might as well be family at this point."

Brian felt the twinge of jealousy before logic reminded him that Wes was head over heels in love with Sarah Hearst. He'd seen that the first time he'd met the cowboy in the Majestic's lobby. "How did your whole life change?"

Faye bit her lip as she considered that. Brian was determined to wait patiently for this answer. He could tell it mattered. "My parents are ambitious. Always have been. They're engineers and work on large construction projects all over the world." She gave him half a smile as if to say she wasn't clear on what that meant, but they could agree that it had to be important. "When I was young, it was too difficult to pack me up and take me with them, so they left me here. When I was older, I just…stayed here. They visit, but Prospect became my home."

Brian studied her face. He couldn't find any of the anger he imagined he'd experience in the same spot.

"Eventually, Wes got here, the others followed, and I

wasn't alone anymore. I felt so out of place, being the kid with parents who couldn't keep her, new to Prospect where everyone else had been born, but then there were these rowdy boys next door who didn't fit with their parents, either."

He had so many questions about her parents. The memory of how she'd asked about his own relationship with his mother made him wonder if they were on her mind.

"I bet the Armstrongs are great neighbors." Brian walked beside her and tried not to press for more information than Faye wanted to give.

"Prue and Walt were always wonderful to me. My grandmother is…intense." Faye rolled her eyes. "We don't have to wonder where my father got his drive, but Prue was so easy to be with."

Faye didn't know that he'd invaded her grandmother's kitchen, but he understood her clearly. Chefs were often demanding, but her grandmother had given him the old familiar feeling of… Fear? Respect? Probably both.

"Yes, so easy," he agreed. "Like Sadie Hearst. I'll never forget this one time she sat me down next to her. The restaurant was still under construction. Hammering, saws, people yelling out orders, but Sadie made me stop and ordered me to enjoy that minute of the process because it was never going to come again."

Faye's eyes shimmered as she met his. "Exactly. Somehow, they know how to live right now. Gran loves the Ace High, and she should be proud of it. That's her focus most of the time. She sets high standards for the food and the kitchen and even the service. I was always desperate to meet her standards."

Brian thought back to the disastrous dinner service and wondered what Faye would say about the state of the Ace High in her absence.

Then he realized why Prue had made a point to tell them that no one was going to share that news with Faye. Not only would she abandon this time away from the restaurant, but she might be convinced that she'd failed her grandmother by taking the chance to try something new.

"Your gran and grandpa and the Armstrongs are all lucky to have you." Brian carefully held the top wire of the barbed wire fence for Faye to squeeze back through. "I've never met a better consultant in my life."

Her theatrical sigh made him chuckle. "You've never met any other consultant, have you?"

She was right, but he wasn't going to admit that.

"How many Armstrong hearts did you break over the years?" Brian asked before another thought hit him. "And did any of them break yours?" Because he wasn't certain how well he would handle that news.

Faye settled back in the saddle and studied him with a narrowed gaze. "Do I appear to be a heartbreaker to you?"

Brian managed to climb up on Charlie with much less grace and pretended to ponder the question before he smiled slowly. "Yep. Isn't every beautiful woman a heartbreaker in one way or another?"

She slowly slipped her hat on her head. "Beautiful, huh? You sure have a way with words. You'll be a true cowboy in no time." When they began to follow the fence back toward the Rocking A's barn, she said, "Wes, Clay and Travis were each boyfriends for approximately two weeks over the course of our senior high school days. Grant and I have been frenemies up until this point. He's in *love* love with Mia, who's helping out at the Majestic with all the preparation for Western Days and researching a book about Sadie's life. And Matt…he's a charming rascal, one that I never got tangled up with, mainly because the line of women in love with Matt Armstrong stretched all the way through town."

"So you aren't pining with unrequited love for an Armstrong," Brian concluded, "or anyone else."

She halted and shifted in the saddle to face him. "Pining? No, I do not pine."

Satisfied, he nodded.

Then she added, "But this is a great opportunity to give you a friendly warning."

Brian tipped his chin up, intrigued at the segue. "Go ahead."

"Jordan saw our blip in the doorway, when we were in the restaurant," Faye said, her expression filled with apology.

"Blip?" Brian repeated as the scene replayed in his head. "Not sure about that term, but okay."

Faye cleared her throat. "There are no secrets in the Armstrong universe. Jordan will tell every single person she meets until there's no one left that there could be something between you and me."

Brian scratched his cheek. It was hard to see a downside, but her serious eyes convinced him he was missing something.

"And that's a problem," he said slowly, hoping she would explain further.

Her impatient huff reminded him of Gemma's reactions sometimes. Was he as dim as his daughter implied?

"Because love is in the air. The Rocking A is so thick with it, it'll choke you when all the couples appear in the same room together." She pointed. "What happens when people find their true loves? They start matching everyone they run across. You and I will be thrown together nonstop if they get serious about us."

Brian urged Charlie along and stole a glance at Faye. He couldn't tell if she was upset about this or…

They rode silently back toward the barn for a while, before she said, "So you understand what I'm saying."

He nodded. "I think so. I just don't see the problem."

She did the huffing thing again. "Your life in LA? Mine here? Entire states between them?"

"Oh. That." Brian held up his hand when she was about to go on. The fire in her eyes convinced him it would be a forceful explanation of what she meant. "Is there any way to stop them at this point?"

That stumped her for a second and she settled back in her saddle. "If we stay away from each other, keep it fully professional, eventually everyone will understand it was a…" She sighed.

"It was a blip. That's all." Brian waited for her to catch up and saw her hesitate. She didn't like the description, either.

"Yeah," she agreed softly.

They entered the barn and slipped off their mounts. "You're forgetting something, Faye."

She raised her eyebrows instead of asking the question.

"I scrapped my teenage daughter's plans for the afternoon, twisted your consulting arm into giving me riding lessons, and endured an in-depth discussion of horses, stalls and their meadow muffins to be right here with you. Alone. Together." He smiled as he watched the realization cross her face. "I might welcome some assistance from the matchmakers. Have you ever thought of that?"

Faye blinked, and they were right back in the restaurant kitchen, paused in the doorway face-to-face, a heartbeat away from a kiss. The steady clop of hooves was their warning that Grant and Gemma were returning, so Brian stepped away.

Another near miss for a kiss wasn't the end of the world.

Eventually, he and Faye would meet in the right spot at the right time. She'd practically suggested that with her warning about the matchmakers.

Her concern about the distance between her life here and his in LA was valid, but they both understood that this was a short-term flirtation. It couldn't be anything more than that, so why couldn't they enjoy it while it lasted?

If it came time to fly back home and he hadn't kissed Faye, that would be a shame.

When their next blip came around, he'd be ready.

CHAPTER NINE

On Tuesday afternoon, Faye smothered a yawn as she stood next to the Majestic's dining room window staring down at the lake. Franky and Rafa, the two chefs Brian had organized to compete to run the Majestic's kitchen, were seated on stools and answering questions Andre had prepared in advance. If she understood the director correctly, this exercise was to help the pair get comfortable in front of the camera. Both were dressed in chef coats, and the shadowed doors leading to the kitchen formed an artistic backdrop.

Luckily, both chefs were comfortable in the center of all the fuss.

Franky, the taller, more outgoing of the two, answered every question enthusiastically and then encouraged Rafa to answer, prodding the quieter chef when his responses needed more detail. Rafa seemed bemused by the hubbub, but it was impossible to miss that he knew his stuff. It would be interesting to see what kind of dishes each of them prepared.

Brian, Sarah and Jordan formed a half circle behind the monitor Andre was watching closely. Franky exclaimed, "This is going to be fun. I'm ready to cook!"

Rafa's lips curled slightly. "It is a good kitchen, Chef. We have a lot to work with." He slung his arm over Franky's shoulder and drew him close.

Faye wondered if the two chefs were only good friends

or something more, and realized the matchmaking illness that inflicted everyone around her might have taken hold in her.

Brian nodded. "We want to see how you'd set the menu here. Remember that teaching something to viewers at home is also going to be a big part of this competition. The Cookie Queen Corporation wants to keep people visiting their site every week to find out who wins and to pick up valuable information, something like Sadie Hearst might have sprinkled into one of her demonstrations."

It didn't surprise Faye when Rafa immediately raised his hand, as if he was back in elementary school and needed to be excused to go to the restroom. Brian immediately motioned for him to lower his hand. "I told you, we don't raise hands in the kitchen, Rafa. Consider this an extension of the kitchen."

The young man tucked his hands at his sides. "Can we get your advice on what would be the right kind of lesson as we cook our dishes, Chef?"

Brian glanced at Andre. "What do you think? We don't want to get to the end of this without usable footage."

Jordan spoke up. "If you're supposed to be an unbiased judge, how can you give advice to them while they're competing? Do we need to see how well they manage on their own instead?"

Sarah bit her bottom lip.

Faye wasn't sure there was an easy answer.

"Let's consider this while we review judges' outfits." Andre swiveled around until he caught sight of Faye. "Let's go, on-air talent." He waved his hand imperiously at her, so Faye sighed and picked up the hanger with clothes she'd carried in against her better judgment.

Andre spread all their choices on the sofa in the foyer and paced back and forth in front of them. Jordan had chosen a black shirt and dark jeans. Sarah's offering was a red sweater and dark jeans.

"This plaid won't do."

That was Faye's choice.

"Chambray? That's a solid blank canvas," he said as he tapped his chin. "Bring a chambray shirt tomorrow. Folksy à la Sadie without being remarkable."

Brian's amusement at the director's sharp orders was easy to see in the curl of his lips. Faye had done her best to avoid getting too close to Brian all day. It hadn't been too difficult because there was so much commotion in the restaurant as they prepared to shoot, but now their eyes locked.

Faye was glad the large distance of the foyer was between them, because if she'd been any closer, there might have been another blip moment.

Instead of arguing, which had gotten no one anywhere all day long with Andre, Faye nodded. Sarah and Jordan left to put on their wardrobe choices and Gemma shot her a sympathetic smile. Faye waved at her before Brian leaned in to say something to his daughter.

Faye tried not to be too jealous as Gemma hurried off.

"Looks like I'll be making a trip to Homestead Market tonight," she muttered to herself as they all trooped back to the kitchen, where Sarah and Jordan settled in front of the camera so that Andre could see how they "read" under the lights.

Andre had planned to ask everyone the same set of questions that Rafa and Franky had answered. The short responses about their favorite recipes, no-go ingredients, hometown restaurants and where they learned to love cooking would be edited in as filler or used as a tease on social media to draw people in.

Not one moment was going to be wasted, according to Andre.

The first inkling that there might be a wrench in the works was listening to Sarah and Jordan navigate the questions. Sarah's nervous smile made Faye think of driver's license photos.

Not the good ones, either.

And Jordan gulped nervously twice during her own answers, forcing Andre to stop her and begin again.

When Sarah and Jordan were finally finished, they stumbled back into the shadows behind the camera while Jordan did her best to wave her hands and stir up a breeze for them both, and the director had pulled out a white handkerchief to blot his shiny bald head.

Were the lights hot? Or was that a nervous reaction hitting all three of them at one time?

"Next." Andre pointed at Faye and then at Brian.

They were going to be interviewed together?

Faye did her best to contain her dismay as she settled onto one of the stools. The heat of the lights hit her immediately, but the racing of her pulse convinced her Jordan's and Sarah's reactions had to be nerve-related as well.

"We're going to need a minute," Brian said as he glanced at Faye. "Nervous about having the camera rolling?"

Since she hadn't been until she'd watched the Hearst sisters struggle their way through an interview, Faye licked her lips. "More than I expected, honestly. This is like nothing I've ever imagined. Hard to believe anyone will be watching *me* on a cooking show." She shrugged. "What do I bring to the judging table?"

Gemma raced into the dining room, a chambray shirt fluttering behind her. "Got it."

Brian nodded and took it from her. "Fresh from the

Homestead Market and our shopping trip. If it fits, it's yours for the show."

Wearing his shirt would be the equivalent of waving a red cape in front of the matchmakers in the room. They would stampede in the rush to push her closer to the chef, but Faye couldn't find a graceful way to refuse without making a much bigger spectacle and drawing more attention.

"Thank you, Chef." She stood and pulled it on over the Ace High T-shirt that she'd put on that morning out of habit and comfort. "It's roomy, but someone told me that looser would work."

He laughed and waited for her to settle back on the stool next to him.

Andre moved closer to peer at Faye. He buttoned the shirt and stepped back. "The shirt is good. Tomorrow, let's find her a Majestic Prospect Lodge T-shirt to wear under the chambray, casual, unbuttoned. Can't be advertising for the competition."

"Then I shouldn't be judging, should I?" Faye turned to Brian for confirmation. "I mean, isn't that the ultimate advertisement, another chef making the decision on who the competition hires?"

Andre pursed his lips. "Chefs are always judges, Faye. They work for other restaurants."

"Faye isn't a chef in title, so…" Brian tilted his head to the side. "But those chefs who are judges aren't choosing their direct competition, either."

Sarah and Jordan put their heads together to confer. Andre joined them before spinning on his heel to return to the center of the room. "I have the answer."

Relieved, Faye shook out her tense shoulders. Staying safely behind the camera would be much easier than judging.

"Faye is out. We'll have Sarah, Jordan and Brian judging. Easy enough. Fingers crossed Brian is more comfortable in front of the camera. He will do the intros, lead the judging, prompt the sisters as needed." Andre snapped. "But..."

He paused for dramatic effect and Faye had a hunch she wasn't going to like where the "but" was going.

"Our consultant will work with the chefs to help them determine what kinds of techniques they can illustrate, helpful tips to toss out as they cook." Andre waved his hand as if to say, "Et voilà!"

So the "but" wasn't as bad as she'd expected. "I can do that from behind the scenes. No cameras." No chambray shirt required. She started to ease out of it when Andre shook his head. "Oh, no, we'll do everything in front of the camera. *Nothing wasted*," he said in a singsong. "I like this. You can ask questions as they stir and chop. An everyman with the work shirt to prove it. That will help draw the viewer in. Our top-rated chef brings the cred. The Hearsts can argue on camera about which dish is better, and if they stumble over their words or have a frozen, creepy smile..." He sighed. "This is going to be good content." His tone was grimly determined.

Andre took his spot behind the camera, checking his sheet of questions. Brian bent closer to do that low-voice-in-her-ear thing that accelerated her heart rate. "Every decision he makes is improving the final product. You have to admit that."

"Let's hold all judgment until the end of day one to see if I can do the things he's suggesting." Faye pressed her hand over her heart. "I'm not a chef or a television personality."

"You cook. You've watched Sadie Hearst in person. She was the most natural teacher I ever met, whether there was a camera rolling or not." Brian smiled. "Channel Sadie.

Do what you believe she might have done, and this series will be great."

He reached over to squeeze her hand and Andre fired his first question at them. "What ingredient should be eliminated from every kitchen everywhere?"

"Easy. I'm eliminating artichokes. They take too much time to prepare for not enough reward. Cutting and peeling and brown fingers from the leaves if you don't move fast enough…what a headache." Brian glanced at her and Faye realized he was still holding her hand. She couldn't decide if it was more obvious to disentangle their fingers or keep rolling, so she…did nothing. "They might be a special occasion food, but I'm going to someone else's restaurant to eat them."

Brian was now focused on her. Cue the heart rate acceleration.

"Lima beans." Faye noted Brian's reaction. His pursed his lips said a lot. "I question the first person who saw a lima bean and decided the flat waxy green thing might taste good. Unbelievable!"

"As long as you're limiting this to lima beans, I'll allow it, but," Brian teased her, "we must keep the *fagioli* or my mother will never forgive me."

"Good," Andre said, businesslike and moving on. "Favorite hometown restaurant?"

"You take that one first," Brian said.

Faye laughed. "Gotta go with the Ace High in Prospect, Colorado. My grandmother runs the kitchen, and you've never had better fried chicken in your life."

"The apple pie is extraordinary, too." Brian spoke directly to the camera. "Believe me when I say your life is not complete until you've tried dessert at the Ace High."

Faye hated the blush that covered her cheeks but the flutter of pride at his praise was sweet. "I'm proud of that pie. It's based on a Sadie Hearst recipe, with something extra in the mix."

Andre nodded. "Who taught you how to cook?"

Faye thought about passing the conversational lead back to Brian, but he squeezed her hand in encouragement. She quickly checked on his attention, but he was facing the camera as they all waited. "Who taught me almost everything I know about cooking? That one's easy. My grandmother. I grew up working at her side at home and at the restaurant. I might never be as good as she is, but I have all the tools to serve up an excellent family meal."

"Family meals. It's funny you should say that. My mother was my first and best teacher, but her hope was that I could have dinner ready before she made it home from work. I don't think she ever wanted me to become a chef, but it was the only thing that fit for me." Brian shrugged. "So I'm still preparing these meals to draw people together. They just happen in my restaurant. I'm pretty proud of that."

"You two are good together. And the camera loves you both. That is a piece of exciting news to wrap up with." Andre scanned down the list before shaking his head. "Let's call it a day. The noise of growling stomachs is going to interfere with the recording if we don't get a dinner break in soon."

Brian eased off the stool to stretch and met her stare briefly before letting go of her hand. Faye wasn't sure what his look signified, but she knew it was silly to experience the weird flash of loneliness before logic reasserted itself.

"All this discussion of family meals has me thinking of making family dinner in the lodge's kitchen before we start taping tomorrow. We'll feed the crew here. What do you guys think about that?" Franky and Rafa immediately nodded. When no one else responded, Brian explained,

"Family dinner is this restaurant tradition where the chef prepares a meal for the restaurant staff. Tonight, I'll cook for you. I'd like to draw in a couple of extra helpers, but a nice chicken and pasta pomodoro wouldn't take long. Gemma and I can handle the main."

"Jordan and I love this idea. Our best contribution would be a salad to go with." Sarah squeezed Jordan tight against her side. Was she trying to prevent a complaint from bubbling on her sister's lips? "We can use the apartment kitchen and meet back here when everything is done."

Faye watched Prue calculate all the angles. Gemma was edging closer to her. Was she hoping to be drafted for a new team in this plan? "I've still got a nice loaf of bread leftover from the lunch fixings. I was thinking I'd try garlic bread for lunch one day this week. Might as well toss that into the mix if I can get an assistant?"

Gemma immediately volunteered, but Brian said, "Hey, I need you with me for Nonna's special recipe. Walt, are you up for light kitchen duty?"

Faye watched Gemma's shoulders slump as Walt nodded. "Yes, Chef, I'd be happy to take some orders from the prettiest cook in these mountains." Prue tilted her cheek forward and he blew her a kiss.

Would Prue accept this plan or find a way around Brian's setup? When she squeezed Gemma's shoulder, Brian's daughter accepted her fate and moved toward the restaurant kitchen.

Faye was interested to see Brian mouth a silent "Thank you" to Prue.

"Let's say, an hour? Meet back here?" Brian waited for everyone, including the video crew, to agree. Then he turned to her. "Can you stay for dinner?"

The weird flutter in her chest was a surprise. Faye rubbed the spot absentmindedly as she weighed her options. She could go home and gather up something for dinner with Grandpa or go into the Ace and be drawn into the loud, busy service.

The memory of Gemma trudging off to the restaurant kitchen convinced her to say, "Actually, could I help out in the kitchen? I'd love to get the famous chef's secrets for juicy chicken."

He visibly relaxed, and Faye understood that he'd been as uncertain of his plan as Gemma, but it was important to him to have his daughter working alongside him in the kitchen. "I would love that."

The last thing Faye saw before Brian took her hand to lead her through the kitchen's swinging doors was the gleam of satisfaction in Prue Armstrong's eyes. If there had ever been any hope of convincing Prue that there was nothing between her and the famous LA chef, it had been burnt to a crisp. Eventually, Faye would need to figure out how to protect her heart against the handsome man who was scheduled to leave Prospect entirely too soon.

But first, she had to prepare dinner.

CHAPTER TEN

Brian lined up the ingredients he'd need for his chicken and pasta dish, aware that his daughter was slumped against the counter next to the sink, the picture of teenage despair at being drafted into dinner prep, while Faye was in the background. They were both waiting for him to give them orders.

And he was hesitating.

Why? Giving orders in dinner prep was kind of his thing.

Though he'd tried cooking with Gemma before, it had ended in tears. More than anything else, he wanted to avoid that.

The whole idea had sprung from being keenly aware of both of these women as they'd orbited the production the entire day. Brian had lost count the number of times Gemma had sighed with boredom. Since that was the first step down the dangerous slope of deciding she wanted to go home and he knew an opportunity like this trip wouldn't come around again soon, he'd been running scenarios of how to reconnect with Gemma.

Cooking together had been his best solution, and it had been weak. Prue Armstrong could have scuttled it easily, but she'd followed his unspoken plea.

So here he and Gemma were.

Awkward.

After drizzling olive oil on the large skillet Faye had

handed him, he said, "Gemma, can you open these containers of grape tomatoes, wash and cut them in half?" She hesitated, so he added, "Please?"

The worried frown creased her forehead immediately, but she straightened and nodded. He had made sure to use his mildest tone. Was that why she was confused? When he was focused in the kitchen, his directions could get… abrupt. For his daughter, he could do better.

"How should I wash them?" she asked, and he turned to her, certain she was giving him a hard time with the question, but she was waiting for his answer.

"Wash your hands first, hot water and soap. Then take the tomatoes out and run them under cold water while you rub the outsides with your hands. Gently. You don't want to bruise them." Brian met Faye's stare over Gemma's head. Her encouraging smile convinced him he was doing fine, so he shifted to searing the chicken. He'd need at least two batches of this dish for a group this size. "Faye, can you find another skillet? This size or smaller is okay."

When it magically appeared on the stovetop, he grinned at her. "I need a consultant in every kitchen I cook in."

"You'll never find another one like me," she murmured into his ear, and he knew she was correct. The tingle her voice sent along his nervous system was hopefully a one-time phenomenon.

"Here's a cutting board, Gemma," Faye said, holding up a chef's knife. "This knife is very, very sharp, so please be careful with it." Brian watched Faye move to the other side of the sink where Gemma was setting up her station. Faye was pulling down plates and gathering all the utensils they'd need to serve dinner, but she was hovering, clearly keeping a helpful eye on Gemma.

Gratitude that she'd agreed to this idea eased his worry.

Until he saw Gemma chasing the grape tomatoes all over the cutting board with her knife.

"Gem, hold the tomato tight with one hand, cut with the other." Brian dropped the pan and ignored the clang as it hit the burner to take the knife from Gemma's hand. "Like this." He demonstrated an efficient cut and the proper way to hold the knife and then handed it back to her.

Her nod convinced him to return to the stove, but he kept taking quick glances at her to be sure. At the rate she moved, he'd have enough tomatoes halved for the pomodoro sauce around Christmas. "Speed it up, honey, okay? We have a hungry crowd waiting."

Brian returned his attention to the chicken and kept reminding himself that it took practice to learn and that this wasn't a timed event and she needed to be slow and steady when she was holding a knife.

Brushing her out of the way to take over was the urge he always had to fight whenever he managed to get Gemma into the kitchen, but he wasn't going to do that this time.

"Hey, I saw this trick on one of the food competition shows," Faye said softly to Gemma. He watched them out of the corner of his eye as Faye held up two plates. "You get two dinner plates with rims." She set one down on the cutting board. "And you arrange the tomatoes like this. Then put the other plate on top so you can hold it firmly without squishing the tomatoes between." Faye demonstrated. "Can I borrow your knife, Chef?" she asked Gemma, who rolled her eyes and laughed as she handed over the knife. "Thank you, Chef."

He couldn't see Faye's smile, but he heard it in her voice as she teased Gemma with the title.

"So the last thing we have to do is cut these carefully between the two plates like this."

Brian turned to see that Faye was slicing slowly and

had Gemma's full attention. After she brushed the sliced tomatoes off onto the cutting board, she asked, "Want to try it with the next batch?"

"Of course. We have hungry people waiting, Chef." Gemma's quick response was delivered in a low grumble that might have been an attempt at impersonating him. Brian shook his head in amusement. Then he noted the teasing glance both women shot over their shoulders at him and he realized he'd accomplished his goal.

Thanks to dinner prep, the three of them were together and they were having fun. No one was bored. No one was ducking him by darting across the room for the exit.

Or worse, crying.

His success made it easy to relax and enjoy his time making one of his mother's favorite recipes for his daughter and their new friends. This was why he loved the kitchen.

"Here you go, Chef." Gemma delivered the halved tomatoes and stepped back. "What next?"

Brian pretended to inspect her job. "Nice. Think you're up to searing chicken?"

The way she immediately shook her head made him pause, but then she said, "Not yet, but I can learn with a good teacher."

He was so proud, he had to resist the urge to call Faye over. "Drizzle oil in the pan, Chef. We're going to season with salt and pepper."

Gemma followed his directions with intense concentration. Brian decided he'd had the same expression when his mother had been instructing him as a kid. Her response to his mistakes had been a loud lecture on the correct manner to do things and an occasional swat with a dish towel, but he'd never worn his heart on his sleeve the way Gemma did.

"Do you and Nonna do much cooking when you stay with her?" he asked.

Gemma was so quiet while she stared at the browning chicken that he wasn't sure she'd heard his question. Before he could repeat it, she shot him a quick glance. "Is talking while cooking a thing?"

Faye's quiet laughter made it easier to wrinkle his nose at her. "For some people. I'm trying something new."

Gemma's slow grin pleased him.

Soul-deep satisfaction rolled through him as his daughter stood there, giving him a hard time but without a trace of worry on her face.

"We have done a little, but Nonna enjoys feeding me more than cooking together." Gemma wrinkled her nose. "There's always so much food. Last time, she sent me home with the leftovers, even though I warned her I was going to share them with Mom and Chris."

Brian whistled. "Nonna holds a mean grudge. Think she's forgiven your mother for not including her in your early years?" After he'd gotten out of jail, Monica had first refused to answer his phone calls. He'd worked through that and now, on the other side of that struggle, he appreciated how diligently Monica had protected Gemma. She'd demanded he prove himself at every step. Any access to Gemma for his mother had depended on Monica trusting him.

Monica's first priority had been what was best for her daughter.

Brian hated that Monica had been put in that position but he understood it. He respected that. And he trusted her to introduce a good man to their family dynamic to be Gemma's stepfather. Gemma had turned out as well as she had because Monica was strong.

"Allowing them leftovers seems like a big step in this

relationship." Gemma shrugged. "Next time we have family dinner at Rinnovato, I'm going to make them sit together. What do you think? Food fight or friendly conversation?"

Brian pretended to consider that carefully.

"There's a third possibility. Frosty silence. But I'm hoping for some conversation." Brian sighed. "We're so close to having the family I've been hoping for ever since I got myself straightened out. Bringing Nonna and Monica together is the last step."

Next, he showed Gemma how to add the ingredients to make the pomodoro sauce that went over the chicken. At some point, Faye had silently placed the pasta pot on the back burner and started the water boiling. Dried angel hair was on the counter next to his elbow. His consultant was good but she was also practically invisible. But then he realized the low-level awareness he'd been experiencing all day was still there. He knew she was nearby.

"I'm not sure Nonna's the last step," Gemma said and he had to rewind to follow her train of thought.

"No? When we get Nonna thawed out, we're one big happy family." Brian dropped the pasta into the water and checked the time. They were running behind but not by much.

"Mom has Chris." Gemma tried to stir the ingredients by shaking the pan, copying his movements, but sighed and reached for a spatula to help. "You need someone, too. Then the family is complete."

There was no doubt in Gemma's voice. She'd already evaluated the situation and knew what was missing.

"You know they're called 'wicked,' right? Stepmothers? Who wants one of those?" Brian asked, prepared to brush this off as a joke if there was any way to do so. Finding a woman who'd jump into his messy life with the hours a restaurant demanded would never be simple.

He glanced over his shoulder at Faye who was washing dishes as he and Gemma cooked, but he could tell she was eavesdropping without a hint of shame. Her wink as she caught him staring made him smile. Finally, he showed Gemma how to test that the pasta was ready and they moved to drain the angel hair.

"Would you like serving dishes, Chef, or do it family style from the stovetop?" Faye asked, holding up a stack of plates.

"Uh, family style. Yeah." That would be easiest. She gave a quick nod and bumped the swinging doors with her hip on the way out to the dining room. When he turned back to his daughter, Gemma was watching him watch Faye.

"Don't pick out a wicked one, Dad." She patted his shoulder as if she was congratulating him. "I'm glad we're on the same page about what kind of woman we're looking for here." Her sunny grin was beautiful. "I'm going to check on the other kitchen to see if they need any help."

The way she skipped out of the kitchen was the complete opposite of how she'd trudged in. The horrors of working with her father were over and she'd managed to tweak his nose in a teenager-ly way, and so her positive attitude had returned.

Brian scrubbed the few remaining pots and pans as he considered how little it had taken to improve Gemma's mood.

A successful cooking lesson without shouting or tears.

A few gentle pokes at her father's ego.

And Faye.

Quantifying how her presence had eased the tension

between them was impossible, but there was no doubt in his mind that she'd made a difference.

Faye suddenly returned. "I'm going to fill some pitchers with ice water and put them on the tables. Jordan said Prue made up some lemonade and tea, so they've got the dispensers set up. Glasses. Ice."

He crossed his arms over his chest and watched Faye bustle through the kitchen, opening drawers and pulling out extra dish towels and a serrated knife.

When she realized he was watching, she straightened. "Prue's going to bring the bread down here to cut it. So it stays warm and soft."

Faye had been working the same hours everyone else had, but she was still moving at top speed. He admired her work ethic, but he also wondered what drove her.

"Sounds like dinner is under control. Want to grab a plate of pasta and have a seat?" he asked. She deserved to sit and relax.

Her eyebrows shot up. "First? Now? Me?"

Given her tone, he might as well have suggested she be the first person to walk the plank or jump out of an airplane. "I guess a good host serves her guests before being seated."

She immediately moved away from the stove. "The chef should get the first plate tonight."

"I can wait." He inched closer to her to evaluate her response. Faye didn't move but she definitely noticed his nearness. "Want to tell me why you've been moving as far away from me as possible today?"

Faye scoffed. "We've been in the same room all day." She motioned between them. "This is far away?"

Ignoring that, he said, "I don't think space is going to throw the matchmakers off the scent."

"Not if you take my hand in front of them, it won't."

Faye tilted her head to the side. "And I don't think it bothers you, their interest. Is that because this is a passing amusement? Because I can understand that. You're here for a short period. There's no real chance your heart is involved. When you go home, though, I'll be the one left here with the consolation of friends and neighbors to swallow."

Brian wondered if she was correct. If he was the kind of man who could treat a temporary flirtation as a game, everything would be simpler, but Faye would have had no trouble keeping her distance from someone as superficial as that. She was too sharp to be fooled into taking such a guy seriously.

"Gemma commenting about a stepmother? That has never happened. Not since she let me back into her life. Not after Monica and Chris announced their engagement or got married. I can't treat this like a game." Brian was choosing his words carefully as he went because he wasn't certain of his destination yet. "The fact that it nearly knocked me over tells me a lot."

"What exactly?" She mirrored his stance, arms folded as she mulled that over.

"That I've never considered adding another person to this mix. Running a restaurant is hard on relationships. The hours. The stress. The finances." Brian realized he was strengthening the case for Faye to hit the swinging door running. "Add to that, our living in different states, and I get all the reasons why we are a bad idea." He looked away and then back at her. "But you're the only woman who's caused Gemma to even consider a stepmother and me to wonder what if there is more for me than Rinnovato."

When the scent of vanilla in the air caught his attention, he met Faye's stare and realized she could smell it, too.

"And here we are again, a breath away from a kiss," she said softly. "And a ghost encouraging us to go for it."

Brian paused. “Ghost? That’s the big secret about the vanilla in the air?” In the kitchen? He had his doubts.

“No one here believes in ghosts, that’s true, but no one would be surprised if Sadie Hearst had returned to her kitchen and her family to nudge things along. The vanilla comes and goes and tends to occur in Sadie-like opportunities.” Faye’s slow smile blossomed. “Don’t scoff until you’ve been here for a minute. I’ve never experienced it before…until you showed up.”

That reminded him of Sadie’s opinion about coincidences again. If anyone could have found a way to pull these strings together, it was Sadie Hearst.

“So all the matchmakers are pushing us together, even the invisible one.” Brian brushed Faye’s hair behind her ear. “Do we have any hope of withstanding the pressure?”

Before she answered, the kitchen door swung open.

“Hot dish, coming through,” Prue called out gaily, “and I’ve got the garlic bread in my hands.” She waited for Brian to laugh at her joke, but he was struck by the fact that Faye had vanished from his side as if she was the one with paranormal powers.

She had hurried out of the kitchen as Prue went to put the pan of bread down on the countertop protected by the stack of dish towels.

“Good job, Chef,” Prue said. She picked up the serrated knife and sliced through the crusty bread quickly.

“My mother’s recipe.” Brian hated the way his conversation with Faye had ended. Nothing was a game to him. Never had been. He’d worked hard to get where he was, and Gemma’s heart was to be protected at all costs.

But life at the Majestic was busy.

He and Prue retreated once the video crew joined them with empty plates in hand and a conversation in progress.

Prue smiled at how everyone had descended on the

stove. She said, "Gemma's pretty proud of herself for her part. I heard she learned a new trick."

"Faye taught her how to quickly halve tomatoes." Brian was proud of Gemma's success.

"And she's got this idea about setting the two of you up to fall in love." Prue raised her hands as if it were obvious. "I had nothing to do with this. I approve, but it wasn't my idea."

Brian sighed. "I don't want her to be disappointed. There are too many people who might get hurt if all the poking and encouragement works. Because she and I are going back home."

"Well," Prue said, "I suppose that's true, but when we come to a decision like this, whether to take the chance on something dangerous or let something that might only come once in a lifetime pass us by because losing it would hurt too much, I always wonder if a life without any heartache really is a good thing. Where would all the best romantic songs and poems and stories come from if we all played it safe?"

He frowned and thought of all the logical problems with her point of view.

Then she smiled slowly. "Safe is you staying in LA, never finding out about fishing lodges and riding horses and haunted kitchens." She squeezed his arm. "Safe means Gemma is still holding you at arm's length because she needs to protect herself. Safe is so boring. We can all do better than that."

Prue moved to take the plate Walt offered her and left Brian with his thoughts.

Why was she making so much sense?

This was what Faye had been warning him about—being caught in Prue's sights. She had already given him something big to think about, something that supported the very thing he wanted to do, instead of the smart choice.

But he was certain that nothing would be settled on an empty stomach, so he grabbed a plate and joined the slow-moving line at the stove. He wasn't sure he could be logical about his attraction to Faye, anyway.

He enjoyed being with her too much to waste any time being "smart." Faye might be fighting this battle to protect their hearts on her own.

CHAPTER ELEVEN

WEDNESDAY HAD ARRIVED. The first round of the cooking competition was ready for filming, and Faye was nervous about her on-camera role. She was unhappy with how she and Brian had left things the night before. She regretted not being at the Ace High. Life there might resemble a three-ring circus at dinnertime, but she'd learned to stand in the center ring and control the chaos.

Here, she was a part of the circus itself.

"Where's Faye?" Andre yelled from the dining room.

The fact that she could hear him as far away as inside the pantry was impressive. She hastened to straighten the cans on the last shelf and hurried into the dining room, stepping over cables and dodging the stationary camera setup that had shrunk the Majestic's spacious kitchen in half.

"Put this on," River said and fussed with Faye's hair.

Faye took the chambray shirt she'd left hanging with the rest of the wardrobe and slipped it on over one of the Majestic Prospect Lodge T-shirts that Jordan had presented her with that morning. River was towing her slowly along until she was seated on a stool in the corner of the dining room behind the host station.

"Close your eyes," River said and Faye did so just before a puffy brush landed on her nose. River worked for approximately two seconds and then said, "Open your eyes." Mascara and eyeliner followed the powder and whatever else

River had applied. "Open your mouth." Faye did that. "Not like that. Like this." River's lips were open but…pouty? So Faye did her best to mimic the look. "You're ready."

"For what?" Faye murmured as she followed River's urging back to the center of the room. Jordan reached over to take her hand as she joined the crowd gathered there.

"Okay, now that we're all here and ready to go," Andre said as he peered at Faye over the top of the readers perched on the end of his nose, "we're about to tape the first round. We'll begin in the kitchen with Brian and the competitors. Faye, you'll start in the back."

"Could I please stay there?" she whispered. Had she meant for anyone to hear her? She wasn't sure but Sarah squeezed her arm encouragingly.

"Brian has a short introduction. He'll read it and then leave the kitchen. We'll cut there." Andre peered around the room to make sure everyone followed him. "Next we move to the pantry where Rafa and Franky make their selections. Faye, you'll be there to make comments and ask questions. It'll be crowded in there with River on camera, so try to stay out of the way if you can. Got it?" Faye immediately nodded. Any other answer seemed like it would be a problem. "We'll cut there. Then back in front of the stove, where we're going to have the two cameras, one getting everything from the back of the room and another next to the walk-in for some side shots of the action around the oven. River will roam and get footage of both chefs as they work. We won't interrupt the action to tape your instructional piece for the viewers at home, but we want to get Faye interacting with the contestants. Chefs, you can answer her questions as long as you keep working, but remember, we will come back and reshoot to get close-ups." Andre waited for both Rafa and Franky to nod. They didn't seem concerned about their part in this. Faye admired that attitude. "You will plate four dishes. And that's another cut.

"Then we move to the judges. We've marked places for the chefs in front of the tables where Sarah, Jordan and Brian are sitting, beautiful lake off to the side. Brian will ask you to describe the dish, why you chose it, how it fits into the Majestic's overall menu. While the judging is going on, the chefs have a break, time to grab something to drink or what have you. We will tape a fuller interview with each chef, a play-by-play that can be cut in with other footage as needed." The chefs nodded. Faye wondered if they'd done TV competitions before, because they were rolling easily with each new revelation. "Judges will score the competitors on taste, presentation and how the dish fits the lodge in style. Before we're done for the day, we'll bring Rafa and Franky back to the judging table and tell them who won the round. Then we say come back for round two and we cut."

Everyone was frozen as Andre finished rattling off the instructions. "Simple."

Franky tentatively raised his hand. "And we'll do the instructional close-ups after that? Or are we doing those on a different day?"

Andre pointed at him. "Excellent question. I can tell who was paying attention. If all goes well, we will tape those after the judging. If all does *not* go well, we can reset that at the end of the shoot. We have extra days that can be filled with shots around town and the lodge unless we get off schedule. If that happens, we'll first finish up the instructional shots and any interviews at the end."

When both competitors nodded, so did everyone else.

"Sarah, Jordan, come with me for a walkthrough of the kitchen." Andre turned and marched through the swinging doors. Both sisters reassured Faye before trotting after him.

So she tucked her hands in her pockets and tried not to smudge whatever it was River had put on her lips.

"You okay?" Brian asked close to her ear. The shiver that went down her spine made her mad.

"No, I'm not." She rubbed her ear, irritated at how little he had to do to draw her in.

"Nerves are normal. Even when you're as good at your job as we are." He waited for her to react to that, so she inhaled slowly and met his eyes. She hadn't been prepared for the impact there, either.

"Best consultant for miles around," Faye agreed and let loose the chuckle bubbling in her chest. She was annoyed again when she immediately felt better, but it was hard to take that out on him. He was helping.

"Exactly." Brian shrugged. "I've only done the one show, but all you have to do is pretend you've never seen anyone cook before in your life. Ask the kinds of questions an alien might ask if they landed in the pantry and go from there."

Faye squeezed her eyes shut. "An alien? So I need to channel a friendly extraterrestrial."

"Friendly is a good addition to that advice. A hungry ET might not be as patient with long answers." Brian tapped her foot with his. "You got this. Dinner rush is three times busier and twice as confusing. TV is simple."

Faye pursed her lips. "I guess you would know."

He waved a finger to indicate the lodge's dining room and kitchen. "I'm the most experienced TV chef for miles around. You can trust me."

Faye laughed. "At least you didn't tell me to imagine my audience in their underwear. I like your variation. A friendly little green guy who has never seen canned corn before is much easier."

Brian sounded serious as he said, "I wish we'd ended

things on a different note last night. I definitely care about hurting you, but I can't stay away from you, either."

Faye nervously licked her lips, remembered the lipstick at the last minute, and closed her eyes. "Did I smudge my lipstick? Andre will kill me."

Brian brushed his hand over her back. "Andre will yell, River will reapply and the world will go on, but your lipstick is undisturbed."

Faye inhaled slowly. "What a relief."

"Yeah," Brian said but the way he stared at her lips convinced her that he was thinking about a kiss.

So then Faye started thinking about a kiss.

And she understood exactly what he meant about being unable to stay away.

"Don't kiss me yet. We don't know if Andre has murderous tendencies," Faye said.

Then Brian's eyes snapped up to meet hers. *"Yet."*

Faye nodded. "Yet. Something about us is inevitable. We'll deal with the fallout when whatever this is, is over, but fighting it the entire time you're here is a losing proposition."

His smile made her wonder if she could reapply her own lipstick before anyone discovered the smudges his kiss would cause.

"Neither of us are good losers. What if there's another option? We just have to find it." Brian took her hand and traced her fingers with his thumb.

Suddenly, the kitchen door swung open and Andre motioned them forward. "Let's go! Showtime."

Brian led the way into the kitchen, which made it easier for Faye to step back inside. Sarah and Jordan were there, but out of the way. Faye went to stand next to them as Andre said, "Quiet on the set."

Brian was centered in front of the longest counter,

flanked by Rafa and Franky, who both stood at attention, their hands behind their backs.

She wanted to ask Sarah or Jordan if that was a result of Andre's direction, but she refused to be the one making noise and ruining a take, so she clenched her hands and watched.

"Chef, in three, two, one..." Andre pointed at Brian.

"For Round One, Franky and Rafa, we'd like you to prepare a family favorite. The Majestic Prospect Lodge attracts people of all ages, so a popular lunch special should appeal to kids and parents alike. It can be a staple on the menu or a seasonal item, but remember cost, prep time, and the restaurant's food and service reputation. What people walk out saying about the Majestic Prospect Lodge's restaurant will factor into the judging decision."

"Cut," Andre said. "That was good, Brian, but you were giving me life-or-death seriousness. I appreciate that, but let's try another take that makes it clearer that this is going to be a Sadie Hearst kind of place."

Faye chewed the top of her thumbnail as she watched Brian nod in understanding.

"Rafa, Franky, you keep that in mind, too. Sadie was easy. Every day was filled with possibility and she would never stand for a formal kitchen. We're all here for Sadie." Andre held his hand up. "Round One, Take Two. Rolling." He paused for the people in front of the camera to settle. "Action."

Faye wondered if Brian would ask for rewrites of the script.

Instead, he smiled. "Here we are in my friend Sadie's kitchen for Round One. We want to see a lunch dish that will keep visitors coming back for more. That means it needs to be unique, cost-friendly and delivered quickly enough that diners wonder how you did it. Running the

Majestic's kitchen is going to be fun, but we're going to take care of the business first. Just like Sadie would have." Brian glanced at Rafa and Franky. "Chefs, are you ready to cook?" After they both nodded, he stepped back. "Shake hands like you like each other and remember this is a job, not life or death."

Rafa glanced at the camera River was holding. "That's how Chef starts each dinner service. 'Act like you like each other tonight.'" The chefs shook hands and ended with a back-clapping hug. Afterward, both appeared looser and ready to cook.

"Two of the best in my kitchen stand before you here. I'm excited to see what they do." Brian took a step forward. "You have forty-five minutes. Your time starts now."

"Cut." Andre clapped loudly. "Much better. Everyone hold here before we get the judges out of the kitchen. We have scripts for a lot of things, but I will promise you that Sadie never met a script that she wouldn't toss out the window when it suited her. We're here to build content that Sadie would love. I guess Rafa and Franky are the only ones who didn't know and love Sadie, so it's up to the rest of us to bring her into the room." Andre spun to make sure everyone got his message. "I want my two competitors to understand this is a family operation. Sisters running the place, neighbors stopping in after a day on the lake, visitors who have found the place they were searching for and special occasions with loved ones. There's no Michelin star or front cover of a glossy magazine. There is freedom to enjoy what you love here as long as you remember who you're serving. The sooner we're all on that page, the faster these takes will go. The script is for guidance. Sadie's approval is the end goal." Andre pointed at the door. "Judges, out."

Brian stopped in front of her. "You've got this."

"Easy-peasy," Faye said with a nod but licked her lips and immediately waited for him to inspect any damage she'd done to her makeup.

"You've got this," he repeated.

"We're burning daylight, people. Faye, into the pantry. River, move in but stay behind the chefs until we tell them to start." Andre took his spot in front of the playback monitor. "Faye, River, stay there until both competitors are done with their shop. Chefs, the clock will start when I say go. Understood?"

Franky winked at Rafa and they both nodded.

Faye realized she was pressing her back as hard as she could against the pantry wall and forced herself to relax.

"Everyone settle. I will count us down. As soon as I say 'action' the clock starts," Andre told them.

Faye couldn't see what was happening outside, but she was happy to have the warning. She smiled at River, who held her thumb up.

"And we're rolling. Three, two, one…action." Andre's word was barely finished when Franky came barreling through the pantry door, elbows flying, Rafa on his heels. Faye watched them both scan the shelves of ingredients, impressed at how calm they both were. That reminded her of her question about whether they had competed before.

"Chefs, is this your first cooking competition?" she asked.

Rafa shook his head. "Well, it's my first time shooting one. I've tried out for others, before I was hired by Chef Caruso. I never made it, so this is all new." He reached over in front of Franky's face to pull down cans of tomato puree and laughed when Franky retaliated by taking down a package of dry pasta from above Rafa's head.

"Premade pasta?" Rafa's scandalized tone was followed by a tsk. "What would Chef's mother say?"

"Time limits, Rafa. Time limits." Franky darted quickly in front of Rafa to move to where the spices were arranged neatly. "Brian had to convince me I was up to this cooking competition, but this challenge is in my wheelhouse. I'm not classically trained. I only learned how to cook food people like, and Brian has done all the rest with me."

Faye managed to duck as Rafa pulled down a loaf of bread and weaved to avoid Franky's wild scoop of onions from the bin on the floor. The chefs were a whirlwind, and then they were gone.

River mimed brushing down her hair, so Faye tried to put herself back together and then moved out of the pantry to see that the chefs were already turning up the heat on the stove.

Keenly aware of her job as the reporter on the street, Faye asked, "Chefs, do you already have a clear vision of what you're preparing?"

Rafa huffed. "Not yet, but it's getting closer."

Franky agreed. "Exactly. Sometimes you have to wait to see what shows up when you're finished to know where you were going all along."

Since that sounded like something Sadie might have said, word for word, Faye thought they were both on track. And she didn't miss the fact that Franky's answer fit more situations in life than cooking competitions.

Like this flirtation with the chef-judge who would be leaving soon.

As the chefs peeled and chopped and diced, Faye realized she was holding her breath. They were moving so quickly in this kitchen that it was clear both Franky and Rafa were professionals used to meeting the demands of a busy restaurant.

When she noticed Andre pointing aggressively, she decided she'd been watching the action for too long. "Rafa, I'm seeing lots of canned vegetables. Do you use those often?"

He immediately shook his head. "No, but growing up, my mother worked miracles with them, so I figured that would be a good place to start here. For family dinners and in a busy lunch service, the clock is ticking, so it's important to use time-saving strategies. The success of the soup sort of depends on how long the flavors have to build, so I'm planning a few tricks to help that along."

Faye immediately leaned forward. "Tricks? I love tricks. I can't wait to see them!" Then she turned to Franky. "And who doesn't love a pasta? Do you have any magic up your sleeve, Franky?"

Franky beamed. "I call this chi-tie because I'm making a hearty chili and including some beefy bow tie pasta to make it a delicious, fun meal that will attract kids and parents alike."

Faye had never seen such a dish, but she was interested. "Is this a family recipe, Franky?"

He laughed. "No way. My family is strictly meat and potatoes, but I like to add flair to whatever I try for the first time."

"This is the first time you've attempted the dish?" Faye asked, hoping she'd misunderstood.

Franky nodded, so she glanced at Rafa. He shrugged, an amused smile curling his lips. "Could be great. Could also be terrible. But you will never be bored when Franky is creating."

"Intriguing, but what are you boiling right now?" Faye pointed down at the clear pot in front of Franky. "I saw sugar and salt. Is that garlic?"

"Yep. I'm going to quick pickle my secret ingredient." He held a finger up to his lips as if he didn't want Rafa to know about it yet, so Faye nodded. She stepped back to check with Andre. His quick nod and thumbs-up signal made her think she was on the right track so far.

River joined them, coming to stand on the other side of Franky as he sliced a large jalapeño. "Pickled jalapeños are a surprise that no one expects but everyone loves." Franky grinned. "Picky eaters can remove them if they like, but the adventurous are going to find a new obsession that they demand for every bowl of chili."

Faye put her finger over her lips as she smiled at the camera and realized how much she was enjoying her role. She didn't have to orchestrate the chaos because Andre had a handle on that. She didn't have to prepare food while her Gran peered over her shoulder to critique her knife cuts. And it was clear that both Rafa and Franky were experts at what they did. Soaking up their confidence and their love of food was easy.

It was also fun.

When was the last time she'd enjoyed working at the restaurant? It was always satisfying because she was helping her family and serving her neighbors, but this excitement and learning new techniques and being surrounded by people who loved the same things…this was so much fun.

She moved back to Rafa as he scooped vegetables out of the stock he was building and watched him blend them into a paste that would help thicken up the soup and enrich the taste. Franky had to dice up some potatoes because the chili had too much salt evidently. Faye asked questions and the chefs gave her simple, clear answers. She hoped the footage could be used for what Andre needed.

And when the buzzer sounded, both Rafa and Franky had four bowls of a worthy lunch special.

"All right, Chefs, that is time. You've completed your first dish for this competition. Good work. I'll watch the scenes tonight to see if there's anything we need to improve for the next round, but I'm satisfied. Go sit somewhere and cool off while we get the judging done."

Franky and Rafa left the kitchen with Angel and River moving lights and equipment as needed.

"What about me, Andre? Anything I can do better?" Faye braced herself. If she had to guess, he was as firm with giving advice as her Gran was. She could take it and lick her wounds in private if necessary.

"This is the first time you've done this?" he asked, clearly skeptical.

Her eyebrows rose. "Definitely. Yes. The first time I've done anything in front of a video camera."

"Well, you're a natural now that you've loosened up a little. It was easy to see that you were enjoying yourself… after you left the pantry. I was afraid we were going to lose you in there."

Faye grimaced. "It was the ferocity of the shopping that got me. Took a minute to adjust."

He laughed. "Yeah. I get that."

"Your reminder that we were here because of Sadie, to honor Sadie and continue her work helped."

"Something about you reminds me of her." Andre nodded when she turned back in surprise. "Sadie never had any training in front of the camera, but she liked people, talking with them, finding out about their lives, even if they weren't celebrities, or there wasn't an audience. I'm getting that same impression with you. She enjoyed her time in the kitchen and made sure everyone did the same, whether they were there or watching at home. You have a ways to go before you match Sadie Hearst, but I see potential, Faye Parker."

Faye was surprised at the way tears threatened at his

critique. That might be the nicest thing he could have said to her. She wouldn't mind being like Sadie at all.

"All right. We're moving camera three and setting up our judges. Come on, Faye, you stay in the back." He turned to add, "Quietly."

Faye fought the urge to salute but was right behind him as he bumped the kitchen doors open and entered the dining room. This whole process was exciting and she didn't want to miss a minute of it.

CHAPTER TWELVE

BRIAN DID HIS best to maintain a professional smile while he waited for Jordan to finish commenting on Franky's unique spaghet-chili dish or chili-tie or whatever he'd called it, but the fifth time she mispronounced "peculiar," she didn't even wait for Andre to yell, "Cut."

Jordan immediately thumped her head on the table in front of her.

Sarah patted her back. "You're putting too many *L*'s in the word."

"I know." Jordan's groan was muffled.

It was painful to watch the sisters struggle but Brian didn't think his advice about picturing a cute little alien guy was going to work here.

"Off the wall. Unusual. One of a kind." Faye had moved into the camera shot under the bright lights and pushed Jordan to sit up. "It's time to dump that word and try a new one. Funky. Unconventional."

"I've never had pasta in a chili like this. It's not a bad or a good thing. That's all I was going for." Jordan rolled her shoulders and pressed her hands to her cheeks. "Good advice, Faye. Let's come at this from a different direction. No *L*'s if I can help it."

Faye met Brian's gaze. It was clear she was struggling to hide a smile. The sisters were an A-plus act without the camera. He hoped they could replicate that soon in front of it. Meanwhile, he enjoyed sharing this silent communication with Faye.

River stepped forward. "Let's fix your hair again, Jordan. Then you nail this take, 'mkay?"

"Okay. Don't fuss too much because after all this, I'm going to run out and dunk my head in the lake, cool off my brain," Jordan mumbled as River powdered the sweat away from her brow.

"I'll be right behind you," Andre said loudly. The loud crack his neck made as he stretched the muscles made everyone wince. "Rafa and Franky have probably decided we've canceled the whole production by now, and kicked back in their rooms, hunting for new jobs."

Faye cleared her throat and shot the director a look and he raised his hands in surrender. Brian decided she and Andre had started to understand each other.

He would guess that meant she was more than adequate at consulting.

"All right. This is it." Jordan nodded firmly. "I can do this."

"I certainly hope so." Andre paced back to his spot. "Brian, you're doing a great job of interacting with both Sarah and Jordan. Keep it up. After Jordan finishes, we're going to come to you to summarize this round and ask each of them to hold up a score. You go last and we'll add an average through the magic of editing at some later date when I've rested and no longer wish I'd become a plumber." Andre slumped. "Out of the shot, Faye. Places. Quiet."

Brian watched Faye step back into the shadows where she could watch the monitors showing the footage of the stationary camera.

"Three, two, one…action," Andre said wearily.

"Of these two dishes, I was impressed by Franky's attempt to incorporate two family favorites, but I wonder if the final result is too…off the wall for a lunch special?" Relief filled Jordan's eyes that she'd made it through the sentence, and Brian, amused, immediately nodded seriously.

"Yes, it was a tasty dish, but I don't know if it's memorable as in so good you have to come back for more, which would be the right thing, or just a gimmick, which is not the way to go here at the Majestic. Sadie's recipes were familiar, but then she elevated them beyond the everyday to out of this world. In that sense, Rafa's dish comes closer to executing the task. On the face of it, vegetable soup isn't very exciting, though. He needs to find the hook, like Franky's pickled jalapeños, something that takes it beyond what you might make at home." Brian wanted to be fair to both of his chefs. Their lunch meals were both good, but for the restaurant to be successful, it needed items that brought people back again and again. He didn't believe either of them were there yet.

"Jordan, do you have your score for Franky's dish?" he asked.

She held up an 8.

Brian wasn't surprised at the score, but it was too generous.

He was even less shocked when Sarah held up the same score.

They both gasped when he held up a 6, and instead of allowing Andre to cut and demand a reshoot, Brian smoothly said, "This is the first round and we have a long way to go here. Good meals are one thing, but we want something special for Sadie's menu."

The sisters seemed to share a silent conversation and turned to argue, but Brian said, "Now Rafa's dish."

They both held up 8s again, and Brian shook his head. "Are you trying to hire both chefs, ladies?" Then he held up a 5 and flashed it at them. "Both dishes were tasty. In this case, the uniqueness of Franky's gave him a slight edge, but neither of them nailed our challenge."

Sarah spoke up. "I understand your point, but are you going to give them advice for the next round?"

"I will," Brian promised them solemnly before facing the camera. "Let's talk to the chefs."

The three of them waited for Andre to yell cut, but Jordan and Sarah both had ideas on how he should be kinder to his chefs. He listened to them talk over each other for a minute and then said, "Who is the expert here?"

Both sisters paused.

"But we want one of them to like working here," Jordan said, clearly irritated.

"They both enjoy working at Rinnovato, but they both also want to be improving all the time." Brian covered his heart with his hand. "I promise, I'm not here to discourage them. They understand what we're doing here."

Sarah's obvious discontent was his only answer.

"Angel, please bring the chefs in," Andre instructed. "While we wait, all three of you think of something short and sweet to say. Then Brian will wrap up with tips for the next round and close this out." He rubbed both temples with his fingers and muttered, "Peculiar" under his breath as he paced.

Once Rafa and Franky were on their spots in front of the table, Andre counted and called, "Action."

The tense silence prompted Brian to ask, "Jordan, what would you like to see next from the chefs?"

She smiled brightly. "It's clear you are both talented chefs. My only advice would be to spread your wings farther and see where that takes you."

Sarah patted Jordan's shoulder. "Sadie told us the same thing." She clasped her hands together. "Sadie was an original, so keep that in mind, but she wasn't big on reinventing the wheel. Her goal was always giving us the very best of the things she loved the most."

Brian could see that registered something for both Rafa and Franky, and it was excellent advice.

"Right now, we have one point between you. Rafa is at 21 and Franky has 22. Both meals were fine, but I can't imagine leaving here and thinking about them again. Creative doesn't have to mean new or strange, but it's an important piece of what we're hoping to find." He waited for his chefs to nod. "There's plenty of room to grow with two rounds left. No one's worried about whether you can run the kitchen. I invited you here because you have proven your skills. We want the best food you have, so you can ultimately step up to take the lead." Brian faced the camera. "We hope all of you will join us for the next round."

"Nice, Chef Caruso. Thank you all." Andre waved a circle in the air. "It's a wrap for today. I'm reviewing the tape tonight and making notes. We'll reschedule the instructional pieces for one of the last days unless a miracle happens and tomorrow goes better."

Jordan wrinkled her nose. "Surely it couldn't go worse."

Andre bit his lip and Brian was curious as to the director's expression, but then he asked, "Is the third sister Brooke any good in front of a camera?"

Sarah wrapped her arm around Jordan's shoulders. The pair offered a stony glare each, so Brian was convinced the sisters had picked up a bit of Sadie's fieriness, too.

Andre pressed his hand to his forehead. "Michael the CEO was hoping that easy, relatable content might come from the family with you two as the obvious choices, but..."

"You should decide what you're going to do for dinner," Faye said smoothly, stepping between the director and Jordan's daggers. "Tonight you're going into town, right?"

"I do not want to stay in this dining room any longer if I can help it," Andre said. "I say it's time to try the apple pie at the Ace High."

"All right, I'll round up Prue and Walt and the others and we'll meet here in…say, thirty minutes? Longer?" Faye asked as she fully blocked Andre's view of the Hearsts.

"I need an hour. A hot shower. And an aspirin." Andre exited before Faye could acknowledge the time change. River stopped in front of Sarah and Jordan before trailing out after him. "Don't let this bother you. Most of Andre's days end in a dramatic fashion, good or bad. By breakfast, he'll be his old self." Then she shrugged. "For better or worse."

Faye laughed and Brian was happy to see Jordan relax.

"Remember to take off your shirts before you leave. I've only seen one wardrobe mishap in my time working with Andre and I don't particularly want to live through that again. Let's keep the shirts here, clean and unwrinkled, please." River raised her brows, looking hopeful.

Faye understood and waited until the crew left before engaging with the Hearsts. "It was your first day, guys. You'll do better tomorrow."

Jordan pressed her hands to her face, while Sarah looked sideswiped. Faye whipped out her phone as if ready to rally the troops. "You're both going to the Ace for dinner, right?"

Sarah sighed and nodded. "We may want to sit at a table far away from Andre, but we're going."

"Prue, could you and Walt be here in about forty five minutes? We have a hungry crew preparing for dinner." Faye pulled a chair out of the shadows and plopped down while she waited for the answer. "Yeah, I'll call ahead and give Holly a number to have a table ready. Thanks."

Brian realized he was staring at her as if she was a star

on a stage, not someone tired after a long day of hard work. The way the light hit Faye made it impossible to look away.

"Holly, how's my assistant manager today?" Faye brushed her long hair over her shoulder as she listened. Brian had his fingers crossed that the crowd had thinned out at the Ace High and that Holly remembered Prue's command that no one spread the tale of the first night's dinner service. "Busy?"

Faye stretched out her legs and crossed one ankle over the other as she listened.

About halfway through the discussion that settled on nine people for dinner in about an hour, he realized that Sarah and Jordan were watching him closely.

Almost as closely as he was watching Faye.

"What?" he asked.

"What?" Sarah repeated innocently.

The words *matchmaker* and *danger* flashed in his brain at the expression on each of their faces.

"Don't you need to get ready for dinner?" he asked patiently. He'd learned that the only way out of a situation where someone else had the upper hand was to avoid engagement at all costs.

"We do, but the show is finally getting good," Jordan answered.

With Gemma, he could Dad-voice his way out of tight spots. Bring up homework or laundry or whatever was next on the agenda. That wouldn't work for Jordan and Sarah.

So he folded like an omelet. "I haven't seen enough of her today. I can't look away now."

When both of their mouths dropped open, almost as if they were controlled by the same mechanism somehow, Brian tamped down his grin. That was how Faye found them when she ended her call.

"You two, leave him alone. He's not used to the pressure

folks in Prospect are capable of." Faye moved around the judges' table to urge Jordan to stand and then Sarah. "Go hang your shirts up for wardrobe, ladies. We can't cross Andre. Then get ready to head on over to dinner with the crew. Entertaining's your specialty. But Jordan, stay as far away from Andre at dinner as possible because I want to have a restaurant to go back to when this is all over."

Jordan and Sarah dragged their feet but they soon exited the dining room. The last thing he saw was Jordan giving him a thumbs-up before Sarah towed her away.

"I did warn you how this would go." Faye's amusement warmed her voice and the small smile on her lips started the weird flutter in his abdomen. "It could have been a blip, but we've moved on to an all-out matchmaking war now."

"Guilty." There was no sense in arguing with her. The evidence had slow-walked out of the room. "But I can't help myself. I missed you today."

Her huff of breath didn't surprise him, either. Learning her reactions was simple. "How? We've been working together nonstop."

Debating the semantics would be a waste of time. She knew what he meant, just as he understood her answer. "It sounds like you did as well in front of the camera as you've been doing behind it. Andre was pleased?"

Her pride hit him right around the center of his chest again.

"It took a minute to get into the game, but then, it was so easy. Franky and Rafa are great at their jobs, and they love what they're doing, so it wasn't difficult to talk to them and I forgot the camera." She shook her head. "That's what I love at the Ace, talking with people. There's no way any news in this town slips by me because I hear bits of all the conversations. I speak to my neighbors at least once a week and more often for the frequent diners. I guess asking questions comes naturally at this point, but the passion those chefs have for what they do makes this experience fun. You did a good job choosing those two."

Brian smiled at her. "I've gotten pretty good at judging people, especially for kitchen jobs."

She moved closer to him as if she was about to tell him a secret. "Meanwhile, Sarah and Jordan?" She grimaced. "Think they'll loosen up more in front of the camera?"

Amused at how Faye had moved herself over to the professional side of the equation, Brian said, "I have my doubts. Michael does want to have more content made here. This is a test to explore potential issues and come up with a plan, but…" He shook his head to make his uncertainty about them clear and she nodded. "Is their sister any better center stage?"

Faye shrugged. "I've only met Brooke through video chats. She's got Sadie's style, but I don't know what will happen when cameras are rolling. Plus, she lives in New York. I'm not sure she's a valid option."

Brian slipped his hand in hers. "No Ace High for you tonight?"

She offered a weak grin. "I promised no interference this week. The temptation to take control would be overwhelming. I'm heading home to figure out a nice warm dinner for my grandfather, and…" That she laughed when she couldn't fill in the blank made complete sense to him. They didn't have free time often.

"Good. Enjoy a night off." He studied her face. "Here we are at another blip. You and me in a quiet room, and I'm thinking about kissing you again."

Instead of retreating, Faye took a step forward. "You know, we might be bad at it. So bad that it settles the question of anything between us forever."

Brian fought a smile as he moved closer. "Could be the

thrill of the unknown causing all the tension between us." Neither one of them believed a word they were saying but they were both enjoying themselves.

And one more inch would bring them together. Would she take it?

"We owe it to ourselves, our friends, our family to answer this question once and for all." Faye stepped to close the last bit of distance between them, the edges of his chambray shirt that now belonged to her brushing against his chef coat.

"A truly selfless act," he murmured as he slipped his hand slowly under the fall of her hair to draw her to him. Her laugh turned to a gasp when he pressed his lips to hers.

Brian didn't expect the sensation of falling when his eyes met hers, but the instant her arms slipped around him, he knew this would be a kiss he'd always remember. Her lips were soft against his, their breaths tangled up.

"Now what?" Faye asked softly. "That test was a failure. We're doomed to repeat it often."

Brian chuckled and rubbed her silky hair between his fingers, reluctant to let her go. "Others might say it was a smashing success. Depends on your perspective."

The wrinkle of concern between her eyebrows reminded him of Gemma's anxious expression. The last thing he wanted was to add to Faye's list of things to worry about, so he forced himself to step back. "Go home. Do something silly or fun or get a full eight hours of sleep for once."

She pressed her fingers to her lips before she headed off. "Good advice, Chef. You give good advice. I appreciate it."

Brian refused to imitate Jordan's and Sarah's foot-dragging exit, but he didn't want to leave Faye. "Tell everyone at the Ace I said hello." Faye moved to push in all the chairs behind the judges' table and line up their notebooks.

Because being busy was her answer to her jumble of emotions. He understood that.

"I'll see you in the morning," she said. Their eyes met and she forced a smile, so he pretended to be satisfied with that.

As he hurried to his room to change and avoid Andre's ire by making the group late for dinner, Brian wondered what the solution could be for him and Faye. Nothing was clear, except that he already missed her.

CHAPTER THIRTEEN

FAYE DRIED THE cast iron skillet she'd used to make cornbread for her grandfather and tried to think about anything other than the kiss. She'd managed to push it out of her mind while she'd cooked a big dinner, something neither she nor her grandfather managed often outside of the Ace High. But as soon as the dishwater started running, the whole day was playing through her brain.

So when her grandmother said, "Looks like we've got plenty of leftovers," Faye jumped and dropped the large mixing bowl into sudsy water, splashing the front of her shirt.

Faye grabbed a dry dish towel and brushed at it as she turned to face her grandmother. "Someone smart told me there was no sense in cooking if you didn't have plenty left for lunch the next day." She gave her grandmother an awkward one-armed hug and pulled a chair out from under the kitchen table. "Sit and I'll make you a plate."

Instead of arguing, her grandmother followed directions.

That was concerning, but Faye decided not to read too much into it.

"How was dinner service?" Faye warmed the plate she'd made for her grandmother and put it in front of her before pouring her a big glass of lemonade, tart as her grandmother preferred.

"Busy, the way I like it. Glad I served the meat loaf.

Holly told me that Sam Walker came in for a hearty meal after volunteering at the library. Now that the temperatures are warming up again, maybe he'll be a regular. Hate to think of him in that big house alone since Glenda passed on. Folks who've lost a spouse never take good care of themselves."

Her grandmother had a way of stating opinion as fact.

Since Gran was hardly ever wrong, her statements were often opinion and fact at the same time, but it stopped her in her tracks to hear her grandmother say such a thing when she'd seemed largely unaffected by Faye's retelling of finding Grandpa on the ground.

Faye realized she must have been biting her tongue loudly enough for her grandmother to notice because she said, "Your grandfather has you and me both looking after him, Faye. He told me he was fine, and when he mentioned hiring the two newest Armstrongs next door to help out around the place, I didn't argue. It'll be good for those boys, no doubt." She pointed with her fork. "Your meat's a mite dry. Less time in the oven." Her grandmother took a large bite of the barbecue chicken post-critique, so Faye decided it wasn't bothering her too much. Reminding her that it had been warming in the oven since dinner was over wouldn't change the chef's opinion here, either.

"Did you go out to talk with Sam?" Faye asked as she divided the piecrust dough on the counter. This was her last chore before she went outside to sit on the back porch and stare up at the sky. It was her favorite way to wind down. "Travis Armstrong mentioned the Prospect Rodeo Club to Grandpa. Reg McCall has plans to get all the sponsors from his years involved, including Sam and Walt."

She rolled the dough out carefully as she waited for her grandmother to answer her question.

"You're overworking that." Her grandmother shook her head.

The urge to ask how many pies her grandmother had made flitted through Faye's brain, but she folded the first crust and spread it in the pie pan, reminding herself that baking was something she loved. Even if Gran was disturbing her peace, Faye could successfully do this with her eyes closed.

"You know I can't leave the kitchen. Gotta keep an eye on things, especially since we're shorthanded." Her grandmother leaned back and Faye decided not to probe whether that was a poke at her for taking time away from the Ace High. "But Britt may have the makings of an adequate server with a few more shifts. Still no sign of Toby."

Faye mounded apples over the bottom crust. "I'm glad to hear things are going so well." That was almost true. A little bit of struggle on the team while she was out might have stroked her ego, but this success should mean a bit of freedom for her even after the video crew left town and took the handsome chef with them.

"Tell me all about this good-looking chef out at the Majestic." Her grandmother stepped up to the sink and washed her plate and silverware before putting them in the dish drainer to dry. "That's Prue's description of the man. I'm sure I couldn't say."

Faye paused. "He was in the Ace tonight. Couldn't you take a peek?" She smoothed the top crust out over the apples. After she trimmed the excess, she started crimping the edge with her fingers as Sadie Hearst had taught her.

"Oh, I've seen the man." Her grandmother grinned. "But I would never pass judgment on his looks. Or on anyone's appearance. Redo that side right there."

Following her pointing finger was easy enough, so Faye fussed with the perfectly fine crimps. "This is the last of the dough in the fridge here. I'll need to come into the restaurant at the end of the week to mix up some more and refill the freezer there."

"Only if you have the time. If we run out of apple pie, I'll find something to keep the people from rioting." Her grandmother picked up her glass and sipped. "Seems your new friend, the chef, is a pie fan. Holly told me he insisted on buying everyone at the table with him a piece of apple pie tonight. The whole video crew, Sarah, Jordan, everyone."

Faye wrapped the pie and slipped it into the chest freezer in the mudroom next to the kitchen. "Wow. He was like you, Gran. No fan of dessert, but that pie has converted him. His daughter asked me to teach her how to make it before they go home."

"Hmm."

Faye studied her grandmother's face. "What does that mean?"

"Nothing. Doesn't mean a thing." After having another sip of lemonade, she said, "But I'm waiting for you to tell me more. Is he demanding? Critical of his chefs?"

Faye wiped down the counter as she decided how to respond. "Yes. To both, but not in a bad way. I get the impression that Franky and Rafa—" she turned back to her grandmother "—those are the competitors from his LA kitchen, they respect him. He has clear expectations of the quality of the food, and even you would be impressed with his kitchen safety standards, but I'm not getting the temper and the obnoxious behavior you hear about from some of the fancy chefs or ones on the cooking shows."

Her grandmother nodded. "Those chefs weren't as young as I expected. Pretty experienced?"

Faye sorted through the snippets she'd picked up from Rafa and Franky on their backgrounds. "I'm not sure how long they've been working for Brian at Rinnovato, but they were both confident about their skills, so I'm guessing yes. Maybe they were like Brian and started in the kitchen as kids."

Faye dried the counter and wondered if she was answering the real questions her grandmother wanted to ask because she could feel an undercurrent, but she didn't know what she was missing.

Her grandmother sat back down at the table and reached for her glass. "Prue said his daughter had helped out at Handmade all day long."

"Gemma was nervous about traveling with Brian and visiting Prospect, so he asked for help to keep her involved here. Between Jordan and Prue, I'm pretty sure Gemma is having the time of her life during her first small-town experience." Faye frowned. "If you stayed in the kitchen, how did you find all this out?" Her grandmother preferred to let Faye handle the dining room and customers, even though she definitely wanted to stay up-to-date with all the town gossip.

"While they were waiting for service tonight, Prue popped her head through the order window." Her grandmother raised her eyebrows. "As if we need every neighbor stopping by to say 'howdy' while we're making their dinner."

Faye mimicked her grandmother, brows raised. "If you'd make the rounds in the dining room like I suggested, they'd make conversation with you while your line cooks handle the food. Everyone knows exactly what they're doing. If you'd quit changing things merely to shake the routine up, you'd see they can run that kitchen efficiently without you."

"I enjoy cooking new things. Serving the same meals day after day is boring, Faye. If the Ace doesn't need all these chefs in the kitchen, we should let one of them go, then. Don't want to pay someone to do the job I should." Her grandmother waited for Faye to step into the trap of saying she was too old to be working at the Ace.

But Faye was too smart for that. "Or you could hire a third chef, split the shifts to cover their training and enjoy your time in the restaurant you've built over decades by doing only the things you want to do and nothing more. That would leave more days with Grandpa. The two of you could try this new thing called a 'hobby.'" Faye's lips twitched as her grandmother tried to glare at her.

"I want the two of you to have more time together." Faye pulled her grandmother close for a better hug now that her shirt was almost dry. "You both deserve to be eating in nice restaurants instead of running dinner service and taking pleasure rides instead of repairing fence." Faye pointed in the direction of the swing her grandfather had put out on the back porch the first summer she'd moved to Prospect for good. "Want to come stare up at the stars with me? It's a fine way to wind down."

Her grandmother shook her head. "I better turn in. If your grandfather starts sawing logs before I fall asleep, I'll be awake all night." She pressed a kiss to Faye's temple. "Missed you at the restaurant, but all I heard was praise from that movie crew about your work today."

Faye jerked back in surprise. "You said you didn't leave the kitchen."

Her grandmother sighed. "Prue wouldn't take no for an answer when they were leaving, so I walked them out and had the chance to speak to the good-looking chef again." Her grandmother tipped her chin down. "*Brian* spoke highly of you. The director fella started the conversation with how natural you were in front of the camera. He said it loudly and made sure that Jordan heard every word for some reason, but then *Brian* thanked me over and above for lending you to this competition. Apparently, he can't imagine anyone else doing what you've managed, as well as you have." She blinked slowly, as if she was waiting for some kind of response.

"Is there a reason you're saying his name like that?" Faye licked her lips as she speculated what it might mean that Brian was trying to make a connection with her grandmother.

Why would a man who was only in town for a few more days put in that much effort for a…coworker? An acquaintance? A fun-to-kiss distraction who would never be anything more?

"The chef and his daughter have settled in quickly. Might there be something more than the filming going on between the two of you?" Her grandmother's inquisition made Faye groan.

"Not another matchmaker! I promise, Gran, the chef and his daughter belong in LA." Before her grandmother could argue, Faye added, "Good night. I hope lunch and dinner go well at the restaurant tomorrow."

There was an argument brimming, Faye could tell by the expression on her grandmother's face, but Faye could still be surprised by her grandmother because instead of jumping into it, Gran stood and said, "Good night, Faye."

After her grandmother had disappeared down the hallway toward the bedrooms, Faye inhaled slowly and then moved through the mudroom and out onto the porch. The quilt she left folded there for cold nights was soon settled around her shoulders. She swung slowly and tried to relax.

Her grandmother's questions about the Majestic's new visitors were to be expected. Everyone in town was excited about the lodge's reopening, and having another choice for restaurant meals would have everyone buzzing. Prue was doing Faye a favor by insisting her grandmother leave her kitchen command center to talk with her neighbors. If Gran enjoyed it, it would be easier to convince her to step away from the kitchen eventually.

But how her gran had focused on Brian Caruso was a surprise.

Emma Parker had never been the kind of grandmother who urged Faye to settle down. Faye had always believed that was because her grandmother understood that Faye might want to follow a passion. Gran loved her son and her granddaughter, but the Ace was *her* passion.

Could this make it easier for Faye to explain that the restaurant wasn't her own passion? Faye owed so much to her grandparents.

And there had never been a dream career that consumed Faye's imagination, so working at the Ace made sense.

But if she was free to do something new, would she go for it...whatever that might be?

Faye drew her knees up to her chest as she rocked in the porch swing, the stars clear overhead in the dark sky. She often cleared her mind at the end of the day like this.

Tonight her questions about her future were urged aside by the memory of the kiss.

And that Brian had helped her with her role in front of the camera.

It didn't surprise Faye that there was something different about the way her grandmother said his name.

She couldn't remember ever being so in tune with a man.

It was sweet, even if she was afraid she was going to miss him terribly when he left. If it had taken more than three decades to find someone who fit her like this, when would another walk into the Ace High?

"You're being so dramatic, Faye Parker," she muttered.

"He's a handsome man, not the prince carrying your missing shoe."

Her practical self had a point, but only one question cut through the replay of the kiss in her head.

What had Gran meant when she'd said she'd had a chance to speak to Brian *again*?

Had they met earlier?

Maybe Gran had meant a chance other than while they were eating at the table in the restaurant.

Before she could puzzle over that, her phone rang. Since only two people she knew would call her after the restaurant closed, Faye hurried to pull her cell from her pocket. It was a video call request, so she opened it and smiled. "Hey, Mom. Good morning." The time difference between Cairo and Prospect meant her parents were getting ready for the day while she was winding down for bed. "Gran just finished dinner. Want me to go grab her and see if Grandpa's awake?"

"No, baby, I called to talk to my lucky charm. I have an important meeting today, so I wanted to pick up some good vibes from my favorite daughter." Her mother smiled as she finished twisting her hair into a tight bun at the nape of her neck and her father entered the frame with two coffee mugs.

"How is my Bizzy this morning?" her dad asked as he toasted her with his coffee.

Faye smiled at his nickname for her. He'd given it to her because she'd always struggled to sit still.

"Fine, but it's bedtime here, Dad." For some reason, she had to remind them almost every time they called and made a comment about the day. It seemed important that it never registered to them that Faye's world was completely different from theirs, as different as the sun and moon.

"Final review of our bridge project is today." Her dad

made no acknowledgment of her reminder. That wasn't new, either.

But it was hard to stay mad when they were both in such a good mood.

Pride made her mother's face glow.

Faye said, "Congratulations," and opted to leave it at that.

Her father had sounded as preoccupied as her mother when he'd responded, "Who knows what's next for the future. Could be time for another trip home and we'll let tomorrow take care of itself."

It was a good philosophy.

Sometimes Faye wished she had a better hold on it for her own life, but the suggestion that her parents might visit lightened her mood.

"How's the TV show going?" her mother asked.

"Web series. It's…fun. We just started, but I'm enjoying the whole process." Faye gripped the phone tighter and admitted, "I might be good at this."

Her mother leaned closer to the screen. "Of course you are. You're a natural planner like I am. If you'd left Prospect after high school, there's no telling what you'd be doing today."

Because running the family restaurant wasn't enough.

That was the message Faye received.

"But I didn't, so here I am, taking care of Gran and Grandpa." If she wished she had some help from her parents with that, Faye hardly ever mentioned it. Her parents loved their jobs as much as Gran loved the Ace and Grandpa loved his garden. Sometimes it worried her that she'd never discovered her own passion, but being angry at her parents wouldn't solve that.

"That's important, Bizzy, but I'm glad you're taking some time to try something else." Her father pressed a kiss on her mother's cheek, and Faye tried to comfort herself that they were happy together on the other side of the world.

Then he added, "If you weren't there in Prospect, we'd have to make different choices, you know."

"Dad, I..." Faye frowned at the loose thread on her jeans as she turned that comment over in her mind. Did that mean they might spend more time here? "Maybe it's time everyone reevaluated their choices."

Her father scooched into the frame and her mother moved aside. "What do you mean? Talk to me, Bizzy."

The nerves of a vulnerable girl shivered inside her. She didn't want to hurt them, but she had to say something. Gran and Grandpa needed some freedom, and she wasn't enough to fill in the gaps.

"None of us have unlimited time, Dad. We don't know how many days Gran or Grandpa will have." She covered her chest. "Or you or Mom or me, for that matter. The clock is always ticking." She licked her lips. "Gran and Grandpa are missing out on your lives when you're so far away, just like you are mine."

Silence fell after her last word like a door slamming shut. She knew it would be a long time before she got up the nerve to try this again, so she had to keep going. "We miss you when you're away." And they were always away too long.

Faye remembered telling Brian that making up for lost time could happen. But not if they were never together.

"It's the scarcity principle, right, Mom?" Faye smiled at her mother who had dropped enough buzzwords in their conversations over the years to add up to an honorary business degree. "Time is limited and in high demand, so it's valuable. That means we should make careful decisions about how we spend it."

"Our girl is smart, babe." Her mother checked her watch. "We better run. Don't want to be late for this meeting."

Her father changed his mind about his first response and said, "We love you, Bizzy. Have a good day and enjoy every minute of your fun job, okay?"

Faye blew them a kiss. "Don't forget to call Gran when you have a chance. She loves to hear from you."

Her mother nodded and they ended the call.

Faye stretched back to stare up at the dark sky. She inhaled and exhaled slowly, listening to the sounds around her as she attempted to empty her mind, and waiting for the terrible, nervous knot in her stomach to ease.

Nothing much had changed during that phone call, but she decided to enjoy this break while she had it. Her parents and grandparents both had work that they loved, and for now, she was closer to that herself. An image of the Majestic and the lake and mountains behind it popped up, and she smiled.

Brian would be there tomorrow. So would Gemma. It would be a good day.

CHAPTER FOURTEEN

ON FRIDAY MORNING, Brian could tell that everyone involved in the cooking competition needed the final rounds to go smoothly. Tempers were ragged, with the Hearst sisters on one side versus Andre and all of his moods on the other, pulling Angel and River behind.

Rafa and Franky had been largely protected from the skirmishes, and Faye had never once dropped her professional, helpful attitude.

But he believed it had to be wearing on her, too.

Not that he would know firsthand, because they'd had no chance to spend more than two minutes alone since The Kiss.

Honestly, that was taking a toll on his positive outlook at this point.

The hamburger round had been another close call, with Rafa producing a traditional choice elevated with a sweet barbecue sauce and spicy crunchy onion rings on top. Franky had gone his own way again with a vegetarian choice of a black bean "patty" topped with guacamole and chunky salsa.

There had been a kitchen accident that led to a stopped clock while the chefs regrouped. Then Jordan had gotten tangled up over the word *delicious* and Sarah had sneezed during their best take.

Today, they'd wrap up the biggest piece, the finale of the competition.

If they made it.

"Hair. Makeup. Wardrobe." Andre picked up his clipboard. "Let's get this last round of competition in the can."

Brian caught Faye's arm before she hurried away. "Hey, you're really good at this." He smiled at the pride that lit her face. "And good morning."

She ducked her head before grinning back at him. "I really am, but thank you for noticing."

"I've missed you. These busy days and Gemma… We just haven't had enough time together. Surely we need to make a run into the grocery store for something." He traced the back of her hand with his thumb, happy to have stolen this minute with her.

"We're entirely too good at shopping for that to be true, Chef." She waved at River. "If I don't go, Andre will be back on his pre-rampage routine. As soon as we have a break, let's run away, okay?"

He nodded as she hustled over to the makeup corner.

"I'm going to take a look at the marina and this dock Faye mentioned." He waved his cell phone at Jordan, who nodded. He wanted to call to check on Belvie and Rinnovato. This might be the longest period they'd gone without talking since he and Belvie had started working together. "If I'm in any danger of interrupting Andre's flow, please save us all and come get me."

Jordan smiled. "Fine. I will, but I do get a kick out of the way his eyelid starts to twitch when he's on a roll."

Brian had had a feeling some of Jordan's adversarial attitude had been pure orneriness, so it was nice to have it confirmed. He was still shaking his head when he made it down to the dock.

"Hello, boss, have you become a professional cowboy yet?" Belvie asked as she answered his call.

Brian laughed. "Not yet, although I did ride a horse,

muck out a stall and learn what meadow muffins are, so I expect to be issued my spurs any day now."

"Excellent. If you decide you must now be home on the range, I have settled nicely into the command of your kitchen. Your accountant and I are communicating effectively as to the nightly receipts, and the building remains intact." Belvie's satisfaction with her performance radiated through the phone. "I have already chosen myself another bauble to keep my bonus bracelet company. Rinnovato is in excellent hands."

"I never doubted it. No trouble, then? How is Robbie working out?" Brian bent to sit on the dock and stare out over the clear lake. This was the most beautiful place he could remember ever visiting. Once a man found it, he'd have to return again and again, wouldn't he?

"One might say that being fired from his position caught his attention," Belvie said slowly. "I cannot fault his recent performance, although his arrival time might be improved with further effort. I have kept your philosophy in mind that occasional tardiness is to be expected as we navigate these challenges in life but..." She let the sentence dangle.

Brian knew how she would fill in the blank. People like Belvie overcame life's difficulties without asking for understanding from their coworkers and she'd prefer it if Robbie could get his own act together similarly.

None of that changed Brian's opinion on offering grace, especially on the little stuff, if the big things were being covered.

"I'm glad he's working out."

"I will be exceedingly pleased to have either Franky or Rafa return in a week." Belvie paused. "Do you know which one will be staying in Prospect yet?"

Brian had a gut feeling how the competition would end, but Sarah and Jordan had surprised him with their own takes. "Still a question mark. I was thinking about that today. Do you happen to know if they..." How did he ask the question?

Belvie hummed. "As to their relationship status, I have my own suspicions but it has never been confirmed. As far as I know, we don't have a policy against coworker relationships, do we?"

"No. No way. The hours we work, if we ruled that out, we'd never be able to keep staff in place, but I was wondering about what happens when it's time for the loser to go home."

Belvie hummed again. "I see. That is a hard question. Do you feel I should talk to the staffing agency to determine if there are any line cooks waiting for their opportunity to step up to our level?"

Brian frowned. "Our level...as if we're superior to other kitchens?"

"We are, Chef. Never doubt it," Belvie immediately returned. "It wouldn't hurt to ask. I could set up a couple of interviews for when you return."

Something in his gut was warning him that they were about to be permanently shorthanded, so he said, "You're right. Let's see if we can find a good replacement to join Robbie."

"Of course, it will be done," Belvie said. "What about Gemma? Is she also waiting for her official spurs?"

"Hmm, she's about to take over a quilt store and shoot for global domination, but she did take to riding as if she was Annie Oakley in a previous life."

Belvie chuckled. "The world domination we always expected, but quilting is new. You are fitting into Prospect perfectly. Should I be worried you won't be returning, either?"

"I appreciate your faith that I could become a full-time

cowboy, but this is a visit, not a stay. My life is in LA, that restaurant, Gemma's school, my mother… It's all there." Brian knew it was true, but there was still a big empty space in him that wanted something to change.

"Why do you sound as if you aren't completely satisfied with that?"

It was easy to imagine Belvie's suspicious stare searching his face for clues.

"Is there, perhaps…a woman?" she asked slowly, as if all the pieces were falling into place.

"If there is, this is when you tell me that LA also has many, many women, some of the most beautiful women in the country, in fact." Brian knew his answer would only confirm her suspicion, but he wasn't interested in lying about his feelings. Not to his best friend, who'd been with him through serious ups and downs.

"Oh, dear, none of that matters if the one you want is in Colorado, does it?" Belvie asked.

Since that was what he was afraid of, Brian didn't answer. She would understand.

"Thank you for taking care of the restaurant. Maybe I'll force you to take a couple of weeks off when I get back," Brian said.

Belvie scoffed. "What a way to repay my dedication. Throw money, please."

They were both laughing when he ended the call.

It was tempting to sit there on the dock until someone came to get him. Instead, he stood and walked slowly to the lodge. He sat down next to Sarah at the judging table.

"Any loud noises, shouting coming from the kitchen?" he asked.

Jordan shook her head. "You know we're the problem, not Franky or Rafa."

"Some of us work hard at being the problem, so we

enjoy being appreciated." Sarah cut her sister a glance out of the corner of her eye.

Jordan shrugged. "I heard on-camera talent was supposed to be difficult. At least I'm not spacing out while filming. Were you thinking about the rest of the lodge reno that still has to be done before Western Days? If I do that, my stomach hurts. I've made Clay confirm three different times that the guys who are going to repair the siding are still on schedule for the week after next and I'm not sure it's the right decision to wait on the bathroom upgrades until next fall."

"Western Days should be on my mind, but I've been preoccupied with Sadie's estate finally being settled. I texted Brooke yesterday after Howard Marshall called to say the funds from Sadie's estate would be released next week." Sarah leaned over. "Other than this lodge, Sadie left everything to her nephews and great-nieces and -nephews in an even split. Selling her LA house in the hills and the Manhattan condo took some time, and there were so many other pieces..." Sarah waved a hand. "Well, that is done. Our sister in New York has been going through a messy divorce, so that money will change her life."

Jordan made the continue motion. "So, what happened after you sent the text?"

"That's it." Sarah sighed. "Nothing. She didn't respond. She liked the text to let me know she'd seen it, but I expected questions or...something by now."

Jordan nodded as she pulled out her phone. "And you'll be no good to film unless we find out what's going on right now."

Brian would have asked if they wanted privacy, but Brooke Hearst answered before he had a chance to excuse himself.

"Hey, now's not a good time, Jordie."

Brian had never met Brooke, but even he could tell that she'd been crying.

"What's wrong?" Sarah asked. "Are you hurt?"

Brooke immediately shook her head. "No, I'm fine. That was good news you sent. Thanks. It's going to fix everything here, I promise. I just have to be patient." That her face immediately crumpled suggested she needed more than money and patience.

Before either Jordan or Sarah could ask for more details, someone knocked on the door on Brooke's side. She immediately straightened her shoulders, and Brian was struck by her resemblance to Sadie Hearst. "It's okay, everything is under control. I'll call you this weekend and catch you up on what's happening here. Meanwhile, do not worry."

She ended the call before Sarah or Jordan could argue.

"It's time." Sarah pulled out her own phone. "We'll be flying out Thursday. Andre needs to have the shoot wrapped up no later than Wednesday afternoon." Sarah scrolled through what looked like an airfare booking schedule. "Oh, good, we have nonstop options. I do not want to be toting you around the airport, rushing to make a connecting flight if I can help it."

Jordan huffed. "The flight to New York is pretty long. Drugs will definitely be required." She closed her eyes and waited for whoever she was calling to answer. "Hey, Reg, it's Jordan. How is life at Prospect Family Practice today?" She waited for him to answer. "Well, I was hoping I could get Keena or Dr. Singh to prescribe something that will conquer extreme fear of flying without making me a zombie. Sarah and I have to rescue our sister in New York next week, and nobody wants me to be fully alert for that flight."

Sarah smiled at Brian. "We used to keep our problems to ourselves. Then we came to Prospect and embraced the fact that nothing here stays secret for long. Jordan hates flying. Brooke might be the only person in the world who could get her on an airplane, but we've been worried about her for months. This is the first time we've seen tears. We can't wait any longer."

"I hope everything is okay," Brian said as Jordan ended the call.

"It will be. Mia can keep the lodge open with Dad's help, and Clay can meet the crew who'll be working on the exterior. What about the museum, Sarah? What do we need to do there?" Jordan said.

Sarah rubbed her forehead. "We're still assembling pieces of the interactive exhibit, but Wes will..." She shrugged. "Wes will help. We have help."

"Of course he will. And you and I will go, straighten Brooke out or bring her home to Prospect. Those are the only choices. Everyone around here thinks two Hearsts is a lot to handle." Jordan smiled. "But Sadie shaped all three of us. There's nothing we can't do together."

Brian considered the lodge they'd rebuilt and how they were recreating Prospect, and it was easy to believe her.

Whatever switch had been flipped by discovering their sister's situation, Jordan and Sarah flew through the last judging round with ease. Frank and Rafa presented their signature dishes, the showstoppers that would be the entrées that diners would likely order to celebrate special occasions.

Rafa was first to present. "Today our challenge was to prepare a standout dish, one that makes us think of celebrating with family and friends. I've made roasted duck with a cranberry-ginger glaze. In my mind, this would be a fall special, with roasted butternut squash, crispy smashed potatoes and a cornbread muffin served with maple butter."

Brian was impressed as he checked the cook on the

duck. It was perfect, and every bite exploded with flavor. If Rafa had wanted to impress them with technique, he had pulled out some impressive moves.

"What made you think of duck?" Sarah asked.

Brian realized he might be the one missing his cues, but Rafa's offering was delicious.

"To me, home is about holidays, but since I have moved to the States, I don't celebrate the way I used to. Then someone I admire invited me to come home with them for Thanksgiving. I have never been a fan of duck, but it's a family tradition there. They shoot and prepare their own wild duck every year." Rafa didn't glance at Franky, but something about his tone convinced Brian that he was the subject of the story. "Once you eat this, you become a duck fan for life. Through trial and error and frequent begging for the recipe, I have learned to make the duck and glaze. Everything else is something I learned at Rinnovato, home of my other family, or dreamed up right here." He tapped his temple.

Franky patted Rafa on the back. "Couldn't have made that any better myself."

"It's absolutely remarkable." Jordan smiled. "I can't stop eating this. I don't want to stop eating this. Someone make me stop, please."

Sarah said, "That's exactly the reaction we're looking for. Good job, Rafa."

Brian reluctantly pushed his own plate aside as Franky brought his offering to the table. It was a pizza.

"Growing up, I prepared many interesting family dinners." Franky clapped his hands together. "I've always enjoyed having fun with food, and I found a job and a place that encourages that. Today, I prepared one of my biggest hits—a cast-iron skillet carbonara pizza with scallops and spinach on top. First, I fried the bacon in the skillet, I sautéed the spinach in the bacon renderings, and then I baked the pizza in that skillet."

After the first bite, Brian knew the judging was going to be impossible. Franky had prepared this before at Rinnovato, and Brian had never been able to forget it. There were no flaws today. The scallops were seared to perfection, and each bite was better, richer than the last.

Sarah and Jordan both sighed happily after they took a bite.

None of them spoke for so long that Andre bypassed pointing and went straight to jumping up and down to get them back into motion.

"Franky, your combinations are always creative, but you took us seriously when we asked for a signature dish." Brian pointed at his plate. "This is unforgettable. It is definitely the kind of dining experience that will bring people back to your restaurant, whether it's here in Prospect or anywhere in the world. Good job."

He watched Rafa throw an arm around Franky's waist to pull him close. Whatever he whispered in Franky's ear made him blush.

"You've made our job very hard. I never expected it to be like this." Sarah rubbed her forehead as she turned to her sister. "How do we keep them both?"

Jordan laughed. "The first thing we'd have to do is fight Chef Caruso to steal both away."

Brian nodded. "I knew you would both do well here, but this exceeded my expectations. Well done."

When his chefs exchanged a high five before falling into a hug, Brian turned to the camera. "Now comes the hard part—choosing one chef to run the restaurant in the Majestic Prospect Lodge."

"Cut." Andre immediately clapped Franky and Rafa on their backs. "Good job, Chefs. Go take a break while we watch the judges arm-wrestle over who the winner is. We'll call you back when there's a score. Are you both okay to find out today who wins? We can postpone this until all the taping is finished if you'd prefer?"

Franky shook his head. "No, let's go. Win or lose, we've both done everything we could do, so there's no reason to have a regret, however this turns out."

Andre motioned them out. Rafa and Franky left the dining room and then he said, "We all know what we're doing here. Everyone ready?"

"I don't know how we're going to make a decision," Sarah said, "but we're ready."

"Talk it out on camera." Andre stepped back. "We're rolling…and action."

"This has been such a close competition, and neither chef made the final round any easier, did they?" Brian asked.

Sarah shook her head. "I will remember both of these dishes. The fact that I won't be able to visit a restaurant to have both of them is sad."

"Let's hire both. Why choose?" Jordan held up her hands. "Oh, right, things like budget and practicality. Fine."

Brian smiled. "Welcome to life as a restaurant owner. Nothing is ever simple, but what I keep coming back to is that one of them prepares the kind of food you expect to serve here at the Majestic. Elevated standards that people will enjoy and come back for. The other chef sits right on the edge of too much, too creative." Franky needed freedom to create but with someone else keeping an eye on the menu to be sure they didn't outpace their customers.

"How would you score this round?" he asked, although he knew how it would turn out.

Jordan immediately held up a ten. "Both chefs deserve a 10."

"I agree." Sarah did the same.

Then both sisters stared hard at him because they expected him to score too low.

So they were both surprised when he held up a ten. "I agree. These dishes were perfection, but we have to pick one chef." Brian paused as he checked his gut to make sure he was on the right track. "Rafa has consistently produced dishes that fit here at the Majestic. He kept the audience and the ingredients in mind at each round. He's the right chef for your restaurant."

Sarah leaned back in her chair. "It's difficult to argue with that. It feels like the right choice, even as I have every plan to beg Franky to make another pizza before he returns to Rinnovato."

Brian smiled. "Believe me, I will be happy to have Franky back in my kitchen. When you visit, I'll ask Franky to create something special for you." They nodded, and he added, "Are we ready to tell the chefs?"

"Let's do it," Jordan said. Brian waited for Andre to yell, "Cut," and tell her to do it again, this time with less grim determination. Instead, the director quietly stopped the cameras and asked Angel to get the chefs.

"All right. Enough of that sad face," Andre said quickly, "because this is a celebration for at least one person in this room. Rafa deserves a big announcement with hearty congratulations and Franky should hear everything you loved. Brian takes the lead here. Heartfelt congratulations and positive comments from Sarah and Jordan and we have successfully finished the hardest part of this project."

Rafa and Franky took their spots. Faye stopped behind the stationary camera. She had a bottle of champagne in one hand, and two flutes in the other. Brian watched her hold them up to show Andre. He immediately struck a dramatic pose. "Yes. That's what we needed. We'll announce the winner, Faye will step into the frame with champagne and we'll cut. Then we start drinking."

Everyone laughed and relief immediately settled over Brian. After the cameras were rolling again, he made the announcement. Franky cheered while Rafa cried happy tears.

"To Rafa and Franky, two of the best to ever come through my kitchen." Brian raised his glass of champagne. "You both deserve every bit of the success coming your way."

After the glasses clinked, Franky threw his arm over Rafa's shoulders. "I'm so proud of you."

The look the two of them exchanged resolved any question in Brian's mind about their relationship. He did wonder how well they would do long-distance.

"Has this competition got you thinking about opening your own place, Franky?" Faye asked. "What kind of restaurant would you open if money was no object?"

"No object..." Franky sipped his champagne. "A bakery. It would only be open at acceptable hours of the day, say eleven to twelve, and then I'd have the rest of the day to bake and...sleep." Franky sighed. "Sleep is so nice."

Surprised by the answer, Brian asked, "Why a bakery?"

Franky shrugged. "Who doesn't love bread? It's always been my favorite. There's plenty of room to be creative, but there's also a part of it that's kind of...magic? It's hard to explain."

"Sadie used to say that putting dinner on the table is life but adding dessert is love. She would have loved you both." Faye wrinkled her nose. "Sorry. It's natural to quote Sadie. She understood that magic."

"I only met her once but her enthusiasm was contagious.

I hope I can do her proud here." Rafa shook his hands and scoffed. "Now the nerves are hitting?"

"You'll have plenty of help," Brian said. Rafa could count on his advice for as long as he needed it.

Andre polished off his champagne. "Tomorrow, Angel, River and I are going to meet with the editor through the miracle of a video call. Michael wants to have a rough cut on Monday to see what we've got in case we need to change course."

"Video calling at the Majestic… What would Sadie think about that?" Faye murmured as she crossed her arms over her chest. "I bet she'd have loved to have the chance to work like this, from her first kitchen."

Brian met her stare. "It's a whole new world, right? People can live and work almost anywhere without losing touch with their family." He hadn't intended to suggest that Faye might leave Prospect, but the closer he got to leaving, the more tempting it became to ask her to consider the possibility.

"On Sunday, let's run through as many of the tip segments as we can." Andre pointed at Franky and Rafa, who nodded. "Continuity is going to be a nightmare. We can't reset the dishes as they were when you were competing, but the magic of editing better build a bridge to get over that."

Franky immediately raised his hands in the air and trotted around the kitchen. "Does that mean we have a free day? What do we do with it?"

Rafa laughed. "We're unfamiliar with the concept! If we were in LA, we could do laundry or buy groceries."

"Or forget all that and try something touristy or even… sleep. I like to sleep." Franky yawned.

"Believe it or not, we also sleep in Prospect." Faye grinned at Franky. "That option is on the table. Or I know Jordan could set up a trail ride if you'd like."

The frown on Franky's face was a quick answer, so Faye said, "No horses, got it."

"Fishing!" Franky exclaimed. "I've got to get out on Key Lake before I head back to the City of Angels. I love fishing, Chef. You know that week I always take off in August? I head home, back to Idaho. Gotta go fishing with my dad. It's tradition. That's also why I know a million different ways to serve trout."

Brian tried not to let his immediate dread show on his face but smiled when he saw the twist of Faye's lips. She was as unenthusiastic about fishing as he was. He was glad they were on the same page.

Rafa said, "Fishing could be a good excursion. A lakeside restaurant should serve fish, I suppose. I could add trout to the menu as a special." Then he frowned. "Are there trout in this lake?"

Jordan pulled out her phone. "I have just the guy. He's going to be managing the marina when it reopens, but I think he finished up his job running the sporting goods store in Fairplay last week. Who is up for a fishing trip?"

Brian was amused when only Franky and Rafa raised their hands. Franky tsked. "You're all missing out. Fresh-cooked trout tastes twice as good when you've caught it, cleaned it and served it with your own two hands."

"We believe you, Chef," Andre said before waving his arms. "That's a wrap for today. Go. Be free. We're leaving for dinner at the Ace in one hour."

When everyone moved toward the lobby, Brian put his hand on Faye's arm. "Hey, I wanted to ask you something."

She glanced over to the doorway, where Sarah and Jordan had paused to wait for them.

He smiled as the women tried to pretend they weren't staring until Jordan cleared her throat. "Fine. May I suggest a visit to the romantic firepit for your conversation?"

She sniffed. "There's lighter fluid and matches behind the front desk if you'd like to—" she waggled her eyebrows "—light a fire."

Sarah dragged her sister away before he or Faye could answer.

He offered Faye his arm and relaxed when she immediately slipped hers through it. Mindful of Andre's ire regarding their on-camera clothes, Brian stopped at wardrobe so they could change into comfortable wear and then led the way outside.

This was what he'd been missing since The Kiss: time with Faye. It had been difficult to work with her but not touch her. How much more difficult would it be when he went back to LA? When he had more time, he'd worry about that. For now, he was just going to enjoy every minute.

CHAPTER FIFTEEN

FAYE SMILED AS she finished stacking the logs inside the firepit. Brian had settled in one of the comfortable chairs Jordan had arranged in a semicircle to maintain a view of the lake, his hands shoved in his pockets as he watched her.

"Are you having trouble with the division of labor, Chef?" she asked as she lit the kindling. "Want to take over the job?"

He shook his head. "I know next to nothing about campfires. You and I both know that."

Faye teased, "It's fire, Brian. There's not a lot of difference in how it works from one place to another." Her lips twitched as he held out his hand.

She offered him the box of matches she was holding, but he wrapped his hand around hers to tug her closer. When he pulled her into his lap and let out a sigh, she realized how much she'd needed this time with him.

"Is this comfortable?" Brian asked. "I just wanted you close."

She stared into his eyes. "Sure, I know what you mean."

He ran his hand in circles over her back as they sat there in the darkening shadows, the fire crackling behind them.

"Happy with the results of the competition?" she asked. "That had to be a difficult decision."

"Yeah. There was no real way to go wrong. I hired those two the first week Rinnovato opened. One of them has a fancy culinary degree, and the other one made a savory *sfogliatelle* from fresh mozzarella and prosciutto." The look of awe on his face convinced Faye that it must have been delicious even if she had no idea what it was. "Best bite I remember putting in my mouth. Ever. Don't tell my mother I said that."

"I'll twist Franky's arm to make me one of those before he leaves. Was that one of his crazy inventions?" she asked.

Brian chuckled. "Nope, that was his master plan. He saw a newspaper article about my food truck and how people lined up and my plans for the new restaurant, and..." He shrugged. "He landed on a recipe, practiced until he had it down, and then talked his way into an interview. It worked."

Faye smiled. It was easy to imagine enthusiastic Franky throwing himself wholeheartedly into the plan when he made his mind up to accomplish something.

"And Rafa has this shockingly good palate and the kind of creative vision that no culinary school taught. Together, they've been a lifesaver for Rinnovato," Brian added. "I don't know how well they'll do apart now."

"You're really going to miss the team in your kitchen, aren't you?" Faye asked. It was proof of his affection for Sadie that he'd let her relatives break up this team.

Brian cleared his throat to dispel the silence that fell after the reminder that the competition would be breaking up a good thing when one of them moved to Prospect. "That's the way it goes. Chefs learn as much as they can from me and go out in the world to build their own place and teach others. Then I go to their restaurant, order something that isn't even on the menu and tell everyone in the place I taught them all they know."

Faye rested her head on his shoulder as she studied his face. It had to be bittersweet to repeat that process over and over.

"We'll all get through the sad part and come out better on the other side." Brian sighed. "I've fired plenty of cooks who better not ever show their faces in my kitchen again, but there have also been the ones that love the job as much as I do. To me, that's the key to being a good chef, not their background or how many good references they can provide. Do they love the kitchen? Restaurants are hard work, front and back of the house. If you don't love it, you won't last. I'm going to invest my time in whoever comes in. I want them to last."

Faye brushed the worried frown on his forehead. "Have you actually been a nuisance at these new places run by your protégés or is that an idle threat?"

Brian laughed. "The threat comes from experience. The guy who gave me my first break, the one I messed up in such a painful way by taking cash from the register as a stupid, desperate mistake, he came into Rinnovato the first week I opened, ordered the short-rib dish that had been his most popular entrée and hadn't shown up on my menu at all."

Faye's mouth dropped open. "What did you do?"

"The waiter hurried back to the kitchen to find me because the chef was insisting that was what he'd have or he'd speak to the owner to know why." Brian chuckled. "She had probably tried to politely convince him otherwise for ten or twenty minutes, so I went out to explain. When I saw him, it was this… It's hard to describe the emotion of seeing someone you've hurt, after all that time, but he hugged me close, told her to bring two of whatever could be prepared without me and poured me a glass of wine."

"Wow," Faye said slowly, "that's an amazing story. Still talk to him?"

Brian said, "Not often, but I did get brave and show my face back in his place not too long ago. He gave me a chance to apologize, to try to make things right between us, so I hope I can always remember to do the same in my kitchen."

When they'd walked out to the firepit, Faye had expected some awkward conversation about the kiss or their future. His comment about how people could work anywhere they wanted to today convinced her he was as preoccupied with the question of what kind of future they might have as she was. But this conversation was so much more powerful because she wanted to know him.

What happened in the future was a problem for next week. Tonight, she settled back against him to stare up at the stars.

"Can we stay here all day tomorrow, too?" Brian's low voice next to her ear sent the sparks down her spine that she'd come to expect. "I don't want to go fishing."

She laughed. "I understand the feeling, but maybe there's a better option. How do you feel about painting?"

Brian blinked at the change of topic. "Walls?"

She chuckled. "Canvases. Gemma's an artist. You told us that. I could ask Prue to see if she could set up a class for the two of you tomorrow afternoon. Patrick Hearst, Jordan and Sarah's dad, is a laid-back teacher."

"Even for students with zero talent?" he asked uncertainly. "This will be one of those things I'm not good at. You don't want to miss that. Join us. Gemma would love that." His relief at finding a valid excuse to avoid fishing was cute.

She'd enjoyed her first Sip and Paint with Patrick, but she didn't want to interfere with Brian's time with Gemma. It was too important.

"You wanted to strengthen your relationship with Gemma while you were in Prospect. Think of how much fun this will be for the two of you." Faye's lips twitched as she patted his chest.

He sighed dramatically. "Your idea is perfect. No kitchen crisis or business calls or texts from her friends. We can talk and Gemma can correct the way I hold my brush or mix my colors or both if she wants to. It's a good suggestion."

Faye smoothed her hand over his flannel shirt. "Make sure to wear something casual…now that you own something casual. Wouldn't want to get paint on your silk ties."

He caught her hand. "Okay, Ms. Consultant. Say you had a client in town who wanted to make a good impression on a beautiful woman. What would you suggest he plan for the two of them, perhaps for tomorrow night, after a painting class ended?"

Faye tapped her lips as she considered his question. "Does this person enjoy movies?"

Brian frowned. "Who doesn't enjoy movies?"

She nodded. "Well, here, that means you have to enjoy them enough to watch old Westerns from the silver screen era." Then she held up a finger. "Plus, it's budget friendly. Tickets are half price for this one night only. Amanda, the Prospect Picture Show's owner, is training her volunteers for Western Days. Dinner at the Ace, a nice movie where everyone in the theater watches you as you experience the finest exploits of legendary cowboys. You can enjoy your date's company and everyone else can enjoy retelling every scandalous thing that happens between the two of you. That's a successful date night in Prospect."

Brian nodded. "What time should I pick you up?"

Anticipation immediately filled her. "Let's say six. That should give us enough time to eat and promenade along the sidewalk while I give you a tour of the town."

"That's a date." Brian pressed a kiss against her lips, lingering to stare into her eyes, and she finally understood all the wordless conversations shared by the couples in love that surrounded her. He understood just as she did that none of their questions had been solved, but still, they wanted every minute they could grab while they were here together.

THE NEXT DAY, Brian wasn't sure who was more relieved when he called a halt to his first attempt at acrylic painting, himself or Patrick Hearst, but it was clear that his daughter had relished every second of being the prize student.

Faye had been right to suggest this time for him and Gemma.

"I've enjoyed this lesson, Mr. Hearst," she said politely as she rounded up the paints they'd used. "I know exactly where I'm going to hang this mountain landscape in my room at Dad's house."

"You can take yours to your mom's house. I'll be happy to let you hang my attempt at columbines in a meadow in your room." He covered his heart with his hand as if he was making a heroic gesture.

His daughter patted him on the shoulder. "Wherever it hangs, there should also be a sign next to it with an arrow that says, 'These are flowers, not Easter eggs.'" The giggles that trailed behind her when she moved to stack their chairs against the wall softened the blow.

"Think I have any future in landscapes, Patrick?" He handed the man their used paintbrushes for cleaning.

"Well," Patrick said as he turned on the water, "on the one hand, some students have talent." He held out his left hand. "And others enjoy creating for the sake of the experience." He waved his right hand. "My favorite students, like Gemma, have both."

Brian could see where this was going. "And probably

your least favorite students have neither of those. That's my group, I guess."

"Not quite." Patrick rinsed the brushes and laid them flat to dry. "My favorite people take time out of their busy schedules to spend an hour or two with my favorite students because they love them and might not even care about the painting. Your flowers could use some—" Patrick stared into space as he chose his words "—refining. They need refining, but the way you care about Gemma is right on track."

Caught off guard, Brian dropped the roll of paper towels he'd plucked from the supply cabinet. "Thank you. That means a lot to me. I haven't always been that kind of father, so I'm trying to make up for lost time. It's not easy. This was Faye's idea. I owe her for keeping me on track." He picked up the roll of paper towels and watched Gemma bustling around to arrange the chairs in neat, matching columns. He hoped the clatter she was making didn't disturb Prue on the first floor.

Patrick crossed his arms over his chest. "Speaking as a father who has a few regrets, I can say it's difficult to do alone. Sadie's the reason I have a real relationship with my daughters, and now that she's gone, I can't even say thank-you for this life she built for us."

Brian wanted to know more, but he hesitated to push for details. The sadness on Patrick's face was easy to read.

"If I can help you, I better do it or Sadie will be sure to make me sorry. I don't believe in ghosts, but if anyone could pull off hanging around to straighten us all out, my aunt would. Sadie rearranged her whole life to buy me time to deal with my grief after my wife died. I couldn't function like myself for far too long, and Sarah had to pick up the pieces while Jordan fought all their battles and the baby, Brooke, learned to pretend everything was fine. Not even Sadie could unteach them that, but she showed them how to be brave and chase dreams and stand up for themselves. She also held the door open for me to step through when I could."

Brian paced, thinking about Patrick's admission. "So there is hope? I will be able to catch up with Gemma?"

"There's enough Hearst in me to say there is always hope. Your daughter enjoys time with you. That's something you can't conjure up. And something else I learned later than I should have is that no matter how old we get, there will always be times when we want our parents. You and Gemma will be okay, but you're going to need someone to keep you on the right path. Sadie did that for me. I hope there's someone at home you can lean on."

Brian hoped it was true that Gemma would love him enough to miss him when he wasn't around, and realized that even his relationship with his ex meant too much to him to lose. Repairing it had taken time, but they had both worked at it because it was important.

For some reason, that made him think of Faye's description of how her parents had left her behind in Prospect. If they changed their minds and returned to town, would she invest the time and effort to build a better relationship with them? In her spot, he wasn't sure he'd hold the door open for them any longer.

He'd gotten used to Faye never being far from his thoughts. He was worrying about something that might never happen for a woman he'd just met… What did that say about him? About them?

Patrick held out his hand. "Hang that landscape with pride, Brian." He held on when Brian would have let go. "But Gemma's suggestion to put a hint next to it isn't a bad one."

Brian nodded, although it didn't erase the temptation

to hide his landscape behind the trash can on the way out, but Patrick said, "Don't dump it."

Surprised, Brian stopped. "Are you a mind reader, too?"

"I've been teaching for a long time, but I've been learning to paint even longer." Patrick shrugged. "I understand being disappointed with the final product, although I have come to understand that with time and distance you may see something there that makes it perfect in your eyes."

Brian tilted his head to the side as he pondered what that might be. Patrick smiled and said, "Try *a lot* of distance and squinting. See if that helps. If not, then hand it to Gemma to create something new."

Amused, Brian waved in surrender and headed down the stairs to Prue's shop.

He wasn't prepared to be center stage when his boots hit the bottom step, but Prue and Gemma were gathered at the spot.

They'd obviously been waiting to ambush him, but he wasn't sure why.

"Gemma tells me you have a date," Prue said in a singsong, her hands clasped under her chin.

He frowned at his daughter.

"You told me not to mention it in our painting class, but that's over now." Then she pointed at Prue. "We're wasting valuable time. Prue can help us."

Brian leaned his painting against the wall. "With what?"

The long-suffering glance his daughter shot Prue would have been funny except it was clear he was the cause of her suffering.

"Faye can't eat dinner at the Ace, she practically lives there, and there's no room in the kitchen at the lodge for you to do something impressive," Gemma continued. "And a cowboy movie?" Dismay was written all over her face.

"This is going to be a special night over at the Picture

Show. Romantic. We all want to be there." Prue tapped her lips. "But dinner... What if you had a picnic? A charcuterie board and some wine from the Market? There's a pretty little park behind the Mercantile here." She pointed over her shoulder. "If you want to avoid a busy dining room with everyone trying to read your lips, it's a better choice."

"Yes!" Gemma jumped up and down. "Sophisticated. I like it. I can help. Let's go."

Prue was grinning as he tried to slow Gemma down long enough to grab his painting. "Gemma's hanging with us, okay? She's going to the Picture Show with me and Walt. We'll get her back to the lodge."

He agreed and it wasn't long before Gemma had maneuvered through the nearby grocery store as if she'd mapped out all the aisles in her mind. He had bags of food for the picnic and an empty passenger seat as he drove away from the Mercantile a half hour later, while Gemma waved from the sidewalk.

Thanks to Gemma's efficiency he had enough time to change his clothes three different times before he had to pick up Faye.

He could have used a consultant but Sarah, Jordan and Mia were all waiting in the lobby for him.

Almost as if they'd been tipped off that he was on his way for a date with Faye.

"Do I look all right?" he asked before he could stop himself.

"Very handsome, Chef." Jordan gave him a thumbs-up and he didn't hang around to listen to any other comments. When he pulled up in front of Faye's grandparents' house, she was sitting on the front steps.

Since he was ten minutes early, he wondered if she was as nervous as he was suddenly.

He slipped out of the driver's seat and noticed his painting in the back seat next to Gemma's.

On a whim, he pulled it out. Faye might see something redeemable in it.

"I'm a little early," Brian said as he closed the SUV door, "but I couldn't wait any longer to see you. You look beautiful. Sure you're ready? I mean, if you aren't, this is good enough." Then he closed his eyes, humbled. The pain in his gut at being so uncool was immediate. "If I've ever wondered if my dating skills are rusty, now we both know the answer." He made the rewind motion with his hand. "Starting over. I hope I'm not too early, but I wanted to see you. You look beautiful." He firmly closed his mouth against any other foolish words that might tumble out.

"If you knew how relieved I am that you were the first one to break the awkward ice, you might start all first dates like that in the future." Faye moved down the steps to meet him. "I might have been excited to see you, too. I almost went out to the barn so I could do some cleaning to get rid of all this nervous energy. Thank you for saving me." She pointed at the canvas. "What's that?"

Brian grimaced. "Okay, so fresh flowers would have been a better option, but I had this and..."

Faye took the canvas from him. He tried to gauge whether she could tell what she was looking at.

"Um, I love abstract art." When she turned it upside down to see if that translated better, he grinned. "Is this what you did during your class with Gemma?"

He ran a hand down his nape. "Yeah. Hers is better. Obviously. Her columbine is actually flower-shaped instead of vaguely roundish, but for my first attempt, I decided it was almost passable and then that I would give it to you. We'll hang Gemma's at my house. You'll have this one in a closet or in the attic somewhere, but we'll have that connection."

Faye shifted so she was close enough that he could see his reflection in her eyes. "I love it. I've never been given anything this beautiful."

The warm glow in the center of his chest surprised him. "I guess it really is the thought that counts for you, huh? Even Patrick, who might be the nicest guy I ever met in real life, was at a loss for words. He mildly complimented my ability to choose colors. Gemma told me to stick to plating food with an artistic flair."

Faye sniffed. "Everyone's a critic, but what do they know? Art is in the eye of the beholder. Everyone knows that. I love it. When you come back to Prospect, it might even be hanging in the Ace's dining room in a place of honor."

He shook his head. "Please, do not hang that picture where you have to tell anyone else that I painted it. This is what we call a grand gesture more than a proud moment."

Faye chuckled as she took his hand and led him up to the porch. "No one has ever made even an extra-large gesture for me, much less one that was grand. Let me hang this where I want to."

"Okay, but when I get better and can replicate flower-like shapes, let me replace this with an improved effort."

"I'll put my painting inside and we can stop by the Ace to see what Gran is serving for dinner tonight."

He nodded and followed her into the house.

Brian stopped suddenly and pointed at the bird clock hanging over the kitchen sink.

"The birds sing when the clock strikes the hour." Brian waited for her to agree. "I got the same clock for my mother the first Christmas after I started working in kitchens full time. It's hanging on the wall opposite the stove to this day."

"Doesn't sing anymore," they both said at the same time.

"Sometimes you get a weird croak to remember the early days," Faye added. "That one was a birthday gift for Gran. I saved tips from the Ace the summer between my junior and senior year."

"I've told my mother I would buy her a new bird clock or even a fancy smart thing that will run the lights and play her Nat King Cole as she cooks, but she refuses." Brian took the jacket Faye reached for and held it out for her to slip into. "I can't believe we both bought that clock."

Faye smiled. "I didn't expect to have anything in common with the hotshot LA chef, but every day I discover something else that we share."

They walked out to his car and he waited for her to climb inside. "Yeah. It's sort of special, right?"

"Yeah." Faye nodded and he shut the door.

Brian understood the nervousness he was fighting was totally silly. He and Faye knew each other too well for the jittery first-date nerves, but there was something about seeing her home and sitting there next to her in the peace and quiet of the car that changed how he felt about this time with her. This might be their first date night, but he couldn't imagine it being their last.

CHAPTER SIXTEEN

FAYE'S DESCRIPTION OF a perfect evening would never have included a charcuterie board or a picnic table before Brian Caruso had rolled into Prospect, but she knew it was unforgettable even as it was happening. The food was good, the wine was perfect and the conversation had been mostly light banter about what the subject of his next painting would be: basically a list of round-ish blob-ish things.

She vaguely recalled that date conversations were supposed to be about career and family and plans and travel, but they already knew all those things about each other. So it didn't matter to her what they talked about.

He was just easy to be with.

As they strolled down the wooden sidewalk in front of the Mercantile, he asked, "What's playing at the Prospect Picture Show tonight?"

Faye stepped into the street to see the marquee better. "*The Virginian*. Have you seen it?"

He pretended to think. "Doesn't ring a bell."

"There's a lot of courting of the beautiful new schoolteacher in town, and the bad guys lose and our happy couple ride off into the sunset. Joel McCrea is the cowboy. That's pretty much how I characterize most of the movies at the Prospect Picture Show, by who plays the hero." Faye took the hand he offered her to step back up onto the sidewalk and smiled when he tangled their fingers together instead of letting go. "Can you name many silver-screen cowboys?"

"John Wayne. Roy Rogers?" Brian paused. "That might be it, off the top of my head, but I do know Roy had a horse named Trigger. I once had a job handing out flyers in front of Grauman's Chinese Theatre in Hollywood where the stars leave their handprints and footprints in the cement? He and Trigger are memorialized there."

Faye stopped in the middle of the sidewalk to study his face. When he rubbed the back of his neck, she realized she was making him nervous. "You and I have led very different lives, Chef, but I keep being surprised at how well they intersect over and over. Roy is fine, but let's talk about his wife, Dale Evans. He was her fourth husband, did you know that? Can you imagine what a scandal she was?"

Brian grinned as he made a point of watching her flapping gesture with her free hand.

"What? There was even less entertainment here when I was a teenager. I spent a lot of time with old movies." Faye pointed at him. "Dale Evans is the one who wrote the song they're known for. 'Happy Trails'…that's all her."

"Four husbands. That seems like a lot of work." Brian grinned at her immediate nod. "Way too much courting required."

"She was Roy's third wife. Hollywood takes a toll on romance, I guess," Faye said.

"It does. The whole LA area is challenging to find and hold on to love, in my experience." Brian shrugged. "Monica and Chris seem to be on track to beat the odds, though, so I think it still happens."

They strolled in front of the Ace High. Faye tugged Brian over so she could peek inside at the dinner rush. Her grandmother was carrying a tray to a booth, so Faye waved. When someone called out to her grandmother, she glanced over her shoulder to acknowledge it and met Faye's stare. She pointedly glanced around at the crowd and tipped her chin up before hurrying back toward the kitchen. Holly hurried past the window with a tea pitcher.

"Everything okay?" Brian asked.

Faye wasn't sure how to answer that. Service was moving, but neither Gran nor Holly seemed…okay.

And where was Britt?

"Yeah. They're busy." Faye followed him as he wandered down past Bell House, the town's bed-and-breakfast.

"Gemma mentioned that Rose Bell ran the B and B in town. She and Prue are best friends, I guess."

Faye didn't comment. Instead, she realized she was staring over her shoulder at the restaurant. The urge to march inside and check on things was strong.

But she'd said she wouldn't cross the threshold until the video crew left town.

Determined to get details out of Gran when they were both home again, Faye cleared her throat. "Yes, the two of them are usually at the center of whatever happens in Prospect. Rose's family dates way, way back, like to when the town first existed. She and Patrick are doing some courting of their own."

"I didn't know people still did that." Brian pursed his lips. "Are we courting? I don't know what's involved."

"According to the movies, people who are courting put on their finest duds." Faye pinched her shirt between her fingers. "Check. And the gentleman offers a bouquet of flowers."

Brian made a motion with his hand. "Check."

"They make genteel conversation about the weather, I think," Faye said.

"Nice night. Think it will rain?" Brian immediately asked.

"But…" Faye shook her head. "I believe the end goal

of courting is wedded bliss." She motioned between them. "This is..." She didn't know the answer, so they walked on.

They reached the unofficial border of the old part of town. Brian stopped in front of a small building on one corner. "What was this place?" He stared inside the shadowy interior. "Some kind of store?"

From their spot, they could see a long wall lined with wooden cubes, as if it had been set up for storage, and a counter-high solid wood partition in front.

She pointed at the sign on the wall beside the counter. "Prospect Post Office. It's never been renovated into a modern space, mainly because it's so small. It's hard to figure out what could go there, but I love that all these old features remain."

"It's perfect for a coffee shop," he murmured and let go of her hand to cup his fingers on the glass to peer inside. "Interesting mugs could be displayed in those cubbies on the wall. There's enough counter space for all the machines, and that wood would gleam if it was refinished properly." He turned to look at her and Faye shrugged. She wasn't sure how to answer. It seemed he could see it clearly, so it was impossible to argue with.

"If you wanted to make it a grab-and-go spot, like for people on the lake, you could put in a glass case to hold baked goods or sandwiches. To do that, you'd need a commercial kitchen close by, though," he added.

Faye wasn't certain what was happening, but she took his hand to tow him reluctantly from the front of the small building, around the corner and down the first side street. "As you can see, there's such a space available." She motioned at the empty structure that had once been an insurance office. "The exterior is a boring box from the eighties, but if it's space you need, it could work."

She leaned her shoulder against the signpost and

watched him repeat the steps of shading his eyes so he could see inside better.

"Are you thinking of opening a business in Prospect, Chef?" she asked. Curiosity was natural, right? It wouldn't hurt to ask if he was making plans for the future. Why was her heart beating faster?

When he slowly shook his head, she knew that she had been harboring a hope that he might find Prospect irresistible.

"I don't know what I'm doing." He took her hand again and they turned back toward the center of the old town. "Belvie and I have been talking about opening up a second version of Rinnovato in San Francisco, but neither of us wants to go and run it. What I should do is invest in her the way Sadie did for me, help her find the perfect spot for her own concept in LA. We both have lives and family in the city."

Faye kept silent and the distance between them stretched back out. "We should head for the Picture Show. We definitely need to get popcorn to enjoy the movie."

"Lead on," Brian said as he moved away from the window.

She had his attention again, but the reminder that his future plans didn't include Prospect was welcome. They had tonight and she would enjoy it.

AS SOON AS Brian stepped inside the lobby of the Prospect Picture Show, he knew he was going to have a memorable experience.

The history of the place had been preserved, and the interior gave him the impression of vintage glamor. Deep red walls were dotted with framed black-and-white posters. He recognized John Wayne and possibly Roy Rogers. The wooden railing on the small gallery above the concessions area displayed brightly colored quilts. He knew nothing about the patterns, but the one in the center featured a giant patchwork star in bright yellow fabrics.

A miniature covered wagon in the corner of the lobby was draped with another quilt. This one had velvet ropes preventing people from getting too close. It was faded, some spots worn. Was it an antique?

"Prue and Gemma have been here, helping Amanda Gipson get ready for Western Days." Faye told him as they waited to order. "Every business in the old town will have similar displays. Quilt show, crafts, a parade, that sort of thing, but this year, the Armstrongs are cooking up a new event, cowboy games with coed teams. I can't wait to see how that turns out. I hope I'll be able to take a break from the restaurant to catch some of it."

Brian said, "Gemma's already trying to find a way to get back to town for the festival. She showed me Prue's photo albums. There was a picture of you riding a float. You haven't changed a bit."

Faye huffed out a skeptical breath as she held up two fingers for the young girl filling popcorn buckets. "Since high school? I can't decide if I want that to be true or not."

Instead of arguing, Brian took the drinks on the counter and followed Faye through the lobby and into the theater. He nodded at everyone who was tracking their progress. He recognized Armstrongs scattered throughout the crowd from his visit at the ranch. Faye stopped to make conversation with a redhead who was sitting next to Travis Armstrong. He smiled as she introduced the doctor who she'd promised could reassemble Gemma if her first side-by-side ride went awry.

"Hey, Damon and Micah!" Faye waved at the boys sitting next to Dr. Keena. "Are you going to be helping my grandpa out in the barn?"

Damon immediately checked to see what Travis thought, so after his foster dad nodded, Damon said, “Yes, ma’am, I’m considering the rodeo club and that will take some cash.”

Micah patted Damon’s arm. “Not so fast, miss. We’ll need to discuss terms, payment schedules, things of that nature.”

Brian wondered if his mouth dropped open. It was surprising to hear a kid who had to be fighting his way through fifth grade math mention “payment schedules.”

Faye’s lips were twitching but she kept a straight face. “I’ll let you gentlemen come to a fair agreement with my grandfather, but he’s hiring strong fellas to help around the place. Grandpa’s also talking about working with the rodeo club, so you might have other things to discuss as well. Stop by after school and see if you can strike a deal.”

Micah nodded solemnly, as if warning Faye that he was no pushover. Brian glanced away to swallow his chuckles.

Then Brian noticed Walt and Prue Armstrong. His daughter waved happily from her seat next to Prue.

Was there a place in the theater where it would make it harder to spy on him or…? He decided he didn’t need to know the answer to that question and moved down another row to claim a seat.

“Decided you needed to stir up the gossip, did you?” Grant murmured from the other side of the aisle. “You two will definitely be the talk of the town tomorrow.”

“You and Mia could take the heat off us.” Faye patted Grant’s shoulder. “You like to be the center of attention. Do it for me. I can’t believe everyone’s here. Who’s watching the Majestic tonight?”

Brian wasn’t sure what Grant’s conspiratorial look at Mia seated next to him meant, but he answered, “You’ve made an excellent choice for your first public outing as a couple. Nothing will save you from all the talk, but you won't be the front-page story."

"Jordan and Sarah left Andre in charge of the place." Mia covered Grant's mouth. "Enjoy your movie."

Faye obviously wanted to dig for details, but Mia shook her head firmly.

The houselights went down and Sadie Hearst appeared on the screen with a welcome to town. He hadn't considered how much a part of Prospect's history Sadie had been. To him, she was the wily firecracker who'd helped him build his career. Since he'd spent so much time with Sarah and Jordan and even their father, Patrick, he'd come to understand how she'd left her mark on her family, but here she was the town's claim to fame, a warm, inviting celebrity. She was young in this video, but her vibrant personality still jumped off the screen.

"It's always nice to see Sadie like this," Faye whispered in his ear.

He understood. Whenever he missed Sadie, it would be easy to find a reminder of her in Prospect. Before he could say that, the countdown rolled on the screen and then the movie started. He wasn't certain what he expected of his first Prospect Picture Show event, but it was hard to be bored when there were cowboys and courting on the screen. For more than an hour, he held Faye's hand and enjoyed movie popcorn for the first time in years, possibly decades.

It was absolute perfection and he didn't want it to end, but the lights came up before he was ready. The credits were still rolling.

Then someone called from the back of the room. "Folks, if I can have you stay in your seats for one more minute."

Brian's gaze caught Faye's as they turned to face the double doors at the end of the aisle.

The woman there said, “Is Wes Armstrong in the room?”

The oldest Armstrong stood up and drew Sarah Hearst to her feet. Whatever was happening, she had not been a party to the planning. Her confusion was clear.

“Oh,” Faye said softly.

When Wes knelt down and Sarah covered her mouth with her hand, Brian finally connected the dots.

“We’ve been waiting for the first proposal. Of course, it’s Wes and Sarah,” Faye said, smiling ear to ear.

“Finding the perfect romantic occasion to make a grand gesture in Prospect is difficult,” Wes said as he opened the lid of the jewelry box. “Even with the cagiest planners in town helping me. If you were surprised by the size of the crowd, it’s because you were the only person in town not in on the plan.” Everyone in the audience laughed when Prue held her hand to her chest as if she had no idea who he might be referring to, and Brian realized he was part of the Armstrongs’ extended family tonight. Everyone in town was. “A woman like Sarah Hearst deserves Paris and the Eiffel Tower or the Empire State Building at midnight, something amazing and jaw-dropping. Unfortunately, this Sarah Hearst has too much to do before Western Days to take a weekend trip anywhere and I don’t want to wait any longer to ask this question.”

Faye clutched Brian’s hand tightly as they waited.

“You’ve changed my life. You’ve changed this town. And all for the better. I want to keep you close to watch whatever you accomplish next and support every step along the way. Will you marry me?”

“Yes. Yes. Yes!” Sarah pulled him up to stand and kissed him as romantically as if they’d been staring out over New York City lights from the observation deck of the Empire State Building. The whole theater applauded and yelled their congratulations.

It took a while to make it through the scrum of people crowding the happy couple, and eventually Faye directed him toward the lobby, promising she'd follow as soon as Jordan let go of her. He couldn't make out her words in the excited conversation, so he expected it might take a minute.

He stopped to study the poster of Roy Rogers, safely apart from the flowing crowd making their way out of the theater. He knew Faye was getting closer before he could see her, like there was a part of him tuned to her presence, so he leaned a shoulder against the wall and saw her head pop up above the crowd.

"It's not every night that the movie ends in a real, honest-to-goodness proposal. Our timing is amazing." She smiled up at him and led him out onto the sidewalk. "What do you think about Prospect's nightlife? Not quite as boring as you expected, is it?"

Brian shook his head. "Believe it or not, that's the first proposal I've ever witnessed. I was impressed."

Faye stopped. "Britt? Were you in the theater? Why aren't you working tonight?"

Brian recognized the server he'd met the night he'd helped out at the Ace. "Mrs. Parker and I agreed that I needed to quit. I've been trying my best ever since the first night when I dropped the tray of food, and Chef here and everyone had to save dinner service. Then, she wouldn't let me quit, but last night, she didn't even tell me to stop crying." Britt sighed. "I mixed up her orders and we ran out of mashed potatoes, so she couldn't finish the table and…it was scary for a minute."

Finding the right words seemed impossible as Faye stared up at him with obvious confusion.

"Chef, thank you for everything you did to keep the kitchen on track that first night. Mrs. Parker might not have been super grateful, but I sure was." Britt gave a big smile before she trotted off after her friends.

He wasn't sure what his expression was, but Faye's hurt was easy to see.

Prue must have noticed, because she stopped next to them. "Everything okay?"

Faye blinked. "Have there been problems with every night's service at the Ace? Why didn't anyone tell me?"

Prue took Faye's hands in hers. "Oh, honey, they were only growing pains. That's all. You needed to be free to try something new, and if you'd come running back every time there'd been a bump in the road, you'd never have that space."

Faye licked her lips and stared across the street at the restaurant.

"Wait! Before you go over there, think about it. You've enjoyed working with this crew, haven't you? And life has gone on at the Ace. Whatever the problems are, they've found solutions," Prue said.

Instead of replying, Faye ran her hand over her forehead. "That doesn't explain why no one told me what was going on, not my friends or my family. It's like stepping out of the restaurant changed who I am or something." She stepped off the sidewalk. "I need to talk to Gran."

Brian watched her go, uncertain of what to do. It felt wrong to let Faye leave on her own, but stopping her would be worse.

Prue covered her cheeks with her hands. "Oh, no, I've truly stepped in a mess, haven't I? This is all my fault."

Walt wrapped his arm around Prue's shoulders. "Faye's levelheaded. She'll see there's no harm done." Walt's eyes briefly met his as he urged Prue down the sidewalk. "We'll catch up with everyone at breakfast. You'll see to Gemma?"

Brian nodded. He noticed that Gemma was staring at the Ace the same way Faye had been before she'd left. Gemma's frown and her worrying her bottom lip with her teeth looked like red flags to him, so he said, "Hey, Walt's right. We'll be okay with Faye once she has a chance to get answers to all her questions." He squeezed Gemma's shoulders and hated the tension there. She had been doing so well, just being a kid in Prospect. "Let me take you back to the Majestic, and then I'll call and check on Faye."

Gemma nodded. But he wasn't certain either of them was convinced that they hadn't ruined their chance with the restaurant owner.

CHAPTER SEVENTEEN

FAYE WAS STILL trying to work through her confusion as she stepped inside the Ace. The Closed sign swung behind her, but since the door was still open, Gran or Holly had to be there somewhere. She skirted the host stand, bypassed the empty dining room and headed for the small office off the kitchen.

Gran was pacing outside the doorway while Holly was seated behind Faye's desk watching her. When the younger woman saw Faye, she sighed with what appeared to be relief. "Hey! I wasn't sure Emma—" Holly glanced nervously at Gran before clearing her throat.

"Was ever going to call it a night. The bank deposit is done and all the receipts are off to the accountant. We can lock up." Holly raised her eyebrows at Faye as if to urge her to go along with this plan.

Another time, she would have, but this situation suited her needs perfectly so she urged her grandmother to sit in the chair wedged in the corner of the office.

"I ran into Britt over at the Picture Show tonight." Faye crossed her arms casually and leaned on the door frame. "Why didn't anyone tell me she wasn't working out?"

Holly immediately opened her mouth but Gran interrupted. "It wasn't necessary. It's only for a few more days and you'll be back. We can make do for that long."

She crossed her own arms in a move meant to punctuate her answer. The statement was a period, not a question mark. Gran had decided that was the correct decision and no one would change her mind.

Holly cleared her throat again. "What I was going to say is that Britt spread the word that she wasn't going to last as a server. We've already had two of her friends come in and ask to apply."

"It's an unnecessary expense and a waste of time. Faye is coming back." Gran nodded once.

This had been exactly what Faye was afraid of, but before she could intervene, Holly tilted her head to the side as if declaring her intention to enter the fray. "Even when Faye is back, we could use the help. Western Days is coming up and then the summer season on the lake. We all know that the reopened lodge is going to increase the crowd in town." Instead of backing down, she leaned forward. "This is smart business, Emma." Her voice shook this time when she said Gran's name, but Faye was impressed with Holly's backbone. She was young but she was obviously both smart and brave.

"Extra staff means extra the cost, when Faye and I have done fine on our own." Her grandmother grinned as if she'd won the round. *"Smart business."* Her snort was worth a thousand words.

Holly's shoulders slumped in defeat.

Faye sighed. "Okay." She rubbed her forehead. The problem was that they were both right in different ways. How many times did her own arguments with her grandmother boil down to the same issue? "Holly, you should go home and get some rest. Tomorrow, please set up interviews with both those friends who'd asked about the job." She made a stop motion when her grandmother opened her mouth to say something. "There's no rule in the world that says we have to hire them because we interviewed them, Gran. If neither of them meet your standards, we'll regroup." Even as she said it, she knew she was giving her grandmother an out. Holly knew it, too, because she shook her head. "But Holly is right about the workload coming this summer. It makes sense to start interviewing now. Right?"

She and Holly both waited for her grandmother to nod reluctantly.

"Good." Faye stepped out of the office so that Holly could vacate the desk and make her escape. "Thank you for everything this week, Holly. Gran couldn't have done it without you, which she knows, but might never say."

Holly slung her purse over her shoulder. "I don't need thanks, but working for someone who listens to my opinion would be nice." Her side-eye at Gran was an extra clue if anyone was missing her point.

"Yeah," Faye said softly.

That was a viewpoint she knew very well.

"How is filming at the Majestic?" Holly asked as Faye followed her to the dining room.

"Good. A little harried at times. Egos, attitudes and all that. But everyone wants to do their best for Sadie, so it's coming together."

Faye paused and asked Holly to do the same. "I'm so impressed by how you've handled all this, Holly. It took me a lot longer to speak up so that she hears me, and it looks like you've already learned that lesson."

She grimaced. "The first time I suggested something to her, I nearly croaked in fear. It's getting easier, but my heart still races."

Faye grinned. "That's impressive. Believe me, I know."

"I'll lock the front door on my way out," Holly said in singsong before she left.

Back in the office, her grandmother had crossed her legs,

the one on top swinging back and forth. Faye had decided years ago that the speed indicated the level of irritation.

Her foot was stirring up a light breeze, but Faye was annoyed, too, so it might be time to finally hash this out.

"I had my doubts about promoting Holly, but she has proven her gumption this week. Gives her opinion almost as freely as you do." Gran sniffed. "But I'd rather she called me Gran than Emma."

"That's what coworkers do, Gran. They call each other by their first names. Sometimes they even share their opinions." Faye stretched back in her office chair and studied the calendar she'd pinned up with all the deliveries marked and the invoice due dates. Holly had picked up on her shorthand and had continued her notes into the next few weeks.

Her grandmother said, "Holly is an employee. The cooks are employees. Not coworkers. This is my place. No one here loves it like I do." Then she patted Faye's hand. "Except you."

"We do love it, but you're underestimating how much your employees care about the Ace." Faye squeezed her grandmother's hand and realized that her insistence on being addressed as Mrs. Parker was tied to her pride in her restaurant and business, not some stubborn refusal to bend with the times. With a little patience and Holly's continued backbone, her grandmother might go with being called by her first name.

Photos of her parents were tacked next to the calendar along with an unfortunate school photo of Faye's that should be destroyed immediately. She'd worn her grandparents down that year and finally gotten her hair "highlighted" by her best friend. Stark white tips grew out to show dark roots in time for picture day.

Her grandmother's pride in her family had withstood even a very bad hair day.

"Holly's great. And I bet she'd call you Gran if you told her to," Faye added softly.

Her grandmother tilted her chin up. "I guess if my real granddaughter is flying the nest, I should audition a new one to take over this place I've built."

At first, Faye thought she had to be making a strange joke, but her grandmother's somber expression while she waited for Faye's answer convinced her that Gran was really waiting for Faye to pack her things and go.

"Gran—" Faye paused to get control of the hurt and anger that bubbled under the surface "—I haven't gone anywhere. And even if I did, I would still be the only granddaughter you have. I love you. You love me. Pretending otherwise is silly."

Gran put her hand over her heart. "Seems like you're making plans. Suggesting your grandfather hire help for the garden and adding waitstaff here when you've been equal to or better than any crowd we've ever had in the place." Her eyes darted to meet Faye's. "I want to keep you here. I do. Your grandfather and I have built a successful business and farm. Through some hard times, we worked and we pulled through to hold on to both. We've done that for our family...and they don't want these things we've sacrificed for. That hurts."

Faye rubbed her burning nose, aware that tears would derail the important conversation that she'd never managed to have with her grandmother. When she was sure she could speak without a shaky voice, Faye said, "I'm staying, Gran. This is my home. But if there were a way to enjoy more of this life instead of working until we're exhausted, falling into bed and doing it again the next day until forever, I want to do that."

Her grandmother's bottom lip trembled. "That's all we've ever done, Faye. Changing that now feels like...giving up or losing." Then she stood. "I need to head home."

Faye closed her eyes as she heard the swoosh of the swinging doors. If she hadn't bumped into Britt, she would still believe that everything was going well here even though Holly was struggling and her grandmother feared Faye was leaving ASAP.

She pressed her hands on top of the desk to still the trembling.

"That could have gone better, but it could have gone so much worse." Faye stretched her arms out as far as she could. The office was so small that it seemed like she should be able to span it with her reach, but she was still too short. The stretch made her shoulders feel better.

Tired, Faye moved through the kitchen, scanning the countertops and floors as she went. Everything was spotless. So was the dining room. When she made it to the front door, she realized she might have no way home. The plan had been to finish the date where Brian would drop her off and kiss her good-night.

Gran had already sped away from the restaurant by this point, but she could see headlights parked in front of the Ace.

Brian rolled his window down and stuck his head out. "Please let me take you home."

"You waited." Faye watched him slide out and move around to open her door.

"I came back. I took Gemma to the Majestic, but I couldn't leave things the way they were between us." Brian waited for her to climb in and then moved back to the driver's seat.

She wasn't sure what to say as they drove out of town.

Again, as if reading her mind, he said, "Yelling might

help." He gave her a rueful smile. "My mother seems to prefer that method when I've messed up."

Faye propped her elbow on the door, the hurt too fresh to let him off the hook. "You've had so many opportunities to mention a little thing like running the kitchen at the Ace High but didn't. This definitely explains the weird comments I've picked up on here and there. Gran saying she'd had a chance to talk to you *again.* When was the first time, I'd asked myself. Gemma mentioned having fun pouring drinks." Faye stared out at the dark roadside. "I puzzled over that."

"Prue made us promise not to tell you about the disarray the first night. She had the best intentions. We all did, but I understand that it's not fair to keep you in the dark. If Belvie tried that with Rinnovato, I'd have a hard time trusting her again."

Faye nodded. That was the point she kept coming back to. With all of them. Brian and Gemma weren't the targets of her anger, but both Prue and her grandmother should have understood how much Faye had sacrificed to build the Ace. She was a part of its success, so solving its problems mattered to her.

"But…" Brian parked in front of her grandparents' house and she was glad to see Gran had already made it home. Then she realized he'd stopped.

As if he had something uncomfortable to say.

"But what?" Faye unbuckled her seat belt.

"All this time, we've been finding all the places we're the same. We understand each other…"

"But…"

"Rinnovato is my dream. I imagined it. I worked for it. I built it, not alone, but every piece of it belonged to me before it was anyone else's." He cleared his throat. "You can love your grandparents without chaining yourself to the Ace High."

The emotional punch to the center of her chest caught her by surprise.

"They're family, Chef. The only ones who ever made a place for me." When he reached to take her hand, she pulled it away. "You asked strangers for help because your relationship with your daughter was so shaky. Do you remember that? What if you'd sacrificed any of your own dream for Gemma, Chef? Think you'd be making up for lost time now? I doubt it."

He inhaled slowly. "I didn't have a choice. Your parents do. Your grandmother does, and so do you, Faye. You're telling yourself you have no options here except keeping the Ace up and running, but that's not true." Brian held out his hand. "Sadie told me to take a minute to imagine what I wanted most and then work to make it happen. Can you imagine what your life in LA might look like?"

She huffed out a frustrated breath. "Of course, I can. And all I'd have to do is forget all my responsibilities and leave everything I've known to make it happen. Simple!" The sarcasm felt wrong on her tongue, but he had to understand her point of view.

Brian pulled his hand back. "No, not simple, but it could be so worth all the hard work."

The hurt tangled with the frustration and convinced Faye it was her turn to escape. "And you'll always find a way for someone else to make sacrifices for your dream, won't you, Chef? First, it was Gemma and now it's me."

She hopped out of the SUV and slammed the door before marching up the steps.

When he didn't follow her or try to stop her, she knew she'd landed her own blow.

Winning a point should have felt better, but she hadn't

absorbed all the pain yet that his words had caused. It was going to be a long night.

And in the morning, she'd have to work out how to finish the job she'd been hired to do.

CHAPTER EIGHTEEN

THE THIRD TIME Andre yelled "Cut" while Faye and Franky were discussing a tip on how to perfectly sear scallops every time, Brian could see the frustration on Faye's face. Throughout the competition, she'd been capable.

Dependable.

Almost unshakable.

This Faye was struggling to get through every shot.

Since his sleepless night had left him with a pounding head and the certainty that anything he might have had with Faye had been wrecked by their last discussion, he understood her difficulty.

He realized his concerned sigh was louder than he expected when Franky, Rafa and the entire video crew turned to stare at him. Only Faye kept her eyes on the outline they'd drafted before shooting.

"Is this a romantic tiff?" Andre asked. "Because the most consistent member of our on-air talent has lost her mojo and I need her to get it back immediately." He braced his hands on his hips. "What is the problem?"

Faye smiled. "Sorry, Andre. I have a lot on my mind. I'll get the next take." Franky squeezed her hand.

Brian said, "Should I go?"

Andre's eyebrows shot up but he waited for Faye to answer.

"Of course not. I can do my job with you standing there, Chef."

"Chef," Franky mouthed, picking up on the change in tone.

"You're too good at this not to stick the landing, Faye." Andre moved back behind the camera. "Final take. And we're rolling." He held up his hand. "Action."

"Franky, scallops on a pizza? That's something only a bold chef would try," Faye said. This time, there was more life to her voice, so Andre made the "continue" motion.

"Scallops are easy and quick. Here are five things that will help." Franky stepped up to the counter. "First, make sure they're dry. Pat them well with a paper towel before you try to sear them." He demonstrated. "Second, you'll need hot oil to get a proper sear." He poured a small amount into the cast-iron skillet on the stove.

"Not butter?" Faye asked as she picked up the bottle and examined it. "This is vegetable oil."

"It's easy and works well. Butter and olive oil are both delicate and not the best for this task." Franky plopped the scallops into the hot pan. "Three and four are all about the pan. Cast iron is the way to go, and always leave plenty of room around the scallops. Don't overcrowd them." Franky pointed at the scallops. "You want to turn them over now, don't you?"

Faye nodded immediately. "Aren't they burning?"

Franky shook his head. "Wait a second or two longer than you think, then flip them, but don't pick them up and put them down and pick them up to check again. That will keep them from browning and increase the chances that you're overcooking. Rubbery scallops will definitely ruin your pizza."

Faye grinned. "I've heard it said there's no such thing as bad pizza, but I don't want to test that theory with rubber scallops." Then she smoothly turned to the camera.

"And there you have it. Use your handy iron skillet and give this a shot."

"Cut." Andre stepped up to the counter. "How are we feeling? That was a good take. Do you have another in you? I'd like to try to get this last tip wrapped up. Michael has requested a meeting tomorrow where we can all review the short clip the editor has worked up and critique it." He glanced around the room. "We need a full day to get Sarah, Jordan and Brian out and about in Prospect, so the schedule is getting tight."

"Franky, I'm up for your last tip. Are you?" Faye straightened her shoulders. "I want to find out more about making pizza in a skillet." The way Faye glanced at him convinced Brian that he needed to take a walk outside. He wanted her to relax.

The large audience waiting when he stepped into the dining room made him wonder if there was a back door somewhere he could use.

"How's it going in there?" Gemma asked before she returned to worrying her bottom lip.

Sarah said, "Prue and Gemma caught us up on what happened after the big proposal last night because the tension between you and Faye is so noticeable."

"It's like you stepped in it somehow." Jordan winced and pinched her nose.

"I thought that when you went back to pick her up, you might've been able to talk it out." Gemma hugged her arms tightly over her chest. The signs of her shyness returning heaped more guilt on his shoulders, and he'd been dealing with so much ever since Faye's parting words.

Before he could find the right words to reassure his daughter, Franky and Faye joined the group.

Faye said briskly, "We wrapped up the tips to Andre's satisfaction."

"He's still muttering and rubbing a red spot on his forehead as he watches the playback," Franky added. "Surely that's a good sign!" His forced enthusiasm provoked a few smiles, but the response was underwhelming.

"What's next?" Prue asked. "Are we ready to get some footage of Brian riding one of our great trails?"

Andre joined them. "Since we need to be in town tomorrow to meet with Michael at the museum, we're going to start there." The red spot on his forehead was fading. Brian hoped that was a good sign. "We'll need Jordan, Sarah and Chef Caruso there after breakfast. Change of wardrobe, please. Wear what you want." He raised his hands as if he was over the whole thing.

River spoke up quickly. "No, stick with your approved wardrobe. Brian, you change it up. No chef's coat, jeans, bring a couple of options for your shirt so we can test them on camera like we did before." Andre nodded and walked away. Everyone turned to watch him trudge through the lobby. River shook her head, a smile curling her lips. "The tortured artist sees the final product doesn't match with the image in his head, but the rest of us are always pleased with the results." She squeezed Faye's arm. "Don't take his feedback personally. Tomorrow, all will be well."

Faye scrubbed her face with both hands. "Since I'm not required for this part of the project or the meeting with Michael, I believe..." She smiled at Gemma. Brian was happy to see none of her usual warmth had faded. So was Gemma. She immediately brightened under Faye's focus. "It's time for the supersecret passing of the confidential recipe for the Ace's apple pie. Are you ready?"

Watching his daughter jump with excitement reminded him of how much he loved Faye's relationship with her. When Gemma had to cook with him, she wilted as if the world was ending, but the opportunity to work with Faye filled her with joy.

It was humbling but also…

He didn't want to ever lose that.

"Come by the Ace when everyone else goes to the museum, okay?" Faye said as she started jumping up and down to match Gemma's hops.

Gemma nodded wildly.

"If you have the time," Sarah said slowly as she bobbed her head up and down with the jumps, "I'd love to have you at the table for the conversation with Michael. In case there's any discussion on what we might add or improve if we try this again."

Faye stopped jumping and caught his stare for a brief second. "Of course. I'm still on the job and ready for whatever you need, Sarah." Then she pointed at the kitchen. "Today I'm going to clean up the mess in there and call it a day."

She returned to the kitchen, Gemma hot on her heels.

"Okay, we have some work to do," Prue said slowly as she pointed at Faye retreating. "Any ideas?"

Silence was her answer.

"I was afraid of that." She tapped her lips with her fingers.

Ignoring the pitying looks of Sarah, Jordan and Prue while he did his best to pretend his heart wasn't gripped in a hard fist reminded him of how Faye had told him that she would be the one left behind in Prospect when he and Gemma went home. She would have to face this reaction from everyone until they forgot about this flirtation and moved on.

He hated that.

What had started off as fun and new and invigorating in so many ways had trailed off to end in bad communication and a sadness he couldn't shake. He owed it to them both to step back and make it crystal clear to all that they were both fine.

Lying had never felt so wrong.

THE NEXT MORNING, Faye was happy to have the Ace High kitchen to herself. Times like this had always been her favorite. The kitchen was spotless, and she had everything she needed to put together enough pies to get the restaurant through at least a week. Now all she had to do was peel, chop, mix and bake. It was effective therapy.

And she needed something to clear her mind after two sleepless nights and a truly dismal day in front of the camera.

All that was missing was her assistant.

Faye heard the bells ring above the front door and headed for the dining room.

The déjà vu that swept over her as Brian and Gemma stopped inside the sunshiny entryway caught her off guard. They were the same as the night they'd arrived, but everything was different now.

"Hey, are you ready to learn my secret?" Faye asked as she shoved her hands in her pockets. She wasn't exactly sure what to do with them. On that first night, she hadn't had to worry, thanks to their lateness and the to-go containers, but today she was hyperaware of them and how she was standing and the fact that her face might also be doing something she couldn't explain while she waited for Brian to speak.

"Put me to work, Chef," Gemma said. The perky tone didn't exactly sound like her usual voice, so Faye guessed they were all out of sorts that morning. Gemma glanced between Brian and Faye before clearing her throat. "I'll go wash my hands for however long this takes."

Faye had to get some of this tension between them out of the way. "I'm sorry for the low blow about Gemma. I didn't even mean what I said. I just…" She winced. "I just wanted ammunition."

He nodded. "Well, I needed to hear it, and it helped clarify things for me, so I should thank you."

She waited to see if he had an apology for her, but she didn't want to fight anymore regardless. Their future was already clear, anyway. A clatter from the kitchen reminded her that they had an audience nearby.

"I'll bring Gemma over when we're done." Faye forced herself to turn away from him. Nothing had changed.

Cooking was going to help her get through.

She rolled her shoulders before bumping the kitchen doors open with her hip. "All right, Chef. First things first, grab an apron and a paring knife." Faye motioned broadly and watched Gemma scurry to follow her directions. "We've got some peeling to do." Then she pointed at the radio. "Assistant gets to pick the station today."

Gemma fiddled with the radio dial until she was happy and then returned to the counter. "Dad gets upset because I never peel thin enough. Do you want to lecture now or later?"

Faye grinned. Sadie used to give her a hard time for the same thing. Practice would fix that issue for Gemma someday. "If there's one thing I have in abundance, it's apples. No lectures today as long as there's no bleeding."

They settled in to peel and chop the apples, and Faye was silently waiting for Gemma to broach the subject of her dad's love life. She braced herself as Gemma said, "I'm sorry we upset you by not telling you about helping out. I don't like it when Dad keeps things from me because he thinks I worry too much. I bet it was something like that, how you felt, right?"

Impressed with how perceptive she was, Faye answered, "Yeah, because it's important to me, so I want to know."

Gemma nodded quickly. "Exactly." Clearing the air made it easier to enjoy their time together.

When they had a mound of apples, Faye said, "Here's the first trick to perfect apple pie." She scooped them all into a large mixing bowl, went to the refrigerator to get lemon juice and sprinkled them all before covering them and putting everything back in the refrigerator. "Everything needs to be cold, so all of my ingredients are in here until I'm ready."

Gemma moved closer to inspect. "Which one's the secret?"

Faye held up a finger. "Patience, young one. Let me show you the real key to all my success first." She led Gemma into her office and pointed at the chair before she opened the desk drawer and pulled out her copy of Sadie's first collection of broader baking recipes, *Colorado Comes Home*.

"Sadie made her name on these delicious cookie recipes, right? I would never try to change those, but she gave me her copy of this the first time we baked together." Faye opened the book and was not surprised when it fell open to the apple pie recipe. "Do you see? All of these notes?" She paged slowly through so that Gemma could see all of Sadie's annotated directions, doodles in the margins, the funny little comments she'd left. It was a perfect capsule of Sadie Hearst, and priceless because it was the only one in the world like it.

"Wow," Gemma said as she tapped the cheeky chicken Sadie had drawn peering up over the edge of the page on a recipe for sweet cornbread. "She was fun."

"Yeah, she was, and she thought time in the kitchen should be, too." Faye turned back to the apple pie recipe.

"Here you'll see the standards. Brown sugar, butter, salt, cinnamon…" She ran her finger down to the piecrust recipe. "Some people add vinegar to their piecrusts, but you won't find that in the recipe. Sadie added apple cider vinegar for this one. See the note?" She pointed at the circle Sadie had added to Faye's special copy and then tapped the margin.

"'Try a dash. Balance. If you want something good, you gotta find some balance, Faye. Strong but not hard.'" Gemma frowned. "What does that mean?"

"Good question," Faye exclaimed. "I asked it, too. So, in cooking, the vinegar helps to firm up the crust, make it stronger so it holds together. A tough crust, one that's been overworked, is no good, but a flaky crust that holds together, with all the ingredients correctly mixed, is perfection. But for Sadie, I think the note was more about life."

"Balance," Gemma murmured to herself. "Like you can't focus your whole life on work, I guess. There's family and fun things like painting or riding horses." She chewed her lip. "But which one is the vinegar in this metaphor? Work or fun?"

Faye's shock had to show on her face, but in all her years of pondering Sadie and her advice, that question had never occurred to her.

Gemma laughed at her expression. "Is the vinegar the secret ingredient?"

Faye cleared her throat as she realized she still had some learning to do about balance herself. "No, I didn't write down the *secret* secret ingredient. It's too powerful. See the heart?"

"Next to two tablespoons of lemon juice?" Gemma scanned the page. "There's no note."

"That's the secret secret. Only you and I know it now. When you run out of lemon juice and lemons in the kitchen and you need to make a whole bunch of pies for a restaurant," Faye said, "sometimes you get desperate and try orange juice. From concentrate." Her scandalized tone made Gemma giggle. "Then you wait anxiously to see if anyone complains, and they all rave about the flavor instead." She bent closer to Gemma. "The other secret? Anyone who bakes often enough will be able to figure out my secret substitution. I'm sure Sadie knew what I was up to, but no one has proclaimed it to the world, so this is just between you and me."

Gemma mimed zipping her lips. "Are you going to write a message there? Like one of Sadie's?"

"I am, because I am handing over this treasured guide to you." Faye nodded when Gemma shook her head. "I am, and when you have the chance, you come back to Prospect with this book and we'll cook together again."

The teenager immediately leaned forward. "Do you have other secrets in this book?"

Faye mirrored her pose. "I might." Then she waggled her eyebrows. Gemma's giggles made her feel light and free. "Go take the piecrust out of the refrigerator. Let's get a pie in the oven."

Gemma hopped up to run to the refrigerator, so Faye grabbed a pen from the cup on her desk as she stared at the heart she'd added to Sadie's recipe and considered the balance advice. After a minute, she wrote, "Don't be afraid to try something new."

It was good advice. Was it as important as balance?

Faye closed the book and stood to join Gemma as she thought about the question. Then she decided that, like most advice, it would all depend on how it was applied. Like Sadie, she'd have to trust that Gemma could use Faye's advice when she needed it.

Pie-making with an apprentice was more enjoyable than Faye had expected.

She and Gemma were having so much fun two-stepping badly around the kitchen to the country station that she lost track of time and had to speed-walk over to Prospect's new Sadie Hearst museum for the meeting with Michael Hearst. She'd sent Gemma over to the Mercantile to continue Western Days planning with Prue, and she didn't even pause to wonder at the impressive interactive exhibits of Sadie's life and memorabilia now stationed around the large open area. Sarah had already given several folks a sneak peek at the displays, but Faye wanted to come back when everything was final to spend more time.

Faye was out of breath when she entered the conference room. It smelled so new that she was afraid to brush up against the walls in case the paint wasn't quite dry.

But it was clear no one had noticed her late arrival.

River and Angel were helping Sarah figure out all the tech pieces to get the video conference going. Every now and then, Michael Hearst would pop up on the screen and then he'd go away. Sometimes there was sound. Eventually, the image of Michael stabilized on the screen that covered the wall of the small room and answered, "Hello" to Sarah's greeting.

Everyone clapped at the success.

"Are we ready to start?" Michael asked. "I feel like I've run a marathon."

"And you weren't even doing anything," Jordan replied with a wry smile. Faye had picked up snippets about the Hearst family's dynamics since Sarah and Jordan had moved to Prospect, so she knew Michael was the oldest and bossiest of all of Sadie's great-nieces and -nephews. He had enjoyed that position and tried to boss Sarah and

Jordan around for a lifetime. They'd expected his being named CEO of Sadie's empire would make that worse, but as far as Faye could tell, he'd supported everything the sisters had wanted to do.

Still, they were family. No one could humble a person like family.

Michael tipped his chin up. "Good point. Count on Jordan to keep things real."

"We all have our talents." Jordan pulled out a chair and sat at the table.

Faye maneuvered around the room to an empty spot next to Brian, but she didn't glance in his direction as she settled in her seat.

Michael braced his elbows on his desk. "Gotta say, I wasn't sure what you'd be able to do on such a quick turnaround time, but these chefs are both impressive. Andre, you and your team are the best, as always. Everything I saw is rough, but the shots are tight. The food looks delicious. And the interviews you've added make this personal. That was the piece I was afraid we were going to miss, the Sadie connection, the thing that keeps her fans coming back for her content week after week, but Faye did it. Really good job. We definitely have to find a way to work Faye into our plans for website content and new streaming series ideas going forward."

Faye managed to contain a huge, embarrassing delighted grin but she knew her cheeks were flushed with pleasure at being singled out because of her performance. She'd had her doubts about stepping in front of the camera, but she was so proud of herself for saying yes.

Sarah scratched her temple. "Any feedback on the judges?"

Michael grinned. "Brian is a professional. Nailed it

every time and I'm not sure which way I would have gone, Franky or Rafa, but I know I've got to get to the Majestic to try their food for myself. I hope Jordan's ready to be booked up with Cookie Queen fans and new converts anxious to give Rafa's restaurant a try."

"Not yet, but I will be before Western Days," Jordan mumbled.

The lack of comment on her own performance was obvious to Sarah. "Jordan and I might get better with more practice."

Michael tilted his head to the side as if to ask, "Really?" but he politely kept the question to himself. "What we have will work for this series, but we don't have the answer yet for ongoing content or the live sessions we want to host."

"There's no way to tape anything in that kitchen when it's open for business. Too small." Andre chopped through the air with his hand. "We'll have to use the studio at the Cookie Queen headquarters. Faster. Easier. More cost-effective overall."

Faye tried to imagine how working in LA would ever fit with her life in Prospect. Every scenario seemed impossible. The slow deflation of her excitement must have been noticeable because Jordan said, "Or maybe we don't do that, either."

No one had another suggestion to offer.

Michael frowned. "Let's table this discussion about future content for now. Have you got the file that was downloaded or uploaded or beamed up into the cloud? I want everyone to see what you've managed so far."

The video began by showing Brian standing in Sadie's kitchen, Franky and Rafa flanking him. This was the first thing they filmed for the competition rounds, where Brian had introduced the rules. He was handsome in his chef coat. Obviously.

Then everything that Faye had experienced in fits and starts rolled seamlessly together. There she was on the screen, wedged in the pantry while Franky and Rafa teased each other about using dry pasta. The camera angles expanded when they were back in the kitchen and Franky and Rafa were sharing their tips and tricks, and through it all, Faye could see her own enjoyment of the process on her face. When the clip ended, everyone clapped.

Michael said, "It's good. We'll need to add a short intro, the three of you in front of the lodge with the title, and any graphics, like teasing about a tip coming soon with Rafa or Franky, that kind of thing. We set a tentative date to post this on the website and start promoting on social media in two weeks, with fresh content coming every week after that until we have a winner."

Sarah frowned. "That pushes us past Western Days. We're hoping visitors to town will meet Rafa then. Is that a problem?"

Michael replied, "I don't think so. More buzz is good for us. And the lodge."

"All right. We've got our orders. Time is money, people, and we have to finish this pronto." Andre stood. "Daylight is wasting away. Let's get some shots of the lodge and tomorrow we'll saddle up."

In the commotion of people standing to leave, Sarah scooted into Brian's empty chair. "Listen. This LA versus Prospect question of taping more content with you… don't give up on that yet."

Jordan leaned around her. "Or on your chef, either."

Faye nodded, even though she'd much rather pretend

all was well. "You better get over to the lodge. I'll meet you there."

They were still watching her sadly when she left the conference room.

ON WEDNESDAY, Faye realized she might as well have been sleepwalking during the remaining days of the shoot for all she remembered of the time before Brian and Gemma's last day in Prospect. Brian had kept his distance, and they'd established a professional but stiff relationship.

None of it was easy, especially since multiple sets of worried eyes were glued to them wherever they went.

But they had successfully wrapped up the series, Andre and his crew were on their way back to LA, and Gemma and Brian would be following the next day, so Faye forced herself to pretend she was fine, just fine, in order to return Brian's freshly laundered, starched, pressed and spotless chambray shirt to the Majestic.

Mia was bent over the computer at the lodge's reception desk when Faye walked into the lobby. Mia smiled and said, "I'm so happy to see you and your smile, Faye! The mood around here is tense. Everyone is packing up and no one is very happy about it."

"I guess Sarah and Jordan are pretty worried about Brooke and getting to New York," Faye said.

Mia nodded. "And Gemma and Brian have been at odds all day."

She hadn't expected saying goodbye to be easy. "I need to get this shirt back to him before they finish packing."

Mia held up her hands, her fingers crossed as Faye moved down the hallway. When she arrived at Brian and Gemma's rooms she heard Gemma say, "If I forget to pack something, I'll just get it the next time I'm in Prospect." Each word was as sharp as a weapon.

Whatever Brian might have said was interrupted when Faye stuck her head inside Gemma's open door. "Good afternoon, Carusos." She met Brian's eyes as Gemma flew across the room to hug her. She read his expression as relief, but she wasn't sure whether it was about seeing her or hoping Gemma would put down her knives for a minute.

"I was afraid I wouldn't get a chance to say goodbye," Gemma said softly as she squeezed Faye tightly.

Faye handed Brian the shirt as she rubbed Gemma's back. "No way. You are bonded to us by the secrets of the Ace High now. We're never saying goodbye for good. When you get ready to bake, call me and we'll do it together. I promise."

Gemma nodded and stepped back. "And when I come back to Prospect," she said as she shot a look over her shoulder at her father, "we'll try something new, another recipe with a secret ingredient."

Faye smiled at her. "This is a good plan."

Gemma turned from Faye to her father. "I'll finish packing all my stuff without you." Then she raised her eyebrows and gestured broadly at Faye.

She understood that to be a hint that she and Brian needed to speak privately, so she pointed in the direction of the firepit. "Could we go outside and talk for a minute?"

"Yes, please, let's do. Get me out of this room," he said before he went to Gemma and smacked a loud kiss on top of her head and followed Faye outside.

She sat in one of the empty chairs and waited for him to settle next to her without knowing how to get the conversation started.

"For me and Gemma, Prospect has been every bit of the magic I was promised, but being this close to her heartbreak because we're leaving has been rough." Brian rubbed his forehead. "Not only do I feel the ache myself, about saying goodbye, but I can see it on her face." Then he braced his elbows on his knees. "Thank you for coming."

He was so close that she was tempted to inch forward to bump his legs with her own. "Had to return the shirt."

His crooked grin as he met her stare tightened the knot in her stomach. "It looks a lot better on you than me. You should keep it."

This time, she did scoot closer to touch him. "I have faith that you have turned over a new denim leaf. You're going to need it in LA. I can always pick up another at the Homestead Market."

His smile faded as he studied her face. "I'm sorry I hurt you."

Faye nodded. "But not for what you said."

"I'm sorry I hurt you," he repeated, "but I am selfish enough to want you close. At the same time, I want you to have all the space to do whatever it is you're passionate about. That's all. You deserve that. We all do."

Faye inched even closer. "I hope this is just goodbye for now."

Brian slipped his hand under the hair at the nape of her neck. "I hope that you'll brave LA's traffic to visit me. Rinnovato will feel incomplete until I get to show it to you."

The ache in her chest and tears burning in her eyes didn't stop her from enjoying the sweet kiss he pressed to her lips.

"Tell Gemma I'll text her after you guys make it home," Faye said as she stood. She hurried back through the lodge and hopped into her SUV, proud of herself for holding off the tears at least until she was driving away.

CHAPTER NINETEEN

TWO WEEKS AFTER his return to LA, Brian sat at the bar of his restaurant with Belvie as they sampled the pasta their newest line cook had made. Slipping back into the routine at Rinnovato had been simple, thanks to Belvie's leadership, and hiring this addition to their kitchen staff helped.

"I am not certain she has the same palate Rafa does, but then, I am not certain anyone could match him there," Belvie murmured before she sipped her ice water. "This is technically a sound dish, boss."

Brian agreed. "Overall, yes. But it lacks some color, doesn't it?"

Belvie sighed. "I could say the same about this entire operation lately. My once passionate boss has become positively boring gray. I miss one of my favorite chefs and the other one has me worried. I don't like worrying, Brian."

Before he could ask for details, the front door swung open and Franky entered. The way his shoulders slumped and he studied the floor as he went was unnatural for the eternally happy chef.

"Sorry I'm late," Franky said before pulling the strap of his bag over his head. "I'll do better tomorrow."

Brian nodded and they both watched Franky disappear into the kitchen.

"There is no fire in the place. I worry that customers will find we have lost our spark. I had hoped teaming up the new line cook with Franky might loosen the situation a fraction," Belvie said slowly, "but I believe a trip to the mountains has broken my best chef. I don't appreciate that."

"I guess we have the answer to how well they'll do apart, don't we?" Brian asked.

"Have you heard any reports about Rafa's behavior? I am concerned. Franky was punctual, energetic and creative. Now..." Belvie waved a hand as if it was impossible to summarize how everything had gone so wrong.

Brian was having trouble focusing. Sleeping hadn't been easy since he'd come back to LA.

"Do you think Franky would like a chance to open a new restaurant in San Francisco?" he asked. "Maybe another change of scenery will be the boost he needs to rebound."

He tapped the file of information on their plans for a second Rinnovato. It was time to decide. Waiting wouldn't solve anything. He needed movement. Distraction.

That reminded him of Faye's comments on how restaurant life was good for people like them because there was always work to do, but the last thing he wanted was another reason to miss her.

Brian opened the file to study the figures the accountant had pulled together with a conservative estimate of profit and loss over the course of five years. He would be foolish not to pursue such a sound investment.

When Belvie smacked her hand over the paper, he realized that there hadn't been much of a "they" or a "we" about this plan.

Not the same way there had been with Rinnovato.

He could remember showing Belvie the sketches he and Sadie had drawn on napkins, and how she and Sadie had shot down his idea of a "minimal" restaurant.

"Nobody pays top dollar for 'minimal' for long, Chef," Sadie had said with a hoot.

She and Belvie had been correct. Rinnovato was classic but comfortable and diners returned with their families over and over.

"Chef. Listen to me." Belvie turned to face him, clearly wanting him to understand that this was important. "No one is going to San Francisco. I don't want to. You can't go. And there is only one cure for Franky's disease. That cure is in the mountains of Colorado. In fact, I am coming to understand that the fix for all of this…" She stopped and blinked several times. "It's in Colorado. I am quite content with our thriving restaurant here, but if you must grow, you will have to find a way to do that in the cold mountains. I'm sorry to say it, but there it is."

Brian propped his elbow on the bar as he faced the fact that Belvie had been saying this all along. It didn't matter how smart the project was, how much money they might make, if it made neither of them happy. At this point, Gemma was his priority, not another thing that would take him away from her. He checked his watch. Monica would be dropping her off soon.

San Francisco wasn't anywhere close to his dream, either.

The longer Brian stared at the figures, the clearer it became that he'd gone about this the wrong way. Sadie had taught him to find the dream first, then build it. Instead of doing that, he'd asked what he could build and was trying to make that a dream.

In that way, he wasn't too far from Faye's situation at the Ace High.

Luckily, he'd courted a woman in Prospect and stumbled across the kind of place that would be perfect for a new thing. The post office's potential had been so clear to him at the time.

But he was going to need help.

"Hey, Franky," he called and waited for the chef to come out of the kitchen and join them.

Belvie noticeably relaxed against the bar. "Finally," she muttered.

Franky asked, "Yes, Chef?"

"If I wanted you to go to San Francisco to open up a new restaurant for me? To be my newest executive chef? What would you say?" Brian ignored the slow shake of Belvie's head.

"San Francisco?" Franky asked in a voice that creaked like a rusty door hinge. "I would do anything for you, Chef. You know that."

"But you would not be happy there." Belvie raised an eyebrow as if to say, "See?"

Brian raised his eyebrows at her to tell her to wait a minute, so she relaxed again. "Now, what if I moved the opportunity to Prospect?"

Franky's shoulders immediately straightened. "A Rinnovato in Prospect? Yes, Chef. I would love that shot. Is there another competition because I am prepared to cheat to win this one."

Brian chuckled. Feeling amused made it easy to smile for the first time since he'd left Prospect and it was welcome. He pulled out his phone to show Franky the shots he'd taken on the way out of town his last day. "Tell me what you think of this."

Franky scrolled through the photos of the Prospect Post Office. "It's too small for formal dining, Chef." He covered his heart with his hand. "Which pleases me. You know I don't have the flair for that sort of service, but I love the character, the details." He glanced up at Brian. "It would make an excellent pizza place, depending on the size of the kitchen behind it. Every town deserves a good pizza place. With the lake there…" He nodded as if everyone could see the potential in pizza.

Brian took his phone back and offered it to Belvie. "The problem is there's no room for a kitchen. It's part of Prospect's Old Town, so the facade is historical, and can't be changed." He scrolled to the next set of photos, pleased at the way they both shifted so that they could see the photos better. "But there's this office space behind the post office that isn't historical. My idea was to—"

"Convert this to a commercial kitchen to supply the storefront." Belvie pointed at the doorway of the office building. "If we could get permission to build some kind of covered passage here, connecting to the back of the post office, it would be an easy distance."

Relief immediately filtered through Brian. Belvie could see the potential. It wasn't a foolish idea.

"I had considered a coffee shop with baked goods, grab-and-go sandwiches," Brian said slowly.

"But pizza is the winning idea." Belvie smiled as she handed him his phone and offered Franky her hand for a high five. The loud smack of their celebration seemed to splash color across the whole restaurant, a vibrant spirit that had been missing since his return.

Gemma entered at some point in their celebration, her backpack slung over one shoulder. "What's going on?"

Brian drew her into a quick hug. "Hey, we came up with the best idea for a new restaurant in Prospect."

Franky danced in a circle. "I'm going to make pizza in Prospect!" He danced away after twirling Gemma in a circle, singing "pizza in Prospect" under his breath. Then he pulled his phone out of his pocket and pressed a button, then paused. "Rafa, guess who's opening up a restaurant in Prospect? Me!" Franky raced back toward the kitchen and hit the swinging door at full speed, talking so fast it was difficult to decipher his words.

Belvie clicked her tongue. "Dinner service may be erratic tonight, Chef, but I cannot complain."

Brian had expected his daughter to be as happy about the idea because she'd loved every minute in Prospect, and some of the sadness of leaving it clung to her, too, but Gemma's uncertain frown and the way she fiddled with the ends of the backpack strap told him otherwise. "What's wrong? I thought you loved Prospect?"

"I do. I just... Opening up a new place takes time. When are you going away? How long will you be gone?"

Belvie faded away so Brian urged Gemma to take her seat. "I'm not opening it." He frowned. "I mean, I will need to go sometimes, Belvie can go others, but Franky will be running the place. Rinnovato is mine. My home is here. You're my home."

She moved closer to wrap her arms around his neck, and he held her close. "What's wrong?"

"I like having you here, Dad," she said softly, "but I know you miss Faye, so we can figure it out. You should go to Prospect. I will visit. A lot. I know you need balance in your life. Remember?"

Brian frowned as he tried to follow the last part. Then he sniffed the air. "Do you smell vanilla?" Because if he now had a ghost, even if it was Sadie Hearst, he was going to be upset.

"Yeah." Gemma leaned back and opened her backpack. "Faye gave me her copy of this cookbook that Sadie made all these notes in. I thought I might try cooking something from it this weekend. If you wanted to help me?" She offered him the book. "Maybe we could try something new together?"

Brian held the book and watched it fall open to the apple pie recipe. He knew Sadie's handwriting well, but he could see Faye's under it with a note about trying something new.

At least one part of the answer he needed was crystal clear. "We should definitely give one of these a shot this weekend, and we can talk about the new pizza place. What if we hold off on the renovations until this summer? We could both go. You and I could decide how it should look, get Franky to work on the kitchen. We'll have to run it past your mom, of course, but..." Gemma hit him with a surprise hug as she said, "Yes! Yes! I want to do that!"

More color splashed across his vision as he realized how much their relationship had changed. There was no threat of calling her mother for rescue this time. She was already listing all the reasons she would present to her mom about why she should go with him to Prospect for the summer.

"And we will convince Faye to give you another shot, Dad." Gemma patted his shoulder as if she was prepared to calm all his nerves.

"Hey, don't get your hopes up there, Gem." Brian waited for her to meet his stare. "Nothing has changed between her and me, but the two of you are still friends. She will be happy to see you and bake with you again, I know it."

Gemma paused before agreeing. "Okay, nothing is different. Yet." Then she waggled her eyebrows at him.

Which was concerning to be sure, but he couldn't work up much energy to worry about that. Yet.

He felt good about this plan for his future. It was nice to dream again.

ON THE SAME day in Prospect, Faye was experiencing a bit of her own blah workday. Holly had the day off, but Toby had stepped up to take the lead in the dining room. He and the other server Faye had insisted on adding to the payroll had managed the dinner rush without any difficulty.

Leaving Faye entirely too much time to sit in her cramped office and ask herself if this was all there was.

Ordering supplies.

Paying bills.

Submitting receipts and payroll numbers to their accountant.

Listening to her grandmother lecture her line cooks about things they already knew.

"You keep sighing like that, I'm going to think you're unhappy about something." Her grandmother plopped down in the chair across from her. Before Faye could come up with a suitable answer that might be somewhat true but not enough truth to send her grandmother back to watching and waiting for her to leave, Faye's phone rang. She saw Sarah's name on the display and answered. "Hey, when did you get back to town?"

"Last night. Driving across country with Jordan and Brooke was one of those ultimate tests, like the gods used to set for heroes. I'm not sure whether I passed it or not, but all three of us are still alive, and speaking to each other," Sarah said. "Michael sent us the first episode, and I want to introduce everyone to Brooke, so I was thinking of hosting a small family party to watch it together. What do you think? Can you get away from the restaurant tomorrow night for an hour or so?"

Faye considered how much she'd actually contributed to the Ace High that day and automatically said, "I wouldn't miss it. Is it okay if I bring Gran? And Grandpa, if I can get him into town at night?"

"I love that idea. Yes! Let's do it at the museum. It'll be a crowd, but we have that screen, and I can show off the latest interactive display that was finished while I was on the road trip from Hades," Sarah said with a laugh.

"Gran will definitely be there tomorrow night." Her grandmother's eyebrows shot up, but she didn't immediately argue, which felt like a small win. She might mutter down the street about all the chores left at the Ace, but Faye could count on her grandmother to show up. "Did you need food? Snacks?"

"I'll put Prue in charge of that." Sarah coughed and cleared her throat. "If you only knew how much I appreciate that you are so easy to talk to, Faye. Thank you for this—it's the simplest conversation I've had all day."

Now Faye laughed. "It's tough being the older sister, I guess?"

"I love them both. And Jordan would commit criminal acts to keep Brooke safe, but when it's a… Friday? No one's in danger? The two of them require a full-time referee. When Western Days is over and the lodge is fully open and the museum is done, I'm taking Wes far away where there is no cell phone service."

Faye didn't believe it would happen, but the urge made sense. "I wish you good luck with that."

"Me, too." Sarah chuckled. "How about eight o'clock tomorrow? Dinner service should be mostly wrapped up by then."

"Perfect." Faye was still smiling when she put down the phone.

"First sign of life I've seen in you since your chef went back home." Her grandmother sniffed. "What did you get me into tomorrow night?"

"Sarah's putting together a watch party on the big screen at the museum. We were able to videoconference face-to-face with Michael Hearst in LA and watch the rough cut of the first segment in the conference room there. She has the first episode of the web series, all final and ready for the website." Faye tangled her fingers together as nerves hit. "I'm proud of what I did, Gran. I'd like for you to be there with me to see it for the first time."

Her grandmother straightened in the chair. "You don't think I'd miss it, do you?"

Surprised at her answer, Faye shrugged. "Well, you'll still be busy at the restaurant, but it's at a good time. I'd appreciate it if Grandpa was there, too. This feels like a big accomplishment to me. I'd like to share it with my whole family."

Her grandmother stood. "Like I said, I wouldn't miss it. You don't ask for much, so you better believe I'll move mountains to get your Grandpa out of his barn. We're always proud of you, you should know that." Her grandmother gently touched Faye's cheek. "You do know that? I believe you can do anything you dream up, Faye. Selfish me, I want to hold you close, but more than anything, I want your happiness. If that means you need to fly away, then you just know you can always land safely right back here. Anytime."

FAYE WAS SURPRISED at the jitters that popped up now and then throughout the next day, but when it was time to head to the museum, her grandmother took the lead and they met her grandfather outside.

He had even taken off his barn hat and smoothed down his hair.

"Well, don't you look nice," her grandmother said as she wound her arm through his and motioned Faye to his other side. She knew her goofy grin should embarrass her, but it felt nice to be escorted into the museum in such a way.

Prospect's own version of a red carpet event.

"Oh, Emma, I am so glad to see you! I can't wait for

you two to watch Faye shine. Your granddaughter was a natural in front of the camera." Prue nodded wildly. "It's true! Michael Hearst has been dreaming up all kinds of ways to keep her busy on content for Sadie's channels." She leaned forward to add, "Sarah and Jordan got none of Sadie's ease center stage, let me tell you."

"You don't have to tell all our secrets, Prue," Jordan called from the doorway to the conference room.

Sarah arrived and welcomed them. "Come on in. I saved you seats at the table. Mrs. Parker..." Sarah stopped and threw a glance at Prue. "Oh, Emma, I managed to get your son and daughter-in-law connected, too, but it was a miracle, so don't be surprised if I can never repeat it." She motioned them all forward.

"You got Mom and Dad to call in?" Faye said to her grandmother. "And Grandpa? You must have been calling in all kinds of favors."

Her grandmother stopped. "The way you asked..." She shook her head. "Like you weren't sure what the answer would be. I didn't like that, Faye. I am always so proud of you, but it's clear we don't say that enough."

Faye hugged her grandmother. "I'm proud of you, too, Gran. We make a great team."

She would have moved on, but Gran held on to her. "Why didn't you tell me you were going to be doing more of this? That the Cookie Queen president has you in his sights? Prue says you're a natural."

Faye blinked. "I'm not sure I will be doing more?" She brushed loose hair behind her ear. "I can't, Gran." Explaining about the time commitment and being away from Prospect for so long was a conversation for another day.

"Are you coming?" Sarah asked from the conference room doorway. "This connection is stable but I'm treating it like magic. It could wink out at any moment."

Faye nodded and together they found their seats front and center. The crowd settled. Sarah and Jordan were off to one side with a beautiful blonde who had to be Brooke. Rafa was seated to her left. He waved and Faye waved back. Prue and Walt and all the Armstrongs looked hopeful and anxious.

And her mother and father were staring back at her from the screen, smiling.

"Hey, Bizzy, this is the first watch party I've even been invited to. Thank you for including us." Her father's proud grin wiped away any of Faye's temporary embarrassment over his use of the nickname.

"I'm glad you're here." Faye squeezed her grandparents' hands. "All of you."

"Hit the lights." Jordan pointed at Grant, who was closest to the doorway, and as soon as the room was dark, the screen lit up.

The first image was of Sarah and Jordan standing in front of the doors at the Majestic Prospect Lodge. Then she and Brian joined them and "The Majestic Menu" rolled out across the screen.

The professionalism of the title and the shots and how easy it seemed finally convinced Faye that everything Andre had said was true. The shots were good. This was going to work.

Her grandmother's gasp next to her as her photo popped up with a short description convinced Faye that the whole thing was becoming real for other people in the room, too.

No one said a word through the introduction of Chef Brian Caruso, Sarah Hearst and Jordan Hearst. A short clip of Key Lake was narrated by Sarah to explain that the Majestic had been Sadie's home, and then Brian was on the screen with Rafa and Franky flanking him in the segment they had watched with Michael. Each contestant delivered a brief outline of his experience and favorite dishes.

Then the competition began. Graphics were added to list each chef's pantry ingredients; the list was updated to show what made it into the final dish as the round went, and the final scene for this first episode was of Brian seated behind the judge's table, asking the chefs to present their dishes.

The final screen teased the next episode with the question: "Who will win round one?"

Even though she knew the answer, it was exciting to imagine how the polished episode would draw viewers even further into the competition.

The loud applause surprised her, but she laughed at the way Sarah and Jordan encouraged it to keep going.

"Michael is so pleased with this, Faye, Rafa. I hope you're proud of the final product." Sarah hugged Rafa as he wiped his eyes.

"I am. I am very proud." His lips twisted. "I wish Franky was here to see this with me."

"Well, Emma, what did you think?" Prue asked, her eyes locked on Faye's grandmother. "Your girl is a natural, isn't she?"

"She is."

Faye turned away from her grandmother to see her father answer instead. "I had one idea in my head, Bizzy, but this is so much more than that."

The emotion in Faye's throat made it impossible to speak, but her grandmother said, "Seems a real shame you won't be doing more of that, Faye. Your father's right. It's one thing to hear how good you are, but an entirely different thing to see it right before my eyes. You loved every minute of that and the camera loved you."

The recognition she had wanted was nice.

But then she realized all the Armstrongs and Hearsts in the room were waiting for her to do something, say something, and she had no idea what.

But her grandmother understood. "And you turned down the chance to do more. Why?"

"The offer was to do it in LA, Gran. You need me here. This is home." Faye shrugged. It was that simple.

Then Sarah leaned forward. "Brooke, could you do me a favor and cover Jordan's ears?"

The mean glare Jordan shot both of her sisters made the Armstrongs laugh, so Sarah said slowly. "We aren't doing anything else before Western Days, Jordie. Did you hear me? This idea I have, it's for later." She inhaled and exhaled slowly, encouraging Jordan to do the same. "No new ideas before Western Days. I promised and I'm keeping that promise."

"We get the idea is for after…" Brooke smiled. "Go ahead. Spill it."

Sarah wrinkled her nose. "None of us can afford to spend months in LA shooting more new content. LA doesn't work, so… I was thinking…" She pointed dramatically at the wall behind the screen. "What if we made this space, beyond the wall, a test kitchen? We could put in a replica of Sadie's set, with full working appliances, and tape there? The large glass window could draw a crowd while we're working, a sort of behind-the-scenes glance at Cookie Queen processes. Faye might still need to spend some time in LA, developing content with Michael and the staff there, but a studio here shouldn't be too difficult." She glanced around. "Should it?"

"After Western Days. Not before," Jordan said firmly.

Sarah covered her heart with her hand in a solemn promise.

"You could put a sign up in the window to let visitors

know it's coming." Brooke grinned at Sarah's expression. "Already on it, aren't you?"

Sarah brushed that away.

"And we'll take care of the Ace and help out with the farm while you're gone, Faye. You know that," Wes added from his spot behind Sarah. "Family helps family. You can do this. If you want to."

She didn't even have to hesitate. "I want to. I want to go to LA and see Brian and Gemma. I want to be here to keep the Ace going and rescue Grandpa when he gets tangled up in the barn." She rubbed her forehead. "I don't know how to make it all work."

"Faye, girl, you don't have to do every bit. That's what they're saying." Her grandfather squeezed her shoulder. "What we're saying. All you have to do is what makes you happy. That's what we want."

Faye glanced around the room and couldn't find a single person who seemed to disagree with that take.

"I need to book a flight to LA. I have an idea for a series to discuss with Michael." She inhaled slowly. "And Gemma."

Sarah, Jordan and Prue immediately leaned forward. "Say more," Jordan ordered.

"Cooking with her reminded me of the way Sadie taught me how to love baking. A series for beginners like Gemma could be fun." She held her breath as she waited for a response.

Gran patted her hand. "The world needs more bakers, that's for certain."

"You can stay in my apartment in LA. I'll find you a flight." Sarah held up her phone until Faye agreed.

"You're going tomorrow, right?" Jordan pulled out her own phone. "Gemma said she'd text me after the Caruso family dinner tomorrow night so we could watch our favorite show together, you know the one with celebrities who sing and hide their identities by wearing wild costumes? Wouldn't it be cool to surprise her and Brian? I'll get her to reserve you a table at Rinnovato and you can figure out the rest."

Faye hesitated. "I don't know. Brian and I didn't leave things in the best spot. He told me I needed to find my own dream instead of living my life for someone else's."

Gran sniffed. "It's not bad advice."

"And then I told him that he should have made a few sacrifices in going after his own dream so he wasn't having to make up for lost time with his daughter." She shot a glance up at the screen to see if her parents registered the comment. The way her father's lips tightened convinced her he'd taken the hint.

Walt grunted. "Sounds like you both got a good lick in."

"We were both right and both wrong," Faye said quietly.

"It happens like that when you fight with someone you love." Prue brushed her hand down Walt's chest. "If you're lucky, you have a chance to strengthen the spot where you broke it, with apologies and time."

"And you need to do that in LA," her grandmother said.

Faye met her stare before nodding. "Okay. Reservations at Rinnovato and a meeting with Michael if I can. Guess I better make sure Holly can run the Ace High dining room tomorrow, because now that I've got a dream of my own, I have to try to make it come true."

FAYE BRUSHED HER hands nervously down the skirt of the dress she'd borrowed from Sarah's closet. The Hearsts had made all the arrangements for her, including providing her keys to Sarah's apartment and free use of anything in the closet there. Even if she'd never eaten at Rinnovato, Faye knew that the style of the place would fit Sarah's wardrobe much better than her own, so she'd chosen a deep blue, simple sheath that immediately boosted her confidence.

Until she was seated at her table for two, all alone.

"Act like you know what you're doing," Faye murmured to herself. It was sound advice that Sadie had delivered often enough to show that it applied to a variety of situations.

"Are we still waiting on someone or would you like to order, ma'am?" The young woman standing beside the table smiled. "Could I answer any questions for you?"

Faye licked her lips. "I'd like a piece of apple pie." The story of how Brian's mentor had gotten his attention had been floating through her mind ever since she'd decided to take this shot. Was she brave enough to make herself a nuisance to make her dream come true?

The frown that wrinkled the younger woman's brow shook Faye's resolve.

"We don't serve apple pie, ma'am. If it's dessert you're in the mood for, we do have a vanilla crème cannoli that is popular." The server moved to point it out on the menu, but Faye shook her head.

"No, I know the pie isn't on the menu, but if you'll take my request to the chef, I'd love to discuss apple pie desserts with him." Faye nodded firmly in the same way her grandmother delivered an order, certain it would be followed. "Apple pie. Mention it to the chef."

The server glanced over her shoulder and back at Faye before walking slowly away.

Faye crossed her fingers that the next person to approach the table would be Brian, because her courage was disappearing and she still had a big apology to make before she asked if she could have another chance to work at this thing between them.

The cycle of her thoughts stuttered when she saw a chef

coat out of the corner of her eye, but she glanced up to meet a beautiful woman's dark eyes. "Belvie?"

The chef's slow grin made her feel welcome. "Ah, the mysterious woman from Colorado has finally made her appearance. What a relief." She crossed her arms over her chest. "Brian told you that story about tormenting his chefs after they go out into the world, I see. How did you get a reservation on short notice?" Then she tapped her forehead. "This is the secret Gemma has been desperate to share all day long. Of course."

Belvie motioned for Faye to stand. "I forced Brian away from the kitchen to enjoy time with his family. Ever since he has returned from the mountains, he has cast a sad pall over my kitchen. Even his new business idea cheers him only in fits and starts."

Faye followed Belvie as she wound through the tables toward the bar. "New business?"

Belvie stopped. "In Prospect? Pizza? With Franky running the show?" She clicked her tongue as she resumed her march. "We have the perfect reason to reach out to our friends in Prospect to celebrate, but do we do that? Of course not. We have to continue to suffer and bring down a contented Belvie in the process." She covered her heart. "I am thrilled to send him away to the mountains, you understand. I have this place exactly as I like it. I will miss Franky, of course, but we grow, we change, we fly away. It's life, is it not?"

Faye wasn't sure an answer was required but she agreed, so she nodded.

Belvie pointed at a door with a small plaque that said Event Room.

"Every Sunday, all the Carusos in one place." She patted Faye's arm. "It's lovely to meet you, Faye. I hope we have plenty of time to plot against Brian in the future."

Belvie was gone before Faye could decide whether that was a joke or not.

Then she realized the nerves would only grow worse the longer she stood there, so she eased the door open and stepped inside. Gemma must have been watching for her because she was the first to notice. "Faye! You made it!"

Gemma's arms were wrapped around her instantly and they swayed back and forth until Brian stood up from the table. "Faye." Then he noticed everyone else had frozen in that moment. "You're here."

"I am. You're wearing jeans." Which had absolutely nothing to do with her goals for this surprise, but it seemed like a development that needed to be called out. She desperately wanted something smart to add here, but nothing came to mind. She was locked in his stare as he left the table and came toward her. "I want…us. I don't know how it works. Sometimes I may be in LA because I'm also here to get that job that Michael offered, and yet it's pretty far from Prospect. Our families are so important to us. Gemma, if I get the job, I have an idea for something we could shoot together using Sadie's marked-up cookbook for inspiration and a guide, but there's still so much to figure out."

Brian grinned when his daughter squeaked with excitement at the suggestion that she might be involved in a cooking show. "Have your people contact her people and let's get something on the books. We'll be in town this summer."

Faye knew her mouth had dropped open but she couldn't come up with the right follow-up questions.

He gently nudged her chin up. "Our next battle may be with Chef Emma Parker because Franky and I are bringing authentic gourmet pizza to the Prospect Post Office. Do you think she'll start a war?"

The bubble of relief that filled Faye escaped in happy giggles. "I have no idea, but once she tries Franky's pizza, the war will be won." She touched his cheeks. "We can do this, can't we? We can imagine the life we want, here and there and with Gemma and my grandparents. We can build it. Together."

"We have to." He slipped his hands under the fall of her hair to draw her closer. "Nothing is any good anymore. It's just not the same since I've met you."

"Balance," Gemma whispered loudly from her spot at the table. "Like Sadie said, that's balance."

Brian looked worried, but Faye shrugged and smiled. "Apple Pie Club. We can't talk about it with you, but she's right."

He sighed. "I'm going to be outnumbered for the rest of my life, aren't I? You and Gemma are an unbeatable team." He pressed a kiss to her lips that proved to her he wasn't concerned about whatever ideas she and his daughter might cook up together. The thought warmed her heart.

"Does this mean we can start courting again?" he asked, a bright gleam in his eye, his expression open and hopeful.

Faye couldn't hide her smile any longer, knowing her dream was coming true. "Sadie always said we need to know where we're going if we want to get there, Chef. The path's not entirely clear, but I can see exactly where we end up. I guess we've been courting all along."

* * * * *

A NOTE TO ALL READERS

From October releases Mills & Boon will be making some changes to the series formats and pricing.

What will be different about the series books?

In response to recent reader feedback, we are increasing the size of our paperbacks to bigger books with better quality paper, making for a better reading experience.

What will be the new price of Mills & Boon?

Over the past four years we have seen significant increases in the cost of producing our books. As a result, in order to continue to provide customers with a quality reading experience, the price of our books will increase to RRP $10.99 for Modern singles and RRP $19.99 for 2-in-1s from Medical, Intrigue, Romantic Suspense, Historical and Western.

For futher information regarding format changes and pricing, please visit our website millsandboon.com.au.